NOWHERE NEAR YOU

leah thomas

BLOOMSBURY
LONDON OXFORD NEW YORK NEW DELHI SYDNEY

Bloomsbury Publishing, London, Oxford, New York, New Delhi and Sydney

First published in Great Britain in February 2017 by Bloomsbury Publishing Plc
50 Bedford Square, London WC1B 3DP

First published in the USA in February 2017 by Bloomsbury Children's Books
1385 Broadway, New York, New York 10018

www.bloomsbury.com

BLOOMSBURY is a registered trademark of Bloomsbury Publishing Plc

A CIP catalogue record for this book is available from the British Library

ISBN 978 1 4088 8537 6

Typeset by Newgen Knowledge Works (P) Ltd., Chennai, India
Printed and bound in Great Britain by CPI Group (UK) Ltd, Croydon CR0 4YY.

1 3 5 7 9 10 8 6 4 2

To all the friends I left behind:
you deserved better.
To all the friends who won't let me go:
I don't deserve you.
To all the friends I haven't met:
What's it like being you?

chapter one

THE BILLBOARDS

Moritz, you know me.

You know that usually I'd be the first person to say I'm awesome.

Behold! The Teenage Lord of Glockenspieling! I've got the astronomical charts for the next six months memorized, at least for the small patch of sky that hangs over northern Michigan. Did *you* know a comet's going to be soaring over my cabin in seventeen weeks? The Teenage Lord of Glockenspieling knows.

Keep on beholding, though! Because thanks to all the letters we've written this year, when it comes to getting epistolary, I am basically motherfluffin' Alexander Hamilton.

But here's my slice of humble pie: I've never been all that awesome at *patience*.

How did I handle the suspense of knowing I was actually on my way to meet other experimental kids like us, Moritz? With hazmat pants full of proverbial ants.

And how did I handle riding in a car out of the woods into real-life society for the first time?

Basically, I smeared my gas-masked face against the window for hours while Auburn-Stache chauffeured me down the freeway. He wouldn't let me turn on the radio (as if I could figure out the buttons!) and slapped my hand away whenever I reached across him to point at things.

"Whoa! Those windmills! They're moving! I can see them *moving*!"

"Glad I packed tranquilizers," murmured Auburn-Stache, but his goatee twitched.

"I thought windmills were little wooden houses with wings! Nobody told me they'd be white and *electric* and look like, like *gargantuan futuristic spaceship flowers*, 'Stache!"

"*Ollie*, I'm going deaf in my right ear. Spare me."

Although my allergies are still my ultimate kryptonite and electricity loves clouding my eyes with puffy swatches of color, I've gotten better at seeing past the swatches to what's underneath. I do this sort of squinting thing and scrunch my nose up in a way that might make Liz want to dump me for real. Then I can actually see almost like normal people do. The modified hazmat suit, the womble, absorbs the worst of the electricity, so these days I'm mostly only sneezing in the face of glowing screens. Sneezing beats seizing, so I'll take it.

And, Moritz, I have to tell you how outclassed my old power line nemesis was. For years I thought of the cable halfway down my driveway as actual Voldemort, burning orange in my aura, but that thing was only the lowest level of Death Eater (think Wormtail). Now I've seen power grids! They light up every horizon. I can't get over the towers that support those fiery lines in almost every direction. During that drive, to me they looked like stick people holding out cable jump ropes made of lava, and those lava ropes could have caught the world on fire if those other tower-people didn't help out and lift those ropes away from the fields—

Squinting too hard made me hiccup.

Auburn-Stache put a firm hand on my shoulder and shoved me back down into my seat.

"Ollie, I'm not daft enough to ask you to sit still. But sitting *down* would be a start."

"I'm just appreciating the beautiful things in life, you kook. Hey, do you think the kids we're going to meet will mind if I'm unfocused? Because I can't help being unfocused, but I don't want them to realize I'm less than cool. I have my hermit pride."

"Cross that bridge when we come to it."

"I want to seem *suave*. I should try to be aloof like Moritz." I sat up straight. "If I'm documenting their lives, they have to take me seriously. Right?"

Moritz, I'm on a storytelling mission. I figure being raised a woodland weirdo without even electric-coffeemaker experience to my name means I'll never be a good applicant for, you know, *office jobs*. But you told me I'm a good storyteller, and plenty of writers are antisocial! Some of them go off to live in cabins on *purpose* and do crap like stare at ponds for weeks. If you really think about it, my whole life's been a writing retreat. The TLoG is very qualified in this area.

So I'm going to conduct interviews. I'm going to write authoritative accounts of the lives of our fellow weirdos, the kids created in the laboratory and then scattered around the world. I'm going to meet them and tell their stories, and tell them right.

I like them all already. And I know it shouldn't matter, but I've always been a halfway-friendless electro-sensitive hermit, so I also want them to like me back.

"Do you think they'll tell me what it's like being them, Auburn-Stache?"

"Ollie. Wait and see."

"But—"

"Ollie. Please. You're doing my head in."

He really won't say much about the kids we're going to meet, Moritz, which is typical in an obnoxious sort of way, since that's the whole reason I'm *on* this trip. Aren't we all done with secrets already?

I guess old habits are vampires, immortal and hungry to exist. Because yeah, Auburn-Stache *is* like the dad I never had, but he's the kind of dad who spent a decade and a half of my life lying to me about basically everything important. I don't know. Maybe all dads do that, Moritz? Maybe if you cut anyone open, secrets wriggle out? (At least you and me are way past that!)

Right now it doesn't matter. Right now there's a whole world falling open in front of me instead, making me queasy in all the brightest ways. If I were serious and aloof like you, I'd sit still and let it wash over me.

My shoulder blades hit the passenger seat for maybe the first time.

But two milliseconds later, I rested my head on the dashboard, trying to angle the womble gas mask so I could get a good squint at the overpasses we kept driving under. The smog of cars flowed over the sides of bridges in gunpowder waterfalls, but for moments after we drove through them, the clear air underneath made me feel like we were floating in hidden caves.

"Spelunking!"

"Ollie! Seat belt!"

"How can anyone see anything with a seat belt on?" I twisted to look out the rear window.

"Not everyone is so thrilled by the panoramic views of a freeway commute."

"Holy crap! Is that a motorcycle?"

"What else would it be, Ollie?!"

Heck, it could have been anything. I didn't have time to focus on whatever lay beyond the electric clouds. All I saw was what looked like a severed head, speeding by on top of a black smog-horse.

"Can I get one? I shall name it Brom Bones, and it will strike fear in the hearts of mopeds!"

"Pissing Nora, no! Sit. Down. Before you overheat."

"I'm not an engine." I made a huffing noise through the filter of my gas mask.

He smirked. "The little engine that could."

I tried to ignore the doomed, unrequited desire to wipe sweat from my forehead. I considered napping, but that seemed risky.

What if I missed something miraculous?

Moritz, basically everything in the world is miraculous.

The countless colors invading my aura started mimicking autumn: those power lines draping orange curtains, planes miles (or kilometers, Mo) above trailing wisps of bronze through the clouds, blackened RVs and HOLY CRAP SEMITRUCKS roaring next to us with their twenty-something wheels and magma-colored diesel engines. Puffs of umber bled through the cracks in the pavement—dissipating as cars tore through them—especially as the scenery shifted from woodsy to industrial.

Northern Michigan has pine trees and lakes, but downstate is no great beauteous shakes. The farther south we got in Auburn-Stache's Impala, the flatter the roads, the grayer the scenery, the more overpowering the vomity bouts of electric color stabbing my pupils became. Glowing signs on massive posts told me that restaurants are a pretty big deal, but the signs became distorted when they merged with electricities: fast-food restaurants in yellow turned to sulfur in my corneas; green gas-station signs browned like dying leaves. Again, kind of vomity.

Actually, after a while just about everything felt vomity.

I put my hand on my stomach, and when I squinted at the next billboard, an advertisement for the Detroit Zoo, my hiccup tasted like . . . you get the idea.

"I have a pickle for you, Auburn-Stache," I said, voice muffled by the gas mask. "You know how you told me to stop writing Moritz while you were driving, and how I wasn't allowed to read or paint or glock in the car because I might get carsick?"

"Ollie, you're noisy enough without glockenspiel accompaniment." He was tapping his fingers on the wheel with one hand, biting his nails with the other. (And he gets mad at *me* for fidgeting!)

"Well"—I shut my eyes—"turns out the carsickness doesn't think those qualifications matter. Maybe you should stop the car."

"I can't simply stop the car, Ollie." Why was he sweating? He wasn't the one encased in layers of rubber.

"Sorry. What's the phrase for nonhermit car people? Oh. Pull over, *pretty please*." We overtook a minivan. It reminded me of Liz and the Ghettomobile and leaving home; the reminder made me queasier. "I'm gonna be sick."

"I can't," he said. "There are too many cars around."

"Look, I'll whip the mask off and do my sticky business and whip it back on in a flash. It won't even take long enough for me to seize." I tried to laugh but burped again, and I really didn't have time to talk about this. "I'll be just dandy!"

"I'm sorry, Ollie." He glanced at the wing mirrors, at the line of cars behind us. "We're half a mile from a rest area. Hang in there for one minute. Just one minute. To avoid any accidents."

I wanted to shout at him that I was about to have an accident right here in his car, but when I opened my mouth, something sicker than words came out and splattered onto my own face, and I realized the accident had already happened and this suit was never going to smell the same, and it hadn't smelled like lilies to begin with.

"Ollie!" cried Auburn-Stache. "Ollie, breathe. Chin up." He signaled left.

"Fluff you," I mumbled through burbling spit, nostrils burning. I tried clawing the mask away from my face. He grabbed my hand and held it tight.

"You *can't*, Ollie. You're wound up enough that you might short us out. Not just my car but the batteries in the cars on either side of us. The cars behind us. Do you know how disastrous that could be? If even just one car stopped without warning?"

I swallowed a teaspoon of vomit and coughed, and I couldn't reply because, aside from my disgust and my anger and my scorching throat, what tasted worse was knowing he was right.

Moritz, if I'm not careful nowadays, I could send out a pulse just like I did during the Halloween dance. Like how I blew out all the gymnasium lights and people's phones and ruined the evening for the DJ. This is what happens when you're an electromagnetic loser and you don't have any say in the way you impact the world.

This is why Mom wanted me to never leave the woods.

I gasped again, a hot sob that came from nowhere or from the dark inside me.

"Ollie, we're almost there." His hand on my chest wasn't restrictive anymore, but more like he was trying to hold me in one piece.

But then I was thinking of her, and I don't think I would have been breathing right even if I weren't dealing with a mask full of puke. This felt like a brand-new kind of seizure.

Did she die, Moritz? It seems as unbelievable as giant stick people draped in cables. As impossible as four lanes of steel machines surrounding me in parallel lines, machines moving fast enough to bend metal and pulverize bones during collision.

Moritz, if things as deadly as cars can be part of the world, why can't I?

"You'll be all right," Auburn-Stache said as he turned onto an exit ramp and toward a brown flat-roofed rest area. He parked the car while I breathed hot acid through my nose.

No one was around to see him drag me out into the parking lot and across a narrow strip of grass, into the line of trees beyond a few picnic tables. No one but a scarred old man, leaning on his truck and chewing jerky, who blinked at us like he'd seen much stranger things in his life than a goateed doctor tearing a dripping gas mask off a sobbing teenage loser.

"Ollie, Ollie. Now, stop that, kiddo."

"Why did you . . . let me leave?" I gasped, stomach rolling, eyes streaming. "If you're so afraid I'm going to wreck the world, why did you agree to take me on this . . . trip?"

Auburn-Stache didn't reply until he'd caught his breath. I guess dragging me out of the car was a bit hard on him. He's older than ever and I'm taller than ever, and my legs felt like lumps of dead weight, even to me.

"Neither your mother nor father would have wanted you to spend your youth with only ghosts for company."

"Me and my dead parents." I wiped my mouth on my sleeve and stared up at the darkening sky. "Someone should write a book about an orphan named Oliver."

"Enough, Ollie," he said gently.

"The bright side, 'Stache: a lot of superheroes are orphans." I laughed weakly. "Maybe I'm just fulfilling an epic destiny."

"There's that fabled optimism." He patted my back.

"Hey. Do you think the kids we're going to meet will mind me smelling like damp compost?" And then, all hoarse: "Do you think they'll mind *me*?"

Liar-Dad's detailed, heartfelt answer? "Wait here. I'll go clean your mask."

I winced. "Do I have to wear it again?"

"I'm afraid so. For now."

Auburn-Stache soon returned with the mask and more: my toothbrush, a tube of toothpaste, a warm bottled water, and a washcloth. I rinsed out my mouth, brushed bits from my teeth, and washed my face. Auburn-Stache helped me wrap the damp cloth around my nose and mouth inside the mask, but that thing still reeked enough to knock approximately seventeen skunks unconscious when I shoved it back on. In the parking lot, we found the old man sitting in his truck, trying to start his engine. Is that called revving?

Revving and revving, but it wouldn't start. That was almost definitely my fault.

So was his dead phone, probably, and his semifried hearing aid. Where before I'd seen the usual smattering of electric shades, now there was nothing. And his bumper sticker said he was a veteran and everything.

Go, me.

While we waited for someone to come along and jump our batteries (because of course I'd shorted out the Impala, too), I sat in my stinking womble at the picnic table on the edge of the narrow line of fake woods, holding my knees and staring at the litter underfoot.

Moritz, I know *you* get it: there have to be dark parts in origin stories.

I just hope the other kids like us will get it, too.

Once or twice while Auburn-Stache laughed with the old man about how bizarre a coincidence it was that both of their car batteries died in the same parking lot, the old man craned his neck to peer at me and my suspicious radiation suit. You hardly ever see superheroes wearing suspicious radiation suits.

When we finally left the rest area, the sunny first day of our road trip had given way to an amethyst November evening; I wish electricity got darker with everything else. Instead, all the colors only seemed brighter, and nausea caught me again.

Auburn-Stache took his hand from the wheel and placed it above the womble goggles, the approximate area of my forehead.

"Bet you regret this already," I murmured. "This insane road trip."

"I won't if you don't."

"Fair deal, Auburn-Stache."

I'm still impatient, Moritz. Even if I'm finally getting a little taste of how terrifying strangers can be and a bigger appreciation of what it is to be you, alone in a crowd of people. This must be what it's like to go out without your goggles on.

I told Liz I wanted to take this trip to figure myself out, but it's not easy. My electromagnetism might always freak me out. Maybe I can't control my life if I can't control my own body. Maybe I really will short you and your pacemaker out, and I don't think it's as easy to jump a person's batteries as it is to restart a car.

Even knowing that, I still wish more than anything you were here to talk to. You said you're not worried about me hurting you, but honestly, Moritz? Maybe you should be. Because I might be willing to hurt you a little if it meant I'd get to meet you!

I want to meet *all* the kids like us. I want to write their origin stories, too, dark parts included. I want to give them a shorter nickname than "kids I'm going to meet." Oh, and help them with their emotional teenage nonsense. I want this to be my new life purpose!

But what I want most is one of those amphibious vehicles. Then Auburn-Stache and I could just drive right off the coast and aim straight for Germany. I'm sure there'd be gas stations along the way, floating on buoys out in the middle of the Atlantic. We could stop off at oil rigs, right?

That'd be the cherry, Moritz Farber. You're the ultimate cherry. And we're serious about cherries in Michigan.

Now! Shut up and tell the Teenage Lord of Glockenspieling what the sounds of your life look like, Ultimate Cherry Dolphin Mo-Man!

I know you're sighing in exasperation. Just like Mom used to.

Focus, Ollie.

~ O

P.S. Hey, since we're on the move, you can e-mail (!) your next reply to the account Auburn-Stache set up for me, and he'll go print it out. (Did you *know* about the existence of print shops? I stood outside the door when Auburn-Stache went in, and when he returned, I swear I smelled watermelons. Does ink come from all those black seeds we spit out?)

Anyhow: oxenfree@stache.org. I'm not even joking. *Stache.org*

P.P.S. There may be a handful of us weirdos stranded here in the colonies, Moritz, but after the eighty-seventh time I asked him, Auburn-Stache confessed there are more in Europe. Unlike me, you have access to the magical realm known as the *Internet*, with all its maps and search machines. You can use electricity to meet the X-Men (real nickname pending)! What d'you say?

chapter two

THE APPLICATIONS

You remain as overwhelming as ever, Oliver Paulot. What a garbled mess your last letter was. Oh, the *humanity* of your vomit-laden grief.

Chin up. Soon be Christmas. It is late November after all.

If you wish to speak about your mother, don't hold your tongue on my account. Be nonlinear and remember her. We have spent enough time *talking about* talking about our feelings that we can omit the first "talking about" and simply talk about them.

Now you've got me speaking nonsense again.

If I could remove my pacemaker and simply run, I would run to meet your amphibious vehicle when it arrives on the coast. Though I do not hug, I might hug you. I am not the toughest of cookies yet, but I am not without my crunchy almonds. When we meet, my electric pacemaker and I will withstand the milk of your presence. Without crumbling into soggy despair.

Your penchant for terrible metaphors has infected me.
As ever. The things you do somehow change me, Ollie.

As for Kreiszig.

In my life, I have endured my fair share of dark parts.
One might think after having survived heart failure I should
be able to tolerate no small degree of misery.

One might think.

I have rarely felt the same sense of being beaten as when
Frau Pruwitt laid three *Gymnasium* applications on the
kitchen table before me.

"Go on, then," said my librarian.

"At this very moment?" I stood up from the chair.
Adjusted my lapels. Pulled my goggles down from my hairline to obscure my eyelessness.

"Got a date this morning, Peter Parker?"

"Is that such a surprise?"

She stared. I coughed.

"Your MJ can wait. You aren't leaving until I see your
name and address on these forms." She patted the chair
beside her. "You've been avoiding this for weeks."

Not untrue, Oliver.

Her infamous eyebrow rose. I sat. She jabbed a pen into
my hand. I clicked my tongue at the text on the first docu-
ment. Sound waves echoed back to my ears. MBV—*Magic
Brain Vision*; see how I've entirely adopted your nonsensi-
cal shorthand!—informed me the application was for Myriad
Academy, a fine arts school on the western side of the city.

The wealthy side of the city.

Father's face tightened while he leaned over the stove. The noise of the coffeepot illuminated him. I do not need to turn to see, if I can hear. Echolocation reveals everything. As ever I am listening. I hear what's unspoken:

We can't afford Myriad.

"That's a school with a creative focus," Frau Pruwitt said. "They offer extensive music, art, and performance classes."

"You may have noticed that I lack creativity on all fronts."

"That's not true, Moritz." Father spoke slowly. Pouring coffee at the counter. I scooted my chair in so he could fetch milk from the fridge. "You're very good at hip-hopping."

"Spare me. I mimic. I don't create. I lack the capacity." I am certain you have written beautiful songs on your glocken-spiel, Ollie. I long to hear them all.

I shuffled the forms. Clicked at the second application. A *Gymnasium* far from Kreiszig, in the rural sprawl of Rhinluch.

"That is an almighty commute. Should I learn to apparate?"

"It's a boarding school. Your father thought you might like the countryside."

"Despite the undeniable appeal of attending school in an isolated swamp, I would prefer to remain in the city, where there's enough sound to see properly. There are other con-siderations for eyeless monsters."

"Moritz, what's wrong?"

"Don't indulge him." Frau Pruwitt tapped her nails against the plastic coating on the table. Flecks of breakfast toast, vividly magnified to my ears. How irritating. "He's decided to be difficult."

Father turned away from the stove, mugs in hand. Had I eyeballs instead of blank sockets, I might have rolled them. How he smiled at her.

You won't see me making doe eyes when I meet the one I love, Ollie.

"The deadline for Myriad is only two days away. Begin it now. You can type the essay portion out after you get back."

I wrote half my name. Frau Pruwitt hissed between her teeth. "Gracious, is that really your handwriting? How did you even pass the transfer exam?"

"I colored in a large number of bubbles."

"We can help you apply online instead."

I pushed away the stack of paper. Stood. "Perhaps I should remain at Bernholdt-Regen. I have made a friend or two there. Sometimes the cafeteria food tastes almost edible. It hardly matters where I spend my last semester."

"It won't be your last. If you're accepted at one of these *Gymnasiums*, you'll take part in an expedited education program. After two years of hard work—work we all know you're capable of—you'll be qualified to do what you please."

Two *years*, Oliver. How insignificant she made it sound!

"Moritz, Frau Pruwitt has spent hours on the phone with financial aid programs. With representatives of these schools. We will help you, whatever you decide." Father took her hand.

Perhaps she blushed. I cannot see blushing.

"I will consider all of this."

"Why are you upset?"

"I'm not in the least. Beg pardon. I have elsewhere to be."

"Hogwash," shot Frau Pruwitt.

"Beg pardon?"

"You *are* upset. Your father and I can feel it."

I clicked on impulse. Then wished I could retract the sound.

Of late I am denied any sense of privacy. Of late my emotions emanate from me whenever I echolocate. Living, bee-stinging things. You would not need to cut me to see my secrets. I have no say in the trajectory of my emotional transference, Ollie. As you have no say in your electromagnetism.

Of late I suspect every individual within yards of me feels what I feel. When I fret, those closest unconsciously bite their lips. When I am livid, fists clench in my vicinity. Father and I believe this is more than coincidence. It is an actual consequence of exposure to the pseudoscientific disaster known as Moritz Farber.

Why has this transference suddenly worsened? A mystery. The one instance when Father murmured "*Ist es der Pubertät?*" we both cleared throats. Exited the room. Perhaps blushed.

Ollie. Forget automobiles. If the world can suffer my oddities, it can welcome you.

I gritted my teeth. Doubtless, so did they. "I'll be nineteen by the time I graduate?"

"In the grand scheme of things," Frau Pruwitt replied, "nineteen rather than seventeen can't make much difference."

"I disagree. We've reached an impasse, Adamantium Pruwitt."

I spun on my heel.

"Moritz!" Father's temper, rising alongside mine. *Because* of mine?

I closed the door behind me. I did not slam it.

That would have been rash.

I inhaled mildewed air. Walked to the stairwell. Even from here I could feel the familiar traffic far below, clarifying the tiers of the concrete apartment complex. Today the symmetry of angled steps, parallel railings, and diagonal staircases did not soothe me.

Cold gusts foretold imminent winter. I had neglected to grab my cane. I would only swing it into the pavement. Wielding a sledgehammer. When I passed smokers, I did not hold my breath. The burn of cigarettes seemed less cancerous than the taste already in my throat. Once, I strayed from the sidewalk and into the road. MBV tiptoed me out of the path of honking vehicles.

I tried not to let the smallest smidgen of my feelings dribble out into the atmosphere. I'm convinced strangers sensed my frustration. They hung their heads at my passing. Did their hearts hitch?

My pacemaker had difficulty steadying me.

I am so accustomed to pains in my chest, Ollie. Those pains are infinitely trivial beside the notion of not meeting the boy I love.

I will not wait two long years to see you, Ollie. *Gymnasium* be damned, I won't.

I stopped under the *Südbrücke* between the Abend residence and my own, where I maimed Lenz Monk in that ill-considered fight many months ago. I listened for my reflection on rippling water. Of course I could not hear it. I considered leaping into the canal. Not with any reasonable goal in mind; the canal does not lead to the ocean. It is man-made and filthy.

It could never take me to you.

Or even to Owen.

We spend a great deal of time together. Not only in the *Diskothek* and the Sickly Poet, but also during hours spent after school "volunteering" in the *Bibliothek*, under the oddly lenient eye of Frau Pruwitt. She lets us linger between shelves with nary a snipe. Once we saved up for the cinema. That amounted to a great deal of noise and the feel of Owen's hand in mine. You have asked what films are to me. Now they are his warmth.

Despite his tonguelessness, he tells me he cares for me. Speaks with his posture. His touch. I am abysmal at sign language. It takes me eons to read the notes he writes me. But there's a rhythm to Owen: the tapping of pencils on the edges of things, quiet footsteps, and gentle humming. Sounds that make him immense to me.

On Friday he put himself on pause while we waited in the school courtyard for his sister.

She stayed after to speak with an instructor. Serious, then, about attending some of her classes. This may portend the apocalypse. Fieke, tucking in her blouse to demonstrate her newfound scholarly dedication. She still looks and sounds like a hellion in high boots, with her ceaseless "fluffin'" cussing.

But she wears twenty-three piercings rather than fifty now. That is almost like making an effort.

Owen and I, on the steps. Made an art of hand-holding. My cane rested across our laps. We engaged in people-watching of the highest order. Bernholdt-Regen's delinquents did not disappoint. Watching an adolescent in braces inflict a wedgie on his weed-thieving minion is not romantic. We made do.

Lenz Monk has made it apparent since his return to school that no one is to disturb us. A week after Owen, Fieke, and I visited the laboratory that raised me, Lenz appeared in my peripheries. I waited for him to shove me. He nodded. That was all. Later someone tried to cut Owen in the lunch line. Lenz grabbed the unfortunate line cutter by the nape of his shirt. Dragged him away. Lenz might make a passable bouncer.

On the steps. The wind blew the city into our faces. It felt not altogether miserable to be alive. Owen pulled my arm toward him. Traced my skin with his forefinger.

Tomorrow, he spelled. *Come over.*

"Why?"

I am forever amazed at the volume of his laughter.

Überraschung! he traced with aching slowness. "Surprise!"

His touch. So jarring I forgot where I was.

Now, under the bridge, where was I?

Ollie, you and I have been working on standing up. But those undead habits: for years I dodged projectiles before they could come close to hitting me.

I sent Owen a message. *Gutschein?* ("Rain check"?)

After only a handful of heartbeats, my phone trembled. A synthetic voice read his reply aloud: "Is everything okay?"

He did not demand an explanation. Only asked after my well-being.

I sucked cold air between my teeth. Moved my fingers on impulse: *I've fallen ill. So sorry.*

Not strictly a lie. Perhaps the brother of one.

If Frau Pruwitt and Father could feel my anxiety, Owen would feel it also.

Understand. Owen has been helpless enough throughout his life. Our relationship is growing, but doesn't that make it fragile? A woodland metaphor for you, fellow hermit: while the boughs of trees expand into magnificence, the tips of branches break at the slightest pressure.

Recently I felt one snap.

Owen and I stood shoulder to shoulder in the library. Books in the children's section are placed in *rainbow order*, whatever that signifies; the concept of color remains irrelevant to my ears. Every time he slid a hardcover into a gap, Owen tapped the spine with his forefinger, mouthed the shape of a shade: *Orchid.*

"How is *orchid* a color? It is already a plant. Is that not enough for a thing to be?"

Owen smiled through pursed lips. I elbowed him. None too gently. I felt warm when he rocked back into me and used his careful hands to tap a tattoo onto the bindings. I could see the books even more clearly through the intimate echoes of his fingertips.

"If you can't handle work this simple," called Frau Pruwitt from the upper level, "how do you expect to get along in a respectable school?"

My breath caught. Owen's fingers halted. If only for half a beat, the books dissolved in my ears.

His tapping resumed, meter ever so slightly off.

If I went to see him after this spat about applications, I'd be no kind of company. Me, leaking pains that don't belong to him. Tragic enough that my emanations impact strangers.

If I can no longer be certain whether people in my proximity are feeling their own feelings or feeling mine, how can I help but mistrust their dismay? Their surprise?

I am an unnaturally manipulative creature.

I can only trust you. Only trust the letters of someone never tainted by meeting me. Yet meeting you is all I want. Even if it would mean sabotaging your emotions as well.

More happened on that very same day. Events that will set you bouncing in your rubber womble. But you seem content to be a storytelling tease. I will follow suit.

As for finding the children like me in Germany, I can't bring myself to make the pledge you have made. To call this my *Lebensziel*, life purpose. Not because I fear they would not like me. I don't like me, either.

Oliver. Has it occurred to you that there's purpose in simply being alive?

Life's enough of a thing for life to be.

Love,

Moritz

P.S. Recall that computer screens frustrate me. You'd be better off asking someone like Owen for help in the "magical Internet" area. Beg pardon.

P.P.S. A word that is the same in both our languages: *Idiot*. The ineptly named "kids you are going to meet"? They will be smitten by you. There's no alternative. *Idiot*.

chapter three
THE BEANIE

PEP-RANT INCOMING!

Moritz! What are we going to do with you?

You stood up your *beau*? Because of *feelings*? Bejeezus, man.

I want to grab your shoulders and shout in your ears to just let yourself BE HAPPY for once. You've finally got good things in your life! Maybe I never should have told you my theory about echolocation and emotional transference. Your *emolocation*. You're overthinking it, dingus!

I know you feel like an angsty blob of moods. (You're talking to a kid who kills phones when he's scared.) But here's the deal: Owen *cares* about you. Adamantium Pruwitt and your dad, too. They aren't worried about you manipulating them. It's *normal* for people who care about you to feel for you! That's not you foisting your emotions on people. That's just how people act. If Owen's sad about you changing schools, it's probably because *he'll miss you*.

Besides! Think about it, Moritz: If you're *really* infecting other people with your feelings, well, how amazing would it be if you infected them with something upbeat? Ask Owen! I bet it doesn't feel like bee stings when you *laugh*! Maybe that's more like, I dunno, getting your ears cuddled by a dozen ghostly kittens! Maybe when you smile, people melt like molten lava cake!

Idiot. You make me feel better even when you're a grump. So imagine the possibilities!

And now that you've survived this latest PEP-RANT, here's a promise: WHEN we meet (I'm always gonna say WHEN and never *if*), I'll be the happiest person in the world. So if you feel scared or sad, I'll grin hard enough to even us out.

And dang it, Mo. I'll hug you first.

I woke up blinking under white stars, breathing soil and antiseptic wipes, womble half peeled off my face. Green leaves scraped my skin, and stiff stems of massive stalks of some plant dug wedges into my spine.

"Where are we?"

"In a cornfield." Auburn-Stache perched on a pillow beside me in orange lantern light. "We crossed into Indiana an hour ago, while you were snoring."

"We're in *Indiana*? Fluff!" I sat up.

"Language."

"I spent my whole life alone in a cabin just so one day I could sleep through a border? *For shame.*"

"You only missed a signpost."

"I *know*! A signpost I've never seen!"

He picked at a leaf on a broken cornstalk, stripping it to restless ribbons.

"I can't smell any pine." It felt like losing a part of me, a pinkie maybe.

"Places nearer cities smell like petrol. A mite more industrial. More like where I grew up."

"Really?"

"Years before I was born, there were a lot of mines in Salford. The smell of coal hit your nostrils, permeated clothes. Perhaps that's why so many kids took to smoking."

"No lakes? Or forests? Or anything?"

"Dingy canals." Strips of leaf fell to his shoes.

Auburn-Stache's upbringing is as much a mystery to me as social networks are. "You've never talked about this before, 'Stache."

"I suppose I'm picking and choosing my secrets."

Another innocent leaf met its demise.

For once, I didn't push for honesty. "So whose cornfield is this, Auburn-Stache?"

He coughed. "I've no idea. An opportunity to leave the road and pull unseen into a field presented itself."

I laughed. "So you just drove crop circles out on some guy's farm!"

"Elkhart County is home to a small Amish population. I thought there might be fewer power lines here."

"Liz used to think I was Amish." I rubbed my cramped legs. "How do people sit in cars without turning into mummies? I feel crusted over."

"More toilet humor?"

"Auburn-Stache, I'm too classy for that kind of talk. I am not the one who pooped."

"I won't try to fathom you today, Ollie. I'm exhausted."

"See, me and Moritz have this joke about people who worked at the laboratory being metaphorical poopers."

Naturally, he shut up when I mentioned you, Moritz.

"You know. *Moritz?* That zany batboy you've known for years? Sort of mopey but in a sophisticated way? My best friend who you never talk about?"

More torn leaves.

His obnoxious vow of laboratory silence includes you, too. I never get to talk smack, Moritz! Yet another classic youth pastime denied the TLoG. *Forsooth.*

"I swear it was funny." But we both know it wasn't really, because that was the kind of desperate stuff we talked about right before Mom—

I clapped my hands, stood on my tiptoes. Cornstalks grow so tall! You wouldn't believe it! But I could see stars overhead and I could hear crickets, and this wasn't so unfamiliar after all. Impala aside, the only electricity in sight came from the power line near the road, orange tendrils. The circle Auburn-Stache had made was like twenty feet in diameter. I have no idea how I didn't wake up while he was steamrollering corn. Now his car murmured brown on the opposite side. I could *just* stomach it.

Moritz, I think it's interesting (and not just embarrassing!) that your dad suggested puberty maybe triggered your emolocation, because I've read that some kids outgrow epilepsy during puberty. That hasn't happened to me. I'm trying to build my tolerance, but now I'm not using just a little book light; I'm using the world. It's always going to be a gamble which of us will cave: me or electricity. But I guess I'm in a gamblin' mood.

Guess I don't want to die alone in the woods.

I picked at the womble. "Maybe I can try sleeping without it. . . ."

"Oliver, when you seize, where does the aura strike first? Where do you feel it?"

Seizures hit me like cloudy bricks, numb tongue and cinnamon and garbled words and aching head, but pinpointing the first casualty? "I get pressure here." I put my fingers on my temples. "Railroad spikes."

"I thought so." Auburn-Stache twitch-walked to his car.

"Digging for treasure?" I kept my distance when he popped open the trunk. Womble-less, I'm not as tough a cookie as you are, Moritz, and we didn't need me stalling his car out in the middle of some pitchfork-wielding man's cornfield.

"It won't stop your reactions entirely, but covering your temples and crown should prevent you from projecting electromagnetic pulses, at the very least. That suit is becoming inconvenient."

"Praise A'tuin the Star Turtle!" Mo, I'm glad you sent me the womble and sorry I blew chunks in it, but that thing made me feel like Joseph Merrick (a cool person, but not known for enjoying his teen years).

Auburn-Stache kept scrounging, up to his armpits in his portable supply of medical equipment. He tossed my fishbowl and several of my books out onto the crushed cornstalks. I hurried to pick up my copies of *Hard Times* and *Femme Felines from Frolix 8*, but right then, Auburn-Stache cried "Aha!" and pulled something from the recesses of the trunk. "Catch!"

I caught it, this bundle of scratchy gray clothing.

"A *beanie*, Auburn-Stache? Couldn't you give me a fedora? This thing is mayor of Uglytown. If I wear it, I'll definitely become some sort of pariah!"

"Ollie, it's time I tell you something."

"No way are you going to tell me things!"

"Fedoras are dreadfully uncool. This hat is knitted from rock wool. It's a great insulator."

"I didn't know rocks were anything like sheep. . . ." I trailed off, because there was something very familiar about the hat. The way it was put together, I mean. "Mom knitted this, didn't she?"

Wind rustled the cornstalks. "Yes, Ollie. She suspected the aura hit your temples first. Mothers sometimes notice things scientists overlook."

"Oh." I ran my fingers along her knitting, so tightly woven virtually no space between the fibers for electricity to slip through. "She made this just in case I left home, huh?"

"Most likely, yes."

"I never realized she actually meant it. I mean, about letting me leave."

He stepped forward, but I backed away. I pulled the hat down over my head and tucked my ears inside it.

Before going to sleep, I pulled the old book light from my backpack and turned it on. The familiar buzzing set my teeth on edge, and the green puff of electricity did, too, but it didn't exactly *hurt*. I pressed it to my head, pushing it into the hat. The light didn't even flicker.

It was an unseasonably warm night. Too warm for a wool hat, but I wasn't taking it off.

I had one angry motherfluffer of a crick in my back in the black early hours of the next morning. That's what you get for sleeping in shoddy crop circles. We feasted on bottled water and granola bars. I blinked at the womble.

"We meet again, my friend, my foe."

"It should be the last time," said Auburn-Stache. "I've thought of an alternative."

"An entire jumpsuit made of rock wool!" God, that would be itchy.

"Not far off, actually."

Uh-oh.

I did my business between cornstalks. (Farmers of the world, forgive me. Other people don't have to deal with this crap.) Then we skedaddled before the Amish could find us out. I felt bad about the ruined corn, so I left that copy of *Femme Felines from Frolix 8* in the middle of the circle. Maybe it would blow some kid's mind. There are some mighty-fine-lookin' cat people on that cover.

Auburn-Stache stared at billboards with all the intensity of a hunter.

I can't believe how quickly the novelty of face-planting car windows wore off, Moritz. It made me feel like a huge liar or something, since I've spent my whole life talking about how much I wanted to see the electric world, and now it lulled me to sleep. Liz would say "Told you so, doofus" and bop me on the nose, and you'd say "Did I not forewarn you of the underwhelming reality of society's blanditude" and bop me on the nose. If Mom's hat can prevent major car wrecks, maybe it can prevent your nefarious bops.

Eventually, Auburn-Stache cried "Aha!" and took us down a winding exit ramp beside yet another field, where a green tractor puffed Dijon clouds of electric gunk. I waved. A hand emerged from the gunk, waving back.

We pulled into a dinky parking lot in front of a bizarrely pink building. At first I thought it just had a really weird brand of electricity suffused around it, from the wiring inside the walls or something, but no. The little shack was actually painted BRIGHT FREAKIN' PINK. I squinted through the coiled light of the sign across the door frame to read "Adult Superstore" in huge red letters. A cartoon lady wearing rabbit ears and not much else was groping the letters pretty strangely. I guess she was really hot for the word *store*.

"What does being an adult have to do with rabbit ears and leopard print?"

"You'll have to stay in the car." I *can* see blushing. This was some prime blush-worthy material for our old doctor friend, Mo.

Another sign in the shop window claimed it was a "pleasure" having customers. And *pleasure* was italicized.

"Whoa. Wait. Is this a SEX SHOP?"

"Yes, Ollie. Yes, it is. My apologies."

My mouth dropped open, and then I was grinning like you wouldn't believe. "I don't think I need this sort of male bonding. Gee, Auburn-Stache. You old *perv*."

"Please don't."

I laughed a little. "Um, well. Happy birthday to me, I guess."

"You won't be saying that in a moment."

And yeah, sitting there, waiting for him to come back, getting bored, and realizing that a car seat was never going to feel comfortable after all, I did get sorta nervous. By the time he emerged carrying a glittery plastic bag, I was cringing.

"It's not ideal, but preferable to the womble. You'll need something less conspicuous, where we're going."

I opened the bag and laid eyes upon a thing unholy: a full bodysuit made of *black rubber.*

32

"*Tch.* I'm sure it'll flatter my curves," I said, dubious. "And look—complimentary handcuffs."

Auburn-Stache sighed. "All the questions you ask, and you haven't asked the biggest one. You unfathomable pretzel of a child. You haven't asked *where we're going.*"

"We're fulfilling my life purpose. We're going to see kids like Mo. We're going to help them, and I'm going to write their stories and—"

"Yes, yes. But where *are they*, Ollie? Growing on trees? Geographically. Where do you think we're off to first?"

"You're not gonna let me ask and then go all cryptic on me, are you? Because I'm armed now. *With fuzzy handcuffs.*"

"Ollie. Where?"

"You said Ohio, right? Or was it Mordor? Does it matter?"

His smile got sad. "I suppose, Ollie, you're just impatient to go anywhere at all. Yes?"

I shrugged. "Wherever my fellow weirdos are."

Moritz, if you've literally never gone *anywhere*, and you've never *seen* anywhere, how does it matter where you're going? Until we hit the road, I never knew there are rows of candy at gas stations. I never knew about "Walk" signs at intersections. No one ever told me about the eerie, disembodied voices of drive-through speakers, or how every stranger you meet for two seconds at drive-through windows says "Have a nice day!" and how great is that? (It's greater than the fast food itself; I'll say that much!) When there's that much world out there waiting for you, you're not picky. Everywhere there be amazing monsters.

Auburn-Stache could say the name of a place, and it wouldn't matter. I can't associate places with anything but books, maybe photos. What were the odds we were going anywhere I had read about? I'd ruled out Hogwarts. (I swear I didn't *really* dream about it. Everyone knows Hogwarts is in Scotland. And even if Hogwarts is (a) *completely electricity-free* and (b) full of perfect weirdos, it's fictional. *Supposedly*.)

"I guess setting *is* important in storytelling, 'Stache."

He clapped his hands. "So ask the bloody question!"

He looked like the kook he used to be—nothing like the tortured scientist stripping cornstalks to death—so I crowed, "Fine! Where are we going? Geographically?"

He smiled, held his arms out. "The Windy City. *Chicago*, kiddo."

Okay. Jaw-drop, et cetera. I *have* read about Chicago. In DC Comics, Metropolis *is actually based* on Chicago. Moritz, we were headed to Superman's hood.

The idea of me having anything in common with Superman is impossible.

Or it might not be. Because I have a sexy catsuit (meow, dude), and now I'm part of the *same world* you're part of. Moritz, even if you don't need a life purpose: I know you have strong feelings about Matt Murdock.

Tell me you don't want to read about my adventures with *actual superheroes*, the kids like us (but cooler), and I'll tell you your pants are on fire.

Sorry, let me translate the idiom: thine lederhosen are aflame.

I can wear my coat on the outside, even if that glorious, shiny bodysuit pinches pretty awkwardly in my crevices and makes my fingers sweaty. I definitely won't take the hat off.

But I wasn't off the hook yet.

Auburn-Stache started sad-side-eyeing me. He reached over and flicked my overgrown bangs.

At a hardware store not far from the, erm, *sexier hardware store*, Auburn-Stache picked up double-sided duct tape and a length of rubber tubing. From there, we went to a pharmacy for shaving cream and razors. Waiting in parking lots meant I couldn't help noticing how empty and vast the world seemed. Fields surrounded this little town, but no trees.

That seems kind of lonely, Moritz.

My first-ever park was outlined by power lines (those things will always stalk me) but empty apart from the statue of a soldier. The lot next door was full of tombstones—my first-ever graveyard. And in the lot next to that, someone had posted a "For Sale" sign outside a beige house. Do signs like that work in the real world? Back home, I could have made "SOS" signs in the front yard and no one would've ever seen them.

"Would people want to move in next to a little cemetery?" I asked, sitting on my first-ever park bench.

"Maybe, if next door was a park."

America is weird.

I eyeballed the swing set. It's terrifying to think people push their kids on those things. What if those kids are anything like Liz, and they have springs on their feet? What if you push a kid on a swing and then that kid goes up, up into the sky and never comes back down? (Don't get me started on the teeter-totter.)

Shaving foam never dripped past the nape of my neck, and Auburn-Stache never nicked the skin of my ears. The rubber tubing taped to my temples never got dislodged. He might have been a great barber instead of a mad scientist, if he'd wanted to.

I almost made a joke about that, but he was so quiet as he

toweled away the last remnants of foam, and, gosh, was my naked head cold. I stared at my hair, stuck to my shoes. You'd think being bald would make me lighter, but that tubing weighed me down like a demented crown.

"Now, there's a clean seal, right, Auburn-Stache? Good riddance to the rooster cut of yore!"

Auburn-Stache sniffled. I think it was only because the wind blew autumn-icy at last. Just in case, I didn't look at him.

Hitting the road was supposed to be an adventure, Moritz. But what if I left everything that was Ollie UpandFree back home? What if I got lost in these new woods?

"Do you want to have a go on the swings?" Auburn-Stache tore off a final piece of duct tape, secured the beanie, and pulled the edges down over my ears.

"Maybe not the swings." I felt like an ass, so I turned and smiled and said, "But I am definitely gonna wreck that slide."

This time I saw the signs at the state line. One read, "The Land of Lincoln" (which is pretty great by name-dropping standards). Another one read, "The People of Illinois welcome you." Would they welcome me if they knew I could kill their phones?

Maybe, Mo. After all, we were two hours away from meeting my first fellow mutant. Maybe there really is room for all our emotional nonsense.

And I can't *do* subtle. Subtle takes patience! I'm saying it again— *not* ALL-CAPS-ING, but saying it with entirely *mature enthusiasm*, because shouting doesn't really work with you.

If meeting these kids can help them like it's helped us, what have we got to lose? If Auburn-Stache won't talk smack, well, let's let them do the talking. Join my quest, Moritz!

Don't give me the whole "let me/them rot" spiel, Moritz. You act like you resisted my charms for ages, but you started caving after two letters. (I counted!) It's not betraying me, you know, meeting them. If you're thinking something like that!

There's room in us for more friends. Moritz, there's room in us for the world! And vice versa!

~ Ollie

P.S. So! Send me Owen's address, so I can write him about using the magical Internet!

chapter four

THE CURLS

Oliver. Much as I find it, ah, *adorable* when you cheerlead me, your selective delicacy is disconcerting.

Of course we're allowed other friends. Trust you to be entirely fine with my eyeless horror of a face and somehow uneasy about my potential for *hurt feelings*. Once again you are not practicing what you preach. If *I* am not responsible for the feelings of others, how can *you* be responsible if I feel . . . what? Jealous of your friends?

Oliver, if I am honest: I envy anyone who has heard your voice. Touched you.

But.

Surely you've read John Donne? I am not threatened by these dull sublunary anyones. Our relationship is not determined by proximity. We are boundless, Ollie.

Leaving home is frightening. Beyond parks are often graveyards.

Date or no, I would not go home. Frau Pruwitt might sit in the kitchen until the cusp of dawn. That eyebrow lost in the back reaches of her hair, waiting for me to finish filling out applications.

I cannot read bus numbers on digital screens; I climbed aboard the fourth after the driver confirmed it went west. Nearly pulled the emergency-stop lever before the bus even began moving. Every horrid centimeter of that vehicle seemed to contain a body. No question of getting a seat.

I clutched a dangling handle so tightly I felt my knuckles would burst. At least I am not tall. Bodies could hold me in place once the motion of the bus distorted all sound waves into an incomprehensible slurry.

The doors squeaked shut. The machine shifted into gear.

The world dissolved in my ears.

I breathed deep. Reminded myself that this was no anechoic chamber. I would soon be on solid ground once more. My pacemaker would not allow my heart to fail. I could survive disorientation for thirty minutes.

Oliver, if I am incapable of conquering a simple bus ride across my city, surely I am incapable of meeting you.

The bus had only stopped twice in a span of six minutes. Bodies pressed against either side of me, indifferent to my silent agony. Elbowed in the back, with nary an "excuse me."

How is it, Ollie, that the greatest trials in my recent memory include something so mundane as a bus ride?

Had you only been aboard, smiling with Chiclets on your teeth.

By the third stop, I must have been emolocating my misery. Someone prodded me in the chest. Through grainy feedback, I realized she had gestured me to take her seat. An elderly woman. I clicked in her smiling face. Counted enough wrinkles to shame me.

I shook my head. Thanked her. Disembarked seven stops too soon.

A sailor returning to land. I wanted to kiss the ground. I would walk.

I will walk to you if need be.

Will you ask where I was going? Or doesn't it matter, as long as I arrived?

Ollie, I have always enjoyed public radio. One program I'm fond of, *Die Speiselokal*, records local shows. Once while I wrote you at my desk above the city, the announcer proclaimed that, after a message from his sponsors, he would stream a live performance taking place at the *Kulturmesse* (culture fair).

The tune itself was initially unremarkable: an up-tempo choral reimagining of Debussy's "Clair de Lune." No glockenspiel accompaniment. I imagined the shape of the cathedral. Halfway through, the choir fell silent. The pianist took command in a reprise. I thought the song lacked a well-timed rap solo—

And that's what happened.

Rhythmic speaking. Free-form poetry. A gorgeous voice. Rapid, precise. Such an outburst should have been incongruous in a piece so delicate. But no. These performers saw a piece of music as I thought only I could.

Students from Myriad Academy. Where such things are mundane.

If we want to find room in the world for us, perhaps the *where does* matter, Ollie.

Afternoon arrived shortly before I did. I paid the wind nipping at my earlobes little mind. Paid mind instead to the lawns stretching before me.

Located on the city's edge, Myriad's campus is as much a park as anything else. On weekends, the gates are opened and the public may enjoy the trees and gardens. There are two auditoriums, an outdoor amphitheater. Myriad (ha) study halls. A large library. A famous *Literatur* department where, it is rumored, the students have no chairs. They gather on fireside beanbags during lessons.

To sit on a beanbag at school would be to taste heaven, Ollie.

Myriad's tuition is essentially criminal, despite what Father pretends. It is especially beyond our means if I intend to save to come see you. I had decided. Even before Frau Pruwitt dropped off the applications. In the secret hours when I trudged through Myriad's illustrious history, my computer's digital voice ringing in my ears.

I had decided I could not go.

Yet here I was.

It may be dolphin-wavy, Oliver. But *verdammt*! I want to go to art school.

I wandered from the stone path. Sat down on a manicured lawn beneath a large willow tree. Permitted the reverberations of dancing and singing from two auditoriums to float past my auricles and illuminate the leafy whips draping above me. Illuminate the mites on the leaves and the veins in the leaves and the fluid in the leaves and the splendor in the leaves—

Someone was *looking* at me.

She stood near my feet. Posture stiff, guarded—I could almost taste her aggression. I fought the strangest urge to lift my goggles.

"Do I . . . are we acquainted?" Knowing the answer.

"Prince Moritz." Her voice fell soft on my ears. She, dressed primly in a lace dress and a broad summer hat. A mane of curls hung loose on her shoulders. "It can't be. It can't be you."

I drew myself up. Clicked my tongue at her, once. She didn't flinch. Only hitched her smile higher.

One of her smiles.

Not *both* of her smiles.

The second mouth on the nape of her neck, currently hidden beneath her locks—hidden from almost everyone but not from my ears—did not smile. The corners of it turned downward. Her eyes widened. The smile on her face remained fixed.

There stood the girl who once tried to drown me in my mother's laboratory.

"Molly," I said. "What are the odds?"

Molly's eyes betrayed her, her perfect smile a sheen that existed on the surface of her like a layer of sweat. She wore it too closely, the girl who tried to drown me.

"Did your mother send you?" She tiptoed near. No matter how docile she seemed, she bared her back teeth. Curls bounced; I smelled cherries. "Is that it?"

"No," I blubbered. "I've no idea where she is. Haven't seen her in years."

Molly bit her lip. "Oh . . . ?"

Understand, Ollie—for you, being an experiment once seemed better than being sick. For me, having been an experiment keeps me awake. Embracing the kids like us means bringing nightmares to my waking mind. Bringing me back to near-death experiences, Ollie. I have wanted to forget her second mouth. Along with the rest of her.

"So what are you doing here, Moritz? Here, where I happen to be."

"It's a lovely day. This is a lovely place," I replied. Perhaps too quickly. Did I sting her with my unease?

"Do you—have you enrolled here?"

"I—I am considering it." She need not know I couldn't afford it. "I had no idea you—that you would be here. Beg pardon."

A group of students in choir robes passed by on the sidewalk. A girl called out to her. Molly didn't take her eyes off me. I smelled cherry once more. Realized her second mouth sucked on a lozenge.

"You weren't stalking me, then?" Molly's brow furrowed.

"*Gott in Himmel*. Not at all! Why should I ever want to?"

"Then you don't have anything to apologize for." She put out a gloved hand. I dodged it like a hit. "I can show you around campus, if you'd like."

What might you do in such unsettling circumstances? Was I to run from this girl in dance slippers? She was nothing I could solve with my reflexes. Nothing I could manage by being quick on my feet. I may as well be as clumsy as you are.

"Beg pardon . . . I should go."

She put her smile back on. "Do you live nearby?"

I began to nod. Halfway through, I shook my head.

"You're acting as if I'm going to dunk you underwater again!"

The teeth in the back of her skull were all but grinding together.

"Your second mouth is not smiling."

"It's not smiling," she whispered, "because it has a habit of betraying what I'm really feeling. Most people don't know. But you can see it even now, right? I can't hide from the prince."

"It reveals your subconscious? So you truly feel like baring teeth at me."

"Honestly?" She exhaled. "I'm *frightened*, Moritz. I'm scared to see you here."

My throat constricted. This is so like what others have suggested: *I* am the terrifying one. I am my mother's son. This suggestion, even from the girl who once held my skull down in a heartfelt effort to fill my lungs with water.

"I'll frighten you no longer." We are trying to stand, Oliver. I fall down easily. "I'm expected elsewhere."

"You have friends waiting for you? That's nice, Moritz. I mean. It's nice, how we can all get on with things. We Blunderkinder."

"We *what*?"

"We're more a blunder than a wonder." Both mouths carried the same small smile.

Did that make it genuine?

"You've got friends as well? Here?"

Two grins. "Yes. Would you care to meet them sometime?"

Would you believe I nodded? "Yes. Yes, that would be lovely."

The distant slap of dancers' footfalls. Wind in the branches.

"You're still here, Moritz."

"Yes. I may have, ah, exaggerated the urgency of leaving. I wish . . ."

"What is it?"

"I wish I could trust you."

"And I wish you'd take my arm, Prince Moritz, and let me show you the campus."

There were so many bystanders. Surely she could not drown me. I took her arm, precisely because it was so hard to do. You would have done it.

The midmost theater smelled faintly of lemon polish. Of hair spray. Incomparable to the putrid sweat stench of Bernholdt-Regen's stairwells. Music ignited wide hallways. I saw by laughter that had nothing to do with inflicting grievous injury. Were there no Lenz Monks here?

Molly beamed with her front mouth. Her back teeth chattered. Nerves? Or hunger? I could no longer hear her lozenge clicking. She introduced me to students as we traversed the building. All of them greeted her with smiles.

"Nice shades." This from a jocular boy. He towered over me in costume. A trim 1890s preparatory school uniform. "Who's the new fish, Molls?"

"This is Moritz. And *no*. Come along, Moritz. If you do enroll, watch out for Max. He doesn't even pretend to mean well."

Max smirked and squeezed both my shoulders. "*Hey*, you. *Moritz*."

I started. Such overfamiliarity!

(Ollie, a brief lesson in tongues: upon meeting someone new, I'm accustomed to being addressed with the polite form of the word *you*. *Sie* rather than *du*. Call me antiquated, but months passed before I greeted Owen as *du*.)

Max *duzen*ed me as if my name belonged to him.

"Beg *pardon*?"

Max released me. Nearly knocked me askew. Soon he spun around to watch us leave. Molly's unseen hind mouth stuck out its tongue at him.

From a grand hallway with high, echoing ceilings covered in ivy motifs, Molly led me down a narrower hallway and then backstage. Her arrival was met by raucous *Hallo!*s.

To think one of my mother's monsters is genuinely popular. No one smashed her face into anything. Not a soul seemed to bear her ill will. She held herself with grace.

I lacked her presence. I waited for someone to shrink me down, Oliver. To inquire about my goggles. To mock my fringe. To shy away from my fears projected.

But they greeted me with friendliness. Curiosity. If anything, I was underdressed: many students wore theatrical costumes and makeup. Those who did not clothed themselves in shawls and drainpipe pants. Peculiar art-school garb. An *Aladdin Sane*–era David Bowie lookalike named Chloe complimented my choice of wardrobe.

"There's a brand-new boy, but I don't know his name. And he's wearing four patterns at once? That's *bold*, and I *dig bold*, son."

Several students in canvas coveralls carried hammers on their belts. "Not sure why there are stagecrafters building here on a Saturday," tittered Molly. "It'll interfere with Year Two dress rehearsals."

"When else were we supposed to finish all this work?" called a stocky, scraggly-haired boy from atop a particleboard staircase. Sharp eyes darted to Molly's arm, looped around mine. I heard his grip tighten on the handle of his hammer. "Hey! Golf pants! Who are you supposed to be, anyhow?"

"Beg *pardon*?" I clicked in surprise, snapping my ears his way.

"Moritz is an old friend." I jolted at the exaggeration. But her second mouth didn't refute her words. "And you could actually meet your set deadlines during school and there wouldn't be any trouble. As class representative, I am responsible for hounding you, *Liebling*. *Cat on a Hot Tin Roof* premieres on Friday. Where's the tin roof, Klaus?"

"If you paid any attention," said Klaus, pointing with his hammer, "you'd know that there is no tin roof in the play."

"*Liebling*, I was being *sarcastic*."

"Perhaps he was, ah, waiting for that click." My contribution.

Plays aren't your strongest suit, Oliver.

47

Tennessee Williams's *Cat on a Hot Tin Roof* tells the story of Maggie and Brick, a dysfunctional couple. "Waiting for that click" is how Brick describes the uncertainty of existence: waiting for an indefinable moment. Some existential click to remedy his life.

Klaus leapt from the summit. Sawdust took violent flight upon his landing. A mighty boom, not a click.

"How gay are you, on a scale from one to rainbows?"

"Ah. I can't comprehend rainbows."

"What?"

Molly sighed and began to lead me away; Klaus's frown returned.

"I'm no threat," I blurted.

He coughed into a muscled forearm. Not looking at Molly. Suddenly cowed.

Her second mouth pinched.

I'm no matchmaker, Oliver.

My footsteps echoed up a wooden staircase. A flawless stage faced a gaping cavern of a room. Nearly perfect acoustics. I whistled a note, high and clear, toward rows of cushioned seats extending into the distance. In that whistle's recall, I saw the curvature of the layered walls around the stage. Panels precisely placed overhead. Architecture made to exemplify a cappella singing. This was the opposite of a soundless room. This room *celebrated* sound.

I sat on the edge of the stage and breathed. Even my sighs made music here.

"Well, Prince?" Molly sat beside me, crossed her legs.

"Thank you for showing me this place."

"It is wonderful, isn't it?" Molly adjusted a pin in her hat. "Sometimes I forget. I'm glad to see you so pleased."

"The girl who drowned me, glad to see me. *My*."

"Well, I think I knew all along that it was a bit unfair." She sighed from both sides. "You were a lonely boy, not a cruel one. *You* never would have tried to drown *me*."

"I might have. And my mother drowned us all."

"Maybe. But you *aren't* your mother."

Could she feel my gratitude? "No, I'm not."

She bit her back lip. "So. Have you ever wanted to find her?"

"Never." My purpose in life, Ollie, isn't to search for anyone.

Molly, carefully: "You won't find her here. And you'll already have a friend."

I swallowed. "You say that word so easily."

"Or you don't say it easily enough." Her second set of lips revealed nothing. "Living in the lab, I never imagined having friends. But you know, Prince Moritz. Most people really do try to be good to each other."

A Blunderkind found me first. A reckoning, Oliver.

Always I'll greet newcomers with caution. Waiting to find out which of their organs exists in duplicate or not at all. Forever listening for evidence of my mother's soulless workings.

I don't imagine you found a hero in Chicago, but someone more complicated.

Meeting Molly reminds me that the improbable occurs.

Impossible really is not so very far away. Our lives seem comprised of meeting strange people under strange circumstances. Perhaps that is what all lives are like. Your optimism remains infectious. Perhaps you are emolocating as well?

When and never *if*, Ollie.

P.S. I will *never* ask Owen whether my laughter feels like "ghostly ear kittens." You insufferable, perfect idiot.

chapter five

THE FOG

Drop the acoustic-to-electric transducer, Moritz.

Because I did find a hero. Not in Chicago. In *Kreiszig*. You're *textbook* sometimes!

Embarking on a quest! Overcoming the fearsome Cyclops known as the city bus?

(Stop it, man.)

Journeying to a mighty hall and facing down the Medusa who haunted your childhood?

(Moritz, I'm *dying*.)

Befriending said Medusa?

(I'm dead, Moritz, for you've killed me with your panache.)

Good thing you don't have eyes, because when you open this letter, it'll be blinding, reflecting the radioactive hugeness of my smile!

How dare you be so awesome? What, MBV wasn't enough of a superpower? Emolocation wasn't, either? Now you've got to be pristine *and* mature? Also, holy crap. Turns out Molly really has two mouths? I'd find that harder to believe before this road trip. But now . . .

The Blunderkids (I am stealing that punny nickname and 'MURICANizing it) are a wacky bunch. Soon we'll have to start wearing uniforms. I don't vote for the yellow spandex route. Then again, after wearing this damn bodysuit, it wouldn't be such a bad transition. And then all the rest of y'all would know the agony of pinching.

I'm kind of jealous. If we were fiction, you'd be halfway up Mount Doom and I'd still be picking my nose in the Shire. (Or lounging in Rivendell, because why the heck were the hobbits so eager to leave a land of beautiful people, waterfalls, and delectable foodstuffs?)

Moritz. It's HUGE that you took Molly's arm. What *are* the odds? Auburn-Stache says there are only twenty-seven of us in the world. And you ran into one in your own city?

Looks like you're all aboard the *Lebensziel* train, like it or not!

Even if she's kind and flowery, you tell Molly something from me: she tries anything like that drowning bullshit on you again, I'm gonna swim over there and electroshock her ass.

Fair warning.

Moritz, can I take you to the city with me? As a storyteller? Not that I have words for the sensory overload known as Chicago. Good thing being lost for words has never stopped me from talking!

As we approached the Windy City, so many more cars crowded so many more lanes, and electricities became so thick that squinting accomplished jack squat. Describing the car smog without saying brown (colors don't help you, which makes this whole *finding words* thing even harder), I'd say this felt like bathing in a bowl of chunky oatmeal.

Until a shimmering, multicolored fog crept up from the horizon.

"How can you see where we're going with all that fog in the way?"

"Fog?" Auburn-Stache didn't look my way, but he was itching to. I guess being surrounded by speeding vehicles is stressful even for people who don't see ominous oatmeal where cars should be. "Ollie, there isn't any fog. It's a clear day, autumn gray."

"But . . ." It looked so tangible, Moritz. Real, actual weather.

After I tried squinting again (and got subsequently smacked by hiccuping sneezes), I *could* see the outlines of bluish skyscrapers on the horizon. That's probably what most people have to settle for.

But when this Blunderkid *stopped* squinting, Moritz?

"Holy shit."

"Ollie! Is the hat not working?"

I put my hand on his hand, on the wheel. "No, it's good. It's just . . . 'Stache. It's just . . ."

"Then—"

"Shh." I don't think I've ever shushed someone before. (The hypocrisy!)

Once I helped Liz create a density jar for her science homework. We sat in the cabin kitchen and poured milk, canola oil, cola, and cherry syrup into a bottle and watched all the layers separate.

Chicago was the ultimate density jar, this massive glow cloud that crept over us in billowing layers, probably across four or five dimensions. I saw it in every color imaginable. To cater to my batboy audience, I'm going to pretend I saw textures, too.

The orange of infinite wiring in walls sparked above buildings in jagged spears, jagged like bread knives, and beneath them, shining from countless windows, beams of emerald and purples, and if they had a texture, I'd say they were long tubes of glass, and lower down more tangerine stripes coiled like unwound paper clips, more grass greens layered like woven baskets or torn bits of corn leaf, and a blue misting layer of gauze that was maybe something electric I'd never thought about—maybe it had something to do with stoplights? And farther down, Moritz, maybe hundreds of feet, near the foot of the glow cloud, the brown oatmeal of vehicles and machinery, and burgundy strands like bacon-y ribbon underground that I later learned had to do with trains.

And everywhere, like pores on the glowing cityscape? Speckled punctures of green light that made cheesecloth out of air, green pinpricks growing larger as we drove into the city limits, pinpricks like stars in the ether, stars reflecting a million people I never thought I could have shared space with. People who were probably parents and siblings and friends and enemies and police officers with saffron-slashing walkie-talkies and babies in cribs with cottony night-lights warming them, the welcoming people of the Lincoln State?

And I couldn't meet them all.

Seeing so much electricity in one place should have shut me down, beanie or not.

The city was alive, Moritz. Every part of it fought to outshine every other part, and if there were dark parts, I couldn't see them. Instead—oh god, I think I was in *lovesickness*, Mo! This city was like I am sometimes, just screaming to be heard.

A city like this could only create heroes.

Moritz, the *where* really matters.

"Ollie! What's wrong?" Auburn-Stache, shaking me.

"I just want to meet *everyone*," I choked.

The tension left his shoulders. "Steady on. We're going in, Ollie."

But he was wrong. I think the city was going into *me*.

I wish I could share every thought I had in Chicago, but I can't spend years writing about just one city. I mean, after our visit, during the flat drive from Illinois to Ohio, I wrote twenty pages just about elevated trains that travel *over your head* and *over streets* and make you maroon-y sick in trash cans. (No one ever told me there are helpful trash cans on the street corners of America. Bless this land, where man is free to vomit where he may!)

Auburn-Stache saw me drawing maps and reminded me he wasn't going to send "bloody novels" to you every week. He could have told me that *before* I got carsick writing the pages. Auburn-Stache would rather deal with my actual vomit than my question-vomit.

I'm only ever quiet when I'm writing you.

But I need to be more than quiet. I need to be professional. A real storyteller.

(Granted, my audience is probably pretty limited in this case.)

Travels with the Teenage Lord of Glockenspieling:
An Electro-Sensitive Hermit's Guide to Chicago
(SERIOUSLY ABRIDGED, ALAS AND DAMN IT)

Chicago isn't exactly hermit-friendly. However, any electro-sensitive hermits who brave a trek to the Windy City won't be disappointed!

Electro-sensitivity will always be our personal ass-pain to bear, but remember: people are the best distraction. Normally, I can count all the people I know on my phalanges, fellow hermits! In Chicago, every stranger feels like a new species. Inquisitive hermit types should approach this aspect of the world through the lens of a scientist conducting important research!

A man in a long coat? The inquisitive hermit asks: Why so long, coat?

A lady with long red fingernails? Why so long and so red, fingernails?

Oh, bearded man, beating the living crap out of buckets on a street corner—what did buckets ever do to you?

The least hermit-friendly aspect wasn't the noise, either. Fragile hermits might want to pack some earmuffs just in case, but the *cacophony* (that'll be on the vocab test!) melted into a steady hum of activity. Blips when horns honked or music blared in the street. Music through speakers sounds really tinny and staticky to antielectric ears. But remember, brave hermits: the woods are noisy, too. Only instead of the hum of insects you get roaring traffic.

And then there's the gimmick-shattering voice of your intrepid caretaker:

"We can't stay here long. We can head directly to Arthur's home in Logan Square. I've spoken to his guardian. Lately, he's been homeschooled, so he'll be around. Or we could see some of the sights. Millennium Park, the Shedd Aquarium, the *shiny Bean*, et cetera."

I'm losing the gimmick, but the least hermit-friendly part about visiting Chicago: "I have to pick between Superman and the fishes?"

"Ollie, Arthur's not Superman. Quite the opposite. Prone to accidents."

"Wait, you're actually telling me things? What's *Arthur* allergic to?"

"He's really very sick. A bone disease." We crossed a bridge over Lake Michigan and got caught between buildings, swallowed by skyscraper shadows.

"*Very sick*, huh." Having Auburn-Stache say *sick* so bluntly, I had to face facts: maybe all those times our doctor left me moping in bed, he knew other kids with way better reasons to be in bed.

Maybe that's what he doesn't want to tell me.

Moritz, maybe I'm the least heroic of all hermits.

"Let's see more wonderland. . . ." The rubber tugged at my underarms. That's why I was sweating. I don't get claustrophobic. Not about dark parts, not about buildings on all sides.

"This isn't a wonderland. It's a city, Ollie. You're not living in one of your science-fiction novels. You must be careful in the real world."

"I'm not a toddler."

"In a sense you are. The dangers here aren't just to do with your electromagnetism. People in cities aren't worse—but there are *more* people."

"But that's miraculous."

"Of course. But when so many people group together, a few are bound to be unfriendly." He bit his nails. "I *shouldn't* be taking you here, understand? What would your mother say?"

In that second, I wanted to stop the car and run in any direction: over bridges, across city blocks. Just run and find whoever had sprayed their names on the graffiti-slathered bricks and ask them about their families and whether they'd gone a day without electricity and what that felt like.

I wanted to climb up every rusty ladder on every old warehouse-y building, as high and as far away as I could get from this car, with its heaters and sudden quiet.

What *would* she say?

Outside our car, nobody wore wombles. I couldn't just say hi to total strangers. I couldn't ask them things. (Why so grumpy, bus driver? Why so tired, woman with Coney dog?)

Moritz, if I forced my way in . . . how many batteries would get shorted? How many trains might stall, go from burgundy bacon to nothing? How many electric hearts could I stop? Big and worth being in as Chicago felt, there might not be room for me here.

Just like there isn't room to tell you about it.

"Ollie? I worry when you're quiet. Are you with me?"

I nodded.

"*Now* I'm absolutely petrified."

The thing is, Moritz, there *are* people with wombles of their own. And I thought maybe if I met some of those Blunderkids, maybe I'd see how they fit into the world. Selfish again: learning their stories might put me in the world, too.

I wasn't asking to belong. I just wanted to be the good kind of tourist. The sort that doesn't leave traces behind.

"Can we go see Arthur, please?" I had to prove her wrong or right, Moritz.

I'll never know what she would say. She might have said go home. She used to lock the doors.

But she knitted this beanie, too.

We left Chicago two weeks ago. I know my storytelling is lagging behind the present day, but, Moritz, I'll make it worth it. If I'm going to spend my life telling Blunder-stories, I'm going to do them justice. Especially when those stories beat the one I'm living . . .

Moritz, Myriad would accept you in a heartbeat; you HAVE to apply. Even if you think you're not creative (doofus!). Even if you think you can't afford this.

Even if it means waiting two years to meet me.

We'll be okay! We have our letters, and we have all these people filling the world around us, and we agreed that's a *good thing*. (Is there a German word for "delayed gratification"? Delunderisch Gratifikationisch, or something?) Before I meet you, Moritz, I want to finally leave Rivendell. I want to be someone worth meeting. I have a lot to learn from the people of the world, Blunderkids and beyond.

And yeah. Every time we meet a person, it's a potential near-death experience.

But, Moritz, I have to believe in near-*life* experiences, too.

~ Ollie UpandFree

P.S. What gives? Send me Owen's address! This is Campaign Blunder-find. OLLIE WANTS YOU! I am pointing my finger and my eyebrows are Pruwitt-level wacky. It's not just about finding Blunderkids. I also have to ask Owen about your ear-kittens.

chapter six

THE ORCHID

Oliver,

Far be it from me to tell you how to tell a story. But remember, however you tell it, *your* story it remains. I have followed your antics for far too long to shift my affections from my heroic protagonist to some newcomer. No matter how interesting.

Do not think for a second that you aren't worthy of anyone. I am content to hear you rattle on about strangers only because it is *you* who rattles.

If ever I suspect, even for a moment, that you are telling me about Arthur or any of the others to distract me from something that ails you? I will, as DJs say, SHUT THE CLUB DOWN. I won't allow you to hide yourself in woods of words.

There is more to the day I met Molly.

I walked away from the gates of Myriad and Molly's farewells, and the world grew only colder. Grimier. Crossing the canal into Ostzig, I'd entered a dystopian civilization. The eastern side of Kreiszig is half abandoned. Filled with vacant buildings made prey to foreclosure. Or made of stone so old it crumbles when touched. Frigid wind chilled my ears. Difficult, faced with soot-coated churches, tiptoeing under bridges so as not to wake the homeless, to maintain the sense of optimism I'd found in the auditorium. Myriad is a *where* far removed from my home.

Night had arrived. Frau Pruwitt no longer haunted our kitchen.

Father had fallen asleep at the table. I pulled a cold mug of coffee from his hand so he would not overturn it. The applications lay before him. I clicked at the pile.

Father lifted his head as if I'd pulled a trigger.

"Have you eaten?" He gathered the papers. Tucked them between the bread box and the refrigerator.

"I'm not hungry. Thank you."

"Thirsty?"

I shook my head. I wished, Ollie, he would become angry. Punish me like any parent should when his son is awful. My father is too understanding. It has been years since he rescued me from the laboratory. Years since I should have gotten better. Still, he tiptoes. Telling him about Molly would only make him tiptoe more.

(My honesty is reserved for you, confidant.)

Father put the kettle on. "Assam or oolong?"

"Neither. Thank you."

"Owen stopped by to check on you. He left something." Father plucked a tea bag and a cup from the shelf. "In your room."

An ache in my chest. How crestfallen Owen must have been, to catch the brother of a lie.

"Will you ask me whether I've considered the applications, Father?"

The water boiled before he answered. "I didn't think you wanted to talk about that."

"Because you can sense my apprehension? I'm stinging you with it?"

"It's not like that."

"Don't, Father." Maybe I paled. "Don't accommodate me. I don't deserve it."

Father poured hot water into the cup. "You deserve it."

"I—"

Father looked at me, necessary or not. His voice kind. "My *son* deserves whatever I can spare him."

"So you won't get angry. Even if I stay at Bernholdt-Regen?"

He stirred the water. "Not if you want to stay."

"Or if I actually wanted to go to, say, *Hogwarts*, you would not argue. If I wanted to go to that useless art school across town. You would not argue."

He set the mug on the table between us. "We would find a way, Moritz."

I laughed. A pathetic, squawking ibis.

"Moritz?"

"We can't afford proper tea leaves. You darn your socks. Be reasonable."

"Do you want to go to . . . Hogwarts?"

"Yes, I want to go to *Hogwarts*. But I never got a damn owl, did I? As ever, since you took me in. You just have to make do!"

"What do you want, Moritz?"

"Buy yourself some new socks. Stop bothering about me."

I swallowed half the tea in one angry gulp, scalding my tongue.

Very quietly: "That tea was mine."

I set it down. Left the kitchen.

A potted orchid waited on my desk. The note attached? *Überraschung*.

I lay back on my bed. Pulled my headphones on. Checked messages.

Fieke: "*Brille*. You twat! Owen's just told me that you *stood him up*? You'd better have a fluffing good reason; he gives you the benefit of the doubt, but I don't. For fluff's sake! You can't—"

Delete.

"I know you, you *android*, and you deleted that message. So again: this isn't how you keep friends. For whatever reason, he wants to keep you, so you'd better step up and—"

Delete.

"Moritz. My brother fluffing loves you."

I did not delete that one.

The final message came from Owen. I listened, dry-throated.

"Hey, Moritz!" In the voice I had programmed for him. A sort of musical, youthful tenor. Perpetual exclamation marks. "Looks like you decided to surprise me today instead!"

This is what I amount to. Heroic or subhuman, Ollie?

"Frau Pruwitt told me you left angry! But we could have talked about it! You didn't have to lie! You never asked me what I thought about you switching schools! You clam up!"

I have programmed him to sound like you, Ollie. Or how I imagine you sound.

"But I know if I had a chance to leave Bernholdt-Regen, you would send me on my way!"

He knows this? *I* don't even know this.

"I'll miss your frown! But Kreiszig isn't that big!"

I messaged him back:

Some of the schools aren't in Kreiszig.

And, within seconds, the voice answered: "The world isn't that big, either! You can send me photos of your wrinkly forehead from Russia! I'll see the lines just fine!"

I am laughing appropriately.

"Just give in already and write 'Hahaha!' Be like everyone else!"

Never.

"I would send you a winky face, but I'm pretty sure text-to-speech would just read 'SEMICOLON D!' Hahaha!"

TTS wouldn't even enunciate the semicolon. Send me a so-called winky face and I'll only hear "D!"

"D! D! D!"

Laughing appropriately. And, Owen?

"Yes?"

Apologizing. Profusely.

One can sense hesitation through machines. "Apologize in person!"

In person?

"You said 'rain check'! That part better not have been a lie!"

It wasn't a lie.

"D!"

That hardly seemed wink-worthy.

"That wasn't a wink! It was a happy face! Tomorrow?"

I bit my lip, hand hovering.

Owen, do you ever feel what I'm feeling? As I'm feeling it?

"D! Not sure what you mean! But I hope we'll be 'feeling it' together really soon! D!"

I cannot see blushing. I wish this emolocation worked both ways. If only I could understand the emotions of those around me. Through a phone, would it matter? Owen might have been laughing as he wrote me.

Or crying.

I clicked. Traced the outline of the binder that holds your letters. Peeled my headphones down to my neck and my goggles off my head. Rubbed hands against my long forehead. Despite the lateness of the hour, I pulled pen and paper from my desk drawer.

I began writing you.

Three minutes in, paper rustled outside my bedroom door. I stood, opened it. A teacup pinned the Myriad application to the floor. The heat of a teapot steamed the linoleum. All print portions of the application had been filled out in my father's block-lettered handwriting. Only the essay portion remained.

Father's bedroom door was closed. He could be trying to sleep. He works Sunday mornings.

I hoped he could sense some of the feelings seeping out of me.

I took his gift inside. Poured myself a cuppa before turning back to my computer, replacing my headphones. The Streets' *A Grand Don't Come for Free*. Opened my word processor while Mike Skinner shouted at me.

The unimaginative prompt: "What can you contribute to Myriad Academy's rich heritage?"

Did I answer with creativity? Not at all.

But I wrote as if I were writing you.

As for the rain check—a gentleman would not say.

Suffice it to say Fieke was not home. Suffice it to say we did not talk after all. Suffice it to say when I arrived on his doorstep leaking guilt, Owen's gaze scraped me head to toe like a sunburn before he took my hand and pulled me inside.

Suffice it to say I never knew that tapping fingers on the skin beneath clothing could leave one feverish. Suffice it to say the dingy apartment grew stuffy despite autumn's cold outside. Suffice it to say I have rarely been so eager to miss a few heartbeats.

When Owen reached for my goggles, letting my lips free at last, I regained senses enough to grab his wrists, lower them to my shoulders instead.

Suffice it to say.

Afterward, lying against him in the dark of the dank basement apartment, the walls felt paper-thin. The dilapidated couch beneath us. Could it give way?

How delicate were these new branches?

His fine hair brushing the boxy lump of my pacemaker, his breath against my ribs: these things, something nearer than near life.

"Owen," I told his sleeping form, "I haven't apologized."

Air whistled through his nostrils, a soft, keening sound. Musical even when sleeping.

"Owen. The orchid smelled like cinnamon."

Is cinnamon also a damned color, Oliver?

Perhaps I thought this aloud; Owen's eyes snapped open. He pulled me closer.

This December morning I received an acceptance letter from Myriad Academy. Next month I'll begin attending classes alongside the girl who tried to drown me.

Yes, Ollie. Things are going well here. And yes. I am panicking. Emolocating fluttering moths of uncertainty that make my peers swat at their ears.

Perhaps uncertainty is wise.

The German word for "delayed gratification" is *Belohnungsaufschub*. It is not a word I care for. You are not the only one who struggles with patience. Two years until I hold you.

Yours always,

Moritz

chapter seven

THE DRONE

Suffice it to say:

MORITZ, THAT WAS NOT VERY GENTLEMANLY.

Honestly, just because I'm wearing a catsuit nowadays doesn't mean I want to read about your, your—*lusty indiscretions*.

But this is so Moritz. Of course you waited THREE LETTERS after doing the do to tell me you'd done the do. You *know* if I ever did something like that, I'd write it in ALL CAPS.

Um. Actually, while we're on this weird subject.

You write about you and Owen, and how you're getting really close, and I'm glad you trust me enough to share your business. I trust you, too. And you know I hate secrets. So I'm going to tell you something honest at the end of this letter, and I hope it doesn't upset you. Because it's awkward, even by our standards.

But first! Speaking of awkward—meet Arthur.

The first Blunderkid I ever met lives a few miles away from all the skyscrapers, closer to buildings that felt more lived-in. Stoops you could sit on, trees you might be allowed to climb along the sidewalks, in a place called Logan Square. (Another superhero omen— *Wolverine's real name is Logan!*)

Arthur and his caretaker rent the top floor of a duplex, in a row of houses someone chopped in half with imaginary lines. When Auburn-Stache turned onto their narrow street, we passed some sort of purple church perched on the corner. People in teal robes sat outside eating cake, watching children chase one another in circles. I'd have loved to sit with them. We could compare our odd outfits. (Oddfits.)

If I'd grown up in the city, I'd sit on *all* the stoops, talking to all sorts of people, doing smack-talk. Stoop-Sitter Supreme: that's what they'd have called me, Moritz.

We parked farther down. To our right, another stoop spread behind a locked metal gate. I scrambled out of the Impala, grateful for the air even if it bit me (Chicago in November feels like getting slapped with freezer-burned meat), grateful for the smell of cement and smoke.

"Wait a moment, Ollie. I've messaged Professor Takahiro, for what good it'll do. I've heard her call phones *confounded*—"

"Auburn-Stache, look!"

Across the street from Arthur's duplex stretched another park, because Chicago is littered with litter but also little parks. A handful of people wandered around in scarves with dogs in scarves, too. An old woman sat on a bench, holding a steaming beverage in mittened hands.

But I was all about the human cornstalk. This tall, *tall* guy wearing a green flannel shirt with his sleeves rolled back and a goofy yellow earflapped hunting cap. I'm talking *unnaturally* tall, like someone had stretched him on a good old-fashioned medieval rack.

His elbows were large, thicker than his straw-thin arms. And the only forearm in sight was crazy long. If his legs hadn't been just as crazy long, his fingers might have hung past his knees.

But what really got me about Arthur (obviously, this is Arthur, Moritz—I didn't write this suspenseful buildup for some stranger!): tall as he was, he was trying to be taller.

He stood on his tiptoes.

Leaning back, facing the white sky with something electric turquoise in his right hand.

And there in the sky—not a bird! Not a freaking plane! But a flying, erm, thing! That flew! In matching turquoise electricity! A UFO? His ship from Krypton?

"What is *that*?"

"That's—that's *Arthur*, Ollie. Don't be rude. He has, among other things, a disease that affects the connectivity of his tissue. Elongates his limbs, bends his spine with a slight scoliosis—"

"*Tch*. Not 'What's that thing that's obviously a person.'" I rolled my eyes as slowly as possible. "I meant, 'What's that magical flying thing?' Come on, 'Stache."

Moritz—you can't see blushing. Let's just say our doctor burned like a candle.

"Oh. A drone. A flying, ah, toy."

"He builds them himself. Useless things, but he does enjoy them." The voice came from behind us, raspy and tired. I turned away from the drone; a small woman with wrinkled, tawny skin sat on the stoop. She pulled a cigar from between her teeth, twisted it out against the steps, and stood. "Instead of doing his work, he's busy building robots. I hope you're not like that, too."

"Um, I can't—"

"I was talking to Gregory, actually." She adjusted her jean jacket, jerked her chin at Auburn-Stache. "I hope Gregory's been doing his work."

Basically, all of Auburn-Stache's blood was stuck in his face at this point.

"Professor—it's . . . it's lovely to see you."

"Call me Beau. You haven't been my student for years. So, this is your favorite disaster?"

She stepped closer and reached for my shoulders with careful hands. Her touch was gentle, settling like feathers, like she thought she'd break me.

Her dark eyes stared right into me, Moritz. I wanted to look away into forever and beyond.

"Condolences about your mother, Oliver."

I did look away then. Because . . .

. . . Because the drone was really cool, okay! And *so* turquoise! If turquoise had a sound, Moritz, it might sound like water splashing against ceramic.

Beau Takahiro's fingers fluttered, pulled me back. "And that's all I'll say about it, unless you want to talk more. When my father died, I was younger than you. The worst thing anyone could do was bring him up without warning. None of their business, and this is none of mine."

"So why'd you say anything?" Great first impression I was making, squawking like that. And not looking at her, watching the drone hover. Its propellers shook off light like a cat drying itself.

"Because I'm *not* younger than you. I'm a whole lot older now. You'll need practice for all the other idiots who won't think twice about what they're saying."

Her fingers left my shoulders, and she flung one arm around Auburn-Stache's neck, not even close to careful. Man, did he hunker down to accommodate her. "Let's get you inside. Englishmen are hardly men at all until they've had some leaf juice. I'll point you to the teapot and you can do the work. Consider it your makeup assignment. Oliver—"

"Call me Ollie, Professor?"

She nodded. "Ollie, then. You call me Beau. I'm not teaching anymore. Retirement does exist, if you don't mind being broke. Go say hello to Arthur."

"Ah, how's he doing?" Auburn-Stache, speaking from under her wing.

"Bored silly. Naturally. Misbehaving. Also naturally. Looks like he's out and about without his chair again. So he's also an idiot. Ollie, catch him if he falls, will you?" Beau steered Auburn-Stache away, and suddenly the street seemed wider and I—

"Can't *you* call him over?"

I had jitters, Moritz. Unless Clark Kent had been put through a taffy puller, this wasn't Clark Kent. I had no clue how to start interviewing him. Auburn-Stache could probably hear my panic, but Beau spoke first.

"I'm sick of pulling him down from the clouds. Besides, we old people have to talk without young ears around. Have Art take you for coffee or vinyl shopping. Something young and pointless like that. Go on."

Auburn-Stache's face said, *Blazes, no! Don't let Ollie wander alone*. But, Moritz, the whole time we were in Chicago, he never disagreed with Beau. I think they have what people call *history*.

"Tell him to bring his chair." The gate clacked shut behind them.

The trilling pressure of the drone grew louder, bluer. When I turned around, it floated at eye level right behind me, turquoise droplets basically sizzling my cheeks. I swatted with my arm on electro-phobic instinct. The drone swooped up and out of the way with a disgruntled buzz. (Machines seem alive to me, Moritz.)

"Whoa, beanie guy. *Ahuhuh*." Arthur let out a clunky guffaw, laughing on his inhales. He'd crossed half the distance while my back was turned.

"'Beanie guy'?"

"Well, you're wearing a beanie? On your head, there." He pointed to his hat with his remote. The drone dipped when he bumped a button with his forehead. "Did you know? Or did it just creep up there and take a nap when you weren't looking? Beanies, man. They're always up to something shady. *Ahuh.*"

Arthur was probably *weird-looking*. His long neck sort of thrust forward, and his head bobbed loosely on his shoulders like a vulture's. Adam's apple? More like Adam's grapefruit. And his mouth hung slightly ajar at all times, crammed with teeth.

But when he laughed like burping, I couldn't help but laugh, too.

"So you *made* that?" I pointed at his machine, spoke in an awed whisper. (The drone was basically a dragon. Always whisper around dragons, Mo.) "By yourself?"

He shook his bangs out of his face and squinted at me from behind tinted bifocals. "Yeah, I made it. Why?"

"I'm collecting data. And that's awesome! You created *life*!"

He looked at me for a moment, then grinned very slowly, opening curtains on his uneven teeth. "Heck yeah. It is *fluffing awesome*. Wait." He blinked three times in quick succession, then pointed the remote at me. "*Wait. Beanie* guy. Are you UpandFree? Electro-boy? Hey, man! *Hey! I've been *dying* to meet you!"

Arthur of Krypton put the remote between his teeth. The drone plummeted from the sky, and my heart jumped into my throat—no, wee dragon!—

But Arthur's free right hand caught it.

I used to have flipbooks because I couldn't have television, flipbooks showing all sorts of animals in motion (that's how I knew I wanted to see dolphins, because I saw them leap out of the water like gravity can't touch this). Arthur loped like a giraffe, all knees and elbows. Up close he wasn't just taller, but maybe also a year or two older than me. Your age, Moritz?

He held out the drone in his long-fingered right hand. His left arm rested in a canvas sling.

"Hold Vince for a sec."

"Who?"

"Vince Noir. This drone guy."

I put my electromagnetic hands up, Mo. "I really shouldn't."

"Dude. I wanna shake your hand, and my left hand is *totally* out of commission, so hold Vince. Don't leave me hangin'."

"It's just—me and electric things don't really get along. I don't wanna accidentally—"

"Get over yourself, guy. Ass said you'd be *wearing protection*." Before I knew it, he'd shoved the device into my rubber-gloved left hand and grabbed my right, in a loopy sort of soft shake like he was trying to sketch sound waves with my arm.

"You call 'Stache *Ass*?"

"Yup."

I put my finger on something unspoken and spoke it: "Arthur, are you . . . *cool*?"

"What?" He kept shaking my hand, but this slowed the wave right down to a ripple. "Yeah. I *am* cool. I try, you know? Not everyone gets that, man. *Ahuhuh.* Wanna do some tourist shit? Is that what we're doing?"

"Consider me the ultra tourist. But they said not to go far. . . ."

"Bah. Fluff 'em. Let's go."

"Um, Beau told me to tell you to bring 'your chair'?"

A wave of his hand. "It's a bitch rattling that thing down the stairs. Last time, I dropped it from the balcony, and I nearly hit the neighbor's pug. Broke off the kickstand."

Kickstand. I told Mom I'd be her kickstand and look where that got—

Arthur caught the drone-gon as it slipped from my fingers.

"Sorry. I'm sorry! I almost—"

"Nah, it's cool. Even if you wrecked it, I'd make a new one from the pieces."

I stared at my feet. "You can't replace things so *easily*."

"Sure you can, guy." He spoke like he didn't notice me freaking out. "That pug I didn't flatten with my wheelchair? It's the neighbor's, like, *sixth pug*. And the third one named Hector. Twisted shit, to put that kind of pressure on a pug."

I snorted, then one of his words snagged. "Wheelchair?"

Arthur side-eyed me. "Hasn't *Ass* ever told you about me?"

"Not a chance."

"Oh. I'm the guy made of chalk."

Chalk?

Arthur reached one long arm over the fence, tucked Vince in the bushes. "Let's take the 'L' to Union. We can walk down Adams from there. The art institute's got lots of shit in it."

"Shit, huh."

"*Good* shit." Arthur has a favorite word, Moritz. (Is Fieke single?)

"The 'L'? The . . . the *flying trains*?"

"Don't shit yourself, guy."

"I'm—I just—don't we have to tell them—"

"I've got my phone." He patted a glowing green pocket.

So me and my new super(shit)hero walked past bars and restaurants and grungy corners under construction to the train station and then onto the Blue Line train, and from there up and down and underground, back to the middle of the winding Windy City.

On the train, I closed my eyes and asked Arthur if he knew about you. Because Moritz, Arthur knew who I was. Guess Auburn-Stache didn't mind talking about Blunderkids, so long as he wasn't talking to me?

"More-its? Oh, the echolocation boy? Heard about him, but nah, never met him." He went on to say *casually* that he's met a couple of Blunderkids, and the ones he's never met he's heard about from Beau.

The train rattled around us. I told Arthur my quest to write about Blunderkids.

Arthur gave me a thumbs-up. "Neat. But, like, I was little when I left that place. I don't remember it. Most of us are just living life, doing our own shit. Like anybody else."

I pressed my forehead against the cool window. *"Exactly."*

Arthur couldn't really know that I've *never* lived my life. I laugh it off sometimes, saying *everybody has problems*, but, Moritz, you know me. You know my biggest problem wasn't being electro-sensitive or having epilepsy.

My problem was being alone.

If Auburn-Stache had told me about the others from the start, I might not have been.

I opened my eyes and looked at reddish buildings and electricity the texture of splinters and felt like people treat the world like it's no biggie.

When we were getting off at the bustling Union Station, me clinging close to Arthur like some barnacle because I thought the crowd was an ocean that could pull me anywhere, I caught girls by the door staring at him, whispering and giggling. Not *nice* giggling.

Arthur noticed, too, and just waved at them. The giggling stopped.

I *am* getting something out of this. I'm learning from awkward.

So now *our* awkward part, Moritz.

If this is bad timing, what with your emolocation boomeranging, I'm sorry. But gird your loins:

Could you possibly tone down your romantic overtures?

It's not like I have a problem with you loving me. I love you, too, you know. But I don't know how to respond when you talk like you're . . . *in love* with me. Like when you told me you, um, programmed Owen's voice to sound like me? You get how that sounds . . . I don't want to say *creepy*. But if he's so great (and he really seems like he is!), that's not okay!

I'm not asking you to change. I feel lame when you write "the boy I love" and I feel like it would be polite to reciprocate, but I don't feel the same way, exactly.

So I appreciate your feelings . . . but maybe keep them to yourself? A little?

God, this sounds terrible, like I'm trying to shove you into a closet or something. That's not what I'm going for, by the Hammer of Thor!

It just feels like we're losing our even footing, you know?

UpandFree (Not DownandOut)

P.S. How much did *you* know about me before we became friends? When you got that first letter from me, did you already know my story? Was I a fictional character to you?

P.P.S. Okay, this officially feels deliberate. You don't want me contacting Owen about finding Blunderkids?

chapter eight
THE LIBRARY CARDS

Ollie,

Ninety-nine problems, but loneliness ain't one. Yes?

I could lash out bitterly at this latest rejection. Could throw a fit as I once did. Proclaim to the miscellaneous deities of all galaxies that I will no longer speak to you.

But you helped me evolve beyond that sort of cowardice. We've agreed to stand our ground.

I am not offended, but know that I still love you. *Ich liebe dich*.

Certainly, I won't stop saying this. Not after it took so long to find the words in the first place. I refuse to push our relationship backward. Do not presume to counsel me further on this. Or counsel me about my treatment of Owen. I haven't misled him. He knows about you. He understands that adolescent relationships are temporary. He is clever enough.

Ollie, can't you see? You are being hypocritical. You cannot demand honesty from those closest to you and then deny me my single greatest truth.

And so, *I love you*. Even if you are bald. Even if you cringe at the thought. If you wish to challenge me on this again, you had best clamber into your ludicrous, fictional amphibicar. Drive here. Say it to me in person.

This brooks no further conversation.

On the first day of my last week at Bernholdt-Regen, I stepped into my past. Upon entering the noisy courtyard, I thought I'd returned to who I was before you. Students hardly spared me a second glance. They were busy kicking dirt in the yard.

I felt only one pair of sharp eyes.

Not Lenz. Fieke. Perched atop the staircase where first I met her. This time she threw nothing. Only a weighty stare when she heard my cane on the steps.

"I really, really hope," she said, "you realize how lucky you are."

"Quite the luckiest boy who's ever lived."

She raised her legs to horizontal. I stopped before my knees could bump against them.

"I mean it." She twisted a piercing in her nose. "If anyone ever blew me off like that, I'd give them a fluffing boot, not a potted plant. And if they showed up on my doorstep later, they'd get the *other* boot. Nōt whatever you got."

Which emotion emanated from me?

Her posture slackened. "So, when will you be leaving us, *Brille*?"

"I haven't decided that I will necessarily—"

"Oh, you'd *better* necessarily. Don't think for a *second* I want you here for the rest of the year, waxing mopey." She coughed into a bangled wrist. "Spare us your terrible dress sense."

"Fieke . . ."

"Green corduroys and an orange silk shirt?"

"I liked the textures."

She wiped her nose on her hand. Stood up straight on the ledge, held her arms wide. Would she fall? Fieke is precarious, Ollie.

"The air smells like shit here." She hopped down to stand beside me. Squeezed my shoulder. Bracelets chimed, revealed a studded face that would not cry.

I heard Owen's fingers tapping his satchel, heard the quiet of the rest of him behind me. Felt him like he was part of me, another heartbeat. Those new branches. I gave him my hand. It was already his.

There on the steps, I killed a secret. Told the Abends about meeting the girl who drowned me. Spoke of her dual smiles. Owen frowned. Fieke cracked her knuckles.

I think, Oliver, you won't need to electroshock anyone. The Abend siblings are near me.

"Whatever happens"—Fieke cleared her throat—"don't flinch."

I am here, Owen's arms told me.

We answered the summons of the bell.

I handed Frau Pruwitt my acceptance letter. I'm unused to her smile. I shivered.

We began peeling checkout cards from the backs of books. Cataloging digitally now. I felt sorry, tearing those chronicles from jackets. Until then, you could pick up a book and discover who read it in 1997. The last person to check out a waterlogged copy of *Watership Down*: Rachelle Honnell. Who was she?

Frau Pruwitt exhaled. "*Stop* stinging me. Say whatever it is you mean to, young man."

"I have to stop volunteering here," I blurted in a single burst.

"Nonsense."

"I need a job. To help Father pay for Myriad. I can't justify going if I don't contribute."

"You *could* quit. See who wants to hire a boy with the social graces of a pincushion." She tore out another card. "Or you could just keep working here."

"I don't get paid for working here."

"Of course you do. More than you deserve. Direct deposit to your bank account."

"Whose bank account?"

"Why, the czar's!" She put her hands on her hips. "Yours. The one I opened for you."

"But—you've always maintained that this was volunteer work!"

"I've maintained your finances so that you couldn't blow your savings at noisy *Diskotheks*. You've earned a decent sum here. Put that sum toward Myriad."

"That money could go to better use."

"Employees get paid."

I doubted I was a legal employee. Frau Pruwitt was offering charity she knew I'd not otherwise accept. Perhaps I should have protested. But I looked at the ceilings, so dingy and decrepit. Galaxies away from auditoriums.

"Thank you very much," I whispered.

"What else can an old place spend money on?" She stared hard at the binding of the book she held. "An old place with few visitors."

We continued tearing paper from pages in silence.

Who'd have thought I'd ever have reasons to stay at Bernholdt-Regen?

Yet if you must leave your doorstep, so must I.

The holiday break has begun. Owen and I have gone out often since your last letter. We have gone to bookstores. Walked out of Ostzig to brighter places. Visited a museum. I appreciate sculptures. Owen appreciates places where people are as quiet as he. Do not think I am mistreating him.

It is only: whatever Owen is to me does not lessen what you are to me.

December 16 marked Owen's seventeenth birthday. He and Fieke joined Father, Frau Pruwitt, and me for dinner in our little apartment. Warm Glühwein, goose with apple stuffing. Fieke did not put her boots on the table. Owen told us, through his phone, that he wanted to toast my Myriad acceptance. I only wanted to toast him. And when I felt that warm, perhaps the whole room warmed with me.

I am the luckiest boy in the world. Quite.

Ollie, wondrous as Arthur seems, I've never written to him. I've heard of him in passing. How I once heard of you. In passing. Yes, nearly fictional. Unlike you, I did not want to know.

Recall that not all of us lived alone in the woods, Oliver. With me, Auburn-Stache could never deny the existence of the laboratory. It's a place that made and raised me. Perhaps I knew Arthur as a child. He would not have spoken to me. He would have glared across a cold room. He would have hated me.

Meeting people is less wondrous for the son of their tormentor. I need not dig into the lives of those who would rather I not. I am trying to move forward.

Let me be adamant: I am loath to search for the Blunderkinder.

So, Ollie, I *will not* give you Owen's contact information. Nor encourage this flight of fancy.

You are Blunderkind enough for me.

M

P.S. It is almost Christmas. Soon I will start attending Myriad. Yet *you* are writing about events that took place an entire month ago. Is *this* deliberate, Ollie? Surely this can't be in the service of story. Your handwriting has become spindly. I can scarce hear it. When last it looked this way, you were hiding a trauma. A body in the woods. Where are you, Ollie?

How are you?

Truly?

chapter nine
THE SNOWFALL

Okay, okay. Not okay.

First off, you're being paranoid. I mean, where did that P.S. come from?

Have you been talking to Auburn-Stache? I haven't seen him in weeks. If you're only getting his side of the story about how everything went to shit, well, you're not getting the whole truth! And now *I* sound paranoid, too!

I'm fine, Moritz! *Really*. I'm just determined to tell these stories right.

It's not a flight of fancy, thanks. It's my life.

Second off: I'm annoyed about this not-exactly-minor disagreement we seem to be having. And bullshit you're too mature to get upset! Not trying to be a dick. But your response was *worse* than awkward, Moritz. You spent a bunch of time worrying that your emotions may be corrupting people and then purposely ignored my emotions and dropped yours on top of them.

I told you something felt wrong, and you said, "Okay, I disagree. What else?"

Honestly, *truly*, I tried to be tactful and it didn't work, but you *can't* treat Owen like some casual pastime while you wait for "one true love" to show up. Didn't you have sex with him? I mean, I've read some people are polyamorous, and they can love lots of people at once, and that's not necessarily unhealthy for them. But that's *not* me. It's probably not Owen, either.

It took me longer than usual to write you back this time, Moritz. Maybe I had to figure out what to say and how to say it, and the last thing I want to be is mean at Christmas. One time you told me you're trying to be friendly snowfall when you scold me, not cruel ice. That's what I'm doing. I'm being tough on you because this disagreement isn't worth ruining our friendship over. Got it?

Third off: Who cares if I'm still writing about November? Good stories are linear, remember? When we first started writing, I told you about my childhood. Moritz, I told you about things that happened years ago. Why does time matter to you all of a sudden?

I know why it matters to me.

She's been dead for almost two months. But in our letters, she's only been gone for two weeks.

God. How can I explain why that matters? I know it's crazy, Mo. But it matters.

Arthur and I entered a building guarded by green lions: the art institute, with its basement full of photographs and tiny dollhouse displays of lavish homes from around the world (none of them A-frames in Michigan forests), with these halls full of furniture and

Egyptian pillars older than anything America has ever seen and pottery and so many canvases that I didn't even know what to look at, and there was this one awful room—this deafening room that was just ceiling-to-floor television screens on three sides, an exhibit by some modern artist who filmed a bunch of people screaming and laughing at different pitches.

(That's one monstrous sentence, and no way to tell a story. That room got to me, Moritz.)

The installation was called *Tearslaughter*.

The name doesn't even capture how bad it felt, and didn't explain how the artist got footage of children and adults and old people screaming. Is there stuff in movies you can't explain, Moritz? Are actors that good at pretending? I have no idea. I still had my beanie and bodysuit on, and I could barely see the screens through the electric blur, but that meant I could just *barely* see the outlines of *real people* and one of the blurred faces might belong to a middle-aged woman alone in the woods—

Moritz, I wanted it to stop.

I didn't even think about what I was doing, but every instinct told me to just pull my hat off, just do it, pull my hat off and make the noise *stop*, and before I could realize how insanely stupid that thought was, those open, wailing mouths had filled all my bleary vision, and my fingertips were already underneath the wool of the beanie, working themselves under the duct tape—

A brittle grip took hold of my wrist, and Arthur's unusual face replaced the others. He met my eyes through magnifying lenses. "Hey, guy, not a great plan."

I wanted to laugh it off—usually that's what I'd do—but I couldn't budge.

Arthur kept hold of my frozen wrist, playing it cool, ignoring the salt water streaming suddenly down my stupid face. "How about let's check out the Magritte exhibit. This room is *shit*."

I swear I didn't want to hurt him—it's just that when Arthur grabbed my wrist bones (carpi) to pull my arm away from my hat, I still couldn't seem to let it go, and the force of me *not moving*?

That pressure fractured three of Arthur's chalky finger bones.

There came this crackling sound like a line of Bubble Wrap getting popped and his grip vanished along with my paralysis. I let go of my beanie, but Arthur just looked at his hand and sighed under the noise. Just *sighed* at the sight of his mangled fingers.

Did I say *fingers*? I meant twigs. His forefinger bent backward just above the second joint, his middle finger off-kilter, skewed left in almost the same place. And his *thumb*, Moritz—it looked almost flattened at the top, where he'd put pressure on my inner arm.

"Aw, *shit*. What a buzzkill."

"What—Arthur? *Holy*—"

"Let's go. This shit's hurting my ears."

A lady in a business suit hushed us. Arthur waved his former fingers at her, and the hush went back down her throat. "If you're the artist, watching reactions incognito, I want you to know your art is shit."

Arthur didn't need his arms to get me out of there. He kicked the exhibit door open and held it for me with his boot, and after we were out, he turned to me and asked: "You all right, man?"

"*Arthur*, I just *broke your fingers*."

Arthur shrugged. "Shit happens. But shit *art* doesn't have to. Man oh man."

I laughed like shouting, wiping my eyes. "Arthur. *Thank* you."

He showed me every tooth.

I followed Arthur's giraffish gait down a museum thoroughfare full of centuries-old Tibetan altars. (Moritz, I'd never seen anything older than trees before!) Arthur held his right hand close, folded both arms against his chest. The universe snickered, because Arthur stopped right in front of a Sri Lankan cross-armed statue of Ananda that matched his pose. "Shoulda known better. You went human statue. *Ahuh.* Now, let's get to the armory."

I flinched at his attempted fist bump.

"Guy, don't get spooked. Could be worse. *I* don't have to dress like a porn star. *Ahuhuh.* This happens when you've got basically the shittiest case of brittle bone disease."

"*Osteogenesis imperfecta*?" Me, wannabe anatomy expert, learning to unlearn everything I learned here, Moritz. "I thought that was something that babies had. *Not* something that turned fingers into Twix bars."

"Now I want a Twix, damn it."

"Eat it on the way to the nearest doctor? Or Beau?"

That off-kilter laughter rattled his shrunken chest. "Ugh, Beau. Once I came back with a backward knee and she virtually strapped me to my bed. Here's hoping she doesn't find out."

We passed a group of fanny-packed tourists speaking curling languages I never thought I'd hear, found a high-ceilinged gallery full of ivory Grecian statues. Ancient Greeks must have gotten some nasty sunburns, going naked everywhere like that.

"Aha! Stairs!" Up we went, Arthur taking the steps three at a time.

"How could Beau not find out? You gonna wear mittens for months?"

Guffaw. "You gonna knit them for me, beanie guy?"

"Mom knitted the beanie, not me." I bit my tongue. How did her name escape the woods of me like that?

"Your mom gonna knit them for—?" He stared right at me. "Sorry. Not cool."

I looked past him. To the right of us on the marble landing stood an urn deep enough to move furniture into and live inside. But to the left—

Moritz, the room gleamed silver from top to bottom. Medieval spears, once held by people I could never meet. (No one could, because those people are kaput.) Suits of armor posed like ghosts stood inside them.

My legs almost buckled.

"*Swords*," I whispered.

Arthur walked right past them to the far corner of the room and sat on a bench directly across from a huge display case. Inside the case? A trebuchet replica, Genghis Khan era. (Holy shit. People like Genghis Khan existed, people like Joan of Arc and Salvador Dalí and the Wright brothers all existed beyond fiction, Moritz, and there's real, actual evidence of them in the world, so how are people not constantly trying to move into museums?)

"I freaking love shit like this. Before people had, like, real flying machines, this was the closest they got. Good effort, past people. Keep trying. Eventually, you'll throw something up and it'll stay there."

Arthur wasn't taller than me once I sat by him; his crazy height is all limbs.

"What are you going to do?" I looked at his fingers, twitching in his lap—

Here's where it gets Blunderweird, Mo.

I used to pore over anatomy books. Usually, when someone breaks a bone, there's bruising, swelling, and obstruction of blood flow. But these fingers had none of that. They were crooked but whole, like they'd been broken *years ago*.

"Rapid regeneration. You cut me, that shit closes up in seconds."

Cue my shameless ogling. "Does that mean you've never had skinned knees?"

"Can't be a skateboarder. No one takes you seriously unless you got scars. *Ahuh.* Sucks, 'cause I'd have some real cred. One time I broke my *neck*. Did well on a geometry test, skipped outta the classroom, hit my head on the door frame. Stupid shit."

"Stop. The. Phone."

"Ahuh. You mean 'hold the phone.' Or 'stop the presses.'"

"I don't know. I don't do phones. You've broken *your spine* before and you didn't end up paralyzed or *super dead*? What about your nerves?" You probably know this, Moritz, but when bones break near nerve centers, they sever the connections that let us feel things, that keep body parts moving properly. Uncle Joe's not in a wheelchair just because he broke his spine. He severed spinal nerves.

"My bones are brittle shits, but Ass says my nerves are steely strong. Good thing, because I don't really feel pain."

"Actual nerves of steel? Arthur, it's too . . . *punny* to be real." Moritz, would it be okay to get hurt over and over again, if you knew you'd always recover?

"*Ahuh.* Hey, man. I just work here."

"Why do you need sunglasses?"

"Prescription lenses. Doesn't matter if my eyes keep healing if they were crappy eyes to begin with. Myopic all over the place. And they're different sizes, too. Quick healing doesn't make you *purty*, guy. But watch this." Arthur got up and loped his way once around the gallery, scanning the placards, then sat down right next to me again. "Point at some shit."

I pointed at a tapestry on the far wall.

"That's a Franco-Flemish piece called *Tapestry (Moose Hunt and Falconry from a Forester Series)*, circa 1523. Wool and silk, silt and double dovetailed weave."

"No way." I pointed to a cannon.

"Oh that? That baby came from Normandy in 1582. Belonged to a Master Fromont."

He can't have looked at the placards for more than a few seconds each, Moritz! But if the neurons in your head heal on a constant basis, what you could end up with is a perfect memory. (There are things I've forgotten about Mom already, like the smell of her hair after she worked in the garden, the way she sneezed.)

Finally, I pointed at a bust of some man wearing a ruff.

"*Ahuh.* That is *Ugly Motherfluffer*, by Johnson P. Dick. *Ahuh.*"

"Art."

"The highest, man."

"Could you grow limbs back? Attack on Titan–style? Like a salamander tail?"

"Here, chop off my arm."

A middle school girl in a uniform overheard him; her eyes bulged and she scurried to rejoin her class.

"Erm . . . maybe later."

"I'm also totally wearing a wig. My hair grew so fast I had my whole head lasered to forever-bald."

I reached right out and tugged on a tuft—

"Gotcha. That shit's just hair." Arthur's guffaw frightened a few other kids forward, echoed off old iron.

I laughed with him. "Shoulda guessed. Who picks a brownish mop wig? You go eighteenth-century pomp or you go home!" I leaned back, looked at him in all his gawky-as-hell glory. *"Behold!"*

Arthur blinked. "Behold what?"

"You. You're amazing." You still believe we can't be heroic, Moritz? I didn't even care about anatomical impossibilities, because this was classic Marvel nonsense, here.

"Sure, it *sounds* amazing. Especially when someone like you says it, all enthusiastic and shouty!" His lazy smile became a wince. "There are *downsides*, guy. My bones heal so quick sometimes they heal the wrong way. And to reset them—"

"You'd have to break them again?" I blinked. *"Ouch*, Arthur."

"Shitty city." He wiggled warped fingers. "Beats being grounded. Bad enough Beau stopped letting me go to school."

For the first time, Moritz, Arthur seemed less than cool. His eyes locked onto the trebuchet again.

"Um, want me to help?" I tried to forget the Bubble Wrap crunch.

"You a doctor now?"

"Nope. But I read a lot of books. And I have fingers that aren't scary Twixs. I *have* to help you, fellow hermit. That's why I'm out of the woods! My quest!"

"You don't *have* to. Seems like you have enough problems, you know?"

"I'm fine." Nobody ever believes this, which is annoying. "So how do we do this?"

He sized me up. "Reach into my pants, will you?"

"*What?*"

"*Ahuhuh.* My *pocket*, beanie guy." He gestured with elbows at his right cargo pants pocket, and yeah, there were a bunch of thin steel rods with holes in them—the same kind that made up the axles of that flying drone—a screwdriver, and masking tape. "Make splints."

Arthur gave me his hand, and it felt like trying to save a bird, like the ones that used to end up hitting our cabin's windows. "Right. You gonna scream?"

"Nah, man. You?"

"Maybe!" I reached for the tip of his middle finger, trying to decide how much pressure it would take to break a chalk bone, and—*pop!*—the thing crunched in my hand.

"I didn't even—"

"Never mind, just put it back, hey?" I did what I was told, like handling pasta noodles. I pushed it into place, taped a rod against each side of it.

"If your bones are this fragile, how come the weight you put on your legs every time you stand up doesn't shatter you?" If I wanted a distraction, Arthur did, too.

"Well, you're, what, allergic to electricity but fine during lightning storms? Fine with a brain full of electrical shit?" This laugh was not his usual one. "We're all freaks."

"Don't say that." I scratched my head, surveying my handiwork.

Arthur guffawed so hard this time a grown man fled the scene. "Beanie guy, *why are there three joints in my thumb now?*"

"Oops."

Arthur wiped his nose on his shoulder. "It's cool, UpandFree. Stick me with the modern art. *Ahuh.*" He stood all the way up and up. "Let's see *actual* shit, hey? Magritte was definitely *on* something. Imagine having an apple for a *face.*"

"I've actually never imagined that!"

Minutes later, Arthur waited for me near the entrance to a special exhibit. Huddles of people gathered around surreal art, more people I'd never meet. I'm realizing that's something normal people have to live with, too. "This should make up for the *Tearslaughter.* And I thought that room sucked *last* time."

"What was in there before?"

"Videos of clowns playing with toilet paper. No lie, beanie guy."

Broken fingers and all, Arthur faces the toilet-paper clowns of the world. Maybe I can, too. Arthur's showing me that the world doesn't mind weird. What difference does being weird make, Moritz, if we can do everything anyone else does, in our own weird way? If we can snort like immature assholes at some great paintings (especially this one featuring a woman with boobs where eyes should be)?

The best thing we saw, if I had to pick, was a painting called *The Pleasure Principle.*

It's this portrait of man in a suit, a man with an orb of light where his head should be. Just endless golden light, and anything could be under the light, an eyeless face or maybe a face like Arthur's or a face with two mouths. Anything. Didn't matter what was under the light, only that one body was too small to contain all that beautiful, scary brightness.

Moritz, why didn't you tell me up front that you're against looking for the Blunderkids? I feel like you just told me "rain check." I knew you weren't exactly pumped about my life purpose. But I didn't realize you *loathed* the idea. Now who's keeping secrets?

If you'd told me, maybe I would've stopped sending you stories you're not interested in reading. Do you even want to hear about Arthur? If I'm the only part you care about, I mean, I might as well send you sticky notes with my name scratched on them.

Or maybe I could just talk about weather?

It's snowing outside today, but it's hot in the room I'm writing from. There are lots of terrariums in here, reptiles on heating rocks lying under UV lamps, making the place smell greasy somehow. I've been alone for weeks, in the room I'm writing from. Is that the story you want?

Moritz . . . we have to be honest, right? At least with each other.

So, honestly? It feels like one of the branches of our friendship just got hairline fractured.

chapter ten

THE SCHOOL

Oliver,

I am accustomed to the pains in my chest. I am accustomed.

But my stomach churns now. You and I. Though we have always been very different people, we have always fought for common ground. If I have compromised that, I apologize.

Please do not misinterpret me. You are my favorite storyteller, and I will hear anything you wish to tell me. *Honestly*. Only lend me sympathy, Ollie, where the laboratory is concerned.

Perhaps we should kill this ugliness. Revert to a more formal friendship. Find our footing again. *Siezen*, not *duzen*. The world is opening up to us, Ollie, a well at our feet. We will need each other. We must be steadfast.

I've tripped already.

On the second day of the new year, another confounded bus

deposited me outside my new school, half queasy and wholly anxious.

Molly waited by the Myriad gates, as she'd promised in a message. Earmuffs, muff, faux-fur collar. A girl from another era. An era of tea and movie musicals. Parasol tucked into the belt around her peacoat. Affectations suit her. I did not have my cane, did not know what to do with my hands. Until she interlocked her arm with mine.

"There you are! I've told everyone a prince is coming."

"You haven't."

"Of course not. But I put in a good word for you. I really do want to think the best of everyone." Perhaps because she knew I would hear it, she smiled wide in the back. Her second mouth is honest, Oliver. Something reassuring: if she can feel my emotions, I can *see* hers.

"Now we take the plunge. On the count of three. One, two"—she pulled us across the frosted entrance—"*three*! Still breathing, Prince Moritz?"

I straightened my goggles, stepped forward at her urging. Aisles of trees with icicle ornaments. The campus, a separate entity from the wintry city. The cold lessened here. Lessened by *her*.

Everywhere I went across meringue-snowed lawns during my first day, Molly accompanied me. She distracted me from my incessant social ineptitude. Before I could finish spitting garbled sentences, Molly would pat me on the shoulder as if I were the wittiest creature imaginable. Others believed her. They downright adored her.

Molly dominated campus like there was no pleasure greater. She aspires to be a stage actress. Were it not for that second mouth, I would believe her to be the most confident creature that ever lived. I could sense anxiety only when her back teeth clenched. When the lips became chapped and she wetted them with her second tongue.

The scent of cherry lozenges.

At Myriad, students pick two focus areas. I enrolled primarily in *Literatur* courses. And in *Musik*. Vocal, not instrumental. I had an elective hour to fill. I am no actor or painter. I scheduled a block of Stagecraft. All these courses feel like electives.

My favorite course? Music Interpretation. Students create their own musical arrangements and perform them during an assigned hour every other week. This is no glee club—this is a critical audience. Fortunately, because of experience garnered at the Sickly Poet, I survived my introductory performance. By the time I entered the third verse of "The Sounds of Science," I received approving nods from Chloe-Bowie.

My least favorite course? Stagecraft, where Klaus the curmudgeon dwelled. First impressions carry weight. His was less than fond. He couldn't fathom Molly's interest in me.

"We're, ah, *friends*." I smiled, warmly as I could, backstage in our first class together. Other students already at work, smearing paint across a canvas backdrop.

"Don't you smirk." Sawdust speckled Klaus's hair; I could hear the hiss of it slipping down strands. "Friends from where? I've never heard of you, and I've known her for years. And what can you even build with those arms? If I'd wanted a stick person, I'd have drawn one."

"I'm sure you'll teach me a great deal."

"Don't try it. I'm straight."

I puffed up my chest. "I wasn't—"

"Just get painting the grass at the bottom of the skyline. Paint's in the storage closet."

"Paint it?"

"Greens, browns, and swooping textures. Got it?"

"I'm, ah, color-blind."

Klaus cursed, threw up his hands. Walked away, barking at the skyscraper painters.

He treats me as a *rival*. No one else has ever considered me that.

Come early afternoon, Molly showed me to an office beyond a frost-covered tulip garden. In the overheated building, Molly introduced me to the headmistress, a frazzled, bespectacled woman named Laurel Welter. She smiled at my goggles. Told me she used to wear those to steampunk conventions.

"You must do things like this while you're young so that you can do them even better while you're old. We've arranged to give you a proper tour of the campus during lunch hour."

"Molly has been marvelous in that regard."

"A student has volunteered to cover for her. Molly has an audition."

"Really?"

Molly smiled on both sides. "I'm trying out for the Year Two production of *The Effect of Gamma Rays on*

Man-in-the-Moon Marigolds. Frau Welter, who's offered to show Moritz around?"

"Max Fassner. He insisted."

"Oh, I'm sure he did." Her downturned back mouth.

Outside, the crunch of snow outlined an incongruous hole in the sole of one of her furry boots. Molly sighed. "I did warn you about Max, didn't I?" She patted down her curls. "Keep your head on, Prince. He's unsavory."

"I remember." I recalled the boy in the prep uniform.

But what harm could he do during a campus tour?

I met him a few hours later and saw he wore his shirt halfway unbuttoned. Despite the chill. Saw he grinned at me in a manner distinctly predatory.

I understood what harm he might do.

"Moritz," he purred, "let me show you things."

"No, thank you," I replied before I could think.

Max grabbed my hand and pulled me forward down the path and through the gardens. He led me directly away from the crowded mess hall. Into deep snowbanks. The frozen top layer snagged my pants. Numbed my toes in my boots. Max dragged me underneath wisps of a barren willow tree and pushed me against the trunk.

I knew he had no interest in showing me the campus.

Of course I could have dodged his chapped lips. Just as I dodge fists and projectiles. I could have, Ollie.

I allowed Max Fassner to kiss me. I did not protest.

I can't say why. Perhaps because he was warm and the air was very cold. Perhaps because the tension in his body was not quite the same as the tension of a body about to hurt me.

"I'm not," I told him. "By which . . . I mean to say, I have a boyfriend."

Max took one step back. Mustered a grin. I might call it entirely shit-eaten.

"Not for long." Max bowed.

I stood alone in the snow until his departing footsteps faded. My vision dulled with no echoes to ignite it, apart from the creaking of icicles in the branches.

I put my fingers on my lips. No denying Max has a tongue.

A tongue Owen does not have, even if his breath against my chest was soft when we slept together. A tongue Owen did not have, when he whimpered himself awake.

Tell me I'm disgusting, Oliver. Won't you let me rot?

After two rain checks, I met the Abends at the Sickly Poet. Busy on a winter's night. Owen and Fieke sat at our usual table. Owen tapping into his phone, Fieke scowling at the woman onstage currently butchering a rendition of "Not Waving but Drowning" by dumping vases of water over her head after each line (there are *Tearslaughters* everywhere). I could see every tiny piece of that room in the clinking of glasses and the brief bursts of verse as the woman onstage recited the poem again, this time backward. I saw them when they could not see me.

Fieke said my name. I halted between tables and the bar.

"I'm not bothered what Moritz will think, actually. I'm bothered about *you*. You've spent so much time on that fluffing forum this past week. You prefer it to reality."

I heard Owen flick his fingers at her. Signing too fast for me to comprehend, but I could sense his annoyance.

"If you think this is going to get you closer to him some-how—wake up. He doesn't give a shit. He'll think you're an idiot or he'll think you're being *cute*. He doesn't take you seriously."

Owen's grip on the phone tightened. The dreadful thing: this made me want to hold him. As though he really were something that needed coddling. Something cute.

I felt another crack, somewhere near my sternum, some-where in our branches.

Fieke narrowed her eyes and spun around to face me—had she felt it, too?

I pursed my lips and slid in next to Owen. He squeezed my knee. A fragile smile.

"Hey," said Fieke, not kindly.

How is it? Owen signed. An instant ago, I had wanted to pull him close and bury the thought of Max. His damnable tongue. Now . . .

There are many actors at Myriad. I tried to mimic Molly. But the undercurrents of everything I feel escape my juris-diction. Not all of us are so adept as you at wearing cheerful masks, Ollie.

"It is a remarkable change of pace. Everyone is terrible—terribly friendly. And very musical. You would appreciate that aspect, Owen."

He stared. I cleared my throat.

"I've heard Myriad is like a fluffing queer candyland. Take your pick of boys," Fieke said.

Owen picked up his phone. Tapped away. His rhythm trapped on a screen, illuminating something inaudible.

"I didn't find any company I prefer to nights with the Abends."

Fieke bit her lip. "Don't try so hard. Just promise you won't be buggering other boys this year, and we'll be just cake."

"I will promise no such thing." Affronted, Ollie, and who would not be?

The tapping stopped.

"Surely I've earned more trust than that. Leaving Bernholdt-Regen doesn't make me any less your friend. You encouraged me to go."

"Methinketh he doth protesteth too mucheth."

"I'm not the only one trying too hard," I snapped.

"No, but you're clicking at the end of your sentences." Sneering. "That's your tic, yeah? What's got you so nervous, exactly? What is it about the topic of infidelity—or was it what you heard when you were nosing into our conversation?"

"*Beg pardon.* I didn't ask to be discussed behind my back. Our relationship is not your business." I reached for Owen's hand. He pulled away and tapped, tapped.

"I introduced you! It's been my fluffing business from the start!"

"In lieu of having no life of your own to mismanage, Fieke."

"What are you *saying*, you complete prat?"

"I'm saying you meddle in our affairs because your own life is dull."

She slammed her fist on the table—

Owen stood. Walked away from the table. Approached the microphone the woman had abandoned.

He screamed silently on the stage, the same three words over and over. Mouthing them with such quiet rage that every patron in the *Kneipe* turned to bear witness.

"Ich bin hier, Ich bin hier, ICH BIN HIER!"

I am here.

Tell me why I'm still a person, let alone a superhero?

Who knows whether Owen would have "screamed" into the microphone if I had not been feeling ashamed. Who knows what Fieke might have said about queer candyland if I hadn't felt so damned uncertain. Spitting waves of guilt.

Tell me more than weather, Oliver Paulot. Tell me everything you are. Show me how real people behave. I may take notes.

And perhaps if we are not good people, we can at least be better to each other.

chapter eleven

THE BLENDER

Moritz.

Can we put away our recent bullshit? Give it a sea burial? So when we get our damn amphibicars and take on the Atlantic and meet halfway to high-five in the middle of it, our fossilized bickering will be totally buried by the sands of time?

Look. Maybe I'm *not* qualified to comment on what's going on with you and Max and Owen and Fieke, but I'll say this much: I get you, Moritz. More than *you* get you.

You spend a lot of time worrying about emolocation instead of working out *what* you feel and *why* you feel it. It comes down to the same old issue: you're always half convinced you aren't worth loving. That you should be punished for your past. That's been your trouble all along!

So you were born in that place full of needles. Maybe steady footing's always hard if you started life without feet, and your scars don't heal like Arthur's?

But do you really think I'll *ever* let you rot? I mean, really? After all we've been through? Don't be such . . . such a *Moritz*.

There are real reasons why you and I can't stop writing each other. I mean, it's ridiculous! Even when we're annoyed and annoying, we're pen-palling addicts. We write *pages upon pages* at least twice a week just so we can paper-whine at each other.

Person or not, you're definitely good enough for me.

When Arthur and I got back to Logan Square, Beau and Auburn-Stache were *both* waiting on the stoop. I don't know who hollered more. At one point Beau slipped into Japanese and Auburn-Stache slipped into *SUPER BRITISH*! ("A bloody reckless bit of messing about, that was!"), and Arthur and I started guffawing, which *really* set them off.

"Oh, they're trouble together." Beau shook her head. We grinned.

"We'll be leaving in an hour or so, Pro—Beau! Ollie, don't look at me like that—we have elsewhere to be. And Arthur certainly seems healthy enough."

Arthur didn't look sheepish, I swear, and definitely didn't hide any hands behind backs (he'd taken the splints off on the train and wiggled fingers good as new and *not* triple-jointed).

Beau sighed. "You think I'll let you leave tonight? Don't insult me. Ollie, you're in Arthur's room, although you'll have to sleep in that hat because I can't afford to lose the leftovers to another power outage. Greg, the couch is all yours. Art, go get us some Tso's."

Moritz, in Chicago I met a hundred miracles, and Chinese takeout was one of them.

Arthur offered me his bed, but I noticed his comforters and quilts were arranged into a sort of cubby of cushioning. I wasn't as likely to break in half by rolling into a bedpost, so I chose a tatami mat and tucked my feet under his wheelchair.

We didn't sleep. We *shot the shit* for hours, talking about my woods and his city. When I asked about school, his tone changed again.

"If I didn't have this stupid cast . . ."

"Why do you, Arthur-mander? Fashion?"

"I fluffed up, guy."

"You slam it in a door?"

"Nah. I punched a guy and it folded like a bendy straw."

"Punched him? Was he a *Tyrann*?"

"A what-now?"

"A bully." I stared at the wheelchair, all black and silver. "Did he have it coming?"

I could almost see him nodding, maybe by the light of the electrical sockets spitting confetti colors into the room. Or by all the lamps on his desk shining on the glowing blue pieces of robotic machinery, his supertech indoor hobby. Or by the plastic stars glued to his ceiling. (It's never dark anywhere outside the woods, Moritz.)

"Um, I tried to fix it myself."

Here's what happened to Arthur's arm.

His fracture was a total one, halfway down his radius. His arm split clean in two. The bones ended up overlapping and healing that way, in a thick sort of lump where they joined (a bone callus, Moritz). Arthur panicked and broke that callus, but then the two bones didn't line up anymore.

"I never go see doctors. Beau does it all herself—she used to be a badass surgeon. Afterward, she locked me indoors for weeks. Can you imagine how much that sucked?"

"Yeah."

"I bet you can, OllieUpandFree." I heard him roll over. "I'd done a few fixes myself, you know, ever since middle school when I broke my toe on a soccer ball. Usually that shit goes fine. I was off my game. That lump got bigger and bigger, and I just felt . . . smaller."

For two hours, Arthur sat in a dark auditorium breaking and rebreaking bone.

By the time he came home after dark, his arm was a club.

"They tried to replace it. Give me an artificial radius? Ass came over to help with the procedure, but, um, my shitty skeleton was not on board. The fake bone kept breaking the others. So I don't get to have two arms anymore."

I stretched out on the floor, listening to the alien sound of traffic outside. (I guess cities never go dark *or* quiet, Moritz?) "Here's a perk: you're kind of a cyborg."

"A really shitty one."

"Still cool, Arthur."

"Thanks, guy."

"That could have happened to your fingers today." I squeezed my eyes shut. Watched electricity drift in my aura. Like when you press on your eyelids and sparkles refuse to leave you. "If I did it wrong, I could've killed your hand."

"I know." He laughed. "Stupid of me to trust a dope like you, right?"

"So, *so* stupid."

"Yup."

"Arthur?"

"Present, guy."

"Start using this wheelchair, okay?" I tapped it with my foot, felt my sock slip on the rubber. "For Beau."

"She's going into overdrive, man. There's no reason to—"

"You'll regret it. If something happens to her and you didn't listen, you'll regret it." I should have worn the damn coat, I should have stayed close, I should have . . .

"Okay, UpandFree."

"Arthur, why did you punch that guy?"

No answer, because Arthur was asleep even if the city would never be. Even if I couldn't really be, the first night wearing the rubber suit.

I didn't ask Arthur in the morning, and I didn't hug him just in case, although Beau softly held me and roughly held Dr. Auburn-Stache before we trundled off to the car. Auburn-Stache seeming like he was in a hurry, me wanting to move right into the museums or maybe live under Arthur's bed or just *stay*.

"What's this?" Arthur asked me. I'd handed him a crinkled piece of notebook paper.

"Your contract. Sign on the line so I can tell your story."

Arthur laughed. "You still think my story's worth something?"

"Probably not money, but yeah. Something."

He signed it against his armrest with his good hand. "Cool."

Through the side-view mirror, I watched them wave from the stoop I forgot to spend time on.

Arthur, long arms reaching almost as high as Beau's even though he sat in his wheelchair, quietly declaring himself, if not a man of steel, a man of Metropolis.

After five hours of riding and writing and Auburn-Stache totally refusing to tell me about his collegiate shenanigans in Beau's classes (no word on whether they had a sordid affair, because obviously Auburn-Stache never tells me squat), the Impala left the freeway and turned into the subdivision where another Blunderkid lived.

This wasn't the woods, and this wasn't Chicago.

In this neighborhood, all the houses looked identical to one another. Everyone's backyard basically rested on the one next door, or would have if everyone didn't insist on fencing themselves in. I'm not a big fan of fences. And these fences were crazy low. If people cooked out on their grills, they could have staring competitions in four directions while their neighbors burned bratwurst. Is that normal for suburbia? The weird closeness crossed with fake distance?

No one was barbecuing when we drove by. It was late afternoon in November, and hamburgers taste better when peppered with summer sunshine. You'd think I'd be comforted by the trees lining the sidewalks, but their branches were barren. I'm used to underbrush of crinkling brown leaves so thick that you have to dig to find soil. All the people here raked their leaves up and . . . put them away somewhere? Burned them? Stuffed mattresses with them? I don't know. Hid them so their neighbors couldn't make fun of them for being too leafy?

Ohio, Moritz. (Arthur, give me strength!)

"So, Sergeant Secrets, does this kid have a name? Or can't you tell me?"

"She's called Bridget."

I wrote that down in my notepad, like a professional storyteller. "And can you tell me if she knows we're coming?"

"She's the reason we had to leave Arthur so soon." This was floodgates opening, by Ass standards. "Bridget's accustomed to extremely regular monthly appointments."

"Is she homeschooled, too?"

"Not homeschooled, but rarely socializing."

"Well, so long as I can get her story!" I tried to punch the sky and smacked my knuckles against the roof.

"Ollie, you may need to exercise patience. Bridget doesn't always present herself well."

"We can't all be cool like Arthur. I just want to help her with her beef."

"Sometimes there's only so much help to be had. Just because you made headway with your epilepsy doesn't mean you'll never seize again. Yes, we've found new ways to manage your sickness—"

"Please don't call me sick. Here I sit, *victorious* in my giant body condom, overcoming an evil electrified vehicle."

"But we haven't cured you."

"Good. Because I am *living* for this giant body condom, and I never want to take it off."

"And we can't cure Arthur or Bridget—"

"Stop saying the c-word." Moritz, I'm not looking for a *cure*. Really. I can't imagine being someone who didn't see the world how I do. Can you imagine if someone tried to hand you some eyeballs? You'd flush them down a toilet. With dignity.

As a kid, I daydreamed about being *normal*, like kids with glasses still daydream about being astronauts. Daydreams aren't realistic. I only wanted *normal* because I thought *normal* was a word that meant "surviving the world."

But Arthur walked city streets *abnormally*, awesomely. He got my hopes up, and he helped me keep my hat on. I'm going to write him a hundred letters.

"'Stache, I don't want to *fix* anyone. If it ain't broke, you don't."

"Ollie." Auburn-Stache smiled. "I don't regret bringing you."

"I'm irresistible."

"Indomitable, at least."

He slowed by a house like the other houses: gray paneling, boring lawn and all.

"We've arrived."

"How can you tell the houses apart?"

"There're numbers on the mailboxes."

"Oh. Yeah." Things obvious to most people make for hermit surprises. I'd get lost in a cardboard box—anywhere—without familiar ferns to guide me home.

I pushed the door open—

"I HAVEN'T PARKED THE BLOODY CAR YET!"

—eager to get into spaces open enough for fist-pumping. Eager to meet another superhero, Moritz. I kissed the grass, got up, and stared at Bridget's house, iridescent with electricities. The windows curtained, insides shuttered in. Legs tingly from household currents, I pulled my hat over my ear tips and climbed the clean-swept steps to the door. (All three at once, how Arthur would.)

"Well, she's not rushing to meet us."

"She wouldn't. Don't bother with the doorb—"

DING-DONG! DING-DONG!

The first doorbell I ever rang, to the joy of my rubber fingers! I dinged it again before Auburn-Stache grabbed my shoulders and pulled me aside.

"She on the couch like the famous potato?"

"Not likely." I'm as tall as Auburn-Stache nowadays, so he didn't really have to lean forward to talk to me. "Ollie, best behavior."

Auburn-Stache pulled a crowded key ring from his coat pocket. I bet he has keys to the homes of all the Blunderkids. He twisted a silver key in the lock, pushed open the door. We laid eyes on a cold blue living room and a narrow beige hallway. No tapestries here. No autographed album covers like the ones coating Beau's duplex.

The place was spotless. My skin itched.

"Bridget . . . ? It's Dr. Auburn-Stache."

Moritz, Auburn-Stache *never* announced himself at my house. He never tiptoed, either.

"I'm in the kitchen."

Something about that voice was really dull? Like it'd been laced with disinfectant and lost all its character. This person spoke because she was expected to, and at exactly the right volume for us to hear her.

Auburn-Stache's face didn't register surprise so much as resignation. He didn't hurry as he led me down the hallway. Under the floors and in the walls, the wiring hummed. I tugged at my bodysuit.

The walk took way too long.

The second we stepped into the white-tiled kitchen, Auburn-Stache's demeanor changed. His shoulders stiffened, and he put one arm out to block me from pushing past him.

I pushed past him anyhow, because this reminded me too much of Liz and me finding Joe with his spine broken. If this was another accident, I'd rather face it.

I took a deep breath and squinted past the auras of the microwave, fridge, and power sockets to the girl tucked between it all.

Bridget had the straightest posture I've ever seen. She was lean and ochre-skinned, with long ropes of russet-colored hair pulled completely away from her face. She stood behind a counter, hands on an electrical device I'd never seen: a glass beaker with silver blades at the bottom, perched on a base that oozed gravel-gray in my aura. Her tank top hung low off her left shoulder, revealing the weirdest branching slit near her sternum—it looked almost like those pictures you see of cracking earth in the desert.

Bridget held something red and meaty above the electrical device. I remembered our Edgar Allan Poe birthday party back home. I remembered countless nights falling asleep to *Grey's Anatomy*.

What Bridget held was almost definitely, certainly a beating human heart.

The heart looked dry; no blood dripped down her fingers. And her eyes revealed nothing at all. Like she was sleepwalking and no one had bothered to wake her up, maybe not for years.

"Hello," Bridget said, calm as anything.

Tell me the Blunderkids should be left alone, and I'll tell you you're a liar.

Tell me you don't want to hear more of this, Moritz.

chapter twelve

THE STYROFOAM TABLE

There you go dropping science, Ollie. You're dropping it all over.

Set science aside. We are living science fiction.

Oliver, foreboding as she seems, I *am* fascinated by this girl and her removable heart. Certainly, I want to hear more. You dangle the bait, storyteller. I bite.

Whenever we are petty with each other, I want to slam my head into the desk. The world regardless, you have me when you need me. Even if I'm nowhere near.

Perhaps it doesn't matter what opinion I have of myself on dark days. Your good opinion persists. I am not in command of my feelings. But I feel confident that even at my worst, your feelings remain constant. That is no small thing, Ollie.

Consider the bicker-fest shipwrecked.

If my opinions are always low and yours are always high? We even out.

Together we pass for human, Oliver Paulot. Veins pulsing with lightning.

Two mornings after the disaster at the Sickly Poet, I awoke gasping. Wind outside the high balcony screeched. Eked through my window. Coughing beyond my door: Father, preparing for another double shift.

I messaged Owen from bed. *I want to listen. If you want to speak.*

His answer came swiftly for 4:00 AM: "If you're doing this out of pity, forget it!"

I have resolved to reassign him a different voice as soon as possible. (Apologies.)

You shouldn't believe everything your sister says, I wrote.

"Leave her out of it! And you're still talking down to me!"

I'm sorry. It isn't intentional.

"It never is! People think that being silent is the same as having nothing to say! It's not!"

I don't think you have nothing to say. Your actions speak volumes. Tomes of chronicles of volumes.

"You can never say things simply!"

Things: simply.

"And you have a terrible sense of humor!"

I never laughed until I met you.

I realize, Oliver: this is almost precisely what your mother said about your father. I lack creativity. Haven't I said?

"You don't laugh now, actually!"

Ahahahahaha?

A pause.

"Congratulations then! D! God! I can't even stay angry!"

Another pause.

From separate buildings within the same cold city, I nearly told him about Max. But what good could it do? The kiss was an error. I'd told Max I'm spoken for. That tome was closed.

You mean a great deal to me, Owen.

"I need to hear that more!"

Hearing is always the trouble. What were you and Fieke discussing that day?

"Just a school project! Boring, I promise!"

Fieke hadn't sounded bored. But Owen has no reason to lie. He is not me.

I lay back against my pillow.

Too soon I wished him a good night, good morning.

"Love you!"

I found myself in your boots, Ollie. Is there any proper response to that sort of declaration?

I took the coward's way and did not answer.

"I never asked; how was your tour with Max?" Molly took my arm in her lacy glove. Together we headed toward the mess hall for breakfast. "He didn't follow you home and keep you up all night, did he?"

"Of course not!"

"I'm sure he was very accommodating. He always is, with the new students. Especially when the new students are charming Goth boys."

"I am neither charming nor Goth."

"I've already gone ahead and told everyone here you're charming, and *no one* argues with me. And if you don't want to be called Goth, please let me cut those wretched bangs of yours. I won't drown you in lather or stab you with shears. I promise."

I laughed despite myself. "Shears? What beast do you take me for?"

"No more a beast than I am." She laughed in turn. But her back mouth grimaced.

I must have reacted to the sound.

Molly released me.

"You can't really think of yourself that way." After a beat: "You are no such thing."

"Now, now, Prince. How do *you* think of yourself?"

"Our situations—"

"Are virtually the same. I'll forgive myself when you forgive yourself, *Liebling*." Slowly, her smiles returned. "Anyhow. A beastly attitude can do wonders for an acting career."

"Ah! How was your audition?"

"The part's mine." She held up a gloved fist.

"They've announced casting?"

"No." Molly tossed her curls. "But it's mine."

I shook my head. "If I could bottle and sell your confidence . . ."

"You'd be bottling a lie. Imagine where that confidence would be if you offered to give *me* a haircut. Where would I be?" She sighed. "Not here."

I wanted to ask her whether her family—whatever her family was composed of—knew about her hidden teeth. I wanted to ask. I could not.

I haven't bottled and injected curls or confidence.

Any soul would need confidence in my intensive *Belletristik* (fiction) class. Dr. Hoppen is the instructor whose classroom plays home to the legendary fireside beanbags. Ollie, uncertain as I remain of most facets of my life, fiction remains a respite. I won't be humble. I am *good* at listening. Good at assessing stories. I know truth when I hear it.

(And also when I do not hear it, Ollie.)

"Today we'll be reinterpreting *Gläserne Bienen* by creating assemblages from found materials," Dr. Hoppen informed us. Perched on a stool in the center of our circle. Smile as miraculously wide as his unibrow. "And those of you who think this will be easy should note that building minuscule robotic mock-glass bees from recycled plastic is no promenade. Especially as each bee should represent a key theme from the book."

Myriad normalcy. I won't deny it thrills me. I lack creativity. But I am good with textures. With shapes. With strangeness.

I am good with science-fiction novels about technophobia.

And Dr. Hoppen once taught dance to kindergartners in Bulgaria. Dr. Hoppen's sculptures, strung together with human hair, animal bones, plastic bags, and ribbon, have been featured in museums across Europe. Dr. Hoppen respects the odd. He has never once drawn attention to my goggles.

Dr. Hoppen may be the next person I fall in love with.

I sat as straight as my beanbag would allow.

"We'll warm up by reviewing Kafka short stories. A brief bout of creative movement. Three sacrifices?"

I sank back. Willing candidates for acting exercises are hardly in short supply at Myriad—Chloe-Bowie, in capri overalls and a silk blouse, had both hands up. All but wailing to be chosen.

"Chloe-Bowie." Everyone calls her that. "And Max. Max, pick one other student."

I stood. Resigned to my fate even before Max curled a beckoning finger.

I am not afraid of performance, Ollie. I am not afraid of Max Fassner. So why sudden silence descended on the beanbags, I can't say. It could *not* have been my nerves emolocated.

I refuse to believe I blushed.

No time for uncertainty. We three stood front and center. Max's arm against mine. His pulse resonating into me. Knocking me off beat.

"You know the rules. I'll call out a story title and clap. If you've been doing your readings, you should be able to fall into a tableau before I count to ten. *Without talking*."

Tableaus mean extracting a pivotal scene from a story, acting it out, and freezing it. Becoming a living portrait.

"We'll start simple. 'The Metamorphosis.'" *Clap*.

Immediately, I fell to the ground, made myself small and grotesque. I assume you've read Kafka's surreal stories. I don't have to tell you I became Gregor Samsa, the man who awoke as an insect one morning. Elbows on floor. Knees on floor. I can do insect.

I have the goggles for it.

While Dr. Hoppen's clap still echoed, I saw Chloe smile. Then snap into character. She pulled one hand up to her mouth: a feigned expression of shock. Her other hand she pushed forward, palm up, offering me an invisible meal. Gregor Samsa's sister: horrified by the state of her brother. Yet unwilling to let him die.

And that left Max. He ignored Chloe completely. Fell to his knees and, without pause, bent over me. A roof over my cowering form.

Oliver, he is as shameless as he is flexible. He suspended himself just above me, arms rigid, legs rigid in a push-up that urged me closer to the ground. He must be unfathomably strong, to hold himself so steadily. I've heard he belongs to the ballet program.

Hot breath on my throat. I shuddered.

". . . nine, ten! Hold your positions."

Max laughed against my shoulder, shook hairs that stood up there.

"Postulations?"

A small girl: "Moritz is Gregor Samsa. And Chloe's Gregor's sister. But Max . . ."

"Max is a cad," Chloe murmured behind her hand. Laughter rumbled the beanbags.

"No." The girl adjusted her glasses. "He's furniture. The table Gregor's hiding under."

Max snorted, pushed himself off me. "No, Chloe-Bowie's right. I am a cad."

Our classmates snapped applause. Max helped me to my feet. Did not release my hand for many seconds, let his fingers ghost my palm when he did. I did not blush.

Chloe elbowed me on the way to our beanbags. "Moritz Farber, *join my band*."

"Moritz." Dr. Hoppen. "You fell into character before I hit nine. Well done."

I could not stifle a smile.

And, Ollie, I saw it suddenly mirrored on a circle of faces.

You told me. You told me I might brighten a room. You weren't lying.

I've never seen light. But have I *been* light?

In Stagecraft, I used a razor to texture the side of the Stone Table on which Aslan would be sacrificed. Some heavy-handed symbolism in Year One's performance of *The Lion, the Witch and the Wardrobe*. All of Myriad operates on dream logic: living for an endless cycle of performances. God knows what becomes of the graduates when they enter the world and find it devoid of spontaneous musical numbers. We *act* as though that doesn't matter. Today I wanted to act that way, too. Today I *whistled*. Downright unnerving.

I'm a dab hand at textures. MBV ensures that I know what the pores of stone look like better than most. No lion was ever shanked on a Styrofoam table so finely crafted.

I heard Klaus enter the wings. He stood just behind the curtain, watching me work. Aiming for silence, but I could hear his heartbeat. His breathing. The usual sounds of a human body. Klaus peeled his shoes from his feet and slid forward across the floor on swishing socks. Did he intend to scare me? How embarrassing.

"Am I doing a proficient job?"

He deflated. "There's no surprising you, is there?"

I cocked an ear toward him. "Why would you wish to surprise me?"

Klaus folded his sturdy arms and sat down atop the unfinished table. "Maybe I was trying to catch you slacking off. Give me a reason to kick you out of class."

"You're the Stagecraft student supervisor. You don't need a reason." I set the razor down on a brown paper bag beside my knees. "I'm not so popular that anyone would fight for me." I thought about *Belletristik* class. "Well, probably no one would."

"Molly definitely would. Why the hell does she like you so much?" Cantankerous as he may be, Klaus is also bracing. Direct.

"I'm under the impression Molly *likes* very nearly everyone."

"Yeah, sure. But with you it's like—how do I say this? She *treasures* you. She's class rep and she pays attention to everyone. But she looks at you like she can't believe you're next to her. Like you're *blessing* us with your misery."

"We share a close history."

"So tell me what that *means*, Farber."

I found my feet and turned away from him. Headed for the wings. "That's her business. I wouldn't presume to—"

Klaus stood as well, towering above me on the table. He actually *shouted*: "I want her to treat me like that!"

If I put you in a room with Klaus, the room would be full of declarations and completely devoid of shame.

"Then speak with her. Not with me."

"That's the damn problem. Whenever I get close, she shrugs me off. She doesn't—"

I heard his foot lose purchase even before it had.

I spun around.

Klaus's eyes widened and he fell, trying to pull folded arms free.

I heard adrenaline flooding him electric. Muscles clenching.

I became very aware that I'd left the razor blade exposed, there beside the rock.

Unlikely he would land on it, but—

My tongue clicked against my teeth.

I rushed forward with arms outstretched just as he slipped sideways. Slid onto my knees. Would have slid farther if the stage were freshly polished. I took that into account.

The instant my left fingertips pushed the razor spinning away across the wood, I pushed my right palm against his right shoulder. Broke his fall.

Bulky Klaus weighed more than I'd anticipated. My arm caved.

The both of us, entangled on the floor.

"But—you were facing the other way." Klaus dislodged himself. Eyes did not leave me. "And before . . . you knew I was here. So how did you even—?"

"Keen ears." I rubbed my left elbow.

"And I heard you click." He shook his head. "Tennessee Williams, Farber?"

"Oh, I think I'm still waiting for that click."

"What the hell is that supposed to mean?"

"I don't know." I didn't, Oliver. "Beg pardon."

"Why do you wear those goggles, Moritz?" The aggression had left him. His voice imploring. "Tell me."

I shook my head. "It's light sensitivity."

"You're lying." Klaus stared at me. Panting. He recovered his gruff demeanor. "You're just like her. I'm just part of the damn scenery."

"The *where* matters," I whispered.

Hands on his hips, his back to me. "I'm an idiot."

"Everybody trips."

"I'm an idiot because I don't really even know who she is. And I still . . ." He nodded at my arm. "Put some ice on that."

"I will. Thank you."

A begrudging head jerk. "And get back to work. A messianic lion needs to die there later."

The walk home from Myriad feels longer with every day. The snow deepens.

I wrote my assemblage bee captions this evening at my desk. My tea went cold before I could finish tucking minuscule paper scrolls into plastic pockets.

I steeped another tea bag. Set about completing my Trigonometry and Design assignment. All the models you have made, Ollie. Has any madness ever compelled you to construct a freestanding dodecahedron from paper pentagons? I could not hear where I'd placed glue at the structure's seams. Like balancing a house of cards: I could not play music, because I do not play music without bass, and bass toppled my efforts. I could not click at the paper structure, because my breath toppled my efforts. I could not finish my homework.

I journeyed from my room. No sound but the loud ticking of hands in an analog clock. When I was young and new to the apartment, Father hung it over my door. "To show you your way on quiet nights." Did I ever thank him?

Now he is always sleeping or working, working or sleeping.

Dust gathers in our small home.

I washed my exhaustion away under our sputtering showerhead. Illuminated my exhaustion in water patters, found Styrofoam remnants in my hair. Scrubbed my neck. Once and again. Max's breath clung there.

Until I was half asleep, I forgot Owen. Horizontal became vertical. I picked up my phone. Messaged him to say he is not scenery. (I've changed his digital voice to the voice of Christopher Lee. I cannot think of a voice with greater gravitas.)

I waited.

Felt silence.

Owen lives only blocks away. But I dare not see him in

person. With Molly, with Klaus. Max's breath on my neck. I'd only make a mess of it. Sting him.

Ollie. Beautiful as my school is, there remain moments when I long to be a hermit, with only your words rattling inside me.

chapter thirteen

THE STOP SIGN

Moritz, I want you to hear something, right now, and imagine the sort of amazing shapes it would make in echolocation. You ready?

I'm PROUD OF YOU. ALL-CAPS PROUD.

I'm not your dad, so that's a weird thing to say right off the bat. And I know we've been moping like obnoxious teenage stereotypes lately, and you feel more uncertain now than ever before. It's very *you* to feel down no matter what, but oh man—

The fact that you are taking chances on your life, going to a new school, and *owning* being Moritz Farber—Dolphin-Man and Supreme Insect Impersonator—is spectacular!

I would read your comic book, Mo.

You used to be a dorky, begoggled caterpillar. Do you remember? You spent hours slinking around hallways, trying to be meaner than you are, projecting *ennui* (that's French!), and living a life even lonelier than mine.

But now—Moritz, before you seriously consider hermithood (I know you've got depression and you can't help it), you *need* to look at how far you've come. I mean, you've got *friends*. Love interests! You catch falling grouches! You've got a school that will let you *rap for a grade.* And there's even talk of getting your hair out of your face.

I really wish you could see you how I do. I wish you could see that your mistakes mean you're living. And if there are consequences, you'll be learning. Say what you want, but don't give up on the world just yet. We can't *both* spend our lives in bed.

Moritz, what if trying to be better *is* the same as being good?

"Bridget," Auburn-Stache said, "don't."

Auburn-Stache *had* mentioned Bridget before. When he was trying to cheer me up after the funeral. He mentioned a girl who takes her heart out when she doesn't want to feel things.

So here was an unfeeling-looking girl suspending a heart over a machine.

No reason to lose my cool. My weirdness tolerance is growing taller than Arthur, Mo.

"Hey." I pointed. "Is that what folks call a blender?"

Bridget stared like a rock might stare. "Yes."

"*Awesome.* Do you use it for chocolate shakes and whatnot? Can I get in on that?"

"Ollie," Auburn-Stache cautioned. "Your bombastics are not helpful."

"I'm not making shakes." Bridget lowered her arm an inch.

"I'm Oliver, by the way, but most people call me Ollie. What's it like being you?"

Bridget didn't take my hand, what with hers being full of thumping heart. "The electro-sensitive boy."

"Yeah." That threw me, but I kept smiling. "*Everyone* seems to know that."

"Ollie, enough." Auburn-Stache took another step closer. "Bridget, please put it back."

"You don't have to be careful. You won't change my mind."

"Hey, how does your blood keep flowing if your heart's not in your chest?" I eyed the hole near her sternum. It wasn't gory at all. More like a kangaroo pouch than a cut. She could probably pull her heart out like pulling berries from pockets.

In monotone: "I'm a freak."

First Arthur, now Bridget. Like *freak* isn't one of the worst words in the world!

"So you're gonna, what, put your telltale heart in a blender? Is that like some sort of performance art?" (Thanks, Chicago.)

"I'm breaking my heart. I don't want to feel things anymore."

"*Tch!*" I snorted. "Now, that's some poetical love nonsense."

She didn't blink.

"Look, *sure*. I like Shakespeare. I know *metaphorically*, your heart's where you feel things. But anatomically, feelings come from your insular cortex." I tapped my skull. "Basic anatomy. Plus you're totally mixing your metaphors. You're *blending* your heart, not *breaking* it. Blending your heart won't do anything but make a big mess and probably a terrible milk shake."

She shrugged.

"I'm just saying. It's wishy-washy bullshit."

"According to a boy who sees rainbows in electricity."

I frowned, because didn't that sound almost like sarcasm? Like she was being emotional after all, despite what she was saying about removing her feelings?

I was willing to believe Arthur could have accelerated healing. That's very Marvel.

But a *removable* heart? Science fiction, Moritz.

"Hey, now. That's not wishy-washy. Just a bit dolphin-wavy. I was all excited to meet you and now you wanna off yourself? You haven't even heard my jokes yet!"

"I don't care." In the flattest voice *ever*. "And this isn't suicide."

"Bridget, I will remind you, as ever, that doing this *will* kill you. You need your heart as much as anyone."

"I'll die, Doctor." She lifted her heart up again. "But it's beside the point."

You know how I told you about Liz's social worker parents? When Mom got sick, Liz brought over books on mental illness. Most people who really mean to do themselves in don't call anyone. They shoot themselves in bathtubs to avoid leaving brains on the carpet.

But Bridget, she *knew* Auburn-Stache was coming. With or without emotions, she would have known that we'd want to stop her from doing this. Did she *want* to be stopped?

"Fine." I threw my hands up. "I've always wanted to see a blender in action. That was on the list somewhere near humidifiers."

Her eyelids fluttered. Auburn-Stache kept his lips zipped. I sauntered closer to Bridget, watching her set the heart in the blender. She was careful about it. She didn't let it plop.

No emotions, my butt.

"One thing." I held up a finger, leaned back against the cabinets. "Aren't blenders supposed to have lids?" I looked around the room. "You're gonna leave a mess for your family."

"I'm a foster kid."

Bridget reached for the electric buttons.

"Bridget!" cried Auburn-Stache.

I was on it like stink on cheese.

I pulled the blender's plug (my hands tingled!). Good thing quick pressures won't break my fingers.

Bridget didn't emote when the blender didn't churn into life— she just whipped around on me, quick as Barry Allen.

Auburn-Stache leapt forward and held her arms. Eerie composure aside, I'm pretty sure she wanted to claw out my eyeballs. (Would that make us twins, Mo?) She threw a knee back, and her foot landed somewhere between Auburn-Stache's legs.

I capitalized on his distracting yelp by upending the blender.

Bridget's beating heart rolled across the counter—

Auburn-Stache crumpled, and I grabbed that thing and shoved it into the pocket of my coat and sprinted out of the kitchen and down the hallway as fast as I could, grateful to escape into open air even with some girl's heartbeat vying against my own, somewhere near my navel.

My feet slammed against Bridget's driveway as I skidded past Auburn-Stache's car, and then they slammed against the leafless street. While I ran, the heart was incredibly warm and heavier than I thought it would be. It wasn't alive the way organs are.

This heart felt alive like small animals are alive.

Thing is, I'm about as good at running as I am at patience, Moritz.

My feet feel too big and my eyes wander, and my arms flop around like soggy spaghetti noodles. When you've spent most of your existence playing opossum in a cabin or stumbling through underbrush after girls you're lovesick over, sprinting on pavement feels about as natural as walking backward on your hands.

It's even worse when you're being chased, and since then I've learned that Bridget kicks major ass at cross-country competitions in her Fayton high school. I ran like a crippled wind, but she was as likely to catch me as I was likely to eat cement.

And I did eat it. Right in the middle of an intersection. I could blame the four crosshatching power lines overhead, or my stupid feet. But the truth? I totally face-planted when that damn bodysuit got too personal with my ass crack.

Bridget approached at a semileisurely jog. She'd had time to pull on a hoodie and tennis shoes. (How do you say "humiliating" *auf Deutsch*?)

I scrambled to my feet and made a fresh break for it, ran for maybe seven seconds, awkward-bobbing and failing to cut across fenced-in lawns, before she knocked me onto the sidewalk next to a decrepit pay phone. I didn't cuss like a cool kid would when she wrapped her arms around my waist, tackled me to the ground, and sat down on my back.

I said, "Oof!"

My beanie got dislodged, and right away chartreuse veins of electricity (like netting, Moritz) inched down the length of the pay phone, headed right for me. "Um, I might be squishing your heart against the pavement."

She didn't seem bothered. "You stole it."

Not sneezes, but hiccups this time. No, Moritz, I did not come this far to have a pay phone–induced seizure, because Arthur was wrong, I was fine and here to help the other Blunderkids—

To spite me, an SUV approached, and the driver slowed down to ogle us. I guess we were worthy of rubbernecking, but sandpapery car-smog scraped my face as they idled by.

"Can you get off me? *Hic.* Maybe?"

"Why did you steal my heart?"

"Or at least *consider* the idea of—*hic*—maybe getting off me? No pressure."

"Why?"

"You aren't exactly weightless as a cloud."

"No. Why did you steal it?"

"People say I'm impulsive!"

"*Why?*" She dug her elbow into my spine.

"Jegus! It didn't seem like—*hic*—you were taking care of it. I came all this way to get to know you! I can't do that if you're dead!"

"To . . . get to know me."

"Yes! Preferably without being sat on!"

I tried to roll over, but she remained firmly planted, feet flat on the pavement.

"If you'll let me up and promise not to toss it at the nearest lawn mower, I'll give your heart back, and we can talk about the whole blender fiasco and maybe your whole life story?"

"My life story."

"Yeah! I'm collecting the stories of kids like us."

"Collect the heart instead."

What? I mean—*what*?

"Is that really the sort of thing you should lay on someone you've just met?"

"Keep it."

"I wouldn't even know what to feed it." My head pounded. "You know about my—*hic*—electro-sensitive thing, right?"

"I know."

Another car drove past, fast enough to kick up leaves (except there weren't any). I definitely needed to pull my hat back on; my tongue was turning into a heavy slug. Bad sign.

"Well, obviously, you don't *care*, but this turd of a pay phone is creeping on me."

Finally, she got up. I squeaked to my feet, pulled Mom's hat back down quick-sharp. Bridget was already yards away. I hurried to catch up, pulled her heart, fuzzy with lint, from my pocket. "Here! You seem like you're in less of a blendering mood now."

"I'm not in any mood."

"Sure, sure. More Tin Man crap."

She paused at the Stop sign to let a minivan pass.

"That's a reference to a character in an L. Frank Baum book called *The Wonderful Wizard*—"

"'If I only had a heart,'" Bridget sang suddenly. "I've seen the movie."

"There's a *movie*?" I was about to sneakily drop her heart into her hood, but a gigantic yellow monster spewing diesel electricity roared past like a dream.

"HOLY—A SCHOOL BUS?" I tugged on her sleeve. "That was a school bus, right?"

She shook off my grasp and crossed the street. "Yes."

"Can we hitch a ride?"

Bridget paused. "What do you mean?"

"Riding a school bus ranks among my life goals." I stood in the center of the street and waved my arms in the air. It was dang heavy, her heart, and I was scared of dropping it, but I wanted her to react.

She did! Well, kind of: "You'll drop that if you're not careful."

"So you *do* care!" I hurried out of the road.

"Only stating a fact."

"Look, please take it?"

"If you give it back to me, I'll stomp on it."

My eyes found her feet. She was wearing running shoes, the kind with long spikes that could pin tents down.

I tucked the damn heart back into my pocket.

I adjusted my hat again. Walking down the Fayton suburb street felt like moonwalking, waiting to make awkward first contact with leaf-hiding aliens. Here were kids on bicycles headed home from school, men and women pulling cars into driveways, stepping out of smog clouds in suits, teenagers my age loitering under Stop signs and downright glaring at us—

Actually, that kid was *definitely* glaring.

Shortish with freckles like Liz, but his hair was orange. (If orange had a sound, Moritz, it would sound like 88 degrees Fahrenheit— don't mention Celsius!) His eyes were this pale blue, ideal for icy-death glaring.

I stopped and stared right back at him.

"What's your deal?" I called from across the street.

The boy jerked in surprise and then glared harder. Bridget turned to see what I was hollering about and the weirdest thing happened—

Moritz, I think the heart in my pocket missed a beat.

Bridget grabbed me by the hand and wrenched me forward.

"Do you know that kid?" I craned my neck. I thought his eyeballs might pop out and hit us like bullets, but he didn't follow. Bridget's heart started beating normally again.

"That's Brian."

"What's his beef?"

"You shouted at a stranger in broad daylight."

"Sorry, I struggle with *social niceties*. I was only shouting because he looked ALL-CAPS ANGRY. *Shit*, your hand is cold. Is that because your circulation is messed up?"

"My circulation is fine. As long as my heart's within an eighty-seven-mile radius."

"How did you find that out? Did you just leave your heart in the kitchen and then jog away from it until you felt like, oh, okay, I might just keel over if I go any farther? Guess it's lucky I didn't run eighty-seven miles ahead of you just now. How long would it take a person to run that far? I mean, you'd have to have good shoes. Or could you do it in flip-flops?"

"You ask too many questions."

"That's what Mom says—said. Said."

"Your dead mother." In that lifeless tone.

Bridget let me go. Good, because my feet had turned to tree roots.

I guess we'd reached her house. Lifeless, Bridget walked up the steps.

I stood outside with my head bowed, the heart in my chest beating out the one in my pocket by more than eighty-seven miles.

I'll always have to say "said" now, Moritz.

Auburn-Stache waited in the living room, face all twisted up. I sat down across from him. It wasn't a comfy sofa, but it beat car seats.

"You said you wanted an adventure," Auburn-Stache gasped.

Said.

"All right, Ollie?"

I cleared my throat. "Are *you* all right, 'Stache?"

"Parts of me are." He winced.

"There go your equestrian dreams. But hey, we've got a new addition to the family." I pulled the heart out of my pocket and set it on the coffee table.

Weird: once I let it go, I missed its warmth. I couldn't get over how gory it wasn't. Moritz, the aorta fed from the top chamber back into itself. Complete anatomical bullpucky.

"Oh, thank goodness."

"What, did you think I was gonna drop it or something?" No need to tell him I nearly did. "She won't take it back. So what the hell am I supposed to do with it?"

"You sound frustrated."

"I *am* frustrated."

Auburn-Stache sighed. "Remember what I told you. Bridget's not Arthur."

I crossed my legs and uncrossed them again and leaned forward. "Should I just . . . I don't know. Shove it in her mailbox or something?"

"She'll know it's there. Her wireless heart. She can always feel where it is."

"What? How?"

"The same way you always know where your hands are, I suppose." Auburn-Stache rubbed his temples. "Ollie, why did you act so rash?"

"Was I supposed to just watch her make a meat smoothie?"

"She wouldn't have." He shook his head. "Her drive for self-preservation is very strong."

"This isn't the first time you've caught her getting carefree with a blender," I hazarded.

"It's not always a blender. But it's routine. Bridget has never been . . . a stable child."

Obviously he didn't think this was such a big deal. But, Moritz, if someone I cared about started crying wolf—

From down the hallway there came a horrendous grinding racket, a sustained bout of electric shrieking. I jumped to my feet.

"Calm down."

"Why?" I almost hissed. "We're trapped in a house with a—a sociopath!"

"What a thing to say about someone you don't know. And how unlike you."

I felt him trying to catch my eye. I turned away and stared at all the family pictures on the wall. Something seemed weird about the photos, but I couldn't pinpoint what.

"What did she do?"

"She kicked you in the delicates."

"Did she say something hurtful to you?"

Your dead mother.

Right then, Bridget appeared in the doorway with two shakes in hand. She set them on the coffee table on either side of her heart.

"How kind, Bridget." I bet 'Stache was wishing she'd brought him an ice pack instead. "Do I espy bananas?"

"Bananas. Chocolate. And peanut butter."

"Um. Thanks." Like any major asshole, I hid my shame behind a few giant gulps of shake through a purple bendy straw. (Ice cream is serious business, even on cold days.)

'Stache asked Bridget about her heart. She pointed at her spiked shoes again.

"We'll be at the Rustic Bear Campground," he told her, "if you change your mind."

"You should leave. The Tidmores will be home soon."

"You aren't smiling in any of the pictures," I murmured.

That was it. It looked like the blond-haired Tidmores had raised many foster children. (There were at least five graduation pictures hanging up, and in other frames, younger versions of those graduates wore clothing even this woodland hermit noticed were outdated.) Though the wall was crowded with bright faces, room had definitely been made for Bridget. There were photos of her at beaches and parks with her foster parents. Pictures of the three of them posing beside green fields and brown trails, Bridget wearing some kind of athletic uniform. Bridget with medals on her neck. All of them sitting in front of a fireplace at Christmastime. Those foster parents smiled so hard. They overcompensated, became sharks around her.

"What happens when your parents get home, then?"

"*Foster* parents." Her eyes were fixed on my shoulder or on nothing. "We make dinner. We eat it. Sometimes with dessert. They ask about school. We watch television. We go to bed."

I squinted at the TV, which whined a quiet green in Off mode on the opposite side of the room. "Do you watch, like, really violent television? The kind where people scream and laugh simultaneously?" I shuddered. "Is that why you want us to leave?"

"I don't want anything." Her eyes flickered to Auburn-Stache.

I leaned off the couch cushion to see her better. Bridget: another barren Ohio tree. But whatever she'd secreted away weren't leaves.

Were her feelings really trapped inside the pulsing lump of meat on the table?

"Why doesn't my doctor like being seen by your parents?"

"*Our* doctor. *Foster* parents. They would ask questions. They don't know about my condition. It would disturb them."

"Well, that sucks." I stood up and began pacing across the room again. "I mean, really? Doesn't that make you sad? Having to hide all the time?"

(Moritz, that's what you and Molly are doing, too, but Arthur's not.)

"When my heart is out, I can't feel sadness."

"Well, you should get angry about not feeling sad!"

"When my heart is out, I can't feel anger."

"Ollie—our host has asked us to leave."

"I could stand right next to you and hold your dismembered heart out like a bouquet of flowers for your supposedly nice foster parents. Right?"

"They are nice. Not supposedly."

"If I called you a f-freak and told them to submit you for twisted medical research—"

"Enough, Ollie!" *He* sounded angry.

"You'd be cool with it?"

"I wouldn't care."

"But . . . how would that make your foster parents feel?"

She shrugged; Auburn-Stache grabbed my arm. I shook him off.

"No. I came here to talk to her, and all I've heard so far is she's heartless, literally and figuratively! I don't get it. I *want* to get it. I came here to hear your story."

"That's not my problem."

I folded my arms and popped a squat right in the middle of the floor. "Tell me a story or I won't budge."

"You bloody well will budge!" Sergeant Secrets warned.

"Give me the beef, Bridget!"

"Why does he talk like that?"

Seriously-Annoyed-'Stache: "I'm sorry. That's just how he is. He struggles with social—"

"Niceties," she finished.

The heart kept pumping away between two empty milk-shake rings.

I picked it up and shoved it into my pocket. "There. It can have a sleepover."

Bridget walked around the couch and sat down across from me on the carpet, stared me dead in the eyes. "You asked me about the eighty-seven-mile tether."

I swallowed. "Yeah . . . ?"

"When I was five, scientists tied me to a table. They took my heart across the hall and shocked it with low-watt electricity. They increased the frequency until I screamed. A woman next to me made a note, called the scientists, and told them to take it farther away."

My right hand found my heartbeat, my left hand found Bridget's. Moritz, you know better than I do what it feels like when *this* kind of electricity goes wrong. Does it feel worse than bee-stings? Is that the pointless question the scientists were answering?

Bridget didn't blink. "They took it to the entrance. I screamed on the table. To the parking lot. I screamed. The edge of the woods. I screamed. To the town. Nothing happened. They increased the frequency until I screamed. To the freeway. I screamed." Her eyelids fluttered. "My pulse stopped after eighty-seven miles."

"Oh." Is this how you'd have talked if I'd met you in person first, Moritz?

I deserved a snowfall. A whole damn avalanche.

Auburn-Stache's grip loosened. "Bridget, you have my number."

Bridget led us to the doorstep. The wind blew like it had a grudge, and the sky seemed to have skipped sunset and gone with insta-dark.

I patted the bulge at my stomach. "Um. Sure you don't want this?"

"The blender's still plugged in."

For an emotionless lump, that felt almost like a joke. "See you tomorrow?"

Bridget closed the door in our faces. I spun around to give Auburn-Stache the sort of look you give your mad-scientist friend when you're ousted by a heartless girl, or maybe the sort of look you give when you're in shock about what she's just told you or what he's *never* told you.

"You know, 'Stache, no one's ever kicked me in the testicles before."

"You've lived a blessed life, Ollie."

"Better than hers, huh." I turned back to the house, closed curtains. "Is the campground definitely within an eighty-seven-mile radius?"

"Yes."

We closed the car doors in unison.

"Think she'll take it back tomorrow?"

"I hope so. But, Ollie?"

"Yeah?"

"Not all business is your business. I took you on this trip because I believed you could show some restraint. I *warned* you to be patient. It's one thing for you to badger me." His voice was so stern, Moritz. My heart missed a beat that Bridget's made up for. "Heart or no, do you think Bridget should *have* to tell you about the laboratory? She doesn't owe you *any piece* of herself."

"I didn't mean—"

"You disappointed me today."

I had to look out the window.

The campground was twenty miles away, tucked into a pathetic patch of woods.

Once we'd set up camp on a site near the back of the lot, I unpeeled my second skin to rinse myself off at a cold water pump with my hat still on, and then I skirted around Auburn-Stache and went right to my sleeping bag with my book light.

He could say what he wanted. At least *I* didn't dismiss Bridget's suicide attempt. If someone I cared about cried wolf, I'd come running. Like, even if you cried it a thousand times, Moritz. I'd keep unplugging the blender.

I wrote about the Indiana cornfield that night. Auburn-Stache came in, and I didn't say a word. His own medicine, I guess.

I scratched out words for you, one eye on Bridget's heart by my pillow. Our campground was called the Rustic Bear despite being pinned between two sides of a freeway, and I know woodland creatures creep out of the, erm, woodwork when they smell meat. Her heart fogged up my fishbowl. Dew formed on the bottom of the lid (by lid I mean my *Order of the Phoenix* hardcover). I wondered if Bridget could feel the cold glass, miles away, watching TV with her nice, oblivious foster parents. Maybe she heard me tap my fingers on the bowl and apologize to her, to it, and then snort at my own doofusry.

I wrote and wrote as the temperature dropped inside the tent, as I huddled deeper down in my mummy bag.

"Ollie!" groaned Auburn-Stache at last, rolling over in his sleeping bag. "Put the light out. I've just dreamt I was staring into headlights."

I closed the book and watched the heart glisten.

"Hey, 'Stache? Sorry for badgering Bridget."

"Ollie," murmured Auburn-Stache. "The light."

"No. This here's an interrogation. See, I'm *not* sorry for badgering you."

He sighed. "*You get one question*, Ollie."

"Did you . . . back in the lab. Did *you* torture Bridget?"

He didn't answer right away. "Not personally. I wasn't her primary physician."

"Okay." I had to believe him, half asleep or not.

Not. "But I can't say I wouldn't have, given the assignment. If someone convinced me it would help us learn, for instance, more about Moritz's heart condition." I couldn't see him, which made it easier. For me. Maybe for him. "I didn't know Bridget until after the laboratory dissolved. When it came time to place the children in homes."

"And Bridget moved to Ohio."

Auburn-Stache kicked his feet against the canvas. "No. She's lived with a dozen families, and rarely worn her heart for ten years. The longer she leaves it out, the harder it gets for her."

"Years of dusty emotions gunk up the works?"

"Ollie, when you've been numb for a long while, numbness becomes a comfort. Pain is most immense right after anesthesia wears off. There's nothing so frightening as the full weight of who you are."

"This is a sad story, 'Stache."

"It's not a story, Ollie. It's Bridget's life. And I have no right to share it. Her story or the others'. Do you understand? I'm the last person who gets to lay claim to your lives, Ollie. *Your* lives. Not mine."

How many years do you think we were Auburn-Stache's anesthesia, Moritz?

"But she knew who I was." I listened to beats beyond glass. "You said you won't talk about us behind our backs, but Arthur knew about me, too. But until last year, you let me think I was alone." I swallowed. "If that's because you feel ashamed or whatever, why is it just me? Why am I still in the woods?"

People kept killing my questions with snores.

Moritz, it can't be healthy to let pain build up until you want to plug in blenders. If you don't feel things as they happen, those things creep up on you like a rash, and then you can't breathe, and you just want to clutch your stomach and say, "She's gone, she's *gone*," until the words sound like lies. Until you don't know what you're saying anymore, or if you're saying it clearly, or if language can even capture being that alone.

I'm proud of you for feeling things.

Bridget's heartbeat lulled me to sleep, but it took awhile.

Good night,

Ollie

P.S. Okay. So it's January and I'm writing about November, and you've stopped badgering me about why. But more than ever I think you deserve to know what's been going on with me, and, Moritz, I *thought* I was ready to tell you. I picked up the ballpoint and I was so ready to finally get on with my life, unstop the clock, but . . . next time, okay?

chapter fourteen

THE NAPKINS

You are making a habit of stealing hearts. It took me many months to offer you mine, Oliver Paulot. And yet no one near you remains heartless.

I, too, am trying to learn patience. I understand. A heart is a daunting thing to expose to anyone. But whatever you need to tell me, do tell it. *Honesty*, Oliver. Isn't that what we preach? Be honest with me. I'm not just *anyone*.

Am I?

Weeks in Kreiszig have passed as if pursued by something heartless. Scarce time to keep up with my coursework. Our correspondence. My life.

Molly is busy with rehearsals. All I see of her now are brief embraces in the mornings, the gentle hiss of air through her mouths when she greets me.

"Moritz, are you making friends?"

"Possibly."

"I want you to rehearse, too. Practice talking to people, or I'll just be *livid*, Prince Moritz."

Does "beg pardon" qualify as talking?

I stay late on campus with Myriad classmates. Seeking advice from professors. (I have never before been challenged by coursework, Ollie.) Helping at rehearsals, practicing rhythm under trees where sometimes people high-five me. Chloe-Bowie has recently decided I have perfect pitch.

"Only sensitive ears. I do not sing."

"Who cares? Help me tune my guitar!" I hummed for her in the spacious mess hall. She strummed strings. Grinned. "Give me E-flat."

Max Fassner stopped to listen to her plucking out "Life on Mars?" Sucking his teeth. One foot on the ground. The other on the bench. Eyes? On me.

Fluffing conquistador.

"Moritz, wanna tune our instruments on tour? And you could double as a metronome, you click so well."

An affronted click. "I am not portable."

Chloe sized me up with her forefinger and thumb. "Close enough."

Max winked. I ducked.

What was I? Kittens or bee stings?

When finally Owen and I reunited on a rainy Thursday, I arrived drenched at the café. Apologies at the ready—Klaus's barking had kept me late, Chloe's singing had kept me later—

But Owen did not appear for another half hour. I heard him in the collapse of his umbrella, in the scraping of snow off boots in the doorway. He sat down across from me. Proceeded to spend minutes tapping on his phone. I sipped hot water in silence; Owen's coffee went cold.

At last, he pulled a pen from behind his ear and scrawled on a napkin. I took it eagerly and clicked to read:

Why did you want to see me Moritz.

"Why wouldn't I?"

He took the napkin back and poised his pen, but did not answer.

"Sometimes I am preoccupied, but that doesn't mean I don't care for you."

Preoccupied with Myriad. Neat block letters, shoved my way.

"Yes. With Myriad."

Frau Pruwitt asked about you. He flipped the napkin over, wrote furiously. *You're supposed to keep working the library some afternoons. You're supposed to help her.*

"She knows I'm busy."

Owen raised both his hands and eyebrows.

"With what, you ask? New classes. Stagecraft, in particular. Klaus is always hounding me! The dimwit refuses to understand what 'color-blind' means."

Is Klaus gay, Owen wrote.

"He is not."

Owen narrowed his eyes. I saw the resemblance to his sister. His sister. How was she?

I did not know if I could ask. What am I? The eyeless wonder who abandoned them.

"Klaus only has eyes for Molly. And I've got eyes for no one. Ha."

A joke I'm sure you could land. From my lips, it did nothing.

Oliver, was I emolocating? Frosting coffee in cold hands behind me? Raising the volume of voices? I tried not to think about what happened with Max. How I should have told Owen from the start. Why hadn't I? Truly, why hadn't I? Had the barista looked so glum before I sat down?

"That, ah, reminds me. Molly's set to perform in a play about radioactive posies next month. The Saturday before Valentine's Day. You should come. Meet everyone."

You've told them about me?

"Obviously!" (*"I've got a boyfriend." "Not for long."*)

He filled the napkin's final corner: *Have to go, DJing downtown.*

"Tonight? I'll come. And perhaps after . . ."

Owen shook his head. Signed something. I adjusted my goggles, as if that could help my ears. I could not remember the sign.

He repeated himself. I understood this time.

Ich möchte das nicht. More or less: "I don't want you to."

Owen pecked me on the goggles before departing.

I sat. Foolish.

I pulled my damp coat close around my neck and followed him out into the rainy street. Mostly empty, because wise people took shelter from the gale. Rivers and streams formed between the cobbles, trickling glacial capillaries by which to see.

I see so much farther in rain. But I could not see him.

I could scarce keep my head off the beanbag the next morning. Despite or because of this, Dr. Hoppen chose me for Kafkaesque again. This time I was paired with the mousy girl in glasses. Sally? Something inane like Sally.

"'In the Penal Colony.'" *Clap*.

I sprawled on the floor. Outstretched my arms and rolled myself slowly over, imagining that needles traced bloody words in my skin. In Kafka's "Penal Colony," criminals are tortured by a mechanical device. A bed of nails that carves words into its victims. I threw myself into the role.

There is some security in the familiar, even in the awful.

I assumed Sally would take on the role of the lovingly devoted officer who mans the device. But I only heard her back away. Dr. Hoppen had stopped counting. When?

"You're supposed to freeze, Moritz. And you're supposed to be silent."

I frowned. "I didn't say a word."

"No. You didn't." *Clap*. "I think everybody understood this one quite clearly." He seemed unnerved. "We'll be moving on."

I do not know for certain that I darkened the room. But, Ollie. Max frowned at me. Chloe didn't say a word. I hung my head through reader's theater performances of *Die Blechtrommel*.

Before I left the classroom, Dr. Hoppen waved me to join him by the mantelpiece.

"Moritz, I have a question for you."

"Ah. I'm sorry I did not, ah, follow instructions."

"It's not that. Although yes, that whining sound you made set all our teeth on edge. Like a dentist's drill."

Whining sound?

"Why do you always choose the role of the victim?"

I clicked, bit my tongue. "Do I?"

Do I, Ollie? Will I always?

The finished altar took center stage during an after-school performance of *The Lion, the Witch and the Wardrobe*. I helped my classmates follow Klaus's barking orders. Shifted lampposts and sleighs on command.

Applause grew loud enough to reveal a packed house.

You would not know this from Klaus's expression. A single click revealed deepening frown lines. When we began breaking down the sets, Klaus whistled for us to gather.

"You're free to go. I'll take care of this." On paper the words seem a kindness, but in truth a warning. Chloe-Bowie patted me on the back. (I still fight the urge to duck when people reach for me.)

"Come to the after-party, Moritz. After that freak-out in class today, I think you could use a drink. And there'll be cute boys there. Well, at least if you come, there'll be *one*."

Queer candyland. Fieke's sneer.

"Ah, I have homework. But thank you, Chloe."

She shrugged, rejoined her friends. Together, they encapsulated all eras of Bowie.

Behind me, Klaus unscrewed bolts from backdrop stands. The jingling of the metal hitting his palm revealed careful hands, intense focus, despite all his crotchety posturing.

"Farber, if I'd wanted to be stared at, I'd be an actor. Go home."

I looked at the wreckage before us. "You can't do all this alone."

A bark. "Watch me. Actually, no. *Don't* watch me."

I gathered costume debris from the scuffed floor, tossing pieces into bags for dry-cleaning. Velvet to faux fur. Klaus carried on, making enough noise to see by. In an hour or two, most of the lumber had been returned to the storage space at the back of the auditorium.

"I don't know why," Klaus announced suddenly, while I pushed a broom, "but I feel like you want to ask me a question. It's like an itch inside my skull, Farber."

I started, stopped the hissing bristles.

"So spit it out." Klaus kicked off his boots. Sat down under the pulley system between the inner and outer curtains.

"Was Molly not in attendance tonight?"

Klaus grunted. "I work on seven plays a semester. Nobody goes to all the shows."

"But you're upset?"

"Only because I invited her. But I can't expect anything. We aren't a couple."

"And if you were?"

"We wouldn't stand each other up. Obviously."

"Obviously."

He scratched his neck. What was I projecting, that he snapped his eyes my way? "People don't come to plays to see the scenery."

"I would say . . . scenery matters a great deal."

"You're one weird fish, Farber."

"Yes. I've seen worse scenery than this place."

"Has Molly?"

I closed my mouth.

He stood up and pulled the broom from my grasp.

"Go home. Your misery is catching."

He has no idea.

I'd avoided the Sickly Poet for weeks. For fear of Fieke. Any confrontation could only end with one of us incapacitated, by boot or cane. Our haunt was unusually empty, apart from a crooning torch singer at center stage.

And Fieke, sitting at one of the front tables. Crying into her drink. Hands balled into fists, face so gentle she was scarce recognizable. I could not begin to guess what the matter was. Perhaps it was only the music.

If I were you, Ollie, I would have sat down with her. Anyone human would not have turned tail and stepped back into the mire.

Father was not waiting up with tea at the table.

I turned on my stereo. Full blast. Bass that made cats yowl on the balcony, made a neighbor holler. Checked my mail. Phone. Nothing.

There are many words for "loneliness" *auf Deutsch*.

Mutterseelenallein is one that comes to mind. Don't laugh.

The literal translation? Essentially "without even a mother's soul." We share the greatest loneliness.

Don't laugh. Don't be alone.

Tell me what's wrong.

chapter fifteen
THE SCHOOL BUS

Moritz—

Neither of us knows how to do this "living" thing. Sometimes I blame our weird childhoods. But maybe Arthur's right: we live like anybody lives.

We aren't alone in screwing up all the time. So you suck at relationships? That makes you normal. Look at Klaus and Molly! Look at Fieke, crying. (I hope she's okay.)

Maybe feeling alone is what *normal* means. Maybe everyone on the planet is a hermit until they share that with someone else.

So here's what's gone so wrong with me, Moritz:

Turns out I can't keep people near me, either.

Is this legible? Or are my hands shaking?

Bridget's heartbeat helped me sleep, and I remembered a dream for the first time since Mom died. I know human beings dream *every single night*. But I couldn't remember any until I dreamed about wrapping my arm in a bedsheet and woke up in the tent getting pricked by green electricity—nothing too terrible, but enough to make me wish I'd taped my hat back on after my bath, because it was caught somewhere under my sleeping bag.

I sat up in bed, head sliding against the nylon.

Auburn-Stache was sitting, too, holding his phone against his ear, speaking in a whisper.

"What—?" I sneezed a sneeze so large I half expected the tent to blow free of its posts.

Auburn-Stache crawled outside. I could see the green bobbing light of his phone through the tent walls. He was repeating the same words over and over:

"I don't know. Oh god. I don't know. Oh god. I don't know."

I put my hands on the warm fishbowl. I couldn't sleep after that.

Auburn-Stache shook me from grogginess at the crack of dawn.

Does waking up at 4:00 AM make you feel sick? Like you weren't finished digesting your last potato chips and the shards of them are still poking your stomach lining, but you have to get up and walk around anyhow?

On top of that, Ohio's first snow of the season had fallen. I woke sniffling on the smell of cold and stayed halfway tucked in my sleeping bag even when I dragged myself to the campfire to chew stale granola. Auburn-Stache didn't eat, just coughed a lot while he rolled his sleeping bag away. (If it weren't for me, he could stay in hotels. He wouldn't have to rub his hands together like that.)

He had this furrowed-brow thing going on and seemed even

twitchier than usual. Twice he walked away from the campsite, scurrying around the circular gravel driveway like a lab rat in a maze.

"Looking for cheese?" I asked him.

"Pardon?"

"Who called last night?" I rubbed sleep gunk from my eyes. "Got a secret paramour, 'Stache?"

"Of course not," he snapped. "Ollie, you would do well to think before you speak."

My eyes probably bulged to Clamp manga proportions.

See, I can count on two hands and one foot the number of times that Auburn-Stache has been *that short* with me. This felt like getting slapped with a wet fish. And then another wet fish, because he took one look at my face, made a beeline for me and put his hands on my shoulders.

"Ollie, I'm sorry. That was rude. I'm *sorry*."

"Holy guacamole, Auburn-Stache. No biggie."

His face sort of twisted, and he put one hand over his mouth, trying to hold a sob captive.

"What is it?" Beds with tubes, bodies under deer blinds?

Auburn-Stache pulled me into an awkward, one-armed hug.

"Don't worry yourself, Oliver." He let go and started pacing the drive again. When he made it back around, he looked almost like himself. He puffed air up at the frosted oaks. "Plans have changed. We're leaving Ohio this morning. Bridget needs to take her heart back."

"*What?* You think she'll be over suicide overnight?"

"We have elsewhere to be, Oliver."

"Where elsewhere?"

He didn't answer. Of course he didn't, Moritz. Auburn-Stache and his stash of never-ending, pointless secrets.

I pulled Bridget's heart from the fishbowl and wrapped my hands around it inside my front pocket, but it didn't touch the chill in my chest. Why is it so hard to be honest? Moritz, what's wrong with everyone?

I couldn't ask. I didn't know where to start.

"Back in your hometown," I said, "did people get lost in the mines?"

He wouldn't even answer that. God, I wish he would have answered something. Just one question and maybe things wouldn't have gone so wrong, maybe I could have trusted him.

Instead: "Ollie, help me pull the tent posts up."

He coughed again. In the soft campfire light, I saw a glimmer of moisture in his eyes. The last thing I wanted was another freaky sobbing hug. I kicked at the tent posts.

The streetlights outside Bridget's place made those shards in my stomach twist. The faint glow of the sleeping houses, all that electricity lying in wait, pulsing in walls and ready to burst out when anyone flipped light switches. The electricities looked more discolored than ever, blurred by the white sheen of frost.

"We're just gonna leave it in her mailbox after all?"

He didn't laugh. "If we must."

"No way. Not unless she pinkie-promises not to do herself in or something."

"She won't do herself in," he said, though he looked agitated. "She never does."

"What if this time she's not crying wolf?" He didn't meet my eyes. "Hey! 'Stache! What if Bridget finally—"

"Ollie, as much as I appreciate your input, you don't know Bridget."

"Appreciate my input. *Tch*." I shoved my hands into my pockets, to rest against Bridget's heart. "You can't even answer a damn question. You can't even *trust* me. Hey. Would you have told Bridget about the phone call? I bet you would have, right?"

"Ollie." All warning tone. "Let it go."

"I just want to help! That's why I'm here!"

"That's *not* why you're here."

I gaped. "Yeah, it is! I'm here to help the kids who—"

"Enough, Ollie. Enough of this . . . this *delusion*! The reason you're on this trip isn't because you've made it *your mission*." Auburn-Stache stared out the window, raising his voice. "I simply couldn't leave you alone in that house after your mother died, all right? Your behavior is so erratic that—you think I worried what Bridget would do? I worried what *you might do*. Understand? Does that answer a question or ten?"

I can't tell you what I looked like, Moritz. But I can tell you this: if my emotions leaked like yours do, I'd have flooded the Impala right then.

"Ollie?" He closed his eyes. "Don't look so—*bollocks*."

Not drowning, laughing: "Well, you sure got me, Auburn-Stache. Gee, I thought you were treating me like a *person* for once! *Good one*, man!"

"I didn't mean to speak so—"

His phone rang in bursts of green light. I hiccuped.

"It's a phone, not one of my questions, so answering should be *fine*."

"Don't move." Auburn-Stache stepped out of the car and closed the door behind him. He put his hand over his eyes two seconds later. More awesome secret news, I guess. He wandered along the road like he wasn't really seeing it. I watched him reach a curb several driveways away.

I climbed into brisk air.

I popped my rest-area letter to you in Bridget's mailbox and lifted the flag. And I started walking. Just . . . away.

Can you see little puffs of air from people's mouths on cold days, Moritz? I slip-slid over the icy sidewalk, maybe in the same direction I'd run the other day. Who could tell in the suburbs? I'm not sure I was angry. Just feeling the old powerlessness pangs again.

In the gray light of dawn, the streetlights glowed double-bright, porch lights made me cringe. I jumped when an engine switched on in a driveway. Deer in headlights would have mocked me. I stared at my feet after that.

I missed the smell of emptiness and sap, Moritz.

I nearly ran into my apprehender.

Maybe he wanted me to run into him, this angry wall-guy with pumpkiny hair. It was him—that kid I'd shouted at. The Stop-sign loomer!

"Whoa, there. Who are you again? Byron? No, *Brian*, right?"

"Shut up. I know what's in your pocket." Brian shoved me in the chest.

I was too surprised to react.

"Hand over what's in your pocket!"

"Calm down, Gollum." I held up my hands. "I don't even know you!"

Brian flimsy-shoved me again. "You think you're the first person she tried to give it to?"

I held up a finger. "Wait, wait. Here's what's in my pocket." I pulled a BIC pen from my jeans and poised it over my palm. "You seem to know Bridget pretty well. Care to tell me her stor—"

This time when he shoved, I shoved back.

Brian clenched his fists and his uneven teeth in unison, looking like one seriously pissed-off fox. "It's not yours to screw with."

"The pen?" Her heart pumped away. "You want me to sign something for you?"

I guess Brian of the Almighty Ginger Rage was done talking, because he sprang forward, made a grab for the prize.

Moritz, you may have inhumanly quick reflexes, but I've never even played fisticuffs. The only things that ever pushed me before were electrical.

Lucky for me, Brian definitely hadn't been in many fights, either. He bounced back and forth like an angry weasel, swatting his hands at me, trying to grab my sleeve with one hand and reach my pocket with the other. I kept up a good fight. Slapping him away, basically.

You can see how this might escalate into *war*.

We must have looked AWESOME, scrabbling at each other, tugging on ears, aiming knees at stomachs and missing. We drifted into the ice-coated street and I swear "Carmina Burana" (glockenspiel arrangement) chimed in my ears. Dogs in nearby yards started yipping, almost like laughter.

I couldn't blame them.

In my pocket, the heart rate quickened; I guessed that Bridget had started running to school. Would she come this way? No time to wonder.

Brian sucked at squabbling but went for it with gusto, a flurry of clothes tugging and cussing.

I had an advantage—he couldn't get any purchase on my clothes and the slippery body suit underneath.

But I slipped up. I got so worried about the freakin' heart leaving my pocket that I totally forgot about my beanie until he tried to pull it off.

"What the fluff!" he cried.

I winced as some of the duct tape pulled away, but the hat didn't go far before I took advantage of his momentary surprise.

I smacked the palms of my hands against the sides of Brian's head. I've seen that work pretty well in comics, and it didn't disappoint.

Brian screeched and let go of my beanie and put his hands against his red ears and slipped on the icy road and fell to his knees, face puckered into an asterisk as I jogged away.

After twenty paces, I turned around and saw him kneeling in the road, clutching his skull.

Maybe I hit him too hard. I mean, I felt like a shit bag for smacking him in the ears when I didn't know him. What would happen if someone did something like that to *you*, Moritz?

So like a complete doofus, I found myself walking right back to him, saying, "Sorry, sorry. Was that a low blow?"

"No."

Brian grabbed my ankle and pulled as hard as he could, and the tight bodysuit didn't let me catch myself, and the next thing I knew, I lay on my back on the frigid ground, gasping for breath, shoulder blades on ice, head on fire.

Holy *crap*, Moritz. Getting the wind knocked out of you really freakin' hurts! Smacking the back of your head against pavement isn't awesome, either.

I saw stars, and I guess the ice ensured I slipped well and good, and now that I think back on it, I'm even more grateful for Mom's beanie and the rubber tubing, because it probably stopped me from hitting my head even harder and ending up good and truly knocked out or worse.

(Then again, if I *had* gotten knocked out, my hands might not be shaking as I write this.)

I couldn't tell if the lights in my eyes were from inside my head or outside, since neighbors were waking up to see why the dogs were flipping shit, and as they woke up they turned on all their stupid electricity, and it started clogging up my eyes, the numbing tingle of a seizure aura (no, never again, *please*).

The back of my head sprouted gory branches.

I realized that Brian was *looming* over me, reaching for my pocket.

And it reminded me of you reaching to help me up in my dreams, and Liz trying to help me up at the Halloween dance, and that was the night I found Mom full of tubes and dying in the garage and that just made me so angry and the potential seizure on the fringes of my mind and the numbing of my tongue, the "please not this, not here" made the rage burn so much brighter.

In all that scary brightness, I didn't worry about my actions.

I just *acted.*

Even through the sparks in my eyes, I saw Brian pull her heart from my pocket and away, and it was like he was taking something from me, like he was *unplugging my mother*, leaving me *Mutterseelenallein*.

I swung my foot upward as hard as I could, catching him between the legs with all the force my hermit ass could muster.

Brian yelped and keeled over.

I would cite this whole experience as a perfect example of how I live inside a shit-com (two nut-kicks in two days?), except no one laughed, least of all me.

I sat up with frost melting damp into my jeans and rubbed my skull, peering through unfocused eyes at my palm to check for blood, and I gasped for air and saw lights in all directions around me, while Brian moaned on the road next to me and I just fumed at the seizure *taunting* me, the electricity *teasing* me with death, so angry that my heart beat twice as hard as Bridget's, and, *Moritz*, I saw lights in all directions at once, which might be what it's like to be caught in a comet.

Light in all directions except one, Moritz.

When I aimed crossed eyes down the road, I saw a monstrous black cloud of electric smog headed straight for us, and I didn't think about how or if we could get away, and all my instincts screamed that the lights and smog had to *stop*, or I would seize again, seize like I always have in the face of electricity, sick and not worth taking seriously, the sort of person you take into the world only because you can't leave him home alone.

It happened again, Moritz. Just like at the museum, but this time Arthur wasn't here to save me from myself. Maybe Lois Lane was in peril, or maybe I need to stop expecting other people to take bullets for me.

It doesn't matter whether the lights were real or just my broken head talking.

What matters is I wanted to tear off my hat again, and this time that's exactly what I did, rubber tubing peeling away from skin.

I want to blame the concussion.

I'm not sure I can.

That's what scares me, Moritz. I did it without knowing why, and the consequences were so immense and unforgivable, and Mom was *right* to lock me up for years, and I've been trying not to think about this or write about this, but now that we've finally gotten here, I'd better write about how I freaked out and, in one stupid act, I hurt people. Honestly.

The moment the tubing peeled away, that intense buildup of incredible pressure collected at my temples, and this wasn't a typical seizure, nothing tonic-clonic about it.

Electricity from all those identical houses with their identical rainbow-churning power boxes tacked to their sides drilled into my skull, popped a hole, a hole that somehow my inexplicably bright rage shot through with a familiar *tch*. I've painted laser beams, but I've never felt like one before: like every piece of me was concentrated into one horrible point in my head and then just pulled out of me in a single instant, somehow, impossibly.

Going full-blown electromagnetic was so much easier than it had been at the Halloween dance. Too easy.

When the pressure burst from me, every colorful patch of electric haze within sight evaporated; I watched the world go monochrome. The density jar, poured down a drain.

The streetlights on either side of us shattered, raining glass down from above, and Brian had the sense to pull his hands from his smarting crotch to cover his head, and I noticed he shielded Bridget's heart with his torso, too, and the lights all down the street flickered out and the power boxes sparked and burst into flame in a few places.

And this is important, Moritz: the ball of black smog speeding straight for us sputtered, and suddenly with the cloud dissipating, what rolled toward us?

An enormous vehicle that shone yellow through the gray and skidded like mad on the ice as the driver hit the brakes, as his engine died but momentum didn't. The vehicle slid and twisted in the road while I clutched my beanie in one hand and my swelling skull in the other, and blood burned a trail from my nose all the way down my chin.

The school bus slid and, before long, turned totally perpendicular and tilted off its tires, blocking both sides of the road when it ground closer, shrieking like a demon as the remaining tires lost purchase and the entire vehicle tipped onto its side and kept going—

Its tail end struck a car parked along the road with a sound like screaming—

And then it leaned toward both of us, about to flatten us into two-dimensional people-shaped nothings—

In that second, I saw people squirming beyond the windows, people I'd never meet—

A hand grabbed my hood and yanked me away, yanked Brian away—

—and our knuckles scraped sidewalk.

Bridget stood tall, her arms folded across her empty chest, and watched the bus slow. The screeching of steel shaving pavement didn't seem to bother her.

By the time it stopped screeching, the school bus lay at a precarious angle maybe only three yards away from the safety Bridget had pulled us to, its nose wedged against a leafless tree, its rear resting on someone's crushed Oldsmobile.

Hot steam gushed toward us. My teeth ached from clench-ing, and maybe this is the concussion talking again, but the steam seemed to curl around Bridget, framing her like a hero in a comic spread.

And then I heard crying from inside the bus, shouting and tearslaughter. I saw hands pressing the insides of windows facing sky.

I hadn't seen hands that small since I was that small, looking at my own.

There was nothing electric in the area left to knock me out even if I didn't want to hear the screams, and without the electric hazes, the neighborhood felt really too real and a broken arm was hang-ing out of one of bus windows on the bottom and—oh god I did that I *did* this Mom I did that—and god someone could be *dead* in there—

"Bridget." Brian wasn't clutching his ears now, just hold-ing Bridget's heart close. "*Jesus*. What even just even happened. *Jesus*."

I stumbled toward the overturned bus. People swarmed on all sides of me, people who looked like one another hurrying out of houses that looked like one another and standing in the street and some of them rushing, rushing better than I was because my feet weren't being feet—

"Call an ambulance!"

"Trying! My phone's dead!"

The phone killer strikes again. What would Liz say?

"People inside, and she warned me that people in the real world just *hurt each other* and oh *god* do you think any kids in there had a pacemaker—?"

Bridget grabbed my arm. Her grip felt so cold it almost alleviated the throbbing in the back of my head, but my eyes didn't focus right when I tried to glare at her.

"It's my fault, it's *my* fault, I have to get them out and Auburn-Stache should have left me at home and oh god Liz wouldn't love me now and Moritz—*Moritz* wouldn't, it's my fault—"

"Why's he saying that?" Brian wincing, Brian standing. "What's he mean?"

Bridget pushed me down to sitting and the spike in my head twisted and suddenly I didn't have the energy to stand anyhow. I watched the steaming bus turn orange as pink dawn arrived, watched neighbors climbing the sides, trying to pull kids out through the emergency windows and the back door.

"There's a lot of noise," I think I mumbled. "I wonder what Moritz would see."

Bridget looked at me without any expression at all.

Brian maybe looked at me funny, but then again maybe he was in shock. "Oh, shit. Here. I got this back . . . sorry."

She pushed her heart away.

"Stop babbling, electro-sensitive boy." The heartless girl looked me in the eyes. "If only you could take your heart out and run."

I heard sirens in the distance.

Maybe Bridget didn't want me crashing an ambulance this time. Or maybe she didn't want me seizing.

But either option would mean, Moritz, that Bridget *wanted* things.

She decked me and I was gone.

And that's why I didn't want to bring the story up to the present.

Ha! Because I nearly killed people, Moritz! You got me!

You *got* me.

I wasn't trying to keep secrets. It's just, I've been writing you the best story. I wrote and I pretended I was as hopeful as Arthur made me feel back in Chicago. I wrote as the me who thought I'd have near-life experiences. Ollie in the car with Auburn-Stache, Ollie staring at the Chicago glow cloud, Ollie who thought he might be a good tourist.

Ollie who wanted to believe in the beanie and not the padlocks.

Moritz, every time I cheered you on, every time I told you I was *proud*, I knew what I was saying. Compared to me, you're soaring over Mordor, rescued by the eagles.

Combining us doesn't make us a whole. It just makes you limp on one side.

I thought the thing with Liz and Joe was bad. But back then the awful things that happened to me, Moritz, were kind of out of my hands.

This is different.

I single-handedly crashed *a school bus*.

I sent four kids and the driver to the hospital in one go. Lucky thing it happened so early in the morning, because the bus had only just started picking up kids.

Four kids got glass in their arms just in time for Thanksgiving, Moritz, because I got reckless. Because I thought, *Hey, if* cars *can be in the world, why can't* electromagnetic freaks?

I'm sorry for telling stories. I'm sorry for calling them stories and not lies.

But you know what? Sitting here in this room full of reptiles, writing about everything I've been scared to admit . . . somehow it just feels familiar. Did you see it coming?

How's my handwriting now, Moritz?

Is it steady?

It feels way too steady.

chapter sixteen

THE BLANKETS

Of course I saw it coming.

Oliver Paulot. Once again you have crippled me with sympathy and frustration. Once again I am cringing in Kreiszig. Amazed at my petty complaints in the face of your genuine ones. You should have told me. Then again, this is nothing new. How many months did it take you to tell me about Joe's fall in the woods? Why should I be surprised?

Because I wanted to believe that you trusted me completely, implicitly? That we had come far enough together to stop suffering alone? I did wish to believe that. Perhaps, for once, I have been the optimistic one.

And you did tell me, with all you didn't say, dearest fellow hermit. You did not fool me. Your loss of focus all over again, your storytelling pitfalls: these things, diversions from the pain of losing the only parent you've ever had. Even if your persona became a fiction, I cherished it. I cherished your near-life hopes. Brothers of lies or not.

Wavering penmanship aside. Fictions aside:

I know you, Oliver Paulot.

I know you are *good*. You befriended *me*, of all people.

Can you blame yourself for how you behaved after a head injury and grief and fear garbled your mind?

I only blame you for not sharing this burden.

The cruelties of the world extend beyond what others do to us; they extend into the decisions we make when we are in no fit state to make them. Extend into our regrets and remorse's tendency to make the smallest of our mistakes into monstrous walls we cannot clamber over.

Oliver, you tore off your hat when a bus drove at you. Nothing more.

Again, you are in pain and I am in pain. And we are nowhere near each other.

Only honesty can bring us nearer. Please see that.

Yesterday I descended the narrow steps to Owen and Fieke's basement apartment.

Knocked three times. Imagine my profound apprehension when Fieke opened the door, greeting me with a puff of smoke and her noisome, clinking face.

"Fieke! Ah. Hallo."

I waited for her to tear me apart. To roll her eyes, at the very least. I wish she had jostled me as she used to.

Her face revealed nothing. "Is . . . Owen in?"

Fieke shoved past me into the snow, stomping up the stairs. The ache in my ribs wasn't cardiomyopathic.

I stepped inside. Eased the door shut. Owen sat on the couch, looking even smaller than usual, bundled in several raggedy blankets. Laptop warming lap.

He spared me a small smile. I responded with one in kind.

Something unspoken marred the atmosphere. Made me long to contact him through a computer instead. Long for distance.

Last time we were together here . . . broken branch tips.

I sat beside him. Carefully laid my head on his shoulder. Tried to project peacefulness. Owen tilted his laptop away from me. Pointless. No amount of clicking will ever make screens accessible to me.

"Message me before you visit. I've been preoccupied." He had not programmed his computer to sound like anything but a machine.

"Pornography?" I jested.

His smile returned. For a flutter-beat. "Do you really want to know?"

"Of course I want to know. What are you up to?"

"I set up a text-based role-playing forum. Weeks ago."

"*Role-playing*? Really."

Oliver, you may not be aware because of your inability to approach computers. Text-based role-players constitute a tedious subculture of people who adopt fantastical identities online. Turn themselves into characters in collaboratively written stories. These characters populate intricate, invented universes and interact to develop skills and "relationships."

Devotion to these fictions compels players to create extensive imaginary landscapes, down to infinitesimal details such
as the thread count of clothing.

In an RPG, you can write yourself as Amelia Armsworth,
conductor of a sky-train. Another user on the opposite side
of the planet can be Haruka Umi, an undersea captain who
longs to sink your train into the sea and woo you into mar-
riage. Or some such drivel. You can write yourself out of
your own life and into one entirely more adventurous. Or
one duller. There's no law that says you can't role-play as a
sanitation worker in Canada. If you wish to. If a moderator
approves.

We are not the only ones who have tried to escape into
fiction, Ollie. Fruitless as it is.

"Well, I imagine that's . . . fun."

Owen gave me such a look. "I'm not doing it for fun. Yes,
to most people it looks like a knockoff role-play for Marvel
fans. That might be why we have dozens of participants. But
the premise is very specific. The setting is very specific."

"Fine, fine." I settled in next to him, taking comfort in
proximity. "Tell me what sort of world you've invented."

"I didn't invent it. I borrowed it."

I nuzzled into his shoulder. "Do tell."

"This is an MORPG about the lives of superhuman
kids created in a secret laboratory on the edge of Germany's
Tharandt Forest. Set a decade ago."

"Beg *pardon*?" I sat up.

"I'm trying to connect with the kids you knew." He kept
typing; the robotic voice continued its barrage. "With any

luck, this can help you find some of the other Blunderkids. Not all of us are terrible with computers, Moritz."

"You . . . Anyone can read this. This is a public forum? Do we know that some remnants of the initiative won't catch sight of it?"

Owen's smile hitched. *Tap, clatter, click-clack.* "People have to create user accounts before they can view posts, so it's not exactly public. And I'd bet the initiative already knows where every single one of you ended up. Why would they care." His computer did not enunciate question marks.

When he leaned in close, I recalled Max pushing me without permission. Nausea threw me to my feet.

"So we should flaunt ourselves. We should risk reclaiming their attention?"

Her attention. You and I are both haunted by our mothers, Oliver, in very different ways. Must I really meet all the children my mother made in order to meet you? Must I confront her mistakes so many times? Endlessly?

"How could you do this?"

Owen half closed his laptop. "I did this for you. I thought you'd want to meet the others."

Speaking of things done unasked for, on my behalf.

"No." I edged away, hit the wall. "I only wish to meet *one* of them." Just you, Ollie.

His face. Oh, his face.

Owen slammed his feet against the tiles. Typed furiously. "What are you feeling right now."

I swallowed. Turned my back on him. There was nothing

I could pretend to be distracted by in the barren space he called home.

"What am I feeling?" This was dire. Not the reunion I'd hoped for.

"Yes. And turn around. It bothers me when you turn away from me. You can still see me, so that's unfair. I can't see your face, but you can always see mine."

"Fine. I've nothing to hide." I did as he asked.

Owen remained trapped in blankets. Trapped by the machine that spoke for him.

"If you have nothing to hide, why do you always wear your goggles when we're alone."

"I hardly have the capacity for facial expressions. Why does it matter?"

"I don't know. It's like you're uncomfortable around me. It sucks."

I clicked. "Can't you use a different voice?"

"This is the only voice I have." Owen hit return so hard I thought he'd break the key. "You think I like it."

"Oh, you know what I meant!" I snapped. "If you don't want to be pitied all the time, stop acting pitiful!"

There was a moment, not of silence—because what moment ever is silent to me?

"What am I feeling? I don't know. Upset? Perhaps betrayed? How—what—behind my *back*, Owen? I don't know."

"I know," said Owen's computer.

"Beg pardon?"

"You're feeling guilty. You clicked at the end of that sentence."

A dollop of ice. "Don't tell me how I'm feeling."

Owen lowered his eyes. "Sometimes what you're feeling cramps my stomach up. Sometimes it gives me headaches."

I held my arms straight against my sides. "Then why spend any time with me?"

"Why do you think."

I couldn't fathom, Ollie. "I can't fathom. But how terrible it must be for you."

He snapped the lid of his laptop shut and stood up. The cape of blankets slipped from his shoulders. He walked to the door. Held it open for me.

I held my spine straight.

Wintry air seeped into my ears and nose and mouth but could not cool the center of me. MBV adjusted to the echoes of the city street. Wish I could say I did not look. I am always looking.

Owen drew the latch. The *clack* revealed a wordless sob as he threw his hands over his eyes.

That sob has been ringing in my right ear ever since.

Wind blew snowflakes into my face. Flakes I could not see. Snow is all but silent when it falls. Needles poked me as I walked. I did not think of Owen while my face turned numb. I swear I did not, Oliver.

I thought of you. Of all the children as fluffed as we are. Molly and Arthur and Bridget and who knows else. We are *not* science fiction. The scars that mar us: these exist. Second mouths, absent eyes, bones of chalk: we are not *acting*.

Owen cannot reduce our nightmarish pasts to a *game* on the *magical* Internet.

The sob buzzes in my cranium. I want to believe new scars can hardly matter.

Do look after yourself. I am rubbing my face raw with worry.

Moritz

P.S. Before I hit Send: I've recalled something that disturbs me. I doubt I've ever said "Blunderkinder" in front of Owen. And certainly never "Blunder*kid*." Yet he knew the nickname.

Ollie. You asked for Owen's address. I never sent it. I choose to believe you had no hand in this betrayal. Believe that in this instance you have not deceived me.

chapter seventeen
THE SYRINGE

Moritz,

Guess you're not the only one who needs pep-rants. Thanks. It felt a little angry. Maybe sometimes a good pep-rant has to be angry.

The bus disaster was weeks ago. I really am fine now. Just let me finish putting it down? Before you make excuses for me? Give me a chance to tell the truth before you decide I'm a liar.

You haven't even heard the darkest parts.

"You can't put him in a bloody ambulance!"

"Sir, you can't be here right now, unless you're this boy's legal guardian—"

"I'm not, but—"

He's not? Why isn't he? Auburn-Stache . . . ambulance?

Now, *this* was a painful awakening, and I didn't know where I was or why there was so much electricity swarming me or why my jaw was throbbing like someone had hit it with a sledgehammer.

Through bleary fog, I saw Auburn-Stache forcing his way aboard, clutching at the trunk doors. Bridget stood behind him, arms—wait, *sledgehammers*—at her sides.

Auburn-Stache must have seen my eyes open. "Please! He's waking up! Put away those *damn* scissors!" My hoodie was already snipped in two.

"What the—why is he wearing that?" The woman asking had this strong accent, all twang and drawl. She was wearing these clothes I thought were pajamas, which was weird.

Scrubs, my brain supplied.

"Don't you dare cut it! He's very ill! He's deathly allergic to electricity, ridiculous as it sounds, and epileptic! Look, I have identification in my car! Just let me—!"

Concussed? Or confused? I was *confussed.*

I sneezed, except it wasn't sneezing but spasming, maybe, that didn't relieve the temple pressure. Either me or the ambulance was about to seize. I looked to my left and saw dangling tubes and something worse—one of the kids from the bus: a small girl with her arm splinted whimpered into an oxygen mask.

"I'm sorry," I tried to say, but the words got stuck in the woods of me.

The red-haired woman leaned into my face. "Is this man your doctor?"

"Yeah," I managed, numb-tongued, and next thing I knew, Auburn-Stache was yanking my head forward, pulling Mom's hat back down. The pressure lessened. I just hoped my blood wouldn't stain the wool, her useless, hopeful wool.

"Sir!" The woman and a uniformed paramedic pulled him out of the vehicle.

"Mom? Why are *you* here?"

The woman cussed. "*Brian*? Why am I—I'm doing my job; several RNs volunteered to come out when we heard it was a school bus! But the real question is why you're here! You're *entirely* grounded!"

"But—"

Auburn-Stache: "Whatever happens, don't take Oliver's hat off! Please!"

"Sir. Stop shouting. Please bring your identification to the hospital."

Another voice: "Mom, you should listen to him. I think that kid just blew out the neighborhood. I think he's some kind of freak."

"Brian, I've already told you," replied the nurse, "to go home. Enough rubbernecking!"

"I wasn't rub—"

"*You could be dead.* Home! Right now!"

"Ollie!" Auburn-Stache. "I'm on my way there! I promise!"

Before they slammed the doors, I heard Auburn-Stache cuss.

Okay, he *had* to regret bringing me by this point.

"I'm sorry," I told the whimpering girl again. "I took my hat off."

"Calm down, honey." Brian's mother? She placed an oxygen mask on my throbbing face.

"My hat. I took my hat off. I'm sorry. I took my hat—"

"Your hat's on now."

Moritz. I have vague early memories of hospital machinery from back when Auburn-Stache and Mom shuffled toddler me around in the hopes of finding a c-word.

I forgot the smell and the glare of the lights and the awkward mint color of scrubs, and I'd never been wheeled in on a gurney before. And the noise—like my skull was strapped to a car engine.

They wheeled the little girl in ahead of me, through automatic doors that split open and spewed gold. She kept whimpering.

Moritz, I'm a piece of shit.

"I'm fine," I told strangers. "Don't take me in there, please."

But on top of the concussion, that cold oxygen bag on my face left me woozy, and no one would listen to me—

I opened my eyes in a buzzing room. I couldn't feel my jaw or my head or any pain at all. Anesthetic, Moritz. That nurse stood near my head, one plump hand closed around the plastic hospital bed frame. ". . . out of our depth. Where's his personal doctor?"

"In the waiting room, Mrs. Arana."

"It's Ms." She bristled. "And let him in, then, Wharton! This is a patient, not a project!"

"But it's ludicrous. No one's so electro-sensitive that they're magnetic." At the foot of my bed, this youngish doctor. His white coat reflected the grainy electricity of the fluorescent lights; glasses didn't hide bright blue eyes glinting above his face mask. "There's been no real explanation for the massive power outage—"

"Stranger things have happened, Wharton. I haven't seen Brian look that upset since his father left. He may be going through a rough phase, but I trust my son." My defender, this stout woman in scrubs arguing down a man twice her height.

The tall doctor noticed I was awake-ish, blinking a lot. He swooped in close, armed with one of my earliest enemies: a penlight. I sneezed because the hat wasn't exactly secured—

The penlight went out. The fluorescent bulbs overhead flickered.

"Sorry," I mumbled.

"What the—?" Wharton leaned in and pulled a small square bit of electrical machinery from his pocket—I'm not sure what it was, but even before he pushed it close to my forehead I could see it emitted no color.

"It's already dead," I told him. "My bad."

"How do you know?"

I shrugged.

Wharton stared at the object as if he were observing an alien artifact. When he looked at me the same way, I felt like squirming.

"I'm not a big hit at parties." I tried to grin.

Next thing I knew he was holding my eyelids open with one hand and trying to remove my hat with the other.

"Enough, Wharton!" Ms. Arana all but elbowed him away.

"But this is . . . I mean, this is a scientific miracle! A kid projecting electromagnetic pulses? Shouldn't people know about this?"

"Know *what* about it?"

I tried to get up. The nurse—Ms. Arana—restrained me with a single hand. "Hold your horses, honey. Wharton, I want you to sign his release form without a fuss."

"I don't answer to you." Wharton's eyes on me, *needley*.

"*Son*, I was working at this hospital before you had your braces off. I play bingo with your mother at the K of C. I'm grateful you treated this young man—"

"People call me Ollie."

"Fine. I'm grateful you treated *Ollie* because I thought I could trust you not to make a mountain out of this molehill."

"It's already Mount Kilimanjaro, Ms. Arana. I mean, think about the dangers of having a unfettered projector of EMPs walking around—"

Thank god the bump on my head and the pain meds made this terrifying conversation seem like the funniest thing ever, Moritz. "I'm not a mountain. I'm a real boy!"

You'd think I had antlers, the way he stared.

"Please," Ms. Arana sighed. "A regular comedian. A *kid*, Wharton. A sick kid."

"Hey, now." My grin wasn't fitting right. "I'm not sick. I'm a storyteller."

"Sure, honey."

Wharton clenched his fists. Latex gloves squeaked.

"Wharton."

"All right!" Wharton's face was hard to read behind his gleaming glasses, but his shoulders fell. "Fine. I'll sign the release."

He scrawled on his clipboard, handed it to her. Before he left the room, he paused to give me another needling stare. I shivered. Is that what it felt like to be a Blunderkid in the lab, Mo?

"Why?" I asked, once the door closed.

Ms. Arana pulled my shoes and jeans out of a plastic bag. "Why what, honey? Take off that gown."

I pulled the cotton dress (let's be honest: those are dresses) off my head and plucked a little at the uncomfortable neckline of the bodysuit before I realized she was waiting for an answer. I looked at my rubber-coated hands.

"Why would you cover for me?" She started putting my shoes on for me, but I sat up straight and tied them myself. "For all you know, I crashed that bus on purpose."

"You didn't. You're a good kid." She handed me a long-sleeved, cat-hair-coated shirt. "That's from my locker. It's less embarrassing than what you've got on, but you'll be swimming in it. You could do with some hearty meals."

"How do you know?"

"You've got hollows, honey."

"No, how do you know I'm *good*? Can you really tell just by looking at someone?" What if someone could see the goodness inside people, in colors, how I see electricity? Moritz, where would we register on a spectrum?

"You don't know anything about anyone by looking at them. I heard what you said, over and over again. To Tricia. The girl with the broken arm. You said sorry."

"Is she okay?"

"Everyone's fine, honey. Bruises on most of them. One or two with stitches after the glass shards were pulled out. The bus was mostly empty and it wasn't going fast."

"Oh." I stared at my hands.

Ms. Arana sighed and eased herself onto a bedside stool.

"Do you know what triage is, Ollie?"

"I've read about it. Paramedics at the scene of an accident gauge patients' need for treatment and treat the most injured ones first. But I never understood it, right, because maybe someone is covered in blood and it's not their blood but they *look* really gory and someone else has like an exploding hernia in the lining of their abdominal wall that can't be detected, so someone doing triage might go for the bloodier person, which won't actually help—"

She put a finger on my lips. "Slow down, honey. At that

accident, it was plain as day Tricia was the worst off—a compound fracture. But the next biggest injury? For my money, yours by a mile."

"I had a nosebleed and a bump."

"Your eyes, honey. Some of your injuries were on the inside. 'Something terrible has happened to this boy.' And no one's doing anything about it."

"You can see that," I said. "You can see that she's dead."

It should have been weird, having a complete stranger hug me. But her arms were large and she smelled like apples and she was warm like Mom used to be.

My head pounded red hot under the wool, but I froze in the waiting room entrance.

Tricia's parents were there. I could tell. One of her dads had her freckles. And the doctor speaking to them kept pointing at her forearm.

Behind them: Auburn-Stache stood to meet us; Bridget didn't budge an inch.

Ms. Arana urged me forward with a soft shove. "It's all right, hon."

"Thank god." Auburn-Stache grabbed my shoulders. "Ollie. I've been pulling my hair out."

"So long as it wasn't your mustache hair . . ."

"Are you all right?"

"I'm golden! No biggie." My eyes flicked across the room. Bridget, sitting like a statue, sat next to a man coddling a screaming baby, stared back. "Is Bridget okay? Did she get her heart back from that hooligan?"

"Ollie, we've got more pressing concerns."

"Obviously you didn't see this hooligan." He couldn't even answer *that*?

"We're leaving."

No matter how I looked at it, Bridget in that crowded waiting room, holding a college-ruled notebook in scabbed hands, holding it but not seeing it, seemed like a pressing concern.

I raised my eyebrows. "What, straight from the hospital?"

"A word before you go, about Ollie's health. My name is Jess Arana. "

"I've looked after this boy since his birth, thank you."

"Have you now," she said slowly, letting her twang snap. "So you've been keeping an eye on his state of mind, too? Has he seen anyone? A grief counselor?"

"You have my number. We're leaving."

"Hold on. I don't know your situation, but I just did you one *helluva* favor. On good faith, and on the basis that you seemed to care about this boy. But if you're not going to address whatever sick- or sadness that's got him feeling so reckless—"

Auburn-Stache spun me around and pushed me ahead of him. Moritz, have you ever seen him act rude? It downright scared me, like those crazy, dark rings around his eyes.

"What is it? Another secretly devastating phone call?"

"I know you're tired, but don't raise your voice."

Yeah, I was tired. Injuring a bunch of strangers is just really tiring, Moritz. No biggie. And so is getting walloped in the face. You know what else is tiring? Asking valid questions and getting different variations of "shut up" in response.

"So when I get to wherever we're going, you're just going to, what? Blindfold me? Maybe give me earplugs?"

"I'll . . . no. I'll explain everything before we arrive." The thought seemed to pain him; the thought of being honest *pained* him.

"Then just explain it here!"

His head twitched on his neck. "Fine. Yes, fine. Step outside."

I followed him out of the waiting room on shaking legs, into a hallway bathed in electric nauseating rainbows.

"Well?"

I stopped to let doctors push a gurney past; machines trailed it, glowing cerulean, keeping an old man alive.

Auburn-Stache turned to me with his weird, wild eyes. "It's Arthur."

"What about Arthur?" He started down the linoleum, and I dragged my feet after him; bringing Arthur up was the worst bait. "The man of Metropolis was fine yesterday!"

"Arthur did well in school, despite his condition. Beau used to hang his architectural schematics on her fridge. He designed school buildings that would make school worth going to." He sounded almost feverish. "Arthur didn't *have* to be different, Ollie. Understand? His disability didn't disable him."

Sometimes I think Auburn-Stache taught me how to ramble.

"Long after he left the lab and moved to Chicago with Beau, I told her that his regeneration could hold the key to saving lives, essentially, and she laughed and told me he had to get through his own life first. Because he's a person, passing as just a person, and isn't *that* what made him a success story, Ollie?" Sometimes I think Auburn-Stache taught me how to feel small. "Arthur could *choose* normalcy. Bridget could do the same—she *should choose* to be whole. Not all of you have that option, Ollie. Some of you kids will never pass."

That stung, Moritz. "But maybe I—maybe Bridget doesn't *want* to choose normalcy. And Arthur's *plenty* abnormal and still plenty awesome!"

"But Arthur *has* benefited from being adaptable. Arthur belongs to his city, yes? And he belonged to his school, too. Bridget never tries to change. To her eternal detriment."

We were in the foyer, now. Phones rang in every direction and I was just tired of hearing them, tired of hearing everything, so I stopped again. "You're talking about us—about kids like me, kids who are different—like we're experiments! Like I'm . . . I'm Mount Kilimanjaro! If you're telling me that the best way to live is to *lie*, I'm not biting, Auburn-Stache."

"Every human being hides himself, herself."

Hiding. That's what Auburn-Stache was doing. Twisting away from telling me the truth. Not this time, Moritz.

"Tell me what's wrong with Arthur."

He paused. "Nothing."

I was *done* being his anesthetic.

"If it's nothing, let's stay. Because I'm telling you that I'm not going to ditch Bridget because you're bored of this science project. She saved my life. I don't care if she's *passing* or not. I don't care if she's *nice*. I don't care if you laugh at my 'delusions.' She matters!"

Auburn-Stache's eyes went hard and his mouth went hard and he did something impossible, then. He reached for my arm with one hand and swooped his other one up from his pocket.

Something prodded my upper arm, but then came this tiny clicking noise and a *snap!*

I looked down at his hands and saw a needle.

A fluffing *syringe*. Moritz.

He'd joked about tranquilizers.

"God, I'm a fool," he said, hands trembling. "I forgot about your bodysuit."

"You—you were really going to *drug* me?" It didn't even sound real in my ears.

"Ollie—I—" He looked so small and shriveled then. I backed away. "Just—I don't know how else to—"

"You could tell me what's going on! Tell me what's got you so scared! Tell me why I should pick one kid over another! Tell the *fucking truth*!"

He almost whispered: "I'm afraid you'll run the other way."

"On my mark, get set—"

"Enough! Ollie!" He sounded almost unhinged. He made himself into a vise and grabbed my arm, dragging me toward automatic doors. A nurse darted forward—

"I'm his doctor!"

She hesitated.

And I flipped, Moritz. "Let me go! Let go, or I'll pull off this stupid hat and the stupid tubing underneath, and this science project might just go boom!"

Auburn-Stache stopped and stared at me like he'd never seen me before. Nurses and staff whispered at the table behind us. A security guard ambled closer.

I put my fingers under my hat. "What'll happen? Do you think I'll have a seizure, or the hospital will? I'm pretty upset right now. Maybe I could knock out all the respirators in one go." That old man trailing cerulean. "Hey?"

"I refuse to even acknowledge this behavior."

"I'll pull it off. Right here, right now."

"You wouldn't. She raised you better."

"I would. I've hurt people before. You know that, Auburn-Stache." I felt my face twisting. "She was right. I *hurt* people."

Ask yourself, fellow hermit: How many good people blow up hospitals?

"Not on purpose."

"Not like you, I guess." My hands shook on the wool cap. "You hurt so many kids on purpose."

"Ollie." His voice broke. "*Ollie.*"

"Just go without me, then. Leave. It'll be like old times."

I wanted him to choose me. I wanted to think I meant more than all those other kids he made. All the other Blunderkids in the world.

Auburn-Stache's face emptied.

He let me go and slipped the syringe back into his pocket.

"Very well. I'll leave some of your things on the sidewalk. Arrange for someone to, ah . . . You'll have to manage for a few days on your own. I'll leave you cash. Take care, Ollie."

I'd like to say that his feet looked heavy, but no. He twitch-walked away through the yellow-spitting automatic doors, and I just watched him go.

The day before Thanksgiving. Two months ago.

I haven't heard from him since.

Maybe you'll abandon me too, Moritz.

Because yeah, I did have a hand in the forum.

Please listen.

I've spent the past few weeks of my life lying on a dirty couch, feeling powerless, feeling like I'll never meet anyone ever again.

When Owen wrote me (he must have found me in your letters, maybe when he left you the orchid), he typed in German but used some kind of Internet translator.

The way you write about Owen isn't how he seems to me. He told me something really personal and sad:

Sometimes you call him Ollie. And you don't even realize it.

Thing is, he still wants to help, Moritz.

So I told him about my Blundercause.

If you're curious: your username is already set up. It's Dolphinmo. You can join the forum at blunderkinder.de. I'll never see the place. Owen keeps me updated. He prints pages of the role-play out for me to read.

We haven't actually found any real Blunderkids. So far as we know.

There are seventy-three active players on the forum. There are characters who do everything from shape-shift to time-travel. Owen created a fictional fish-girl named Citrus, and last I heard she's going through "training" sessions that players set up for the lab kids. It's not very original, putting teens through weird science-fictional trials, but it is a reliable way to find an audience.

Please give them a chance.

All the characters undergo gladiator trials to escape the walls of the laboratory. The online lab isn't like where you were raised. It's more like the crazy fantastical place I imagined as a kid, this underground virtual reality arena full of agents in suits and high-flying action. All steamy romance and leaping through fire. The role-players don't write about kids being locked in silent chambers. They write about a land of adventure where people don't die in beds.

Moritz, most of the characters have escaped the lab. They aren't stuck in Tharandt Forest. One of them has flown into the stars because he is invulnerable. Two of them have traveled back to Victorian London to catch Jack the Ripper. One started dairy farming in Hokkaido.

None of them are stuck.

Don't tell me fiction is fruitless, Moritz. Sometimes it's the only escape we get.

chapter eighteen

THE SNOWBALL

Oliver,

I can forgive so many of your fictions. I can forgive reckless hat removal.

Now you've turned my tormented past into storytelling? Without my knowledge or consent? We have needles enough without pricking each other.

I know this was never done with malicious intent. You struggle with social niceties.

And again my fingers drift to this keyboard. I am still writing you.

Even this lie won't end us.

I nearly wish it would. Ollie, if I could stop writing to you, then you could never lie to me again. But daydreaming of a day that I won't write you?

I may as well daydream normalcy. And no. I won't do that.

You can rot. You are rotting right here on the page.

But I can only rot with you.

I've gone to Myriad each morning with the pervasive buzz of Owen's sob ringing in my ears. Louder on a daily basis. Performances during Musical Interpretation fail to diminish it. My presence in every room punctures many a buoyant grin. When Chloe stood up to perform today, tears hit her guitar halfway through "Heroes."

In *Belletristik* class, I pulled my beanbag as far away from my peers as I could. Lodged myself in a corner by the window. Forsook the warmth of the fireplace. Dr. Hoppen took two steps after me. His expression changed. He left me to shiver.

Yes. Do keep away. I will only cramp your stomachs.

I did not open my copy of *"Der Sandmann."* It highlights a popular German legend: The sandman does not just put children to sleep. He steals their eyes and feeds them to his own children on the moon.

For all I care the moon can have the rest of me as well.

I ate my pickle sandwich on a bench in the tulip garden beside the clock tower, wishing I'd brought an extra set of gloves. No one else occupied the gardens. January air iced me over.

The buzz. In the mess hall everyone else might hear it. They might sob.

For a heartbeat, I could not see despite the volume of my breathing.

Then Molly click-clacked in heeled ankle boots along the icy sidewalk. Unusually disheveled. Lace scarf partially unwrapped. Earmuffs dangling around her neck. Her sighs revealed droplets of water in her eyelashes, held in place by cold. She scanned the gardens, failed to see me in her peripheries.

She crouched. Put her hands over her eyes.

This sudden display of private grief. I intended to leave her to it. As I stood, her second mouth hissed. She twisted around.

"Oh, it's Prince Moritz." She wiped her eyes. "Didn't I tell you to make friends?"

"And you." My voice rasped. I had not used it in days. "Where are yours?"

"You seem out of sorts." Without ceremony, she click-clacked closer and joined me. Smiled like she hadn't been crying. "Shouldn't you be excited about my upcoming performance in *The Effect of Gamma Rays on Man-in-the-Moon Marigolds*? God, the title really is a mouthful."

"Fortunately, you've got, ah, mouths to spare."

No smile on either side. "Terrible, Prince."

"Beg pardon. You're catching my gloom. Perhaps you should sit on another bench."

"You act like I wouldn't understand when I'm the only one here who really could." Her lips trembled. "You don't have a monopoly on gloom, you know."

A twinge in my ears; Klaus appeared on the path. Hair more mussed than usual. Not even wearing a coat. Beside me, Molly tensed. Clutched my arm as he passed. Her second mouth made a shushing sound. Nearly spoke.

Molly clapped a hand over the back of her head.

"Molly, may I ask what's the matter?"

She lowered her hand only once Klaus was out of sight. "You shouldn't be so polite. People think you're putting on airs."

I bit my lip to prevent myself from spitting a retort.

"The character I portray in this play kills a rabbit. To spite her own daughters, she kills their pet. It's horrible. Why did I audition for that part, I wonder?"

I can't say.

"At least in older plays violence is purer. In Shakespeare, people stab or poison each other. They don't usually go around killing pets. I don't know what I was thinking."

"I suppose older fiction is more . . . direct."

"Klaus tried to kiss me," Molly said breathlessly. "In the wings after first dress rehearsal. I wondered why he was there. There's only one set in *Gamma Rays*. Why would he kiss me, Moritz?"

"He makes no secret of, ah, *liking* you. It's unseemly, even."

"He likes parts of me," she agreed, "but I'd never let him run his hands through my hair."

I started—had the mouth on the back of her head snickered at her expense?

"You want to believe the best of people; the people I told didn't love me less for it."

"Prince, you're sitting alone on a bench in the snow."

"Yes." That flustered me. "Because I'm a fool. I'm not alone because I'm eyeless." I said the words and knew they were true. Forum betrayal aside, Owen cared for me regardless of my flaws. As I've loved you despite yours, Ollie. (We rot together.)

"What's wrong with us, Moritz? Apart from the obvious."

"I find it difficult to say."

"You haven't got two mouths? *Brrr!*" To think there are actually people who say "*brr!*" "Will you really come to my show?"

I nodded. "Would not miss a live rabbit-throttling."

Now a smile played on her lips. "You're terrible."

"Quite."

The heat of city streets is meant to melt snow. Yet the cold beyond the walls of Myriad numbed my ears to nothingness. After a long walk, I found myself outside Bernholdt-Regen.

Who should be standing beside the gate on my way out but Lenz Monk, jabbing broken icicles into snow. He nodded. Handed me a snowball.

"For cars," he provided.

"Thank you?"

"Yeah." He lobbed the ball at a vehicle so tiny it might have slid off the road, but Lenz missed. The driver honked. Not particularly hilarious to me.

Lenz nudged me with his elbow. If my sour mood was contagious in some supernatural way, his chortle was contagious in a natural one. "Go on, then."

"Fluff it." I clicked my tongue at an oncoming car. The snowball hit the sign affixed to the roof.

Lenz clapped me on the back. Handed me another. "Again!"

Once the second snowball landed on the next taxi, striking it in exactly the same spot, Lenz whooped and asked for a third performance. I complied. This left him in such paroxysms of joy that I had to snicker at the way he collapsed into a snowbank.

To think he used to scare me.

Perhaps telling you about disrupting traffic is insensitive. We laughed.

By the echoes of footsteps in the courtyard behind me, I saw the quiet of him.

Owen. Watching from the gate. His mouth a thin, disapproving line. If the waves of my regret reached him, he remained unmoved. He knew I could see him even as I faced the road. He knew. And he went the other way.

I dropped my snowball.

Lenz wiped snow off his pants. "You should compete in our next *Bundesjugendspiele!*" (Intramural sports tournament.)

"I don't go here anymore."

"Oh. Why not?"

I made a conscious effort to turn. Watched Owen retreat. Again, my ears seemed muffled. He faded.

"I don't know."

I descended the library stairs. The windows seemed taller. The carpet ragged. No one sat at the desk. I clicked my tongue and caught sight of a bearded man between the shelves.

"Can I help you?"

"I wish to speak with Frau Pruwitt."

"She's taken some time off."

Frau Pruwitt hasn't been visiting. As far as I know. I haven't really been visiting our home, either. The apartment felt empty, somehow, after braving the tundra.

My ear ached in sharp pulses. Hearing faded, returned. Blind, not blind.

I did not visit your forum. I don't intend to. That is one story I've heard enough of.

Blind, not blind.

You are too good to ever blow up a hospital. But, Ollie, I've decimated that laboratory so many times in my imagination. Destroying a fictional version cannot satisfy me. That would change nothing. Least of all me. It's too late. Born without eyes. Born without.

Here I am. Blind again.

chapter nineteen
THE POISON IVY

Here's another story, Mo.

Back when I was maybe eight years old and my whole world was just the cabin and the woods, I remember one day going blueberry picking with Mom. It was overcast even though it was summer, but Mom had on a smile, and soccer shin guards for kneeling on the damp moss. She assigned me the job of bucket holder and warned me not to wander off, but after hearing about fifteen berries plop against plastic, I got really bored and—you know where this is going.

I didn't get far before she caught me with bramble scratches all up and down my forearms from trying to catch a garter snake. Mom was so blustering angry she left the berries and dragged me straight home by the forearm. I felt like crap for ruining a day outside without even a stupid snake to show for it, and I swear the place where she grabbed me burned. It burned and then it itched, and when she called me down to dinner, I stayed upstairs.

By the next morning, my whole arm was on fire. I was scratching it raw.

"Ollie?" Mom knew to look under my bed. She lay flat on the boards and caught me peering out from behind my Legos tote. "Come out. I want to show you something."

She sat on the bed and waited for me to join her, and when I did, her eyes went right to the bedsheet I'd wrapped around my arm. She lifted her hand: she was wearing an oven mitt. "I'll show you mine if you show me yours."

On the count of three, she pulled off her oven mitt. I unraveled the sheet.

We stared at our matching angry bubbles.

"Poison ivy gets worse if you scratch it. But ignoring it is bad, too. When something's wrong, you have to treat it, Ollie." She hugged me with her clean arm. "When something's wrong, no matter how wrong, share it with me. Okay?"

Moritz, there are probably better ways for me to say I'm worried about you. But this is all I have, all I can think of right now.

I'm scared that with this shit happening, you've wrapped this sheet around the chaos so you don't have to look at it. Owen, Fieke, me, everything. If you want me not to talk about the forum, okay. But that doesn't change that it exists.

Doesn't change that I'm scared you're doing the very last thing we want to—letting things fester. That's the earache, maybe. That's the rot. Maybe *that's* what seeps out of you.

Please, Moritz. You need help. And I'm not enough. I'm never enough.

I sat on my bag with my fishbowl in my lap, needled to pieces as anesthesia faded from my system, replaced with a throbbing jaw and aching bones. As I squinted at the snowy parking lot, it began to sink in.

The Impala was gone.

My head steamed hot around the egg I'd given it, but I didn't want to go anywhere I could hurt people. What I wanted was to be back at Junkyard Joe's with Liz. Hell, I wanted to be locked inside on a rainy day again.

What was I supposed to do?

He *left* me. He actually, really, entirely, and totally—

"You should go inside. It's cold."

I nearly jumped out of my bodysuit. Bridget stood beside me.

"Hey, look who's talking." I cleared my throat. "Do you only own track clothes?"

"This is fine. My heart is only eleven miles away. Brian's house."

"About that. Do you go around, you know, tossing your heart to people? Hot potato?"

"No." Bridget cracked her fingers.

"Are you going to go get it?"

She shook her head. "I have something for you."

I groaned. "*Tell me* you aren't about to hand me your spleen."

"Not my spleen." Bridget handed me the college-ruled notebook she'd been holding in the waiting room. It still had a price tag on the front. I opened the first page and blinked in surprise.

The first line read:

This is the story of a girl called Bridget.

Flabber my gast. "Why . . . ?"

"You asked for my life story." Bridget picked at the peeling toe of her shoe.

"I don't deserve it, though." I pushed the book back and blew on my hands; rubber doesn't feel great when it's covered in snow. "I can't even own my own story anymore. I might be the villain. Which sucks. It really sucks when you leave home and you get this feeling that you're just distracting yourself from reality, pretending to be helping people, pretending you *aren't* worse than cars, but then again, maybe if you mess up enough, you'll be sent back home, and even though it's crazy, maybe she'll still be there and what a stupid *nightmare* you've been living in the real world, a stupid nightmare when maybe someone's waiting for you—"

"She's not waiting for you. Your mother's gone."

I forgot where I was, didn't know I was standing.

"You're right!" I laughed too hard. "Everyone's *gone*!"

"Dr. Auburn-Stache, too." Bridget nodded. Her hair, wrapped in knots around her head, almost like a crown.

"It's my fault."

"It's not always about you. Be quiet."

And for some reason I was. I guess I was just really tired.

"I'm going to run to my foster home. You should go inside."

"You worried I'll get frostbite?"

"Only stating facts."

"You saved my life today." I stared at my fingers. "I thought you couldn't care less?"

She shrugged. "I couldn't."

Before I could think of what to say, Bridget took a knee, counted down from three under her breath, and launched herself into the parking lot. Vanished before I knew it in the whiteout descending on Fayton, Ohio.

I peered at the notebook. Wondered *why* she wrote it. Why she'd tell me the truth when Auburn-Stache wouldn't. Why she saved a disaster like me. Things weren't exactly adding up about Bridget, but my head, my everything, hurt way too much to care.

People came and went. I told an orderly I was waiting for my ride. And because my hands needed to be busy, I peeled open the notebook and started reading.

By the time Ms. Arana scuffed along the sidewalk and stood beside me, my fingers were almost frozen to the pages. Snot covered my chin. Tears burned my cheeks.

"Oh, honey. On your feet." Keys jangled in her hand.

"I'm fine."

"You're not fine. You've got a hankering for hot chocolate, by the looks of it. Come with me. There's always room for strays at our house." Venom filled her voice: "There's *no excuse* for leaving people behind."

"Except dying, I guess." *Mutterseelenallein.*

"*I'm* not dead, and neither are you." She nudged me with her boot.

I sat in her messy minivan with my eyes half glazed over until we arrived at a house that must have been only blocks away from Bridget's; it looked the same. I was so out of it I didn't even snark when Brian opened a front door covered in claw marks. He glared from deep inside his hoodie, a heart-shaped bulge in his front pocket.

I know I've got no right to ask, with the secrets I kept, but if you know where he went—can't you tell me, Moritz? I noticed you were so quick to get melodramatic about you and me rotting for eternity like the worst cheese because *I* lied to you. But what about *your* lies?

I'm not angry. I just want Auburn-Stache to come back and tell me what terrified him so much. I want him to knock on the door, and then I'll run down this hallway full of fish tanks and he'll see I'm wearing the stupid hat and I don't hate him and maybe we can go home (even though she's not there). Maybe Arthur could just . . . come to my house instead, and bring his guffaw with him? Childish, I know. I'm a toddler, remember?

After months of living with Ginger-Rage Brian and Ms. Arana, I've had enough of the electric world to last awhile. And reading Bridget's story didn't make me feel like we have a place in the world. If anything, I doubt it more than ever. I don't blame her for being heartless. Maybe you have to be, fellow hermit. Maybe that's what the world does to you.

Moritz, I'm going to have a normal person copy Bridget's story with a machine that copies things.

Let someone else tell stories for once. Honestly, I'm not up for it anymore.

Arthur hasn't answered a single one of my stupid letters.

chapter twenty

THE GIANTESS

Ollie. I'm not thinking altogether clearly. Something a trifle upsetting happened last night. I may not be myself.

How my head hurts. My ear.

I cannot spare the energy to be cryptic. Auburn-Stache sent me an e-mail in December. Perhaps two weeks after he abandoned you. I heard briefly about the bus. About your grief.

I will be honest: I believe his abandonment is justified. Cruel as that sounds.

Don't ask more of me. It is not my poison ivy to share. Please.

It can't be my story to tell.

I spent yesterday evening all but locked in the auditorium. The stagecraft hive mind murmured under its collective breath, but without threat of mutiny. Klaus did not ask to be backstage building a massive skeleton of a fallen giantess at the very last minute, either. A scheduling conflict between Year Two and Year Three students' midsemester musical performances meant *Into the Woods* would be performed two weeks ahead of schedule.

We had only days left to hammer together trees, fairy-tale cottages, and a life-size wheeled cow. Of all idiotic things, I was tasked with braiding enormous rope into the ponytail of an equally enormous head of hair for a fallen giantess.

The giantess is an antagonist in the second act of the Sondheim musical. When she is finally slain, she will fall across the stage. Back to the audience. Most productions choose to show her feet; some ambitious Myriad student decided to instead create her head and shoulders for the sole purpose of dramatizing her demise. The audience would never see her face, so no one gave her one. Eyeless like me. Let us rot.

Klaus rigged a pulley system that would allow her to fall without damaging the stage. Would allow us to hoist her upright again once curtain fell. A repurposed ladder supported her shoulders from within, to spare us from building her an enormous spine. Someone installed a platform at its top. A fort in the half dome of her skull. Lazy fools hid from Klaus there.

Even as we labored backstage, Year Three performers hurried through their dress rehearsal in partial costume. Scampering about with wigs askew, forgotten lines inscribed on palms. Makeup Effects students chased them with foundation and brushes, toner and spirit gum. Orchestra members scurried toward the pit, violins and flutes in hand.

(Chloe lifted her eye patch and saluted me with her clarinet but otherwise kept her distance.) Max strutted around in furry ears and feet, Red Riding Hood's tailcoated wolf. He might have winked at me while he waited in the wings. Hard to tell under the false eyebrows pasted to his forehead.

"I'm not sure whether I can wait for *Gamma Rays* much longer." Molly ran her hands over curtains cut to form the giantess's collar. "I wish *my* midterm had been pushed forward. There's only so many times you can screech 'Get the wooden spoon!' into a mirror before you start to question your sanity."

Her second mouth whispered the last word. Again she clapped a hand over her head.

"Molly?"

"Not me. *It*." Molly's eyes were wide. Her old confidence seemed a ghost. "It never used to talk. But sometimes when I'm nervous, it speaks up. Whether I want it to or not. I have to wonder what it's saying. I can't quite hear it. Why is this happening? It was silent for years."

"A matter of anxiety, Molly. I'm sure it will pass."

"Farber, how's that—" Klaus came around the side of the giantess's head and stopped.

"Hallo, Klaus." The quietest voice I've heard her use.

I lowered my head. Made a show of braiding rope.

"Here to tell us we should have finished this set a week ago?" grumbled Klaus.

I thought I heard her back mouth whisper into her curls before her smile returned. "Oh no. I've long since lowered my expectations."

"You try working with Farber sometime. He doesn't know a hammer from his hands." He stalked away.

To think the night would only get worse.

We stagecrafters finished the bulk of our work by 7:00 PM.

Klaus vanished the moment we finished tacking on the giantess's dress. Molly followed shortly thereafter. That broken smile.

Those of us who remained sat in a circle in the far reaches of backstage. Picked at sandwiches provided by cast members.

Max Fassner. My constant shadow sat directly across from me. Leaned back against the unpainted model cow. Even I cannot avoid partial eye contact when people stare into my goggles.

He took a swig of whatever filled his thermos. Probably not milk, Ollie. Leaned forward as if about to pounce.

The Year Three director blew her whistle to signal the end of intermission.

"My *Oma*, bless her old soul, sent along some Läckerli." Max popped open a biscuit tin. "She's trying to seduce all the young stallions she thinks prance about Myriad. I don't think she understands we're all geldings here." Max looked straight into my goggles. "Isn't that right, Moritz?"

"Horse metaphors. How novel."

"Go on."

He pushed a biscuit toward me. I closed my fist on impulse. Max grabbed my wrist in his rough hands. Peeled my fingers open one by one and placed it on my palm. I had the distinct impression that other students deliberately wandered away.

Just Max. Myself. The overturned giantess.

"Go on, I said." Max squatted next to me. Too close.

I placed the biscuit on my tongue. Honey, kirsch, and hazelnut. I chewed, swallowed. Did my best to smile. I stood. He pulled me down. I would have dodged his grip, but that disorienting ache of Owen's sadness made hazy my right ear again.

"You know, Moritz." Too close. "You're nervous. You can't hide it from me."

"I can't hide anything from anyone."

"That's fabulous. You're as clear as cool water, but like a river: I can't see through the current to what's actually going on underneath—I can only tell that the water is moving. You're a heartfelt mystery, Moritz, and you're always winding away from me. Why?"

Where on earth was he pulling these godforsaken lines from, Oliver? And why did they almost sound poetic to my tingling ears? Even as I knew they were terrible, they captivated me. My pacemaker strained to steady my heart. Max reached for me.

I flinched—

He only pushed another biscuit into my hand. Set his thermos to my lips and whatever was in it burned, but not with heat. The lights dimmed.

Out on the stage they had begun singing. Usually I hear everything, but lately sounds have been muffled by the sob.

"They're carrying on without you."

"The wolf isn't in the second act. So honest, Moritz, but you always hide your face. I want to see you. All of you."

I pulled away. My, did I feel dizzy. He dropped his hand and smirked.

"Have more, if you want. I'll be back in a bit. Don't go anywhere."

I should have gone anywhere.

My breathing grew loud in my ears. My mouth tingled. I ran my tongue along the film on my teeth. Thought about what colors might look like, if colors were textures. Would red be damp and warm like blood? Would blue be silk?

I counted threads in the curtains. Clicked.

Something more than honey may have been in those damned cookies, something more than whiskey in that flask. I did not care. I wished only that someone would hold me. Tell me that it was acceptable that I am incapable of containing my feelings, that I cannot squirrel them away like Bridget. Acceptable that I left Owen ringing in my ears and you alone in Ohio, and tangled the two of you together in my head.

I came partially to my senses. Uncertain where I was. Smelling the lemon oil used to polish the stage. Wood shavings and drying paint. I clicked my tongue, saw a half-dome frame of papier-mâché arching above. Later I would realize I lay inside the head of the giantess. As it was, all I realized was someone held me, running hands along my shoulders.

"I can't see a thing in here," Max whispered. "But I know you're awake. *Click, click*. That habit is so odd."

"Where is everyone?" Hard to taste the words.

"They've gone home. You fell asleep. Only you and me here, Moritz."

I half tried to get to my feet. I half felt only like lying down. Like laughing. Ears ringing louder than ever before. Clashing cranial cymbals. "I should . . . go . . . too. Father will worry."

He pushed a finger into my lips. "That's not what you really want."

Max ran his hands up my neck. Up over my chin and onto my face. Before I could regain wits enough to stop him, he threaded his fingertips beneath the straps of my goggles and lifted them off my nose.

I cannot wince without eyes. Reflexively, I turned away, but Max held my head in place. Ran clumsy fingers across the surface of my eyeless face. His fingers paused. How dark was it, really?

"That's some costume." Sour alcohol breath wafted to my nostrils. "I don't always give the makeup students credit."

Ollie, I did not correct him. There was a millisecond when perhaps I might have told him the truth. I did not wish to see another face curdle with disgust. Thank god he was intoxicated. Thank god I was. Or something near it.

"I can't even feel the seams." Fingers at my ears. "Is it netting? Can you see through it?"

Before his brow could furrow too far, I leaned forward to press my lips against his. His hands slid away from my vacant eye sockets and back into my long fringe. He dropped my goggles down the staircase (*clack-thump*) and pulled me closer. My heart certainly beat fast. He hadn't realized I was a monster.

"Are you enjoying this?" His lips against my ear.

I wasn't. Or I wasn't certain either way. But his tongue in my mouth was a firm reminder that this had nothing to do with Owen Abend. My chest ached. Pacemaker strained. I didn't want to speak, because I feared I might laugh, might cry.

But I am a monster. And of course it was at that very moment that someone turned on the lights. I didn't feel the electricity, did not hear them come to life, addled as I was.

But oh, did I know.

I knew because Max saw that the face cradled in his handsome hands was no face at all. Me and my absences, absences I believed I'd come to terms with, Ollie, but perhaps not. Perhaps never.

The way he recoiled. The gag at the back of his throat. Handsome hands let me go, the handsome rest of him was suddenly meters away, back pressed against the wall opposite.

"The fuck?" Or some approximation, Ollie. Disgust does not translate easily. *"The fuck?"*

The worst thought—the disgust he felt may have been mine. Because if anything radiated from me . . . it was that. "Now who's, ah, winding away?"

I waited for him to hurt me, to spit or shove. But Max only wished to be gone. He wished an ocean between us, an allergy to me. He did not bother with words. The sound of his heartbeat trying to leave him, the sound of him going down the ladder with all the speed he could.

All this growing you claim I have done, Ollie, all this journeying. But I came to a beautiful place and brought ugliness with me.

I curled in on myself, held my knees. Held my knees but could not convince them to unfurl, could not stand up.

I came back to myself atop the staircase. Moments or minutes later. Head pounding. Initially convinced I was having a nightmare. My right ear ached. Knives. I could not see. Water in my ears? I clicked my tongue for almost a minute straight. Finally came a slight popping sound, a beat of pain.

I could hear.

I sat up, cold and aching. Fumbled for my goggles. Nowhere to be found. I heard shuffling from between the curtains.

"Farber?" Klaus's voice. "What the hell? Get out of the prop. It's after midnight."

Beats of pain, head and heart. "Yes. Um, apologies. Why are you still here?"

"Didn't want Molly to think I was following her. And then I had some work to do." I clicked. Felt him lean against the giantess. "Why are *you* here? Max sure left in a hurry."

I swallowed.

Klaus stood up straight. "Farber, are you all right?"

"Yes. Yes. Could you pass me my goggles, please? They've fallen down."

He scrabbled around, then pushed them into reach.

"Thank you." I pulled them on. Blasted shaky hands.

"Don't thank me. Just come down, already."

I made my way to the bottom of the ladder on legs that felt untrustworthy.

Klaus uncrossed his arms. "You look terrible."

"Oh. I am."

Klaus shook his head. "He tried something, right?"

Oh, he did not want to try. What was more repulsive? That I had wanted him to, or that he could not? I don't know, Oliver.

"That scumbag. He's got a reputation. Last year some kid dropped out and everyone knew Max had something to do with it. Spiked his soup. Did he hurt—?"

"No, no." I tried to chuckle like you might. "I'm fine."

"I know you're not fine, because you *never* laugh. What is that? Damn it! If you and Molly would just be frank, then maybe—"

The exit. To the exit.

"Don't just leave when I'm talking to you!"

I flinched beneath his grasp.

"*Don't touch me!*" The snap in my voice, the blade of my pain. Klaus jerked as if I'd stabbed him. He did not try to stop me again.

That buzz in my ears is getting louder, Oliver. I'm not imagining it. Sometimes when I look at my hands, I cannot count my fingers. Everything is recalled to me in sluggish slow motion. As if I really am underwater again. Tomorrow I have class. I have to see Max again. Do not ask me what I will say. How I will "handle" him. I do not know.

If I met Owen now, he'd drown in the waves that pour out of me.

I can't keep trying to be human. At some point I am a lost cause.

chapter twenty-one
THE HEART

Moritz. I have never so badly wanted to hurt another person like I want to hurt this Max asshole. Ever. I don't even care if doing it would confirm my villain status.

Because I'm selfish, okay, and I don't always spend enough time asking about you on rainy days. But you're one of the things I get most selfish about. Even if that's messed up. There's no excuse for the way you were treated. It makes me want to do something inexcusable. I am training daily to beat up Max Fassner, even if that's totally futile. I don't have a punching bag, but I've been punching couch cushions.

How he treated you: that was all him. You don't *make* people do anything. Remember?

The first thing you'll notice is Bridget's handwriting is better than either of ours. All even block letters. It's better, but it's colder, too, like ice blocks. Maybe if she wrote with her heart plugged in, her letters would curl into one another.

But right now this is the best way to get to know her.

It's kind of how you got to know me.

This is the story of a girl called Bridget.

This is the story of a girl who tears her heart out.

Bridget is seven when she leaves the laboratory. She is awoken by the kind doctor with the goatee. Bridget throws her arms around his neck.

"That's it, kiddo. We're leaving. Too little, too late, perhaps."

Bridget is the last child left in the ward. The girl with two mouths and the boy with the strange throat and the boy with no eyes are already gone.

"Where are we going?" Bridget's heart is heavier than all the rest of her.

"We've made some arrangements." The doctor leads her forward. "You have family in America."

"America," says Bridget. "Is it scary?"

"Sometimes." The doctor takes her through the radiation screen. "But don't worry."

"I won't." Bridget reaches past her hospital gown and into her chest. She pulls her heart out from between her parted ribs.

The doctor sighs. He places the beating heart in the pocket of his coat.

Bridget feels nothing.

"I'll do the worrying for both of us, then."

There are no scientists in the halls now. There are a few men dismantling machines. They put the pieces in boxes. There is a woman at the front desk. She collects papers into folios. A tub of plastic toys sits on the counter. A tub of hazardous-waste bags sits beside it.

The doctor and Bridget go through automatic doors. Bridget has never left the underground laboratory. She has never seen cars until now in the dark parking lot.

She doesn't feel surprised to see them. Her heart is not in her.

The doctor drives Bridget outside. This is her first night sky. She does not feel curious about stars. Her heart is not in her.

"Bridget." The doctor pats his coat pocket. "Don't you want this back?"

"Will I feel scared?" Things Bridget feels scared of are sharp needles, bright lights, cold hands.

"Perhaps."

"I don't want it."

"All right, Bridget."

Bridget falls asleep.

They get to the airport. The doctor drops the beating red thing into her lap.

"I don't want it."

"Bridget. They won't let me carry it through customs."

The taxi driver sighs.

"Leave it here."

"We can't just leave it behind. It's your heart. You only get one, and you have to look after it. Come on. If you are scared, you can hold my hand."

Bridget puts her heart in.

She begins to cry.

She cries all the way through security and onto the plane. She cries and people stare at her. This makes her cry more. Everything is terrifying. Being outside. Being around people who aren't sick children. Climbing into a metal tube that goes into the sky.

"Take it out. You have to take it out. Please take it out take it out take it out!" Bridget tries to reach into her chest. The doctor grabs her arm and says, "I'm sorry."

Bridget screams louder. This is terrifying. She screams so loudly that people ask if the doctor is hurting her.

"Please quiet down your daughter," says a woman. "We can't have twelve hours of this."

"He's not my father!" Bridget screams.

"Who is he, then?"

"I'm her doctor." The people on the plane are whispering.

None of them are kind to the doctor. That is scary, too. Because the doctor is the only kind person Bridget has ever known.

She stops crying.

"He's my doctor."

They keep whispering.

Virginia is beautiful. Virginia has green hills and purple hills and orange skies in the evening. The roads in Virginia are winding. Every time the doctor speeds down one Bridget thinks her stomach is dropping out of her. She smiles.

"Now, your aunt and uncle are wonderful people," the doctor says. "But you mustn't take your heart out while you live there."

"Even when I'm scared?"

"I'm afraid so."

"If a monster comes after me?"

"No such thing."

This is a lie. Bridget can remember many of them. They worked in the laboratory. She is getting nervous. Bridget reaches into her chest—

"Bridget, that can't be your solution. You have to feel things. You have to feel scared sometimes."

"Do you?"

The doctor nods. "Oh yes."

"How do you take the pain out?"

They pull into a short driveway in front of a barn-red house.

"Sometimes you share it with the people around you, and then it isn't so dreadful. You'll see."

People are standing on the porch. They shift from foot to foot. Bridget thinks that maybe her family is scared, too. None of them have pockets in their chests.

The doctor holds out his pinkie.

"Promise me, Bridget, that you will feel things."

Bridget latches her finger with his.

"Mmkay." Her heart beats.

On the porch, a smiling woman with dark hair and eyes takes her hand.

Bridget keeps her promise. Her new family tells her that she has a last name. It matches theirs. They feed her warm food. They take her out to look at the family orchards. There are no ripe apples in midsummer. They give her clothes to wear.

They say they hadn't known she existed.

"If we'd known about you," says Uncle Porter, "we'd've come got you years back."

There is Uncle Porter and Aunt Maribel and also cousin Samantha. Samantha is three years older than Bridget. She teaches Bridget how to braid her hair and put on eye shadow. She teaches Bridget table manners. She sings to her in the evenings. She says Bridget will love school.

She says, "I always wanted a baby sister."

Bridget feels many things. She feels the spicy warmth of pie on her tongue. She feels the dust of fireworks on the Fourth of July. She feels cool fingers of lake water after dark. She feels the sting of sunburn on her cheeks. She feels soothed when Aunt Maribel rubs aloe onto her back. She feels empty when a robin hits the window of the country home. She feels swollen pride when Uncle Porter gives the robin a burial. She feels crumbly when the robin caws in her dreams.

Samantha and Bridget go swimming at the creek to celebrate the last day of summer. Samantha gives Bridget one of her old bathing suits. Bridget shakes her head.

"What are you afraid of, scaredy-cat?" Samantha fixes her hair in the hallway mirror. "You're skinny as a rake!"

Bridget doesn't say: "There's a hole in my chest."

"Some girls have modesty." Aunt Maribel rinses the snap peas from the garden.

"What for? There ain't any boys down at the crick."

Bridget wears the bathing suit with a T-shirt over it. She sunburns easily. Bridget does not say: "I never saw the sun until this summer."

Bridget watches from the long grass with her toes in the water. Samantha sunbathes and waits for boys who will not come. Bridget is feeling hot and sleepy. She stands up. She stretches her arms toward the sky.

Samantha grabs the hem of Bridget's T-shirt. She pulls it over her head. Bridget feels things like white shock and red anger.

"Don't!"

"Why are you strapping your chest? You don't have boobs. I don't even got them yet."

Bridget crosses her arms over her bandages. Her T-shirt is soggy with creek water.

Samantha purses her lips. "Why bother? There's nothing to see."

Samantha does not help Bridget pack her schoolbag. Bridget feels yellow worry. She looks at the notebooks on their bedroom floor. Samantha paints her nails on her bed.

Uncle Porter and Aunt Maribel wish them good night. Bridget doesn't sleep. She feels twitches in her stomach. She feels flutters in her heart. It is dark in the bedroom and the night is cloudy. Samantha starts snoring

Bridget breaks her promise.

She pulls out her heart. Invisible worry and fear cling to it and leave her.

She tucks it under her pillow. She falls asleep.

Samantha shakes her awake.

"Get up!"

"Okay," says Bridget. She holds her heart under her pillow.

"Are you still mad at me?"

"No." Her heart is not in her.

"Say it like you mean it."

"I mean it."

"Last time I apologize to you." Samantha lets go of Bridget's shoulder. She leaves to take a shower.

Bridget puts her heart back in. It itches. It weighs more than before.

Samantha is angry at breakfast. She is angry at the bus stop. She is angry when the bus drives along the winding roads. She says, "I'm only sitting by you so Dad won't kill me."

Samantha leaves Bridget to find her own friends at school. She does not tell Bridget where to go. Bridget is scared. A bell rings. The other children go inside. Bridget stands on the sidewalk by the flagpole. She tries to breathe. Her fingers go to her chest.

A man with a whistle around his neck pushes her inside. "Go to the office."

A woman tells her to smile pretty on her first day. She leads Bridget down a green-tiled hallway to a classroom with owls on the door.

Bridget is scared of the stuffed owls stacked on Miss Pauley's cupboards. She is scared of their eyes. She is scared of the eyes in her fourth-grade class. Some kids smile. Some do not. Bridget doesn't know what this means. She keeps her hand on her chest. She stands at the front of the class. Finally, Miss Pauley shows her to her desk.

"It's all right, dear. We have another Bridget here, too. You'll be Bridget T. and she'll be Bridget B. Bridget B., do you mind showing our new Bridget around the school today?"

Bridget B. is pretty. She has a scrunchie in her hair. "Okay. I'd love to!"

Bridget feels happy. She looks at Bridget B. Bridget B. does not smile at Bridget. Bridget B. looks at other girls and rolls her eyes.

Bridget has never gone to real school before. Other kids recite times tables Bridget has never learned. When other kids were learning times tables, Bridget was locked in an incubator in one room while her heart was tested down the hall. Bridget knows this isn't her fault. In her heart, she still feels stupid.

Before lunch, Bridget B. takes her hand. She leads Bridget to the end of the hall.

"I hate that you stole my name," says Bridget B. "It's so lame."

"I didn't steal it."

"I was here first. So yeah, you did. Doesn't matter. People will forget your name pretty quick. I promise."

Bridget finds the cafeteria by herself. Samantha has a different lunch hour. Bridget sits down with her sack lunch. Two kids ask her to go somewhere else. Bridget finds an empty table. "It's okay." A boy with braces and glasses sits next to her. "I was new last year, too." He holds out his hand. "I'm Josh."

Bridget feels happy. Then she looks at him.

His glasses shine like the goggles in the laboratory. His braces are surgical utensils.

Bridget stands. Bridget runs.

"No hall pass, no dice!" says the man with the whistle.

Bridget is good at running. She used to run on treadmills for hours and days and weeks, even, when her heart wasn't in her.

Bridget runs to the nearest girls' bathroom. She locks herself in a stall. She reaches into her shirt and pulls her heart out. Her head clears. She is not relieved. She is not anything.

Bridget wonders what will happen if she flushes her heart down the toilet. Maybe it will kill her. Maybe it will soak her heart in sewage. Maybe she will smell it even from eighty-seven miles away.

She tucks the heart into her lunch bag. The man with the whistle waits in the hallway.

"I know you're new. But you can't just run around school like that."

Bridget couldn't care less.

They get off the bus. Samantha asks Bridget how her first day was.

"Okay."

"Did something happen?" Samantha stops in the driveway.

"Things happened."

"Fine. Don't talk to me. It's not like you're my real sister anyhow."

Bridget puts her heart back in before dinner. She cries in the bathroom for seven minutes before she can bear the weight of it. She washes her hands. She realizes she should have asked Samantha about her day. Bridget feels so sad about this. She knows she can't eat dinner without crying more. She hides her heart behind a stack of towels.

Samantha smiles for Aunt Maribel and Uncle Porter over macaroni.

"How was school?"

Bridget shrugs.

Aunt Maribel takes her hand. "It'll get better. It was only your first day."

Bridget puts her heart back in after dinner. She waits for Samantha to come upstairs. Samantha stays on the phone in the living room. She wears her headphones to bed.

The next day, Bridget still doesn't know her times tables. Josh doesn't sit by her at lunch. She waves at him in the lunch line. He looks at his feet. He sits by himself on the other side of the cafeteria. Bridget stands in the center of the lunchroom with her chocolate milk.

Bridget B. waves at Bridget. "Come here."

Bridget B. is surrounded by girls whose hands always cover their mouths.

"Do you want to sit here?" Bridget B. pats the seat beside her.

Bridget nods.

"Speak up. Do you want to sit here?"

"Yes, please." Bridget is feeling bright gratitude.

When she tries to sit down, Bridget B. pushes the chair back in.

"Well, what I want is for you to go back to wherever you came from. I guess we don't always get what we want, right?"

Bridget backs away. Her fingers creep to her neckline. Her heart is thumping. She has the sense to ask the man with the whistle for a hall pass this time. Before Bridget can cry, she's watching her heart sink to the bottom of a toilet bowl.

Bridget keeps her heart in her backpack and desk, in a Lisa Frank crayon box with a purple kitten on the front.

In Miss Pauley's class, the owls don't scare Bridget. Bridget B.'s whispers and the boys who tug on Bridget's braids don't scare Bridget. Not knowing multiplication doesn't scare Bridget.

Nothing scares Bridget.

One evening the doctor waits in the dining room with a mug of tea. Aunt Maribel gives him a whole apple pie.

"Bridget, you've broken your promise."

She pulls the boxed heart out of her schoolbag.

He peels off his glasses. "Don't you like it here, Bridget?"

Bridget shrugs.

"Bridget, do you know what I'm afraid of?"

"All the things you've done."

He nods. "But I'm more afraid you'll be afraid of the things you've done one day. You don't care now, but I do. I care so much. And so does your new family. You can't keep doing this. You're not ending your fear. You're giving it to other people. People who love you."

"Why should I care?"

"I should think you've seen enough sadness in the world. Don't create more."

Shining utensils and drills and lights. Even when her heart is not in her, she feels those still. The doctor taps the Lisa Frank crayon box.

"Please, Bridget. Give it a day."

"Okay," Bridget says, because the doctor has always been kind.

Bridget plugs her heart into place in the early hours of the morning. She is done crying by the time she has to get up.

Samantha knows the difference. Samantha talks to Bridget.

"There are rumors going around about you." They walk to the end of the driveway. "You spend the lunch in the bathroom. Are you bulimic now?"

Bridget shakes her head. Her lip trembles. She is not used to feeling things.

"Then what's going on? Why does half the school hate you?"

"Bridget B."

Samantha jogs ahead to look Bridget in the eye. "What, this fourth grader did something to you? You should have said so!"

"Why?"

"I'll mess her up, is why."

Bridget stops walking. Her heart feels too large. "Why?"

"Nobody screws with my family."

"But we aren't real sisters."

Samantha adjusts the straps of her backpack and marches ahead. "Like hell we aren't."

Bridget feels mostly merry-happy-joy-glee-teary-never-take-her-heart-out-again.

Samantha confronts Bridget B. by the fence during recess. Bridget B. is not alone. She is with her boyfriend, Jordan. Jordan is repeating fifth grade.

Samantha drags Bridget with her. "Leave my sister alone."

"I never touched your sister. Who would want to? Your whole family's full of dirty—"

Samantha grabs Bridget B. by her scrunchied ponytail.

Bridget B. screams and Jordan pushes Samantha in the chest. He laughs when Samantha hits the grass. "The skank's been stuffing her bra!"

"Have not!" Samantha screams. Her chest is misshapen.

Bridget tries to help her cousin. Her heart aches. Samantha shoves her back and stands up on her own. She crosses her arms.

"Look at her lip shakin'," says Jordan. "What, you gonna cry now?"

Samantha shakes her head. She can't raise her fists without revealing dislodged padding.

Bridget B.'s eyes are full of tears, too. But she's feeling anger. "Pull her arms back, Jordan. Quick. Teacher's coming."

There are boys watching, boys who know he smokes cigarettes. Jordan reaches for Samantha's arms. He wrenches them apart. The crowd shrinks.

Bridget feels scared. She feels Samantha's humiliation. She feels useless and overwhelmed, and her hand is already moving. When Bridget B. reaches forward to lift up Samantha's shirt, Bridget sobs aloud. She plunges her hand into her chest.

The feelings vanish. Her screeching sob halts. She stands on the playground with a hole in her chest and a heart in her fist.

Jordan faints. Bridget B. screams. She tries to pull him off the ground. Someone is gagging. Children run. Whistles blow.

Bridget feels nothing but the heartbeat in her hands. She feels nothing until she turns around and sees Josh behind her. Josh stands still while kids scurry past him. His eyes are wide behind his glasses, and his braces are shining like surgical utensils.

In the laboratory they strapped her arms down. Not here.

She hits Josh so hard his braces cut her knuckles as he falls.

Samantha is wide-eyed.

"I'm not your sister," says Bridget.

Bridget turns and runs, heart in hand.

The doctor finds her down by the creek at sunset. Bridget holds her heart over the gentle current. It is cold. Even without her heart, Bridget feels that. When she drops her heart, maybe it will freeze overnight. She feels exhaustion in her legs. She feels the places she scratched herself when she ran the miles to get here across pavement and through brambles and downhill.

The doctor kneels on the rocks beside her. "Samantha told me to look here."

"I can't keep my promise."

"Promises are like that. But we can try again."

"Not here."

"Leaving doesn't mean the Touschicks don't care about you."

The doctor cups his hands under her dangling heart. "You can drop it. I'll look after it for now. Is that all right?"

Bridget lets go. "I don't care."

He places her heart in his pocket. "Come along."

Bridget watches the doctor climb the hill. "Do I have to put it in when we say good-bye?"

"Not if you don't want to."

Samantha doesn't help her pack her bag. She joins Aunt Maribel and Uncle Porter on the porch when Bridget leaves.

Bridget doesn't look back. Her heart is not in her.

After Virginia, Bridget can't keep her heart in. She runs.

After Virginia comes Kentucky. Bridget's second cousin is there. When the cousin finds the heart under Bridget's bed, Bridget runs to the edge of town to drop it into a quarry. The doctor is there.

In Omaha, Bridget lives with a great-uncle who dies coughing after three weeks. Bridget runs into deep fields of corn. She buries her heart under the stalks. Hours later, the doctor helps her dig it up. He rinses soil from it.

The Kansas family does not pass a CPA inspection. Bridget sets her heart down in lanes of traffic. The second car that passes is the doctor's Impala.

Maine is running into ocean. And Michigan is running

through the decimated city of motors. In a Florida trailer park, Bridget runs until the swamp hits her knees. In a duplex in New Mexico, she walks into the desert and almost presses her heart into cactus needles. After that, she doesn't care. And after that, she doesn't care.

She runs.

Bridget comes to Fayton, Ohio.

The house in Fayton is the same as other houses. Bridget arrives in time for her second freshman year to begin. The Tidmores are kind like many others were kind. The details are repetitive. Bridget talks when necessary. She keeps her heart outside herself. They don't understand why she doesn't smile. Bridget doesn't understand why people ever do.

Bridget doesn't run to school on the first day because she doesn't know the way yet.

She sees Brian at the bus stop. He says, "You the Tidmores' new foster kid?"

Bridget nods.

"You're like their third one. Guess you guys are collectibles." He laughs but does not smile. "Is that mean of me?"

"It's accurate."

"They're pretty nice, actually. Not like my mom."

Bridget shrugs.

"She works at a hospital; everyone thinks that means we should be rich or I should be a smart kid. It's total bullshit. But she just lords it over me like she wants me to help people for a living, too. I don't want to help people. I don't like people. Are you going to tell me I'm awful?"

"I don't like people, either," says Bridget.

It is late September and time for the cross-country tryouts for the junior varsity teams at Christchurch High. Bridget's heart is tucked inside a bundle of grocery bags at home.

The air is warm. People are warm. Bridget is nothing.

Brian doesn't run correctly. He doesn't breathe correctly. He's not asthmatic. He's only slow. After tryouts, he asks Bridget if he has a chance of making the boys' team. "No."

Brian says, "I knew you'd be honest. Think I'm a loser now?"

Bridget doesn't think anything either way. She shrugs.

Brian tries to keep up with her on the run home. Bridget does not wait for him.

After seven days of trying, he still follows. Bridget does not ask him what he's doing.

She doesn't care.

Brian doesn't have the laboratory excuse. He's just bad at school. He's also bad at friends and bad at jokes. Bridget notices.

Brian sits with Bridget in the cafeteria.

"Most people ask me not to sit with them. I usually eat outside. People don't like me. I'm really boring. I don't like people and I don't like stuff, either. I don't like movies or music or any of that crap that people pretend to like so they don't have to think about how much they don't like stuff. Do you want to know what I like?"

"I don't care."

"I know you don't. That's why I like you."

Bridget blinks. She wonders if her heart is beating back home in her sock drawer. Usually, she only wonders about her heart when Auburn-Stache comes over to save it.

"Do you want to go out with me?"

Bridget looks at him. "No. I don't want to."

"I thought you'd say that. But will you go out with me anyway?"

Bridget considers. "What does that involve?"

"Making out. If I were a romantic asshole, I'd ask you to give me your heart."

"Okay." Bridget blinks. "I never wanted it anyhow."

Bridget asks Brian when she can give him her heart.

He says, "Give me . . . ? Oh. Um, wow. How about after trick-or-treating for canned goods? Mom always makes me fund-raise, but she has to work a double shift on Halloween because it's a full moon this year. All the crazies are crazier in the hospital when that happens. She won't be home all night. Just wear a scary costume."

Bridget dresses in a white lab coat and carries silver utensils. She arrives on Brian's doorstep. Brian is dressed in a suit. He is faking a comb-over.

"So guess who I am?" Brian never grins. "I'm my father. I'll be sure to send his new wife pictures. Maybe she'll leave him for me." He holds out his elbow. "Don't you think I'm awful?"

"You're trying to be."

"Let's get this over with."

The heart skips a beat in her pocket. This is unrelated to Brian. It must be happy to be leaving her.

Hours later, they deliver their cans of creamed corn to the cafeteria at the school, where student council waits. The room is full of boxes of macaroni, tins of Spam, and cans of beans.

"Why have you only got seven cans?" asks the class president, Ariel Ramirez.

"When they asked what I was collecting for, I told them it didn't matter because I would just take the goods and move in with some new family. They didn't laugh."

Bridget shrugs.

Ariel sighs. "You two are basically a thing, then."

Bridget's heart thumps in her lab coat pocket.

They sit together on his couch. The walls are filled with heating lamps and small animals. Brian reaches for her. She holds up her finger. Brian hollers when she unbuttons her shirt and hands her heart to him. He shoves it off his lap.

Bridget lifts her heart up off the floor. So he can see how it is beating with pain she doesn't feel. "It's yours."

"Please just go. Go. Please."

Bridget doesn't put it in; she drops it into her coat and walks out the door and onto Brian's driveway, indistinguishable from the Tidmores' driveway. And from there she runs. She sprints back to the latest house that is not a home and keeps going.

And that's all there is, Moritz. She didn't give it a good ending. Maybe because she wrote it overnight. Or maybe because she doesn't care. She didn't give her story any closure. Maybe closure is something you only get in fiction. It doesn't seem fair. If every Blunderkid has an unbelievable story, why can't we have the upsides of fiction, too?

~ O

P.S. Reminder, because I'm still fuming about Maxhole: You know how you and me are like magnets with the same charge, and we *literally* repel each other with our weird illnesses? That's the only kind of repulsive you'll ever be.

chapter twenty-two
THE MARIGOLDS

You were right about things festering, Oliver. Poison ivy.

Not only in my public life at Myriad, or the private life I squandered with Owen and Fieke. The things I keep from you fester, too. And perhaps the person you should be training to fight really is me. I am worse than repulsive, Ollie.

And can I just blame others? Where is the line where I end and they begin?

I see everything. But not that line.

When the night of Molly's show finally arrived, I waited beside her makeup kit and listened to her pin back her glorious curls. Her second mouth was muzzled with a wool mask. I hadn't smelled lozenges of late. I did not ask. I was not being sensitive to her feelings. I was simply overcome by my own.

That buzzing sob grew louder all the time. Often I could not see through my right ear. I began to wonder if my emolocations were so strong that they were echoing back to me. Perhaps I was blinding myself. Sometimes I could not see the faces of people who spoke to me. Could not hear them.

"I've never known you not to listen, Prince."

"Beg pardon."

"Oh, don't. I'm just nervous." She wrung her hands. "I've done plays before. And I'm the villain. People always love a good villain. I'm just making a fuss."

"You'll be wonderful."

"Did you happen to see—I mean, is Klaus here?" Before she pulled her hair into a bun, I could hear the mouth muttering. Incomprehensible.

"Scowling in the front row."

I'd nodded at him on the way in. He'd folded his arms. Put his foot on the chair beside him. The moment I passed I saw him remove his foot and pat the chair. Beckoning me. Watching my reaction. I wanted to maintain my pace. But my ears aren't so keen now. I had to stop walking to focus on him. Klaus took note of my pause. His frown deepened.

"I saw Max here earlier, Moritz," Molly said.

"Oh?"

"I know that look, Prince. He's a scoundrel. I'm assuming something unpleasant happened, the way you've been acting. Are you all right?"

Max Fassner avoided me when I returned to school. Gone were his winks and his fond, unnerving jabs. I must be ill, Ollie. I almost *missed* the attention. "I don't know what you mean."

"If you say so." Her hands shook when she applied her lipstick. "I just saw him fawning over another boy in the foyer."

Blind again. Molly said my name once more. I had to grab the curtain to regain my bearings. For a moment, I saw and heard nothingness. The old void. Am I standing, Ollie?

"Moritz? Can you hear me?"

My sight returned. I wished her luck. She tapped the back of her head with a finger, said, "Shush, shush." Blinking repeatedly. Ragged breaths. Muffled muttering. I left her alone.

I chose a seat near the rear of the theater. Here, my moods were less likely to disturb others. I clicked my tongue over the gentle rumble of chatter. Listened for familiar faces. Head throbbing. Ears temporarily focused.

Relief. Max wasn't in the audience.

Footsteps onstage. Actors finding their marks behind the curtain. Molly sat down at a kitchen table. A set we'd built to look like a shabby apartment. The curtain lifted; the rest of the audience applauded.

Molly became a stranger. A cold middle-aged woman dissociated from reality. She held a phone conversation with an imaginary teacher.

The Effects of Gamma Rays on Man-in-the-Moon Marigolds tells the story of Tillie, a young girl irradiating marigolds for a science fair. Her family is impoverished. Her mother, Beatrice, is mentally ill and spiteful. Her sister, Ruth, is prone to seizures, Ollie. Beatrice attempts to sabotage Tillie's success in the fair. Tillie remains hopeful.

I have no idea how the play ends.

I found Molly's performance unwatchable. The way she treated her "children" so disaffected. I am sure that is wonderful acting. Fiction that chilled me. Molly based her performance on my mother. My mother who tormented children. My mother, the protean creator of all that's wrong with us. A reason I fail at being human.

My mother may reenter my life soon, Ollie. I haven't told you this yet. Another festering thing.

I left the close air of the auditorium to stand on the quiet stairs outside. Waited for my vision to adjust to the echoes in the beautiful foyer. There was a delay in the time it took me to process my surroundings. That ringing ache in my ears. That's why I didn't immediately see what was occurring in plain sight.

Max. His arms wrapped around a young man, as Molly had forewarned. By the time my vision cleared, I heard both of them staring at me. Max with smug disdain. His new-found paramour with defiant anger. The slightest ounce of remorse.

He was very quiet, Oliver.

"Nice to see . . . Moritz." Max stepped forward to clap me on the back. His voice went in and out of coherence. "This is . . . very quiet. I didn't get . . . name."

"His name's Owen," I supplied.

Of course. I'd invited him. Of course. Some would call this karmic. I call it the final drop that overflowed the barrel.

A year ago I would have crippled Max as I crippled Lenz. With a physical jab in the gut or throat. A few ribs broken on impulse. I may have crippled him in the giantess.

All I wanted was to disable Max so entirely he would gargle blood for the rest of his life.

My ears failed me. I could scarce keep my balance. Anechoic chamber.

Owen's face: What was it I could not see?

Sometimes character growth hurts more than harms us. Sometimes I regret that you are my conscience. I can't be barbaric without anticipating your reprimand, Ollie. I can't shove people anymore.

I only wished misery upon them. Wished they could feel an ounce of the *pain* I felt. I attempted to project "festering" dolphin waves right into their cores. Let them hear what I heard.

I made the loudest possible clicking sound in the void.

Two sets of eyes rolled back. Two mouths gasped. Limbs smacked against the marble floor. Noses trickling blood. I did not lay a finger on them, but when my vision returned, they were both collapsed, splayed on the stairs.

Owen looked like a child. Another child tormented by me and mine.

I gasped. Stepped blearily over them and made for the exit while the world faded in and out of view. The winter air only worsened the pain in my head. I slipped on the ice of the pavement. Perhaps someone called out to me, but while my ears still cooperated, I longed for shelter and the willow stood before me. I passed under its whipping branches and grabbed the trunk when my ears failed again. Tore off my goggles. Threw them down. As if that would make me unsee what I had seen. All the things I have always seen and been with my ears wide open.

I fell.

Time did not matter. The where was nowhere.

Someone lifted me from the snow. Hoisted me upright. Draped my arm over broad shoulders. Oh, cold air, damp snow, numb nose. I could not hear. A chasm of nothingness. Of black. At first I struggled against my captor, remembering Max's hands.

"Calm . . . Farber . . . just me!"

Even through the pulsating pain in my head and heart I could recognize that tone.

Klaus.

I stopped fighting. Put my hand to my face. Where were my goggles?

"Stop that, Farber!" I heard, because he shouted. Even so, the sound was muffled. I was underwater again. I did not realize until he pulled my hand away that I'd raked my skin raw. Scratched my skin to bleeding.

I tried to tell him that I could not see. Could not hear.

"Farber! You don't . . . need . . . shout! . . . don't . . . need . . . hear . . . you hold . . . have . . . fever!" Finally, I let him pull me forward.

"Calm down," Klaus repeated. "It's okay."

Were any words ever less true. I trembled for you, Oliver.

A bacterial ear infection. Likely contracted in the cold. I never cover my ears with hats. The doctor at the emergency room didn't ask about my eyelessness. The infection had crippled me enough that I wasn't feigning blindness anymore. I was halfway blind.

In bursts of clarity and vision, I recall that Klaus refused to leave the room. He reassured the doctor that my collapse could have nothing to do with the inexplicable collapse of two other boys on campus. Two boys currently under observation.

I did not see Father, though I smelled the engine grease. When he arrived, he set my cane at the foot of my bed. Fell asleep in the chair beside me. I cannot remember the last time we had a genuine conversation. Now if he spoke to me I could only halfway listen.

The partial deafness in my right ear should leave me. It may take time for the antibiotics to defeat the infection. The pain may stick around a spell longer. As it is, my vision is patchy at best. Sometimes I thrash my arms. Sometimes I am underwater.

The doctor says I should have come to see her long ago. Before it got so dire.

"Weren't you in pain?"

If you and I went to hospitals every time we were in pain, we would never leave them. We are better at sending others to them.

Auburn-Stache has not visited. He has been busy. Is it so horrifying to think he might care about other Blunderkinder like he cares for you? We all need it. Everyone needs. If what you want is someone who cares most for you, you have me.

Like Molly has Klaus. If only she would see it. He sits at my bedside knowing I am eyeless. Surely he would stay by her knowing she is double-mouthed. Shut up! Have each other.

You have me. Everything really is so tenuous. Any of us can be reduced to nothingness without notice, can collapse or implode without notice. So I will tell you what it is that Auburn-Stache will not. I don't want to be the boy who lies to you. I'm done with that.

Tell me stories, Oliver. I can't bear the thought of future silences.

Oliver, Auburn-Stache has reason to believe Blunder-kinder are dying.

This is why I will never stop telling you that I love you.

chapter twenty-three

THE BRISTLE-BRUSH

Moritz, it's a good thing I'm busy or I'd be flipping out. Why haven't I heard more from you? Please tell me you're okay.

What do you mean, *Blunderkinder are dying*? How can I meet them if they're dying? He told me Arthur was fine, so? What's going on?

Was it your goal to keep me up at night?

Not that I could sleep much here anyhow. *You* try sleeping with rodents on your face.

Ms. Arana forgot to mention she lives in a zoo. The last thing I expected when she showed me to the living room was walking past seven terrariums to get there. She shoved a boa constrictor and two cats off the couch before I could sit down.

"Do you charge admission?" She cleared heaps of clutter from the coffee table. I had to wonder if it was electricity or pet dander causing my runny eyes now. "I bet you could."

"Something to consider, honey! I'm sick of graveyard shifts."

"Yeah, and if you work days instead, you'll *never* have to see me." Brian's attempt at a fierce expression was kind of negated by the several kittens rubbing up against his leg, mewling at him. Maybe they could smell the heart in his pocket.

His fierce expression was kind of negated by what I'd just read about him, too.

"Enough. Go to bed, Brian."

"It's not even noon yet."

"Then go to school!"

"No."

"Don't be such an asshole to your mom." Maybe I shouted, because he didn't argue. Ms. Arana seemed surprised by his silence.

"Ollie, you've gotta be exhausted. I can make up that sofa bed for you. Or get you something to eat. You . . ."

I stopped listening, I guess; I kept nodding off despite the stench of fur. I leaned my head back and something purred under my ears. A big Persian cat. Dorian Gray was also a Persian. So this guy smelled a little like home.

Moritz, I realized something. If I keep living in the past, the distance between you and me only gets wider. The future when we meet becomes impossible again.

So from here on in I'm gifting you with my present. (Ha, ha.)

It's going to be so easy that you'll want to smack me. Because here I go, summing up days and days in one sentence. Ready or not, Moritz:

I didn't do a whole lot except lie in a puddle for that first month. (BOOM!)

I spent hours writing you, making every hopeful sentence fool-proof. Played fetch a million times with maybe five dogs I was too freaked to take for a walk. I wrote Arthur, too (he still sucks at replying, or maybe he just didn't buy my happy-go-lucky act, either, because I wanted to only tell him good things and it got really hard for me to make up details about states I've never been to or stories about people I've never met or happiness I've never felt). I counted fish in tanks. And I tried really hard not to look out windows, especially once people put stomach-churning Christmas lights up every-where because going that way meant madness and buses and kids I might kill by accident, no biggie.

I got to know my housemates. Half of Kingdom Animalia, give or take, plus Ms. Arana and her totally errant son.

Here was the weekday routine: Ms. Arana worked mostly night shifts and slept most of the day, only peeking her head out of her room around 7:00 PM to get herself some macaroni casserole and shoo iguanas off the counter. She always dragged me off my hermit couch and watched me eat, making sure I didn't gag it up like her greyhound, Kushla, who liked licking my feet. Whenever I asked her about Auburn-Stache, she said "Soon, honey," and then pulled on her scrubs and some bizarre plastic clogs and headed out the door until after dawn.

Brian usually got home right before she left, in time to be angry with her about whatever-the-hell: she didn't buy new kibble or she didn't clean up Kushla's latest surprise on the bathroom rug and they were out of 409. He didn't speak to me but fed and watered and walked the animals and then slouched right up the stairs to his bedroom.

He kept Bridget's heart in my fishbowl so that nothing would get at it. That was my idea, but Brian insisted on keeping the fish-bowl in his room. I figured that was probably a good way to stop the pets from pawing at it. Every day I asked him to give it back to her. He sulked.

On weekends, Brian left the house in the morning and didn't come back till dark. I figured he had a lot of Stop signs to stand under. Who knows. To quote Bridget: I didn't care. He didn't care, either, and we never talked to each other.

Ms. Arana did what she called her "weekly catch-up," which meant she went around and cleaned up the worst of the animal messes and picked stray teenage socks off the floor, but she was always too exhausted to keep up with it. Most Saturdays she was asleep again by noon.

And me, I just got stir-crazy and stir-crazier, waiting for Auburn-Stache to come back. And the longer I sat sinking into that hairy couch, listening to the burbling of tanks and the yawning of canines and the scratching of cat claws, the deeper I sank into my own head.

That was around when Ms. Arana handed me the printout of your letter about your acceptance to Myriad, where you said some-thing like, "if you must leave your doorstep, so must I."

Maybe your feelings knocked people out. But they also knocked me back onto my feet.

Moritz, I got off the couch.

During the first weeks of standing and trying to be a living per-son again, I collected all the pet dander around the house into this massive pile. I wanted to stuff pillows with it. Trouble was, I didn't really have fabric to sew the pillowcases, so I dug out my tattered sweatshirt, cut up in the ambulance, and set to work on repurposing that. I wanted to do a whole themed pillow set of Patronuses from Harry Potter, so I had to use my shirt and jeans as well.

"You're nuts," said Brian when he got home and caught me sitting around in nothing but the bodysuit, stuffing fluff into the fourth pillowcase. "And you stink."

These were the first words he'd said to me since our lukewarm Christmas dinner, when he asked me to pass him the crescent rolls and Ms. Arana got toasted drunk on box wine and told me about her wedding day.

"Yeahhh, I do. Truth is your mom set up a kiddie pool and a hose in the shed, but I avoid it most days."

"Go use it. God."

"Aye, there's the rub. Your neighbor's generator is real close, right across the fence, and so I can't actually take off my hat to wash my head, because that sucks for either me, drowning in the tub, or them, unable to watch sport-ball games. So basically there's this like patch of my head that I can't wash, and it's driving me crazy just thinking about it. No bath could ever be satisfying, you know? So why bother?"

"I didn't ask for your life story. I just told you that you stink."

"Yeah, well, I don't know how you can smell *anything* in here, Mr. Ornery."

"Don't be freakin' rude. You're a guest."

"Why? You're rude, too. It's not nihilism, it's Brianism. *Pretending* to hate things."

He skulked away (skulking is like sulking but more action-packed).

When I woke up the next morning, there was this weird sort of apparatus lying on the table in front of me—a little bristle brush that someone had attached to a long, thin wire. Maybe part of a cat toy? Attached was a note: *Take a damn bath.*

Don't tell Brian, but that brush did the trick.

Days after Brian started talking to me, I spent hours tailing him around the house while he fed and cleaned up after things in kennels and cages. I figured learning the routine would give me something else to do, but when I tried to scoop kibble he knocked the cup out of my hand. "These are my pets. I'll take care of them."

Speaking of taking care of things—you and Auburn-Stache may have ditched my life purpose, and yeah, so did I, but habits are still vampires.

"Does Bridget know you're a softie? Hey, are we going to give her heart back soon? Also, does your mom know about this situation? She started using a blender and I nearly blabbed about heart smoothies."

"All Mom cares about is never mentioning Dad ditched us. And I'm dealing with Bridget." Brian locked himself in his bedroom. I guess he was playing video games. I could see sparking particles of electricity popping through the floor over my head.

I finished stitching my pillows. Mom was better at embroidery and detail work, but my sewn-on otter didn't look too shabby.

What the hell was I going to do next?

At the end of January, I reorganized the house from top to bottom because I woke up with my eyes full of dust and gunk and a lizard of some description licking my ear like nobody's business for the umpteenth time and wondered where the heck his tank or aquarium was. Or maybe because I'd just told you about poison ivy. (You wanna be the pot or the kettle, Moritz?)

I went gung ho on the shelves.

I inhaled lots of weird crap that day and ended up getting distracted by the collection of glass bottles underneath the kitchen sink, because they were all different sizes, right, and I arranged them into a makeshift glockenspiel by flipping them upside down and wedging them into a broken chair frame. Instead of a mallet, I only had a spoon and I couldn't tune the bottles, which was frustrating enough to set me back to cleaning up the house again.

It was tricky finding places to put things where the dogs couldn't get them. I jammed lizards and snakes back into cages they seemed to belong in. I felt a little guilty when I latched their lids down.

"Because this is safer. Believe me."

I did my best to sweep all the dog food free of the carpet and out the front door. I used dish soap and water on just about everything and that seemed okay.

When Ms. Arana woke up from her deep slumber, she just pulled out her earplugs and stared at the way I'd arranged the terrariums all along one wall of the living room. Next to the window, so that they could air out: a whole wall of animals.

"Pet shop." She blinked at her carpet as if she'd forgotten what color it was.

"Charge admission!"

"You swept the carpet. Why didn't you vacuum?"

"A vacuum? As in the absence of matter?"

The laugh started at her shoulders and rattled her up and down.

While she whipped up instant mashed potatoes and told me about workplace drama, she looked lost in her own kitchen. Probably because she didn't have to dislodge any hissing creatures from her dishes!

All Brian said when he came home was, "You didn't go in my room, did you?"

"No." I'd broken into his room right from the day I started getting up again and noticed that the fishbowl was empty. He's been carrying her heart around, probably in his backpack. Or in his brown paper lunch bags.

Ms. Arana gave me a hug before she left for work.

When she left, though, the house felt so empty. *Mutterseelenallein.*

I undid all the latches.

Brian came downstairs and hollered when he saw all the lizards stepping over each other.

"God! Get a life!"

"When can we go see Bridget?"

That sent him back up the stairs again.

After two more weeks of this, even Ms. Arana was done.

Which brings us to yesterday, Moritz.

I was whittling the legs of her hideous Swedish box-furniture coffee table into elaborate spiral-motif columns while she slouched on the sofa, trying to yank her eyes open by way of coffee, halfway dressed in scrubs patterned with Dr. Seuss characters. Fox in

Socks peered out of her front pocket while she rested her feet on the table.

"Ollie, as much as I like having a live-in musician/pet sitter/maid/interior decorator around, it's time you get out more."

"But I need to be here if Auburn-Stache comes back."

"That's the thing, honey: your doctor phoned me yesterday to—"

I nearly cut myself with the Swiss Army knife. "He *what*?"

"Let me finish. He called to say he's going to be gone awhile longer. In the meantime, we're happy to have you. Gracious knows I like the enthusiasm. But you can't just sit in the house all—"

"What's keeping him?"

"He didn't say. Careful, honey. There's only so much vinery a table like that can take."

I hacked away at it. "So I'll just stay here?"

"Always room for one more stray."

It was true. But it was also true that she wasn't so great at looking after the strays after a while. She was busy, and sometimes dogs busted out of their kennels or month-old cat spew was discovered under pillows or—

"Ollie, stop—!"

The particle-board leg snapped in two, and the table keeled over, almost pulling Ms. Arana off the couch. She stood up, hands on her hips, coffee down her front. "That's it! No more hangin' around the house."

"You want me to leave?"

"That's not what I said."

"But if I can't hang around the house, what do I do?"

"Isn't it obvious? Go to school."

My jaw dropped. No, it plummeted. It *cascaded*.

I protested, for obvious reasons.

"You know about the bus! I'll blow up the school!"

"Honey, you've had your mourning period." Ms. Arana riffled through the shoe closet. "Time to toss the black dress and get yourself back into gear!"

"But I've never been to school before!"

"You're plenty clever. Didn't you paint the constellations on the living room ceiling?"

"Yeah, but only the ones for the last week of January. And only for this hemisphere! I don't even know the charts for June to December! I'll be a laughingstock!"

She cackled. "Only here, Ollie."

"What about my beanie? People will think I'm a gangster!"

"I've got that figured out."

"But—"

She pulled something gray from under the shoes; Auburn-Stache handing me Mom's hat all over again.

"How long have I known you, Ollie?"

"Not even three months! So—"

"Stop." I followed her as she waddled to the kitchen, smacking dust or dirt from the gray object. "My daddy used to say you could tell the measure of a man by how he tied his shoes."

"My dad couldn't *even* tie his shoes. I'm *doomed*."

"And my daddy was an idiot. You know how you really can tell the measure of a man?"

"With a yardstick?"

"Ha! No. Look: folks who are good spend ninety percent of their time worrying that they might not be. Now, sit."

"I had Velcro shoes until I was seven." I bit my lip and sat at the table; something squeaked beneath me and I had to pluck a kitten from the chair. "Did you know Velcro wasn't invented until 1948, and it was like space-age technology or something, it was so new! And it was invented by a Swiss guy named—"

"Oliver, you are going to school. Try this on for size." She somehow wrangled the gray backpack onto my shoulders and then took a step back to look at me. "It's one of Brian's old ones. Don't mind the Totoro face. He used to be really into that Japanime stuff."

"That must have been back when he actually *liked* things."

Ms. Arana lost all her enthusiasm at once. She turned away and made some crack about seeing a man in the bathroom. Then I was just standing awkwardly in the kitchen with that backpack on.

I almost took it off, but it was easy to pretend. Pretend I was packing textbooks into it. Maybe sneaking in my phone. Like any other kid. I kept the backpack on and went to the living room. I pulled Bridget's notebook out of my pile and tucked it into the bag. Even the sound of the zipper made me smile a little.

I mean, going to school. Me, Moritz.

Maybe I wouldn't hurt anyone.

The door in the hallway opened and slammed shut. Brian entered the living room, took one look at me in his old backpack and swore. "No way."

He carried his usual lumpy paper bag. "What you got there?"

"Don't worry about it. You really think that's a good idea? I mean, *really*?"

I didn't want to answer that. "When are we going to go see Bridget?"

"If you want to see her, go ahead. I've never stopped you."

"I'm not the one who can persuade her to take it back." I adjusted the straps of the bag. *Stupid.* "And I don't know how to get there."

"Electro-kid can't read a damn map, I guess."

"Not really, no," I said, grinning.

"You're just afraid to go outside."

"Not really, no." Not grinning.

"You're afraid to go outside, but you want to go to school?"

"Just because you fail all your classes doesn't mean I will."

"No, you won't bomb your classes. Just the generators, right?"

I glared at him. "If you're carrying it around all the time, why doesn't Bridget have it yet? It's Valentine's Day. Perfect day to pass a heart out."

"I hope you don't expect me to get on a bus with you."

"You could run to school," I said, face burning, "except it'd take you ten years, slowpoke."

"*Slowpoke?* You're not even good at *insulting* people. Go crawl back under whatever rock you lived under."

"I'm not the one who looks like a salamander."

"Are you four? That's so lame."

"So why's it getting your goat? Also, your dumb face matches your dumb hair."

"Fuck you very much," said Brian, spinning out of the room just as Ms. Arana returned. She hollered as he left, but I didn't stop to listen to her cussing. I made for the hallway and the front door and tried not to wonder whether the light flickered.

When I opened the door, someone stood on the step, hand raised to knock.

And because that sort of cliffhanger might make you want to write me back *immediate-fluffing-ly,* I'll leave it there, Moritz.

Feel better, and don't say you're dying. Just write me, okay?

chapter twenty-four
THE STOOP

Okay. I'm going to pretend your silence is because you're sick of my terrible pacing, and not because you're dying somewhere somehow, Moritz. All I know for sure? You dropped an atom bomb of a letter on me, all about emolocation doom and earache doom, and then went grave quiet on me.

We both hate silence, okay?

So here. I'm shouting for both of us!

On Ms. Arana's doorstep:

"Ha!" said the man. "I knew it would be you."

It took me a few seconds to figure out who the hell this guy was. He was tall. He had a crazy snaggletooth. This almost *perfect* smile but just one incisor chipped past his bottom lip. It wasn't until I looked right at his eyes that I recognized him—he'd been wearing a mask before.

The blue-eyed doctor from the hospital.

"Wharton." He put his hand out, but I noticed he sort of tensed up like he didn't know what would happen if I touched him. "Going somewhere, Kilimanjaro?"

"That's a bad nickname. And yeah, I'm pretty much storming out in a rage."

I ducked under his arm with that backpack bouncing on my back, tiptoe-hopping over the ice. He didn't call after me. But I didn't turn around just in case he was looking hungry again.

God, the air outside was so clean, Moritz. I felt like the world was an oxygen mask, making me woozy. Snow reflected light into my eyes. Moonwalking.

In the neighborhood, I passed a few kids making snowmen in the front yard. An old man sitting in a lawn chair in his driveway, people watching in his snow pants. Someone doing a futile snow-shoveling routine.

Bridget's house couldn't be far. I could definitely walk there, no biggie.

After an hour of wandering aimlessly around the subdivision, fingers chilling to needles, I kind of realized I'd been optimistic. Back when I lived in the woods, I never, ever got lost. There were just some things that were huge tells to me: hit the evergreen patches along the creek and turn left into the red pine grove near the fallen birch, and you'd find the driveway. But I didn't have any bearings here. Everywhere, clones of homes spilled electric fog into the evening, electric fog blurred by snow.

Whenever cars crept behind me, I got to the far side of the sidewalk. I waited for someone to stop and yell, "That's the rascal who took out the power! Dagnabbit!" If that happened, I didn't know what I'd do.

Definitely not take my hat off. Definitely not. For years what kept my doofus head safe was the pointed roof of a triangular cabin, Moritz, and then rows of trees and an electric fence and a power line. I was so stupid to think that suddenly I could just go from the woods into the world without needing a new roof. If a hat's all I've got, I have to keep it close. Just because I'm in the world doesn't mean a part of me won't always be a hermit.

Finally, I saw the haze of that stupid phone booth. That, and one or two houses on this corner were completely dark: the empty houses hadn't had their power boxes fixed after my freak-out. I pulled my hat down lower.

Next thing I knew I was on the right street. That Stop sign where Brian had loomed. And there—the house!

I crunched up the snowy sidewalk to the spotless porch. I held my hand up in front of the door. Right then, someone opened it: a small blond girl. She wore a tiny tux and a festive bow tie. Her feet clicked when she stopped short.

Strange meetings under strange circumstances, Moritz.

"Dad! Someone's here!"

"Sorry. I've got the wrong house. I was looking for Bridget." I turned around, but she followed me out, tap shoes clicking.

"I remember you! You were in the ambulance with me! I'm Tricia."

I stopped. The ice squeaked underfoot. "I'm Oliver. People call me Ollie." I noticed her sling. "Um, look. Look. I'm so sorry."

The freckled man from the hospital waiting room stepped up behind her, duffel bags on his arms. "We'll be late for the recital! Your father's already— Oh, hello. Who's this, Tricia?"

"He was in my ambulance!"

His expression softened. "Hope you're hangin' in there."

"Yeah. I'm good."

"You live nearby? You and your family should come by for dinner."

"Yeah. Sure."

"He's looking for Bridget."

"Across the street." He pointed. "You can usually catch her running laps around this time. Wait on our stoop, if you'd like."

"You can come to the recital. I can't dance, but they let me wear the costume anyhow."

"It's totally an awesome costume."

"Nice meeting you," said Tricia's father.

They bustled into the car and waved at me before pulling away.

I wonder if I should have fessed up. But they were "hangin' in there." Sometimes people are happier not knowing things, Moritz.

Maybe that's the sort of logic Auburn-Stache raised me by.

I sat on the stoop and waited.

A sprinkling of snow had fallen by the time Bridget appeared. She wasn't wearing enough clothing to be warm: track shorts and a long-sleeved T-shirt, a headband holding back her hair. She nearly passed the house moving like some machine. The street lamps lit her yellow.

I called her name, feeling like a dingus, and to my amazement she didn't slow down—she just stopped and maintained her balance.

"Um, hey. It's great to see you!"

"Is it," she said.

"Um. I wanna talk to you. But let's maybe get out of the road so that I don't go exploding things and whatnot?"

"You're smiling," she said, "but you don't feel happy."

"Yeah, I guess." Trust Bridget to deliver the facts. "I have something for you. Valentine's present."

"I don't want it. I tell Brian every day." She led me instead to her own front step. She didn't ask me to sit, but I did anyhow, partly because when you're cold it's best to keep your body compact and partly because I wanted to have a real talk with her.

"Not your heart." I pulled that backpack off and pulled out her notebook. "Your story. It wasn't my favorite thing to read. You skipped a lot and I kind of wish you'd written at least one entry with your heart in. I bet that would be some amazing writing—"

"You can stop talking."

"'Can' is a great word. But I wanted to ask. I know writing's therapeutic, but not for people who don't feel things. I've had a lot of time to sit and think, and I've been wondering: Why did you write that for me?"

Did I detect the slightest trace of a facial expression?

"Okay, fine. Second question: Why'd you save my life?"

"I knew you had my heart."

"Aha! But that's what's been bugging me! *I* didn't have it; *Brian did*. If you always know where your heart is, you only *needed* to save Brian. Besides, you were all 'I don't care' about your heart, so why save it at all? Finally, after that you also *knocked me unconscious* so that I wouldn't short out that ambulance." I rubbed my hands together; the rubber palms sort of stuck. "You *do* give craps about the people around you."

She shrugged.

"Maybe you aren't *missing* feelings when you take your heart out. Maybe you just feel things differently. Like in your own way?"

"It's none of your business."

"Nope, you're right."

Bridget surveyed me for a long, quiet minute. "You came outside. And ran away from Brian's house."

I flapped my hand at her and got to my feet. "More sort of wandered. It's a thing I do. You're the one who runs. I dunno. Maybe one day you'll let someone catch you?"

She blinked. "Poetic nonsense."

I laughed. "Yeah, that *was* pretty bad. Nobody should take advice from a guy who didn't leave the woods till he was fifteen."

Like talking to a brick wall, Mom used to say.

Or not.

Because the next second, Bridget said: "You didn't leave the woods so you never had the world. But I never had a mother. We're all missing things."

"Are you . . . are you trying to make me feel better? *You?*"

"Only stating facts."

"*Really?*" To me that sounded almost like she was downplaying herself, and that reminded me of someone else. "Hey, do you know Arthur? With the chalky bones?"

She shrugged. "I've met him. A few times during moves."

My grin got real. "Do you talk to him? Like, does he answer your letters?"

"I don't talk to him."

I gaped. "You don't talk to any of the kids like us? The Blunderkids?"

"I don't talk to other people."

"Yeah, but that's *other* people. We weirdos have to stick together!"

"No." Even stare. "I don't talk to other people. You're still other people, too."

And I could only blank-stare her back, because it seemed like Bridget had just somehow hit on something obvious and genius and true, something sort of like what Arthur tried to tell me on the train, something I keep missing. I'm still mulling it over, Mo.

I felt a twinge in my neck: an approaching car. It sputtered and spat and made me think a fire truck was on its way, but no. The black smog of a beater stopped directly in front of the house and Wharton peered out at me.

"Kilimanjaro! Please get in the car."

"No thanks, Creeps McGee. Get that engine looked at. The smog is thick with this one."

His eyes widened. "Really?"

"Yeah, really."

"No, you can *see* that? How? What does it look like?"

I started walking along the sidewalk. He crept alongside me.

"An unsolved mystery!"

Someone leaned over Wharton in the driver's seat. "Get in, honey!" Ms. Arana. Her exasperation swayed me into the backseat. I waved at Bridget as we pulled away.

She lifted her hand, Moritz.

I squinted through the electric smog of the car.

"Get out of my face," said Brian.

"Bridget actually *waved.* So why didn't you say 'hi'?"

He was doing his skulking act. Definitely not looking out the window at Bridget's house. "Fluff off."

"Brian! Apologize!"

I held up my hands. "Don't do me any favors."

Brian rolled his eyes. I think. It was hard to see in the smog. "Don't worry."

"You two have to start getting along. You're going to be class-mates soon."

Be still, stupid heart.

"Brian told me I'd blow up the school," I said, "and he's right. Also, there's the whole I-don't-have-any-documentation thing. I'm the nameless man."

"That's why I'm here," said Wharton.

"Whatever happened to doctors just being people who pre-scribed medicine?"

Brian hit me on the shoulder. Not hard, but it was a surprise.

"Shut up and say thank you."

The Aranas' house stands out now because of the terrariums in the window, the slow snakes and silent lizards against the glass. Opposite of *Tearslaughter*.

Dr. Wharton brought out his briefcase. Inside were these pamphlets about a program called School Daze, which yeah, was a bad pun. The School Daze program is a sort of exchange student organization for kids with diseases. Seriously.

Basically, a doctor belonging to the program becomes your sponsor and monitors your health. This doctor works with schools to allow terminally ill kids into classrooms on unusual schedules. To give them a chance at normal school life. When kids have to visit hospitals out of state for months at a time, they can attend classes at whatever local schools take part in the program. They can show up on whichever days they aren't coughing up their lungs and they don't do makeup work. (I'm not being tactful.)

"You want me to pretend to be terminally ill? Isn't that kind of morally deplorable?"

We sat in the living room. Dr. Wharton didn't say anything about the collapsed coffee table, but he did seem a little bothered by all the creepy-crawlies. I asked him if he wanted to hold François the Tarantula. He said "Nope" before I even hit the question mark. Brian didn't stick around for the talk; he super-skulked up the stairs.

"It's a program for students who can't have the same school experience as most kids. The way I see it, honey, you fit the bill."

Wharton watched my face. I watched him back.

"What's in this for you?"

Wharton let shine that snaggletooth. "If I sponsor you, you'll have biweekly appointments. You've got to let me test your electro-sensitivity as I see fit."

I raised my eyebrows. "Anyone else getting mad-scientist vibes from this guy? If going to school means I have to get needles stuck in me, I'll stay a delinquent. Thanks."

Wharton put a little crease between his eyes. "But don't you want to get better?"

"You can't cure awesome." I clenched my fists.

"Not cured. *Better*. More in control. Doesn't that appeal to you?"

He almost had me. "If there were ways for that to happen, Dr. Auburn-Stache would have figured it out."

Wharton leaned forward. "Are you sure he ever *wanted* you to get better? That doctor of yours? How do you know he wasn't the one experimenting?"

"He wasn't." I remembered that swooping needle in the hospital. The lamp next to my armrest flickered. Wharton didn't say anything, but those eyes of his definitely noticed.

Soon, Ms. Arana edged him out the door, all "We'll let you know by next week." I stood in the hallway, feeling totally at a loss. Arana didn't tell me what to do, either. She just squeezed my arm on her way to the kitchen.

"Hey." I looked up; Brian was sitting on the staircase, peeking down between the bannisters with Nyanko-Senpai, a fat calico cat, spread across his lap. "What did Bridget say to you?"

"You coulda told me you've been trying to give her heart back. Every day?"

"Today I tried to pass it to her at lunch. She told me she'd start a food fight with it."

I couldn't help it; I laughed. "No *way* she said that."

"No. We don't even talk. We don't eat together. I fucked up. I always fuck up."

"Something else. I think she started caring about her life again after you befriended her."

A creak on the stairs; Nyanko rolled off his knees. "Whatever."

"I think you have to catch her. Don't give up."

"Like you can talk. *You* shouldn't let some loser stop you from going to school."

What kind of loser calls himself a loser? An . . . antiloser?

I spent the next few days not thinking about it. But I kept coming back to your last letter. The "dying" thing. I circled that in pen so many times that I tore a hole in the paper.

Over dinner yesterday, I told Ms. Arana that I wanted to take Wharton up on his deal. She dropped a burrito right past my plate into my lap. Three to five dogs gobbled it up while she hugged me.

Look, Mom. I'm going to school.

Moritz, my selfishness won out. I've decided to go to school. Not because I'm not scared of hurting people—I always will be. But maybe I have to risk it if I ever want to get better. Especially if I might be dying? If maybe I *am* the perfect candidate for School Daze? (I can't sleep, Moritz.)

I have packed and unpacked my backpack seventeen times so far.

Never thought my hands shaking could have to do with a good lie.

I hope you're feeling better. I hope writing all this will make you write enough back to even us out.

I miss you.

~ Ollie

chapter twenty-five
THE RABBIT

Ollie! Did I not say I was crippled by an ear infection?
Patience!

Consider: How could I read a thing when I cannot hear
a thing? Your words stacked up on my nightstand. The only
way to absorb them would be for someone to etch them
into my arm. I could not write you. I could not see *paper*.
Let alone read your letters and respond on blind-handed
home keys. I couldn't even be read to.

There were days when I couldn't be sure whether I was
alone. Father's hand was often on my arm. He spelled out
short messages to me. The doctor suggested it might get worse
before it got better. Perhaps a recently ruptured eardrum.
Severe "swimmer's ear." Had I your temperament, Ollie, I may
have laughed. No one had even tried to drown me this time!

I woke up on the third day insensible. I rely on ears for
both sight and sound, and an infection deprived me of both,

leaving me lesser than paramecium in the sea. I had only my fingertips to help me stumble out of bed. I called out for Father. Did not realize he was already beside me until he was helping me back and humming softly into my less-encumbered left ear. He tucked me in, traced *Schlafen*—"sleep"—into my arm. Then also: *Ich bin hier*. "I am here."

That was such a reminder that Owen was not. That Owen would probably not trace into my arm again. That I had hurt him, predictable as anything.

I gasped and gasped as though something crawled out of me; hands fell on me. There were vibrations. Later, Father told me that the other patient in the room started gasping when I did. They left the other beds empty after that.

I've had three visitors apart from Father.

First came Frau Pruwitt. I knew her fingernails. She told me to take better care of myself. Angrily scribbled that I should help at the library even if she had moved on. I could hardly speak.

Second: on the third day, Father had to work. The boy who brought me would miss school and stay in his stead. I would not have known Klaus was even there had he not propped his feet up on the bed midway through the day. Had he not smelled of wood shavings.

The third visitor came while Klaus was there. I sense the world through my ears but also through movement. Klaus stood when she stomped through the doorway.

The visitor took my wrist, briefly. Perhaps angrily. A familiar hand, a girl's hand. Not Molly's. This was the girl who was there last time I was in a hospital. Could I have forgotten her?

Boot steps, and Fieke was gone.

Eventually, the infection waned. Soon I saw the hospital walls. The dust in the crevices. As if I had opened my eyes. I clicked in all directions. So relieved to have what I'd lost. What I'd taken for granted.

I heard Klaus coming down the hallway. I scrabbled for my goggles on the nightstand. Cursed when they fell to the floor, held my hand over my face when he entered.

"Klaus."

He scowled. "Don't bother. I'm not going to run screaming, batboy. And before you even start, don't bother with 'thanks,' either."

I clasped my hands on the bedspread. "Thank you."

"What did I just say? You never listen to me, Farber." He leaned against the windowsill and folded his arms. "I guess you're too busy listening to everything else."

I nodded.

Frown lines deepened. "Oh, don't be a martyr. You're as bad an actor as you are a stagehand. If you just owned up to things you feel and dealt with them, you wouldn't end up crippling yourself and a handful of others whenever you *sniffle*."

That was something you might have said.

"You are not me. I quite literally cannot control what I feel."

"You think other people can?" A barking laugh. "Do you

think I *like* falling for a girl who pays more attention to some whiny gay kid than she does to me?"

I straightened up. "Where is Molly? Busy, I expect."

"I don't know." The tension returned to his shoulders.

"A safe assumption. She's always busy."

"I don't know," grumbled Klaus. "She hasn't been in school since the play."

I set your letters down on the nightstand. Father had brought them for me. And beneath the stack of them lay my letter from Auburn-Stache, Ollie, though I had not asked him to bring it.

"She hasn't?"

"Something happened. Maybe something you can explain. I was useless."

I remembered the muttering. "What was it, Klaus?"

"She started screaming. Screaming with her mouth closed."

While I was in the foyer knocking intimate friends unconscious, Molly performed her heart out as Beatrice, playing the mad mother, Betty the Loon, with scene-stealing grace. The suspense rose. Imagine the audience: rapt, leaning forward in their threadbare seats.

"Molly doesn't think so," Klaus told me, "but she really could make it as an actress."

He saw through her confident facade. He already saw her second mouth.

The climax of the play arrived. The actress playing Ruth, the daughter with epilepsy, let go a bloodcurdling scream.

Came to the fore of the stage. The audience watched her hold the corpse of the prop rabbit up before she dropped it and collapsed.

"All this was scripted. I saw the dress rehearsal. Beatrice is supposed to sit back and let Ruth seize. But instead Molly got up."

Molly ran forward. Picked up the rabbit. Held it to her chest. The other actors waited for her lines. She didn't say them. Ruth's actress kept seizing. Molly stared at the rabbit corpse.

"That's when the screaming started," Klaus said. "No one knew where it came from."

A scream that tore through the rafters and the wonderful acoustics. A wall-scoring wail. Molly fled the stage. Klaus's crew waited a moment and then let fall the curtain. The audience believed this was the play's actual finale. They applauded. That screaming continued. Beyond the curtain. Perhaps it inspired a standing ovation.

The scream trailed Molly as she fled the auditorium through the wings. Klaus followed. An ambulance out front. Police in the foyer. He left through a fire exit. The screaming had not stopped but faded. As if the mouth had run out of breath.

"I would have caught her, probably. But in the gardens, this agonizing waft of air stopped me dead. Air full of hurt. Farber all over. That's what I felt that night I found you in the giantess. You need to learn to let that out gradually."

"You're an expert on such matters."

Klaus shrugged. "I say it like it is. You're repressed."

I let go a laugh of my own. "So simple as that."

"It *is* that simple. Other people deal with worse things. So deal."

"Other people don't have to worry about incapacitating their fellows."

"All the more reason to get on top of it, then." Klaus stood up straight. "You and Molly both. I'm going to go see her soon. And when I do, you're coming, too."

A twinge of blindness in my ear again. Auburn-Stache's letter on my mind. The letter I buried for weeks. A letter I want not to exist, Ollie.

"How will we find her?"

"I know where she lives."

"You said you didn't know a thing about her!"

"I said I wanted her to *tell* me things about her. Get better and we'll go visit her." He was biting his fingernails. Down to the quick. "She'd better be all right."

When I was released from the hospital, Father helped me gather my things. My clothes. He slipped the letters from my nightstand into my satchel.

My breath caught. "Toss the one from the doctor."

Father tucked it in all the same. "No."

He must have read it, Ollie. He shut my bag and hefted it onto his shoulder. I picked up my cane and followed him into the hallway. I had not asked, but I'd been told Max and Owen's inexplicable collapse had only put them in the hospital overnight. Strange that I looked for them. Knowing they weren't there. Knowing I could not explain myself.

"Moritz," Father said, "you know that I am not a man of many words."

I nodded.

"But this letter. Perhaps you will want to share it with others."

Father uses words sparingly. But each one is a thoughtful thing. I have missed that.

Your copies of Bridget's writing waited in the postbox. Ollie, do you know what I took from it? Bridget has tried to die, but mostly tried to live.

Here's a victory for you. Damned, beautiful you: I went to that dreaded website. You know which one. The one I had ignored. Your words, Father's, Bridget's: the new buzz in me.

I logged into the forum you helped inflict on the world, Ollie.

There are, inexplicably, more than three hundred players. Three hundred strangers intrigued by the fiction of my sad reality! Honestly, Oliver, I could weep.

Threads about love triangles. Children who fly, shoot lasers from their fingertips, and at first I did nothing more than convince myself that this is a farce. But there was one thread, Oliver.

My computer dictating, my ears pinned by all-encompassing headphones. Nothing but me and the words of strangers.

From username thorfinn: *My name is Jon. I live in Reykjavik. I am here to say this is no game. I was raised in this lab. I have scars. I remember white walls, reception desks, smiling doctors. And I remember* her. *A word to remember me by is "owl." If you know me, PM me.*

I sent him a private message: *Are you the boy who turned his head backward?*

The answer came swiftly (the time in Iceland is only an hour behind the time in Kreiszig):

"Who is this?"

The eyeless monster.

"Prince Moritz. I remember you. I remember your mother."

I don't have words, Oliver, for the Blunderkinder. I can only begin with this: *I am eternally sorry for what my mother—*

"I am glad to hear from you. It is good to know I am not alone!"

I gaped at my desk. Words from you, and words from children like us.

Oliver, I've been such a fool.

I don't have control over what I feel. I only have control over how I react to those feelings. How I write my own story.

Enough festering.

Enough of secrets. I am attaching the letter Auburn-Stache sent me. Please forgive me for withholding. Forgive me for hiding.

I called Klaus. "When can we see Molly?"

"End of the week."

"Not today?"

"*Dummkopf*. I have school. You have to rest."

Phone down, laptop open: *Jon*.

"Yes?"

Can you tell me how to set up a profile?

"D!"

chapter twenty-six

THE BONES

Moritz,

I am writing you because I can't bring myself to write Ollie, but I am (as ever) concerned about him. Jess Arana, an invested RN, has been keeping me informed of his well-being, because I worry speaking to him directly will encourage him to do something reckless. You and I both know that Ollie is prone to recklessness, especially when he feels his world is threatened, and the truth is my reason for leaving him so cruelly is threatening indeed!

Of the two of you, Moritz, I don't think you'll disagree when I say you are more mature. You may feel crippled with doubt, but you have a self-awareness Ollie lacks. There's a grit to you. You call it a lack of creativity, but I'd call it wisdom if I knew what wisdom looked like.

Please don't relay what I write to you here to our mutual

friend. You'll understand this request, Moritz, when you read the remainder of this letter.

I was obligated to leave Ollie alone in Ohio. If only he could understand that the last thing I ever wished to do was abandon him. I've always hated leaving him, whether it was alone with his mother in the woods or alone in the hospital.

When it comes to honesty, I'm guilty of years of malpractice.

Many of my hopes were thwarted by his mother's caution. Meredith wished Ollie would find contentment within isolation. But then, it was also only at her urging that I agreed he should start writing you. We reasoned he could never leave the woods for your electric heart. I assumed you would not tempt him with the real world; you loathed it so much. It was manipulative of me. Has any scheme ever backfired so thoroughly?

After speaking with you, all Ollie dreamed of was leaving home.

You may need some context.

Beau Takahiro was a professor of mine in university. After the unexpected death of her daughter, I asked if she'd consider being a foster mother to one of the initiative children. She agreed, with one reservation: she wanted to be his grandmother rather than his mother. "Skip the drama and get right to the wisdom" were her words.

I'm not sure if you remember this boy, or whether Ollie's written about him as of this letter—Arthur passes for normal, despite fragile bones and regenerative capabilities. Time was he could break his kneecaps on sidewalks and minutes later play hopscotch again. I've watched that boy crack teeth on lollipops, hold those teeth back in place for a moment, and bite down again.

Arthur is miraculous and of course Arthur is doomed. You know better than most that there is always a cost to your mother's children—our children. From birth, Arthur has suffered accordingly.

When Beau called me less than a day after we left Chicago, I assumed he'd broken a limb. But Beau insisted that the illness afflicting Arthur was unlike anything she'd seen. She described bouts of vomiting, sudden hair loss, and burns on his skin.

She put Arthur on the phone. Immediately, I could tell something was amiss. His voice sounded unusually raw when he greeted me. When I asked whether Beau was merely overreacting again, instead of his usual chortle, I heard a horror story.

Apparently, Arthur gripped a screwdriver so hard that his fingers broke. Apparently, he couldn't even remember picking it up. And then couldn't remember what a screwdriver was. Repeatedly, he asked Beau where his desk was.

She told me he was sitting at his desk the whole time.

Arthur's memory is usually impeccable, Moritz.

Over the phone, he said something I won't forget: "I know my brain's not a bone, but it's breaking. I'm like a screen that laughs and cries. Am I real?"

I reassured him not only that he was real, but that he was loved, and when he asked me whether I was coming, I told him of course. He requested I bring Ollie. Evidently, Ollie made Arthur feel "chill."

Everyone is "chill" compared to Oliver Paulot, Moritz.

I looked at my charge, tucked in his sleeping bag. Most people look more innocent while they sleep, but with Ollie it's just the opposite: he can't pretend to smile while sleeping. His hair wasn't falling out, Moritz; it was only that I had just cut it. Already I suspected an epidemic; perhaps I've always expected that some grievous illness might await the children whose cells we flippantly toyed with. Or perhaps an epidemic was preferable to the alternative.

The following morning, I received another call from Beau and looked back to find the car empty in Bridget's driveway.

Ollie was about to crash a school bus and put himself in the hospital, Moritz.

Thank god he didn't kill anyone. That is my profession, not his. So I hope, Moritz. The secrets I keep are only intended to protect him, Moritz. I stopper his dreams of befriending the world to spare him.

As for how I came to leave him—I'll let him tell that story.

Winter had encroached on Chicago overnight. I entered the home and discovered Arthur upstairs in his room. He'd become dozy-eyed and pale. He wore more than one cast now. He sat in his wheelchair by the window. He told me he'd shake my hand, if only his hands would stop shaking on their own. Evidently, Beau went out for groceries, though Arthur theorized she was "starting a shitstorm" in the dairy aisle.

He couldn't focus his eyes, and his hands trembled with something like palsy; he winced when I took his blood pressure. Most noticeably his skin was inflamed from head to toe, as if severely sunburnt.

The burned skin itself was not unusual. What Arthur often

neglects to mention, Moritz, is how his remarkable condition has left him with unique weaknesses. Yes, his chondroblast cells heal his bones with speed unmatched. And his red blood cells replicate broken tissue instantaneously. But this, combined with his fragility, works against him on occasion. Arthur's body is in a constant state of flux, making and unmaking itself, breaking and repairing with every step he takes. All of his cells are extremely malleable.

For this reason, he is abnormally susceptible to radiation—UV particles, for instance, pierce his constantly transforming cells with ease. Those damaged cells replicate and proliferate his body with daunting speed. When I met him, I assumed he would be cancerous within weeks, but his case is so unusual. His healing has always *been* a cancer, in a sense, but one that works to his benefit—replicating the exact cells he needs the moment he loses them, going no further.

Even so, when Arthur had his first and only X-ray, his skin peeled from head to toe and the healing process took months. Arthur has been forbidden from approaching microwaves since childhood. (At age six, he wept for the loss of pizza pockets.) For years, Beau only let him outside after dark. Now he wears a skin of zinc oxide.

On an overcast autumn day, how had he sustained burns this severe?

I removed his brace and completed the rest of my examination as delicately as possible, biopsying skin and drawing blood samples, unloading all the equipment I travel with. His temperature remained high even after an ice bath.

Again I thought of Ollie's father, Moritz. The ultimate source of their pain was the same. The lab and the experiments within it. I try and fail to remember who I was before my days in the laboratory. The devastation we wrought there is all that my life is made of now, redeemed only by the children who persist despite it all. But if those children fail . . .

"Who's there?" Arthur asked, again and again.

"Doc," I reassured him, again and again.

Arthur asked me how long this would take, and I told him I should have results very soon. But that was not what Arthur meant by that question, and we both knew it. Finally, he asked me where Ollie was. I didn't answer.

I sat on Arthur's bed, encouraging him to do the same, but I dare not risk touching him. Chalk crumbles so easily. Arthur stayed beside the window, squeezed his eyes shut and braced his hands against the glass. And in an instant, I knew he intended to hurt himself and I ran forward, fearing he might leap through the glass and shatter with it.

Arthur withdrew, sat down beside me on the bedspread, and wept until he vomited on the floor between his feet.

I tell you all this in detail not to pain you, but because I want you to understand how dire this is. I want you to understand why I've left Oliver behind.

I wanted him to see the world, not the demise of it.

Moritz, these past weeks I have committed my every waking moment to visiting the children of the initiative. I've traveled across America and flown to Taipei; from Taipei, Osaka; from Osaka, Hong Kong and Saint Petersburg. Next comes Reykjavik.

I've taken dozens of vials of blood. I cut skin from so many kids who deserve better. I subjected them to the memory of what some had managed to forget. I hurt them on purpose. And I awaited inevitable results: signs of imminent demise and markers in the anatomy that might imply your mother programmed her subjects to die young.

Moritz, I tell you now:

So far, *I've found nothing to support this*, beyond Arthur's decay.

This doesn't mean I should stop searching.

There is another factor I've found impossible to ignore. One I dare not consider because of personal biases, but must consider as a medical professional. I will not address that here. I can't bear to, until I can speak with certainty. There are more of you to examine first.

One of those includes you, and your friend Molly, of course. And think of that! Your father has told me that you and Molly are on friendly terms! I remember the day she tried to drown you; I know you do, too. I remember how that changed you both. When we sent her to the orphanage, she was quiet as a mouse and angry as a cat. Her face betrayed nothing, but how her second mouth hissed. To think that you are close gives me not strictly hope, but something close to it. We couldn't ruin you children entirely, could we?

Expect me soon. Until then, my plea is twofold, Moritz.

If anyone can say for *certain* what ails Arthur, it isn't me. Your mother was involved in the cellular manipulation of the children to an extent I never was. If this degeneration becomes an epidemic, and if there are ways to immunize you all, only she might know the remedy. (And if such is not the case and I need to face the alternatives, she might know that as well.)

Moritz, I'm asking, unfairly, for you to help me find her. I am trying, but I won't stray far from bedsides. I have no addresses. No proof she's even alive. This plea is certainly a desperate, unjust one. I'd never want you to reunite with your abuser—but if you can only *locate* her. If you have any ideas, any memories or maps or pictures that may point me her way, I would be eternally indebted to you. I know this is a terrible thing to ask.

Finally, please look after the boy we love. Do inform me post-haste if you've reason to believe his care is lapsing. As always, comfort him when I can't. Don't tell him of my worries, but let him live to the fullest while he can.

We've encouraged him to seek this world. You mustn't abandon him in it.

Don't become the coward I am, Moritz.

Gregory Auburn-Stache

chapter twenty-seven

THE DAZE

I read your letter and then Auburn-Stache's letter in the bathroom yesterday evening, mostly because the bathroom is the only room in this house without cats lurking in it. And after I read it, I just sat there for a while on the carpeted toilet seat cover and took some breaths and tried not to freak the hell out. I wonder if this is how Bridget feels when she puts her heart back in. I almost hit the ceiling when a cat meowed at me from between the shower curtains.

I wished I could flush it away: the whole stinking idea that we really *have* been doomed since birth! That stupid powerless ache again! And *he* couldn't tell me this? He couldn't let me out sooner? He's trying to do what Mom did. Shield me, or something. But that ship's sailed and sunk! We're already out here, trying to be human.

Poor fluffing Arthur. He never answered my letters. I had already decided not to be annoyed, because he really did seem almost too cool for letters. Now I just hope he's doing better. I hope

Auburn-Stache figured out whatever this is. I don't even want to think about the alternatives. Arthur's kind of my idol.

And poor Molly, Moritz. Do you think she's sick like Arthur's sick, or do you think she's sick the way you and me get sick: falling-down-over-ourselves sick? Sick of the world? There's almost definitely a hyperspecific word for that sickness in German, right?

Poor you, too. I get why you didn't tell me. I've never had any patience for being reck-full. Literally no one will ever call me Lord of Handling Bad News with Grace.

I know you probably feel like it's your duty to find your mom, and I think some of your crazy festering had to do with that pressure, too. But that's not your shit to clean up. No matter what happens, getting involved has to be your choice, not Auburn-Stache's. You get me? He doesn't get to tell you to take your heart out.

I never had a right to do that, either.

Just so you know, Moritz, my hair is growing back, not falling out. My hands are steady. My fingernails are grubby with pet grime, but they haven't fallen off. And I'm the antithesis of sunburned.

Screw worrying about what we can't change. I'm going to be responsible for me. I'm going to focus on not exploding my new school. I'm not telling anyone how to live. And who's gonna care what mistakes a potentially dying kid makes? There are three hundred kids on our forum because people think we could be characters worth reading about. Let's earn that, Moritz.

I want to tell you about my first weeks of high school, but I lost words again. I don't know how to be linear, even, because one thing about school is that there's a routine and the routine makes it hard to tell one day from the next.

Things are pretty mundane: homeroom! Public restrooms! Computer labs (I dare not enter)! Cafeterias! Rancid locker rooms! A football field and a *band* room with a *glock* and people shoving and kissing each other in hallways, and glorious air conditioners and overhead projectors and phones hidden on just about every- body (teachers included!) and a library and drinking fountains and, get this, *vending machines* and a science lab with an anatomical model that is pretty accurate by non-Blunderkid standards, but not as pretty as the one I left back home.

All my dreams in one place. All these things I could break.

The first day I was crazy nervous, but Ms. Arana gave me some great advice: "Fake it till you make it, honey."

Maybe every school is a little like acting school, Mo.

I decided not to go anywhere near school buses and generators. But her words kind of worked. I smiled a lot and said "Hi!" to just about everyone I saw. I went to my first class with my gray hat on and told a classroom full of kids my own age—kids who spooked me because supposedly they were *normal* but I couldn't tell you how, because maybe normalcy really is imaginary—that I have a crippling disease.

". . . and I'd tell you more about it, but it involves gory details about my bowels and blood and things, so maybe don't ask." I gave a bow. "I'm just so *happy* to be here!"

A few of them looked shocked. Then some kid in the back began slow-clapping. I sat down to laughter and a little applause. The teacher, Mr. Elton, pointed at me and said, "There's a healthy high school attitude. See that, kids? Be more like Oliver."

"It's Ollie."

Until you make it.

By the end of that first class, I'd been reminded to raise my hand seven times, and eventually, Mr. Elton asked me to let someone else answer questions about Poe for a change. I waited like ten seconds for anyone to raise a hand for the next question, scanning the classroom with my eyebrows raised. A few people scowled at me and a few snickered before I blurted, "Edwin Drood!"

At lunch I had no idea where to sit. I gather from you and Bridget that it *matters* somehow? That where you sit is where you'll have friends for the rest of the year. So I made sure I ate half my pizza at a table full of punk kids and then said good-bye to those kids, and then I ate two bites at the next table full of kids in basketball jerseys and drank my milk at the next table full of kids in glasses and spat out cold, whitish carrot sticks at a fourth table full of girls in cutesy dresses, and then finally ended lunch with my Twinkie at a table full of art students and a table full of student council members.

I hope this means I'll have friends everywhere!

I do this every day. I don't really have a favorite place to sit. I like the art kids because they remind me of you, even though you say you aren't creative. They say things like that, too. And at the punky table, I found, like, Fieke's soul brother. Gabe, a boy with a bazillion piercings who wears *bondage* pants. I showed him my "medically approved" bodysuit and he looked envious. Pretty funny.

I'm babbling again, aren't I?

Brian and Bridget don't eat together or even in the cafeteria since they stopped getting along, so right from day one I had to dart out early to go find them. Bridget eats in the hallway by the gym. And Brian lurks by the English wing and chews beef jerky from his hoodie pocket.

When I found him on the first day: "Why are you by yourself?"

"I don't like people."

"Why don't you sit with Bridget?"

"She doesn't want me to."

"She doesn't care either way. You read her notebook. You *know* this."

"Who says I read it?"

"You left greasy fingerprints on the pages. *Beef jerky* fingerprints. I'm like a detective."

"Mind your own business."

I noticed he had that suspiciously beating paper bag with him again. At some point every day, he tries to give her heart back to her. He picks the most random moments and holds it out in front of her by the drinking fountains or lockers or by the flagpole. It's the most dedication Brian's probably ever shown to anything.

But once I caught him holding it over a trash can. So much for modern romance, Moritz.

"Hey. No Brianism. You have to keep chasing her."

"Don't worry about it."

He tucked the heart away and signed up for the track team.

In Physical Science class, Ms. Goledge didn't care that I didn't know all the constellation positions for June through December.

"This isn't Astronomy." She was middle-aged, with sunspotted skin. Wheat-like wisps of hair. "But welcome to our classroom, Oliver. Happy for you to be here whenever you can."

"Ollie. Or Liver. That might be funny. And don't mind the terribly ugly hat. I've got miscellaneous terminal diseases."

She bit her cheek. "Miscellaneous?"

I laughed and didn't meet her eyes. "Yeppers!"

I got the hand-raising speech ten minutes in again. Also, I have a hard time sitting still. But I think most people assume that's a side effect of my nonexistent medication, so none of the teachers say much when I stand up in class, or sit with my feet on the chair and hug my knees.

I really like Ms. Goledge's class. We've done some awesome experiments with fire and sound waves and water and sticking marshmallows in vacuums. The only experiments I don't like are the electrical ones, because when I tried to help my lab partner, Whitney, this whispering girl in glasses, wire a circuit board in the back of the classroom, the whole thing sparked and busted three times in a row, and Whitney became totally convinced she was just going to suck at all things science forever. Ms. Goledge scratched her head and told us to take notes on someone else's project.

Two days later, Ms. Goledge proposed some kind of potato-electricity activity.

"Don't ask me to do that unless you want potato goop everywhere."

"What does that mean, Ollie?"

"Let poor Whitney have a nonterminal partner this time, huh?"

I didn't explain. I sat out and took a bad grade. It doesn't really matter what grade I get anyhow. I'm just grateful to be here. Everyone feels bad for me, but I feel bad for everyone else.

A lot of kids here, Moritz, wake up every day *determined* to be disappointed. They drag their feet, moan about homework, ignore all the amazing things around them: They've got the *world* in their pockets and miracles on all sides and they're *fed up*?

Moritz, the first time I got to use an automatic hand dryer, I laughed so loud I cried.

Near the end of the week, a girl from the gym class I sit on bleachers for (can't really run in that stupid bodysuit and I have to play up the terminal thing) walked right up in her gym shorts, all confident and good at volleyball and blond and yeah, hot as hell, and smiled like a bazillion pennies and said: "Wanna go to Winter Carnival with me?"

"Why would you ask a dying kid to a dance?"

"Why wouldn't I? You're cute." She tossed her head, which was pretty impressive. "I'm not shallow."

I remember Liz saying I only loved her because she was the only girl I'd ever met. Liz was always convinced there were girls out there that were better than her somehow. Fact is, that's bullshit. As I sat here looking at a hot girl, I *Bridget*ed—didn't care.

She didn't know me. I didn't know her.

"I didn't say you were shallow. But you've never talked to me. I'm Ollie, by the way!"

"I know." A whole circle of girls behind her sort of stared and whispered, like the girls on Arthur's train. Bridget B. and company.

"In nature, most animals seek out the healthiest partners. Are you intentionally fighting your instincts? Or are your instincts kind of crappy? Could it be a biochemical problem? Or—"

"So much for doing you any favors." She glared at me.

"Oh, I didn't know that's what you were doing!" I smiled. "But I've already got a girlfriend. Thanks for asking! That was a first!"

"Freak." She wasn't saying it because of my allergies. She was saying it because of my personality. So I smiled bigger.

She stalked away, looking more confused than angry.

I didn't think it was a big deal until later. I sat around waiting for my ride after school. Track season doesn't begin until March, but Bridget runs laps on the semi-icy track every day after school. While I was leaning on the fence, craning my neck to look at the massive stadium lights with their giant bulbs, wondering how quickly those would make me seize, Brian slumped against the fence next to me, all sweaty practice clothes and hoodie.

"Rumor has it you have a girlfriend."

"Kind of! There's a girl back in Michigan. Her name is Liz."

He waited a second before saying the next thing. "If you're so in love with this girl, how come you're always making me print out letters from that foreign kid instead?"

"Moritz is . . . there are things Liz doesn't get. She had a normal upbringing, you know?"

"No such thing."

"Fine. But Moritz and I both had especially demented childhoods."

"Maybe that's why Bridget and I don't work."

"You might. You're demented enough."

He spat on the ground at his feet. "I guess. I *kicked* her *heart* across a room."

"Well? I kicked you in the nuts and you're cool with me."

"I don't like you."

"Have you tried just, I don't know, asking her out again?"

He answered me for once. "How can I ask her out knowing how she is?"

"Does it gross you out that much? I mean, it's kind of cuddly, her heart."

He shuffled his feet. "Asshole. I mean, how can I ask her knowing that she might be a completely different person? She's never been her full self around me; she's never *felt* for me. The *actual* her probably wouldn't give two shits about me. She'd just leave."

"Who says she's not her actual self now?"

We watched Bridget zoom by. She did not glance at us as her feet fell. She went for another lap. No way Brian could ever catch her. Why can't people just *talk* to each other?

"Okay," I hazarded, "but you still want her to have her heart back? So she can have the option of being whatever version of herself she wants to be. Even if she chooses a version of herself that doesn't give two shits about you."

"So?" He kicked his spitball with his shoe.

"Just realizing for the first time that you aren't really a loser at all."

"Shut up." He pulled his hood over his face.

There's definitely more to tell you, but I have to go meet Wharton. Turns out when he said "biweekly" he meant twice a week, not once every two weeks. There should be two different words for that. English *is* stupid. I don't know how you deal with it, Moritz.

His so-called experiments are something else. I mean it. I'll tell you more about it soon.

Are we passing for human, Moritz?

chapter twenty-eight

THE VIDEO

We might be, Ollie. Do not jinx it.

Klaus asked me to be more expressive. Still, I thought it wise to restrain my surprise when a chauffeured vehicle appeared outside my apartment complex. A driver held the door for me.

"Get in, Farber."

Klaus sat on the leather seat opposite. Arms folded. I had never seen him so neat. Dress pants and a suit vest. Not a speck of sawdust in his combed hair.

St. Francis's was located in the backstreets behind a multitude of office buildings in the Lustlos district. I will not say it was spotless. I have never heard a thing that's spotless. But clean-swept steps. Disinfected doorknobs. A reception desk clear of debris. The smell of warm nutmeg. This place did not recall a laboratory. An older gentleman in a cardigan showed us to the lobby. Gave Klaus the heartiest handshake.

"Master Blumen. A pleasure to see you! Your mother was in just this afternoon!"

"Was she, Eugen?" Klaus *beamed*. My jaw slackened. "I hope she didn't inconvenience you. She can be a bit . . . overwhelming, I know. "

"Oh, to the contrary! She always makes the children laugh; she arrived dressed as a wizard and taught them magic tricks. And you know, there've been rumors that St. Francis's might have to be consolidated with the Rafner Boys' Home. We wouldn't mind, but there's hardly room for everyone."

"Not for growing boys. What did Mother say?"

"She tapped me with her magic wand and reassured me that for as long as the Blumens have any say, we'd be looked after. She suggested expanding into the next building over, if necessary." Eugen cleared his throat. "Should I ask Molly if she'll be wanting visitors?"

Klaus started. "Yes, please."

"Klaus and . . . ?"

"Moritz. He's a friend."

Eugen left the counter and traveled back into the building. Klaus settled into a worn leather chair beside the radiator. Patted the seat beside him.

"You're a frequent visitor." I sat.

"For years. My parents used to bring me here to play with the children."

"You told me you didn't know Molly."

Klaus shook his head. "She never spoke to me. She never spoke to anyone until she started at Myriad. Then she was like a whole new person."

"Oh?" I clicked at him. "I wonder how that feels. Not to know the person next to you."

"Don't, Farber. If you'd have asked me where I came from, I'd have told you."

"Doubtless. So why haven't you seen her yet?"

"She refuses to see me."

He tells me this now? "You tell me this now?"

"She'll see *you*." A miserable smirk. "I'll wait here."

"The usual seat, Klaus?" A wrinkled woman across the room sat in an armchair beside a box of fabric, clothes. Old coats. Cutting and restitching.

Another polite smile. "And you, Frau Andert. What are you making today?"

"Making do. Some of the girls will be needing thicker mittens."

I thought of Molly's lace clothing. All repurposed from used items. Her patterns and prints bought secondhand. Made vintage, made beautiful. No one would know.

If we could bottle and sell her.

Eugen returned. "Moritz, is it?"

We stood.

"She'll see you. Just you. Sorry, Klaus." Klaus sat back down. "She's been under the weather, but she says it's nothing to worry about. She doesn't like doctors." He led me down a narrow hall. "We find that lamps are just so much warmer than fluorescent bulbs. This is a home, not a hospital. We're proud of our kids. Melchior—who's just turned eight—won a spelling contest. And our oldest, Wendla, was accepted into university!"

We made our way up rickety stairs. The air closer, warmer on the second floor. The change irritated my ears for a moment. The linoleum underfoot was scratched to cardboard thinness.

"Molly does us proud. Full scholarship to that academy. She acted her heart out to get in, now, didn't she? You've seen her. She's wonderful, isn't she? Isn't she just? To think she was so quiet when she came here. Not a word. Refused to be adopted. Got downright taciturn whenever she was interviewed, didn't she? But here we are." He knocked his knuckles against a door that creaked open. "All right, pet? Here's your Moritz for you."

"Thank you, Eugen."

Four cots in the narrow room. The sound of traffic through the cold breeze of open air. Molly stood on a tiny street balcony. Doubtless she'd seen us arrive. Even with hearing slightly muffled on the right side, it was apparent to me that something was awry. Her posture was so still.

"Molly . . . ?"

She twisted toward me. Bedraggled curls. A face wan and tired.

"Klaus wants to see you."

She looked out. "He *thinks* he does."

"You underestimate him. He knows about my, um, nothingness."

"I wish mine were a nothingness. If it were a nothing-ness, I could hide it."

I clicked my tongue. Her mouth wasn't muzzled now. It was *bruised*. Pin-stuck. A needle and thread dangled from the edge of her trembling back lips, the thread tangled in her hair. Her lips were scabbed and scraped.

"Molly—! What have you done to yourself?"

"I tried to sew it shut," she told me. "But it's difficult when you can't see what you're doing. The dratted teeth kept biting the stitches. An awful mess. A real drama."

Someone else might have held her. I waited just inside the doorway.

"Why, Molly?"

"I'm not sure I can keep acting. It says the most awful things." She sat down on the cot closest to the window.

"What sort of things?"

"Only the truth you idiot Molly you utter monster you beast it only says the truth and you know it."

The second mouth's voice was harsh and hideous. I did not want her to see me flinch. But what good does hiding do us, Ollie?

"Don't listen, Molly. We all have voices like that."

"Truly awful, awfully true things." Molly coughed. "Things I'm afraid of. Before I went onstage it said I would forget my lines. It said I would fail. It says I'm destined for a laboratory again. Have you come to take me to one, Moritz?"

I sat on the cot. My back to hers. "Never, Molly."

I could be doing more for her, Ollie. And for you. For all

of us, if I only looked for my mother. There are laboratories we can never leave. Feet we'll never grow.

"What's the matter with me? I stood on that stage with everyone watching, and I felt *happy*, Moritz. I had them." She fingered her lace skirt. "They thought I was a star. And then I saw that poor rabbit."

"The hardest thing to be is happy." You know us, Ollie.

She leaned her shoulder blades against mine. Her mouth at my spine, hissing.

"It talks in my sleep. I've torn my hair out. Soon everyone will see me."

"They'll see you and you're awful to see aren't you?"

I tilted my head. My ear centimeters from the mouth. No scent of cherries; unwashed breath. "Molly, my dearest friend advised me to see the best in people."

"Now who says 'friend' easily." The back mouth whimpered. "Sometimes I still hate you, Moritz."

"You will always hate him and you know it."

If only my hearing had gone out then. "That . . . isn't unjustified." I spoke directly to Molly's second mouth. "Do you believe the best of everyone?"

"Moritz?" She tilted her head.

"Do you believe there was any good in my mother?"

Now it sounded like a shriveled, tiny thing. *"Not her not her oh god not her—"*

Molly shushed herself. "There must have been."

"Don't say I'm evidence."

"I won't. But the day I left the laboratory, she didn't hurt me." Molly closed her eyes. "She took me here. She gave me a home."

Klaus's pacing had almost repatterned the lobby floor by the time I returned. Frau Andert lay slouched in her seat, apparently fast asleep.

"Well? How was she?"

"It's hard to be well, coming from where we come from."

"Right." He looked at my goggles. "Molly isn't missing any body parts, is she?"

"Would it matter?"

Klaus stiffened. "Not even a little bit."

"I didn't think so." I smiled. "Klaus, can we make a bargain?"

He eyed me warily. "Yeah . . . ?"

"Show me new scenery. And I'll tell you a story."

Klaus's posture told me not to comment. But what a home. A town house with dual staircases in the front hall. Cold marble floors. Lofty windows. Old wealth. Klaus thanked a butler and declined refreshments. Asked not to be disturbed before he led me upstairs.

I will not waste space detailing the finery of Klaus's magnificent bedroom. I settled in across from him.

"What *is* this, Farber?"

"Will you believe," I told him, "that I've never spoken my past aloud?"

"I'd believe that." I waited for cynicism. It did not come.

"Standing," I breathed. "Do you happen to have a computer with a camera?"

Minutes later, I watched his furrowed brow lift as he perused the forum.

"What *is* this? An RPG?"

"For me, it's the brother of truth."

"A laboratory," he murmured, scanning the page. "That's pretty messed up."

"You have asked about my history with Molly. Turn on the camera and you will learn a thing or two. When I raise my hand like this, please throw something at me. After we're done recording, can you help me post this?"

"This will help Molly?"

"I won't make any promises."

He nodded. "Ready when you are."

A click and a beeping countdown.

Three . . .

Two . . .

One.

"I am user dolphinmo, and I am not a fiction. This is not science fiction."

I pulled off my goggles and raised my hand. I clicked and caught the miniature globe that Klaus tossed at me.

"Please look at my user profile. Everything you see on it is the truth. This isn't a game. Dozens of children in the world had to undergo torment at the hands of scientists in a laboratory. Some of you may know this. But that is not important.

"It doesn't matter whether or not you're actual Blunderkinder. I am calling you to arms all the same. If you retain any of the humanity that your characters seem to—your characters on dairy farms and in Victorian London. Your characters learning kung fu. If you are half as brave as your creations, I need your help. We all need your help. We have to find her."

I told them all I knew about my mother. Described her appearance. Spoke of her mannerisms and her upbringing in Wien. Mentioned the hollows under her eyes. Her pacemaker. Showed and promised to upload the only picture of her I had: Me, six years old. The two of us outside the castle in Freiberg.

I told them who we are. Not superheroes, but a few dozen teens around the world. A few dozen who have felt powerless. Who may have expiration dates. "We can't sit by. Not if there is hope for any one of us to be happy. Not if a boy allergic to electricity can go to high school. Not if someone might love a girl with two mouths. If a girl without a heart might feel. If we can love, there's hope for us."

Your poetical nonsense. Desperate times, Ollie.

Klaus stopped the camera. I opened my mouth to thank him. He held up a tear-dampened hand. "I felt every emotion you did during that. I don't know how you kept your face straight."

"Let's hope they feel it through the digital veil, then."

"They might, Farber." He coughed, stared at the ceiling. "Two mouths."

Ollie, my mother didn't destroy her soulless workings.

I won't sit by and let us destroy ourselves.

The word for being sick of the world, Ollie, is *Weltschmerz*. I'm fighting that.

I hold to hope. Always and ridiculously. You taught me this.

chapter twenty-nine
THE ELECTROMAGNET

Okay. I'm applauding. I'm laughing. I'm sobbing. I'm dying again. (Kidding!)

Moritz fluffing Farber.

You have to tell me what happens on the forum, Moritz. I would give my three stubborn baby teeth to see that video. To see how everyone reacts to you coming out of the Total Badass closet. Maybe soon! I tried watching TV at the Arana Zoo once, and it was just a messy blob of colors that made my eyes cross, but I'm working up to it. I hardly sneeze when I pass the computer labs at school, even though they make my neck prickly.

Then again, nowadays I'm always prickly. I blame Wharton.

The first time he picked me up after school, I nearly sprinted back inside again. Wharton pulled up to me and Brian and honked the horn. He didn't have to. His car is such a black-breathing beater that I have dubbed it the Dark Lord Morgoth.

"Time to pay up, Kilimanjaro," he called through the window.

"Spare me, doctor!" I cried, clasping my hands together. "Spare me or I'll just kill your car with the fall of a hat."

He looked wary as I climbed in next to him. "If you really want to take off your hat, go ahead. Take a deep breath and do it."

I jokingly tugged at the gray fabric, but not enough to move the duct tape. "Okeydokey."

"Let me drive away from the main road first, just in case."

I let go. "You're serious. You actually want me to just take my hat off. You do know that I'm the AMAZING human electromagnet. If I take this hat off, I'll either seize or kill your car."

"Why do you think I bought this junker? If anything AMAZING and electromagnetic happens, I won't be mourning my Fiat."

"So you're kind of saying you bought a car for me?"

"Guess so." Wharton smirked, heading for Fayton's outskirts. "So you seize when you're overexposed, huh?"

"Well, that used to be how it went. I'd have a seizure and bite my tongue and feel like crap for a few days. I hated that, but at least then . . ."

"At least then what?"

No way the hat was coming off. "It wasn't hurting anyone else."

We stopped at an intersection.

"When did that change?"

"I think the lights change on a timer. Based on my limited traffic research." I peered up at the yellow traffic box.

"No." Those twinkling eyes. "When did you start 'killing cars'?"

"There was an accident in the woods. A friend got hurt." I

squinted out the window. "It's not my favorite day to talk about, actually."

"So it *was* a time of emotional distress. See, it's a matter of figuring out your triggers."

The light switched back to green. He pulled forward. I didn't even want to ask where we were going. Wharton made me jittery.

"Eyes on the road. You can stick me in a test tube later."

"Did anything happen when your mom died?"

The EMP at the dance. I closed my eyes. "I don't want to talk about that."

"I can tell. Look."

He pointed to the digital clock under the dashboard, which was nothing but a blur of green bars now. "I take it that it wasn't your favorite day, either. Okay. I'm just establishing that your electro-sensitivity *is* related to your emotional state."

"It didn't used to be."

"Yeah, well. Puberty sucks for us all."

"Especially if you have a snaggletooth."

Wharton blinked at me. "Not cool, Ollie. We've got to work on your filters."

"Get your tooth fixed and asshats like me can't say a thing."

"Sometimes it's about working with your bad parts, not fixing them." Totally deadpan. "I am doling out wisdom right at this very moment, Kilimanjaro."

He signaled left and pulled into a parking lot in front of a very specific store.

"A death trap," I intoned. "You've taken me to a death trap."

"Kid, by the end of April, I want you to walk right into the Electronics Megamart and take your hat off."

I borrowed your catchphrase: "Beg *pardon*?"

Let's talk delusions. I thought Wharton was the most delusional guy ever to get a medical degree. (Other than your mom, trying to make her superhumans, but that's not even funny.)

Dr. Wharton believes I do have a say in my electromagnetic pulses. He thinks seizures are more likely when I'm anxious or frightened, and EMPs are more likely when I'm flooded with adrenaline. I told him Auburn-Stache kinda thought the same thing.

"He and Moritz say it's about balance. But I've never been very good at balance. I tried using a jack pine log as a tightrope once."

"It's a different kind of balance."

"I was joking."

"It wasn't funny."

The following week, he took me to an ice-cream parlor, despite the snow on the ground.

"The more I hear about your doctor, the more I think he was too close to it."

"What do you mean?"

"He was too worried about your welfare. He wouldn't take risks worth taking." Wharton gestured with his straw. "Mankind has to take risks to move forward."

"He regrets stuff." I crushed sprinkles between my fingertips. "Failed experiments."

"That's what I'm saying. You aren't grown up. You're not a failure yet."

315

"Gee, thanks?"

Wharton never took his eyes off me. Just sucked down his strawberry milk shake like brain freeze isn't a thing.

"I don't need you to explain what your doctor was afraid of. It's the same thing every doctor is afraid of. It's the same as being in an operating room and hearing that long beep. Everyone has to hear it sometimes. It's the reason some people quit being doctors. They get blood on their hands and they back off. You can't be so easily discouraged."

"You're saying I have to stand up," I provided.

"I'm saying you can't be a coward."

Auburn-Stache calls himself a coward, but I didn't like a stranger talking smack.

"Blood is sticky. But I guess you wouldn't mind, so long as the blood wasn't yours."

Wharton did not blink. "It's going to be a struggle, but if we work on it, by the time you're grown up, you could be in full command of this. Walk around without thinking twice about power lines. Just imagine."

I could meet you, Moritz, without worrying about frying your heart. I could take Liz to a sock hop without worrying about sneezing. I could sleep next to a humidifier. Maybe fly one of Arthur's drones.

I don't believe in the c-word. But I want to believe in *better*.

"Ollie, you could be *great*."

"But . . . okay. But how?"

That snaggletooth. "Let's start here. Right now."

"*What?*" I looked at the Dairy Freeze sign. Smoggy cars in the parking lot outside. The blue light of the electric freezers. The purple of the shake machines.

"Ice cream is too sacred to risk. Too precious for this world!"

"See, there's your first problem. You're panicking at just the *idea*. What's the worst thing that happens? There aren't any buses here. If you seize, here's a doctor. Don't panic."

"You gonna give me a towel?"

"Nope. Take a few breaths, hitchhiker." Wharton being a nerd made it harder to hate him.

"You're making it worse. Building the suspense!"

"Why are you so worried?"

"Why do you think? Someone could die." The bored girl behind the tiny ice-cream counter. "No biggie."

"Ollie, you didn't kill your mother."

He kept trying to get me to talk about her, but I won't, Moritz.

"How's this: When you're worried, what soothes you?"

"That's . . ."

Moritz.

You know it's you. Knowing that no matter what, you'll be writing me. Someone out there can talk about all this with me. Even after all the sort of unfair things we do to each other, it's always you. At the dance, where I could have died, you saved me. You've pulled me from lots of dark places, fellow hermit.

"Whatever you're thinking of, hold on to it. And close your eyes."

Very slowly, Wharton pulled my hat from my head.

Tape peeled away.

Rubber tubing slipped.

I breathed in through my nose. Thought of your video to the masses. Thought of the womble you sent me. Thought of you calling me good. Thought of you, just you—

I opened my eyes. Still sitting in the plastic chair at the plastic table.

I hazarded a slow glance at the ice-cream machines and freezers. None of the electricities had reached for me. They kept drifting, like I wasn't there.

A massive convict of a laugh escaped me.

Obviously, that shorted out the fluorescent bulbs, and the girl at the counter shrieked as the freezer gave a rattling sigh.

But Wharton smiled even as darkness fell.

"Told you so."

If he had hungry eyes then, so did I.

Mo, it really wasn't all that different from what Liz and I used to do with the book light. Wharton exposed me to increasing increments of electricity, told me to breathe long and deep, and then asked me to remove my hat.

It began with flashlights and old pagers and digital watches and, later, when he wasn't waiting for me to ruin his livelihood or whatever, he started picking me up in a car that wasn't just a crappy beater from the junkyard-hell dimensions.

Ms. Arana did tell me that if he tried any funny nonsense she'd be having words with his mother before he could say "But."

It was strange; it used to be that Ms. Arana never got up until late, but now she was cooking dinner before she even got ready for work. Brian came home from running laps around the neighborhood and I came home from electro-training one night and found a meat loaf on the table. People in books make a big stink about meat loaf. It's actually dang good, if you ask me. If you eat it with prodigious ketchup, anyhow.

After dinner, I dried the dishes she washed.

"That was great, Ms. Arana." I pulled a python out of a cupboard, shoved the loaf pan in.

"You kids are making an effort to move on with things. It's only right I do the same." She dunked another plate and shook her head. "That asshole isn't coming back. Enough is enough."

My heart missed a beat. But she didn't mean Auburn-Stache.

She poured an insane amount of dish soap onto her palms and began scrubbing her fingers half raw.

"Out, out damned spot?"

"Yeah, honey. I put on some puppies since my wedding day. Oh—there she goes!" I swear I heard the suction-y pop of release as her wedding band slipped from her finger and a clink when it hit the sink.

Brian stood in the doorway behind us. Hoodied as ever. "Can I have that, Mom?"

He held out his hand. She hesitated a second before she handed it over.

We followed Brian into the living room and watched him drop the ring—*ploop!*—right into a fish tank. An angelfish inspected it and lost interest pretty fast.

"It looks nice there," said Ms. Arana, finally.

After I managed to walk up and down a café, hatless, without a single bulb flickering, Wharton upped the game. We went to the back of a small old cemetery, behind a crypt, where there weren't power lines around the graves. He brought a portable generator, the kind for campers who can't handle rustic, and set it up in the grass.

I shielded my eyes, Moritz. That thing was basically a bursting tiny sun.

"You might want to call Doctor Octopus to handle this one, Wharton."

Wharton still had that annoying staring habit. "What color now?"

"Hyperactive peach? I told you, most power lines and generators are in the oranges."

"Maybe that has to do with voltage, or maybe not. Ollie, you say electricity takes on shapes? It flinches away, tries to grab you. Have you ever tried grabbing it back?"

"Wharton, it's not actually tangible. I mean, I know it's just energy."

"Maybe. But you told me sometimes it feels like it has direction or even malicious intent." My old power line nemesis. "Whether or not that's just you projecting, anthropomorphizing something mindless, I want you to *try* manipulating what you see. That's our next step."

"How will this help me drive an amphibicar to Kreiszig?"

"Humor me."

"You want me to just . . . grab the ethereal light? Stick my hands out like the X-Men?"

"Nobody here will laugh at you." He gestured at the tombstones.

"They're a really deadpan crowd."

A gleam of snaggletooth. "That was a *little* funny."

"Fine." I put my fingers to my hat and watched him dart around the tiny sun. He pulled something from his backpack. "What's that thing?"

"Don't worry. Just something electric." It was this little handheld black box, sort of like Arthur's remote control. There was a meter near its center, and it made these sort of light crackling sounds as Wharton tucked it into one of his rubber pockets. (He's got his own dopey suit now.)

I frowned. "What something electric?"

"Don't worry! Just do your thing."

I pulled off my hat and breathed in through my nose. It's becoming so much easier now, Moritz. There's always going to be that slight pressure in my head. Maybe an itch to sneeze. But it doesn't overwhelm me anymore. Even that generator wouldn't get me if I didn't panic. Nothing can get me if I don't think about Mom.

If I think about you razoring Styrofoam tables backstage, listening to the world from your apartment.

Feeling like some kind of idiot, I moved my gloved hands toward the orange light. The arcs of electricity bowing out of the generator didn't exactly snap to attention, but they did start inching my way. Slowly, surely, *creepily*, the tendrils of orange light unspooled from the sun and wound themselves around my rubber arms, poking, prickling. But I thought of you rapping, I thought of you playing metronome for Chloe-Bowie, I thought of you and gritted my teeth over the escalating pounding in my temples, and I let the electricity prod me—

"Wait—Ollie, your nose is bleeding!" called Wharton.

I started, tried to stop the blood, but when I raised my right hand, all the electricity coiled there unspun faster than anything and shot away from me, snapped past the generator, whipping against the wall of the mausoleum.

The force of it flung me back into the grass, jaw slamming shut when my head hit, biting my tongue like the bad old days.

Seconds or maybe minutes later (did I have a seizure?), Wharton's eyes shone bright while he shook my shoulders. "Ollie, I *saw* something. Distorted air! And you scored the mausoleum! Look!" He leapt to his feet, ran his hand over the stone. "You *charred the damn wall.*"

"An accident," I said, sitting up, trembling all over.

"Don't ruin the moment. It'll just take practice." He sounded downright giddy. "Wait until people see this."

I held my nose to my sleeve, tongue throbbing. "Why would anyone ever see this?"

Wharton didn't answer. He held the electric device in his hand close to the charred wall. It let loose a high-pitched wailing sound that made him jerk back. When he held it close to me, it did the same thing. His smile stayed on, but his eyes stopped twinkling.

"What?"

"Nothing. Next time we meet, we're going to the Megamart."

This week, Mr. Elton gave me an A on an open-topic categorical essay I wrote about different kinds of humidifiers (although I used too many parentheses and asides, he says. Whatever, man.) He told me he'd think that someone who could make humidifiers interesting could be a great writer someday.

Ms. Goledge, on the other hand, assigned another electrical lab experiment. It involved electroshocking dead frogs to simulate life. Total Frankenstein rip-off, but kind of awesome. And because of practicing with Dr. Wharton, I just smiled and lined right up with Whitney. We made that dead frog dance, Moritz.

I don't know what's going to happen next, Mo, but I'll keep dancing, too.

chapter thirty
THE GOGGLES (REPRISE)

Oliver. I am glad to know I am your solace. Your towel in times of need. You are mine as well. And yet we have had to walk alone these past few months. We have learned to rely less upon each other and more upon ourselves. Equals, not crutches. This is no terrible thing.

But, Ollie, do be careful of this Wharton and his gleaming eyes. I've seen his kind before.

And your "foreign kid" grows weary of morbid jokes. Our lives are no laughing matter, even if that is how we manage.

Let us see if you will enjoy my gallows humor.

Klaus and I posted my video message on a Sunday night. I anticipated taking a few more days away from school. My medicine in full effect. Drowsiness became me.

I did not expect to be roused in the earliest hours of

Tuesday by the stomping of boots outside my bedroom door.

"Moritz, you twat. Let me the fluff in."

I stumbled out of bed. Took hold of the doorknob before I fully realized the strangeness of what was happening.

Fieke stood in my apartment for the first time in months. Certainly for the first time since her brother and I had parted. Not only that. It was 5:00 AM.

"You'll wake Father." I hurried her into my room. "How did you get in?"

"*Please*, Moritz. Like I can't pick locks."

I paled. "Is it Owen? How is he doing?"

"No, it isn't Owen. Don't talk to me about Owen. That's not your business anymore, is it."

"But—"

"So he fainted. At least you didn't break his ribs like you broke Lenz's."

"It wasn't like that," I told her.

"You think I don't know that? I can feel your fluffing anxiety. Whatever. Accidents happen. Breakups are rough. That's not what I'm here about."

"Then . . . ?"

She sat at my desk, pushing my letters aside. Opened my computer. "You idiot. Shit, Moritz. Come here. Actually, no. Just sit there. Listen. Let me read you some of this."

She muted my laptop and read the comments instead.

"A user called shionezumi: 'Dolphinmo, this forum has

gotten me through some hard times. Knowing it's based on something true makes it mean even more to me! I'm sharing this video and her photo everywhere. We will find her.'"

"A sweet sentiment."

"A user called apples-in-the-orc-yard: 'Moritz, I'm a little older than some of the players. I run a local paper. I'll be running your mother's photo on- and off-line. We will find her.'"

"Very kind."

"Yeah, well, there are, like, hundreds more messages like this. People are posting that photo everywhere. Not just on the forum. I wouldn't say it's gone viral, because that's something dumbasses say, and anyhow this is still pretty low-key, but it kind of has. You've got fangirls, Moritz."

"Oh."

"Don't worry, fanboys, too. And you know what? There are people who want to know more about the lab. Because if it's real, it's fluffing terrible. People love terrible shit."

"Don't they just." Of course Fieke had a hand in the forum. She's expanded my world from the instant we met.

"You blew up this fluffing forum. They're posting possible leads. They want updates! A couple of them claim to be real Blunderkinder." Fieke looked at me. "Wish you could see it."

Rattling breath.

326

"The fluff, Moritz?"

"I can't tell whether you're pleased or furious. Whether I should be happy or terrified."

"Both, you idiot. Both to both statements. But you know what this means? Owen's goofy forum is *working*. It's connecting us to freak kids. And we're going to find your mom. We. Will. Find. Her. It's just a matter of time."

"And then what?"

She smacked the computer closed again and spun the revolving chair around. "Then what? Then you fluffers can start feeling better!" Could Fieke also be emolocating? "You can stop fluffing worrying everyone! Get your shit together!"

"I don't know what to say to him. I do not trust myself."

"I said this wasn't about Owen! Jesus!" Fieke stood. "Look, it's easy. Can you say with any certainty that you're in love with my little brother?"

"I care for him."

"That's not what I asked." She waited.

"It is an unfair question."

"Fine, Herr Emotionally Stunted. Let's try a different one: Can you say with any certainty that you're in love with electro-boy?"

She must have felt the answer.

"There you go. Now I'm going the fluff to school. Some of us are going to graduate this year, damn it."

When we reached the door, I took hold of her arm.

"You came to see me in the hospital. Why?"

"'*Why?*'" She held the door. "*Fluff*. Moritz! You were my friend first. That doesn't have to stop because you suck at relation-shits. Get over yourself." She stomped toward the stairwell. "We will fluffing find her!"

In the wake of the video, the ranks of the experimental forum you and Owen created have swollen to more than two thousand, Ollie.

I spent much of the day listening to messages from our supporters. Wondering what might happen next. Whether shady government operatives would show up at my door. Whether we truly would find her. Whether anyone cared. Perhaps they still thought this an elaborate fiction.

The two who claimed to be actual Blunderkinder gave convincing accounts: there was a boy in England who disgorged his esophagus; I remember him personally. A girl in Taipei with a prehensile tongue. Neither reported any ill effects.

Some users wanted to know where I live. One user claims to attend school with me. Refused to give details. Left this as proof: "Beastie Boys." Someone from Music Interpretation?

Occasional users called me freak. Liar. Cried "faaaaakkkke!" But few and far between. For the most part, strangers helped me. Perhaps Molly is right about people. Perhaps you are.

Before I signed out, I heard a ping. From username thorfinn. Jon, the boy in Iceland.

"Moritz! We will find her!"

Thank you, Jon. Are you well?

"Fine! Are others really becoming ill?"

I do not type what I am thinking.

"Anyhow, we'll find your mother!"

To think. I haven't said my mother may not help even if we do find her. Even if we find her, how can anyone persuade her to do a thing?

For a time I simply sat at my desk. Holding on to hope.

Molly was not on campus when I returned the following week. Klaus waited at the gates and insisted on walking me to my classes, scowling at passersby on my behalf, because he knows I cannot scowl.

"Max has just been strutting around as usual. I don't think he'll try anything."

"I can look after myself."

"If I left it to you, you'd send him to the emergency room again, Farber. And then mope about it."

Inevitably, I would run into the wolf at some point. It was in the second auditorium, in transit to *Belletristik* class. He twisted the hair of another boy around his finger. He saw me, tensed. I considered trying to smother my emotions.

No. Enough.

I made no effort to hide my loathing as Klaus and I passed. The smile dropped off Max's face. He lowered his eyes. Stood as far from me as possible and excused himself from the younger boy's company.

I am ashamed of what I did to Max in the foyer. But if he

is ashamed of what he did to me, I would not be sorry. Not in the least. But he isn't. He'll find others to poison.

We passed out of the building into a sunny spring afternoon. I could smell warmth on the air. I could hear, my ears as keen as ever.

"Beg pardon, Klaus. I may have taken your advice to 'feel things' a bit too literally."

"I don't think so, Farber. You aimed that misery at him, not me. No more excuses about control. He's downright fled the building."

"You're . . . impressed?"

"It's more impressive than your paint jobs. That's for sure."

I stopped walking near the fountain. I could hear someone approaching us. Hesitant, small footsteps. I turned around.

"Moritz." The mousy girl from Dr. Hoppen's class. She held out her hand. "Username sallyringwalden. We *will* find her."

Our slogan. I shook her hand. She nodded, lowered her gaze, and shuffled away.

"Why? Just *why*?" Klaus barked. "You're not even handsome!"

I visited Molly that afternoon. Brought her homework. She pulled off her earmuffs and smiled, but she still looked tired. She's kept herself busy, it seemed. Embroidering.

"Don't worry. Needles in fabric and not in myself today."

"I spoke to your teacher about your midterm. He says

he never sees audience reactions that great for amateur performances. You passed."

"Despite fleeing from the stage."

"Yes. That was considered *dramatic* of you. Full marks."

"You are terrible, Moritz."

"I spoke to Frau Welter also. She said that they'll have you back in your own time. Liberal arts schools. They will stand your foolish drama."

"More than under the weather you're not well at all there's so much wrong with you."

She'd fed her second mouth sticky toffee to muffle it. I found it easier to sit beside her this time.

"How are your ears?"

"Better. Thank you."

"Oh, what's the matter? Don't make me guess, Prince."

I opened my mouth, and she shook her head. "Be direct."

"I'm not Klaus." But I complied. "Molly, how am I better than the ones who hurt us?"

She smiled.

"Don't laugh."

"You say, visiting *me*, the girl who tried to drown you, on her sickbed. How could you not be better?" She shook her head. "Honestly, I think Max could stand to be hurt. I can guess what he tried, Moritz."

"I could floor him with a single click. I know I could." I clicked. "I won't. But can I let him hurt others?"

Molly set down her stitching. She put her hand on

mine. "That boy who dropped out last year—he reported Max. People *laughed*. They didn't believe him. Max is so charming."

"He was all charm today. Until he saw me."

"My charm's worn thin, too." She sat up straight. "Let's wear *his* out for good."

"How?"

Two wide smiles. "How else? Through the dramatic arts."

Her scheme was ludicrous. I did not say so. I projected support, watched her phone legions of classmates. Plan the "event" for the end of the week. Max was more notorious than I knew.

"Did you call Klaus?"

"No, Moritz. He would ask to see me. What an outdated romantic. Real life isn't a stage. Shakespeare was deluded."

"Then your plan is deluded."

"I didn't say I don't *like* delusions."

"Sometimes we only have delusions and sometimes that's better than remembering."

I cannot help but think of her parasols and lace. She would never drown me.

Try to imagine her scheme, Oliver. Imagine from Max's unsuspecting perspective.

Imagine you strut onto campus. Cloaked in cockiness. Imagine you enter the grounds. They are unusually empty for this hour. A few students pass here and there, but no one you know. They do not look at you. Imagine you arrive at breakfast and not a soul is there.

Imagine you are Max and you walk through vacant hallways to your first lesson. And then you enter your first-hour drama class in the auditorium.

There sit more than a hundred students. All of them face away from you. When you laugh and try to reclaim the atmosphere as your own, they all snap their faces toward you. But you cannot *see* those faces. Each and every one of them wears black goggles. Each and every one of the goggles is opaque. Not a soul smiles at you.

Imagine, for the duration of the day, whenever your peers see you, they pull goggles down from their foreheads. They close their mouths and stand still. Follow you with soulless stares. They do not break character. This is Myriad Academy, where such things are mundane. Even the students without goggles don't speak to you. They know you are being targeted. They know something must be wrong with you. You are guilty of something.

Imagine that finally you make a bid for escape. You cannot laugh anymore. Your cockiness has fled you. Imagine that you make for the gate.

But I'm standing there. I'm wearing my goggles. And when you approach me, you are wide-eyed and furious and frightened. Ready to hit me. To bowl me over. When you are directly before me, you realize that the others are all behind you. Watching.

I lift my goggles.

And the nothingness there just screams at you:
"We all *see* you."

I did not pull my goggles back on after Max left my range of hearing. Conversely, the other students, who surrounded me, clapping me on the back or embracing me briefly, did not remove theirs.

I was the only one unhidden. I swear to you, Ollie, I held my head high. Of course, as I made my way across campus, springtime mud and grass clinging to my oxfords, one or two students craned to look at me. Not unkindly. Perhaps because Klaus stood beside me. Or perhaps because something emanated from me in clouds of warmth, emolocating what seeing all those goggles on eyes and around necks and strapped to foreheads meant to me. I cannot see reflections. But I could feel myself reflected in flat lenses. I could feel my relief on the faces of others. And if perhaps I *made* them smile, well, they made me do the same. Does it matter where it began?

Ollie, why has that been so hard for me to see?

In the mess hall, I played perfect metronome and tuner for Chloe-Bowie and her bandmates, and they allowed me to freestyle at the key change in "Ashes to Ashes." I don't know what I said about good and bad things. I've never been one to freestyle. I might do it again. I might try to get better.

After lunch, Chloe threw her glittery arms around my shoulders and walked with me to *Belletristik* class. When Dr. Hoppen asked for volunteers for the warm-up, I put up my hand. There were at least five other hands raised. I was just another student who was not chosen.

But Dr. Hoppen nodded at me.

Perhaps next time.

chapter thirty-one
THE LUNCH BAG

I got chills from reading that, Moritz.

That's the cleverest, creepiest idea. I'm glad you and Molly aren't supervillains. Imagine the world at your begoggled mercy! I'm basically already there, aren't I?

I'm bordering on supervillainy, too. Every day, Moritz, I go to school pretending not to be a ticking bomb. Especially after what happened in the graveyard, it feels like anything could happen.

It almost feels great, doesn't it? Owning the dark parts.

Track season is finally under way!

This Tuesday Bridget and Brian were scheduled to run events at the first district meet at the Christchurch field. Ms. Arana packed up her car with blankets and a cooler of juice boxes and carted us over there in the late afternoon to watch.

"Hey, Danielle!" I waved at the girl at the ticket booth.

"Ollie! I'm going to vote for you." She handed us our tickets.

"Vote for me? What for?"

She sighed. "Student council."

I plucked my shirt like it was a suit jacket. "That sounds very prestigious."

Patrick, a boy leaning on the fence, wrapped an arm around my neck and pounded me on the shoulder. "Bro, you gotta get better and join the team next season."

"I'll just tell the tumors to make way in the name of lacrosse."

We went to the concessions stand for popcorn. Whitney was serving cocoa on one end of the stand and she smiled. I said hi to more kids and fist-bumped Bondage Gabe on our way to the stands.

Ms. Arana was all kinds of bemused. "Honey, you could teach Brian a thing about being popular."

"Nah, I couldn't." I popped kernels into my mouth. "He knows all this stuff. He just doesn't *like* being popular."

"My ex-husband told me I'd be too clueless to raise a teenager on my own. Now that I have two of them, I know he was right."

"Sometimes you talk stupid, Ms. Arana. I'm only here because you gave me a backpack."

Brian wasn't in the first two events, but I cheered pretty hard anyhow because I knew some of the kids running them. Ms. Arana told me off for booing the opposing schools, but isn't that what you're supposed to do? Brian sat on the bench on the edge of the track looking as skulky as ever. Maybe his coach wouldn't let him wear his hoodie.

The 200-meter race is tricky, according to Chelsea, the track captain (I sit next to her in social studies), because it's not exactly long distance or a sprint. It's that awkward in-between. The first heat of racers lined up and Brian was one of them. That meant he was in the fastest group. Go figure!

The gun went off. "FORTH, BRIAN!"

It wasn't over in a heartbeat or two, but maybe ten. Brian came in fourth out of eight, which made him the most awkward and in-between of all.

"He wasn't trying." Ms. Arana wasn't angry, just making an observation.

Brian obviously didn't care about this race. He ignored the drinking fountain and skulked on over to the bench to sit by his stuff.

That was when I noticed that his stuff? It included a *brown paper bag*.

"Ollie! Where are you—"

I was halfway down the stands already, and then I was leaping the bannister and hitting the ground and leaning up against the fence to holler at him.

"Brian! Hey! Come here!"

He rolled his eyes and trudged over. "Come to tell me to try harder?"

"Nah. I want to know why you packed a very hearty lunch today."

Blank face. "Don't worry about it."

"You always say that. It never actually unworries me."

He shoved his hands into his pockets, except he didn't have pockets and he ended up looking like a dope. "I'm going to catch her. But I can't win against her. I can't actually chase her down. I have to do it the loser way."

"Um, what does that involve?"

"Watch." He slouched back to the bench.

"Whoa, whoa," I called, grinning. "Who's this cocky youngster standing before me?"

"Shut up, freak."

I headed back to the concession stand. This was going to require more popcorn.

Bridget took an easy first in the 1600-meter. We hollered and cheered for her, and I came down to the fence for a fist bump. I noticed Brian on the bench, clutching the lunch bag but hardly moving an inch.

"I think you'll be able to stop running pretty soon," I told her. "If you want to. Metaphorically speaking."

She blinked. "Today's not any different. I don't want it back."

"If you say so." I returned to the sidelines. Chelsea said I could watch from the bench.

I grinned. "I'm your mascot! "

"Too scrawny." I high-fived all the girls before they jogged to the starting line. Bridget's hand was cold. I fived her the highest.

She geared up with something like eighteen other runners for the 3200-meter. Two miles. Eight laps around. Spaghetti limbs can't even *consider* it.

Bridget pulled her knees behind her. Stretched her arms and legs like a pro. That expressionless face: tough luck beating Bridget, girls. (Hey, everyone was thinking it.)

And it went pretty much as expected for the first six laps or so. Bridget got way ahead of the other runners. People in the crowd hollered her name! Probably her nice foster parents hollered hardest. Every time she passed I hardly heard her feet pounding like pistons.

I'd almost forgotten Brian was there, until he stood up. He watched racers pass and sauntered closer to the track.

Bridget came around the corner, way ahead of everyone else.

Brian skulked out right in front of her, lunch bag in hand.

A gasp from the crowd—

Bridget stopped on a dime in front of him.

"This is how losers catch people."

"I don't want it back." But she didn't run. She let people pass her. She *waited*.

Brian reached into the bag. I had my fingers on my eyes. The drama! The suspense!

He reached into the bag and pulled out . . .

. . . a sandwich. An actual sandwich without a heartbeat. Wheat bread, possibly.

"Have lunch with me again. I don't care if you're heartless or not. It doesn't matter to me. If you don't want your heart back, fine. And if you do, fine. Whatever. But have lunch with me?"

Bridget blinked.

Four more runners passed.

Bridget took the sandwich from Brian. Peeled the bread apart. "Tuna fish . . . and potato chips?"

A ref hobbled over, blowing his whistle. The audience started booing.

"If you ever do want me to pack your heart as well, I will. Not that I mind holding on to it. I like you not liking things. Or I like you liking them. I guess."

"I'll have lunch with you."

I tore my hat off and whooped and not a single stadium bulb flickered.

This Friday I'm supposed to brave the Megamart with Wharton. I'm not afraid.

Moritz, do you think one day I could play electricity like a glock?

chapter thirty-two

THE BALCONY

Ollie, consider: There are people rooting for us, and people we root for. So many others populate our lives now! They leave their marks. Your marks remain best, tucked in folders. Tears and smears and all, Ollie. You are near me.

I'm not jealous of Arthur, only sorry I've never heard his guffaw. I'm not jealous of Bridget, only wishing I could take the laboratory out of her. Ollie, I want to meet them. I'm sorry I never have.

And you! You've never seen Molly's curls! Her smiles!

If only writing could convey every aspect of all of us.

We take what we can get.

The Sunday after we chased Max from campus, I visited Molly once more. This time she hopped forward to meet me in a cotton dress.

I handed her a set of goggles. "A token of thanks."

She pulled the goggles into her hair, holding the strap in her back teeth before snapping them onto her forehead. Another fetching accessory, on her.

"It's quieter today." I walked to her window and opened it.

"My mouth?" She smiled halfheartedly as I leaned on the balcony. "Yes, well. It's been a happier day. Fewer dark thoughts when things go well. Putting Max in his place is heartening. The progress on the forum is heartening. We will find her."

"You're on the forum?"

"Oh, don't act so surprised. I think half the student population is on the forum now. It was something else we talked about after the goggle scare. Role-players. All those people pretending to be other people! More actors, Prince."

"You can't call me that today."

"Oh, you have to know by now that it's a term of endearment."

"It's not that. Consider the feelings of your other Prince."

I waved her onto the balcony. Molly gasped.

Standing a floor below the balcony. Clad in a cape. Klaus. Not frowning.

"Now, Moritz?" he shouted. "Or what?"

"Yes," I shouted, "but for the love of god, uncross your arms."

Klaus held his hands in fists against his sides and hollered at the top of his formidable lungs, "But soft, what light through yonder window breaks?"

"Shut up," gasped Molly, from both mouths.

From an acting standpoint, it was a disappointment after that.

"What? Don't interrupt!" hollered Klaus. "I don't have it memorized all the way! Just give me a moment!"

Molly held one hand over each smiling mouth.

"Soft! What light through yonder window breaks? It is the . . . *fich*. It's the east and Molly is the sun! Arise, fair sun, because, erm, you're better than the moon, who is really too pale. Anon!"

Hysterical giggles from both sides. "This is terrible!" she called down. "What gives you the right to butcher Shakespeare?"

"I only know twentieth-century stuff. Moritz says you like old, romantic crap!"

She spun to face me. "'Romantic crap'!"

"Beg pardon."

"Shakespeare's fine," she called, "but I prefer *Twelfth Night*."

Even as I backed away, I imagined Klaus scowling and crossing his arms. "I don't even know that one! What's it about? I'll improvise!

"It's about people pretending to be what they aren't." Smiles dipped.

"Fine!" cried Klaus. "Molly, I love you on the tenth night and the eleventh night or the thirty-seventh night. Not just on the twelfth one! Even if you like really old plays by dead guys. And if you wanted me to build a tin roof for a Tennessee Williams play, I would. And if you wanted to hide who you are, fair, um, lady, I'd laugh at you because I would love you even if you had seventeen heads and all of them had hairy mustaches."

"*What about two mouths could you love a girl who was always hissing that she wasn't sure about you and not sure about herself?*"

Klaus didn't miss a beat. "Molly! If that's all it is, then Mother will be chuffed! Someone more outspoken than I am!"

Molly was damn near sobbing. "Can't you at least try to stay in character?"

"No. I'm not an actor, and I'm not acting."

Molly didn't have the energy to hurry down to meet him. And Klaus did not wish to charge through the orphanage. So he walked politely into the building. Politely up the stairs. Politely down the hallway. Stood politely in Molly's doorway.

Molly's hands, clasped in front of her. She bit her lip. And then Klaus rushed to embrace her. Molly tried to clamp her second mouth shut, but it continued chattering. Blurting out random Juliet lines. Klaus hushed her, pulling her head to his chest.

I eased out of the room, entirely forgotten, as I should be in this case.

Eugen stood in the hallway, blowing his nose in a handkerchief. He led me down to the lobby and all but collapsed at the front desk. Two children with pigtails in their hair hurried by.

"Goodness. Since she was a napping child we've worried

about the poor girl. It talked in her sleep. Our Molly, full of sad thoughts."

I should not be surprised by anything anymore. "You all knew."

Frau Andert sighed. "Who do you think knit those muzzles for her?"

She threw a set of earmuffs at me.

"I do hope you find your mother. And keep your ears warm, dolphinmo."

Blunderkinder among us. And us among them, Ollie, for as long as we're able.

chapter thirty-three

THE DEVICE

Moritz, everything went wrong today. Right when I thought I was on top of the world.

I'm scared. I'm scared, and worse than that . . . I'm scary.

Moritz. It's all over.

Everything.

The automatic doors spun open in curls of gold followed by every shade of green, an electric lime sea.

I stepped into the Electronics Megamart on St. Patrick's Day.

Dr. Wharton walked a few paces behind me, doing his staring gig with his hands in his pockets.

I couldn't believe how much *stuff* was in there. Counters full of laptops and tablets and screens, screens every-freakin'-where. Walls covered in screens, too. Tables and tables of phones. I know you remember my thirteenth birthday party, Moritz. How Liz set up a makeshift room full of fake appliances so I could pretend to have what everyone else has. But now I was in a room of actual electrical appliances, and I couldn't think why anyone would ever need them. So many flat-screens. Screens that wouldn't reflect a thing until someone looked at them. They were meaningless until someone looked at them.

Well, I was looking, through green smoke textured like seaweed.

"May I help you?" asked a desperate-looking guy in a polo.

Dr. Wharton smiled. "Sure you can. Show us to your most expensive items!"

The guy sort of grimaced but smiled at the same time and led us to more and more screens that I guess were bigger and techier somehow.

"Ready, Ollie?" whispered Dr. Wharton. "Moment of truth."

I closed my eyes as Dr. Wharton tugged off my hat. Some of the heaviest pressure I've ever felt eased into me, then, as I breathed slowly and imagined dolphin waves, it lessened. I opened my eyes. None of the green electricity made a break for me. It just coated everything in emerald. I was on the seabed, staring at a reef that couldn't care less.

I took slow steps down the aisle. The monitors blared sound and color at me. But those things were not reaching for me. Not stretching. Just hanging out like I wasn't there. I *had* this. By the end of the aisle, I was almost smiling, too.

Wharton, right behind me: "It *is* your fault she died, though."

I sucked in air (not water) and pivoted slowly to face him. "What?"

"Yeah. You heard me." He showed his tooth. "Your mom was so busy worrying about you she never took care of herself."

I shook my head and the electricity rippled around me—the screen next to me flickered, and the one next to it, too. I took a deep breath.

Remembered my dreams of you in the deer blind, Moritz, pulling me out. Out.

Prickles on my bare temples.

I needed to get out.

Wharton stepped right up to me, hands in his pockets. I don't know where he put my hat. "Not to mention she was only exposed to the laboratory so you could be born. That's a lot of guilt to carry around."

All the electricity was caught in a new current, the current of me. Wriggling feelers tracing me, making my head pound.

"And you know something else, Ollie?" Wharton pulled the nameless black device from his coat. "This? This device is called a Geiger counter. Do you know what it measures?"

I shook my head; schools of sparks flurried away. "Stop it."

Children were playing handheld games in the aisle behind me. Moritz, I needed out—

"It measures ionizing radiation. See, after you blew out the ice-cream parlor, I went home with this really nasty sunburn. In January! Didn't take much to put two and two together."

I spun on my heel. An ocean erupted around me as I made for the door.

"Do you know what else radiation causes?" he called while people yelped in the aisles, watching screens spark to white and black. "Cancer, Ollie!"

Dr. Wharton increased his pace to match my own. He got in front of me.

"You really should have stayed in the woods."

I tried to think of your face, but her face, her face when she was dead, openmouthed and blank-eyed in bed, came to the front. Her face in the kitchen when she told me that she wanted to keep me. Her face when I was concussed from a bike crash and she told me not to run away again. Her, sobbing outside my door, lying on the floorboards with her wig slipping.

When I shoved Wharton out of the way, he didn't resist. Green sparks obscured my vision. I raised my hands, took hold of the waves, and thrust them away from me. Screens sparked and popped on either side of me; speakers caught fire.

Wharton looked up at the lights and laughed.

You told me to be careful, but I was drowning anyhow.

The automatic doors stayed stuck open for me, and his car was parked near the front of the lot, but I kept walking right past it, to the far edge of the parking lot, the edge of the visible world. But there was no getting away from this. This was a shopping plaza. The more places I went, the more places I would ruin. The more people I'd meet.

I crouched down in an empty space and closed my eyes and fought to remember you.

"Ready or not." I breathed through my nose. "Ready or not."

I was kneeling in an icy pothole puddle, and that brought back something else: the day Liz appeared on our front step, coated in mud. And Mom laughed and shoved me out the door without my coat on, tears in her eyes as she sent me to play in the rain.

Honestly, I don't know why I was so worried, she'd said.

I know now. Do I ever know. Moritz, tell me you didn't. Tell me you didn't know.

Wharton's footsteps crunched cold gravel. Far from us, on the other end of the parking lot, people fled the Megamart.

"Sorry, not sorry. I had to see if that was still a trigger. And it is. If we're going to move forward, Kilimanjaro, you need to accept the facts."

"In a public place? If I'm . . . radioactive." Oh god, Moritz. "People could *die*." Oh god.

"Come on, Ollie." He shook his head. "People *have* died already. And so what? Say what you want, but I know it's worth it. I'm putting up with the burns because science is worth it."

"Science? Oh god. You're *nuts*."

"No. I'm an entrepreneur. And you're what careers are made of."

That gleam in his eyes, that snaggletooth.

"Get away from me."

"Yeah? Where are you going to go? You'll be deadly anywhere you end up, without my help. I'm your shot at controlling this, Ollie. Don't forget."

I watched him go to his car. The Fiat, not the Morgoth monster.

I took a numb, horrible breath. I followed, feeling nothing at all. (Help, Moritz. Help.)

I didn't get in the car. He rolled down the window.

He tossed my hat at me. I caught it and held it tight. "Get in the car, why don't you."

She knitted that, Moritz, because she hoped I might leave the woods. But I *am* the woods.

"Just get in the—"

I let the light smog of his vehicle creep up onto me. I lifted my hand, let the smog lick my fingertips and wind around them, and closed my fist on the threads.

351

If I had your ears, Moritz, I'd have heard him swearing when the engine popped.

I walked. I knew Fayton landmarks now. I could walk back just fine. I knew exactly which gray house was Brian and Ms. Arana's gray house, which gray house was Bridget's gray house.

I hit the road and walked in the exact opposite direction and didn't stop.

Tell me it's a lie, or at least the brother of one.

You can't pull me out of the dark place when the dark place is me.

chapter thirty-four

THE URN

Ollie, Dr. Auburn-Stache canceled his visit. Rain check.

I am forwarding this to you. It is only right. Please know that I am here, even if nowhere near. Please know you've come through all sorts of forests, and the last thing you deserve is to be condescended to.

Ollie, please don't be reckless.

Dear god, I'm worried you've walked into traffic. Ollie.

Moritz,

I apologize for not calling, but some words are hard to say and easier to type. I'm postponing your scheduled checkup. I've been preoccupied with pressing matters in Chicago.

Arthur asked to be cremated. Beau was sure to joke about it at the wake. I don't think many of the mourners laughed. Chicago people are hard. Industry in their blood, the struggle to stand tall in their veins. If they did not appreciate the humor, they could understand it. Arthur had many friends, it seemed. I don't know what sort of people they were, as all I saw of them were confused faces. That's all I often see of people these days; there's a wall between myself and other people, people who've never had a hand in harming children.

Beau said some words, but all I can remember was a joke in poor taste: "Art said he'd been trying to fall to pieces for years and hadn't done it properly."

Morbid talk, but where else is such talk justified? And essentially that's what had happened to Arthur, on my watch. Far from my first funeral, hopefully close to my last.

After the services, she had invited the mourners to her duplex for "scenic views of an alleyway and terrible casseroles."

The urn sat on the stoop between us. Beau smoked her cigar like she might any other day. There were no words worth saying, only inane questions worth asking, and one of them I asked: Had Arthur asked for his ashes to be spread anywhere?

She told me that was none of my business, that my business should have been the business of stopping this outcome. She accused me of playing favorites. All this she did quietly, because the weight of the words was worse than shouting ever could have been. She was smoking, of course, and the smoke is still in my nostrils. I may take up cigarettes again.

Beau is correct, of course. I have been playing favorites. I have ignored overwhelming evidence, Moritz, kiddo, and perhaps I sent you on a wild-goose chase when I asked you to seek your mother. I've spent the last few months in denial, wandering like a vagrant, and Beau's saying so, with smoke on her breath, cold ice under us, made this impossible to ignore.

Beau asked a final question. "Tell me, do you think he'll thank you for this?"

I had no answer, and she told me we'd just have to count the funerals.

Arthur asked for his ashes to be scattered in the sky. But Beau told him no.

"I told him 'You're mine and I'm keeping you,' and good kids don't argue with their grandparents."

I couldn't bear to hear any more, Moritz. I'm always going to be a coward.

I drove down the street, and in the rearview mirror, Beau clutched the urn like an infant.

Moritz, Arthur fell ill within hours of meeting Ollie. In those hours, his unique anatomy experienced in high-speed concentration the selfsame symptoms that eventually ended the life of Ollie's mother.

We've always known Ollie's body emits electromagnetic pulses. But I've often ignored the knowledge that electromagnetic radiation can be as innocent as beams of light, or as corrosive as gamma rays. The niggling suspicion that Ollie could be radioactive as well as electromagnetic was one I've always been eager to dismiss. After all, surely I myself would be cancerous by now. Surely his childhood friend, Liz, would be.

That is the selective nature of denial. Of course I realize that low doses of radiation may take years to accumulate to hazardous proportions. Some people who witnessed Hiroshima died in days, and others lived for decades before tumors developed. After the Chernobyl disaster, exposure to tainted water resulted in birth defects before early deaths.

When Ollie was small, he laughed so loud that birds took flight.

How could I let myself suspect that Ollie could be as deadly as he is lively? How could any world be so cruel as that? How could mankind create such a tragedy, and how could I have a hand in it? How could such consequences continue to devastate, years after my actions?

How can I ever face him? How can I live with knowing that the very moment I tell him the extent of those consequences, he may never laugh again? How can I ever be honest?

Moritz, it isn't that Ollie can never meet you.

He can never meet anyone.

Gregory Auburn-Stache

Oliver Paulot, you are so loved. This is your sickness and never you. You better every life you enter. God, can I attest to that. Please do not be rash. Please stop to breathe. Please.

I have been so happily lost in the woods of you.

chapter thirty-five
KRYPTONITE

Moritz.

Poor, poor fucking Arthur. You didn't meet him but he was IMPOSSIBLE AND MIRACULOUS and cool and he was stoner *superman* and I guess that makes me kryptonite. I can't stop gagging and there's nothing left to spit up. Moritz, can I have Auburn-Stache send my ashes to you? Moritz, I'm wondering if all my letters to you are radioactive too. Like Marie Curie's documents. How can I just keep writing then? What sucks is I want to anyhow. But this isn't about me. It doesn't matter what happens to me. This stupid damp letter and my stupid bad handwriting and knowing that every day only counts because I was counting them and our letters were counting them, me counting you and you counting me and I guess I don't get more than that. But you should get more than that. You should get letters that aren't radioactive and in the meantime you should burn the ones on your desk, please tell me you'll burn them? I could die tomorrow or kill three people tomorrow and I don't want you to worry either way, okay man. I want you to have the world Moritz and even though it's selfish after you already gave me SO FUCKING MUCH of your time and so much of your life, it still wasn't enough for me, I can't think of a future without your sarcasm and I wish I could spend every day writing you and if that's not love, then I don't know what is and I'm sorry I've been so stupid about that. I want to spend today writing you *one last time* but I can't even tell a story, I can't think of anything funny, like I started writing a pun about "urning the future" but I gagged instead. I can't even remember what I'm writing. Moritz, I'm not the superhero. I'm not the villain. I'm walking death. But I'm choosing not to be that. I'm choosing to stop being. I'm going to stop.

Good-bye, fellow hermit. Thank you for the world.

chapter thirty-six

THE RETORT

Oliver Paulot. *Walking death* is the farthest thing from what you are.

I am not confessing love. I'm confessing life.

I was half-dead for years. My heart stopped in an anechoic chamber, and for half a decade afterward, I believed my resuscitation unsuccessful. Every beat of my mechanical heart amounted to nothing but vacuous sound. Convinced me of nothing but my emptiness. Every beat, a hole.

Your letters became another pacemaker. A tattoo to counter the voids. Every damn word plugged meaning into my existence. Reminded me there'd been meaning all along. That even the holes themselves were a sign of life.

We are not dictated by what we are. We become our choices. This was no choice of yours.

So the beanie's been pulled off you again.

Remember the world is full of wonders. Remember there may be answers we cannot guess at. With my mother and elsewhere. Remember the world is vast, Ollie. There will always be a place for you in it. There has been for a long time.

Ollie, let me be your *Geborgenheit*. Your shelter, your safety. The place that contains all the thorny pieces of you. Please accept the confines of my patchwork heart.

chapter thirty-seven

THE MESSAGE

Ollie. The Blunderkinder story continues. I choose to believe you remain part of it.

It's been a while since I heard from you, but you are forever on my mind.

I choose to remain calm. I choose to believe the best, because believing otherwise—

Suffice it to say I know something of what Auburn-Stache felt when he would rather lie to himself than think of a world without you in it.

Of late I've spent a lot of time on the Blunderkinder forum. Speaking to the people there. Learning who they are. Trawling through old threads that have existed for months despite my ignoring them. I think I have been trying to fill the silence you left me with.

Ollie. I want to share with you something I found.

I found a message. A thread titled "Beanie Guy" on the

board. Upon printing the pages, I held them close. I hope you will do the same. I hope you will not recoil from this.

username wrightguy:

Hello World!!!!

Thoght I'd use this space to try to send a message to Beanie Guy who visited me. And he told me about this place in one of his letters that I never wrote back to him on because guys I'm not good at writing, I'm better at bilding shit, I mean I can't even spell for shit

I forgot what I was saying and that keeps happening

Oh Yeah

Basicly yeah I can't build anything anymore and I can't get out of bed to go to the mailbox and send a letter now anyhow so maybe one day when one of you guys meets Beanie Guy you can tell him I wrote this? One of youll definately meet him because hes trying to meet all of you and I think hes like a dog chasing cars and he willll catch us eventuly. No offense Beanie Guy.

So the reason I'm writing even tho I'm shit at writing is because that night you were at my house and you asked me what happened to my arm and I told you and then you asked me WHY I punched some kid even tho my bones are chalk and I pretended to be sleeping and I didn't tell you. Yeah that was Lame of me Beanie Guy but you know even tho you said I'm Cool sometimes I'm really Cool at being lame lol.

And you wanted to interview me like I matter which made you so much cooler but I didn't want to tell you the story because I thoght it wasn't a good enogh story for your collection. But you know now,

362

that i might kick the bucket any day I want to do something nice for you because you did something nice for me. So mano e mano!

Here's the story of why I punched a guy and my arm exploded.

I can never ever win a fight, no way in chalky hell. When people look at me they see skinny arms and ugly legs and people say stupid shit all the time and its so, so not worth getting broken over. But there was this OTHER kid this guy who takes special classes and worrys about shit I never even notice. Like he counts lockers and tiles and he can't step on cracks and he Screams like he's dying when other guys bump into him.

He was differnt and that made me like him. I mean I wanna scream when people run into me because, when people run into me yeah I can break BONES. but beau always tells me to laugh it off and that's what I do. but I guess I liked this kid, Locker Guy, because he dosent front. He just does HIM. That's cool. That's how I wish you were to Beanie Guy but you're more like me, I think you laugh when your scared.

But there are these assholes at my school. They glued a penny to the ground in the hallway one time at break just to screw with Locker Guy because they know it bugs him like drives him up the wall when things are messy. So the bell rang and Locker Guy was late for class and I saw it happen because I was skipping.

Locker Guy started crying waterfalls trying to pull that penny off that ground. He didn't care when I told him it was glued. Maybe if my toes weren't shit I could of helped him kick it loose. But the kids who COULD of helped, the Asshole Guys, just watched and snorted like pigs.

So I didn't care how much it sucks. I punched one of the Assholes. And then I ruined my arm for good and then I got suspsended.

363

THE END

I told you it wasn't a very good story. But I wanted to do something nice for you after you did something nice for me Beanie Guy. If you are thinking what nice thing you did then I'm not surprised Olly because, you are the kind of person who does nice things by accident. The nice thing you did for me wasn't just calling me cool, it was bigger than that. When you met me you didn't care what i looked like, you just cared about what I made and how I lived and shit.

I don't know why I'm only getting sicker and, I just want to say that was cool. Maybe your right. Maybe things that die can't be replaced, maybe if you can't I can't either. Because if I'm gonna die I thought at first maybe it'd be okay, because I didn't want to live in a world where Locker Guy is waterfalls and assholes are laughing at kids like him or kids like us.

But now I feel like if you were in the hallway with me and that crying kid and those Assholes you would of kicked the coin for him and no one would of got punched, olly.

I just wanted to tell you that you make the world cooler. Stay you, guy.

chapter thirty-eight

THE SKY

Ollie,

I am writing you from the sky.

I am typing with trembling hands. Airplanes hum so loudly. The air here is clearer than the air in trains and cars. It is clearer but clogged with pressure. I am grateful for the hand I hold.

I am not alone on this flight.

I thought the events of our lives had sufficiently overwhelmed me for the time being.

But no. Allow me to copy another message to you, received while I've waited for any sign of life from you. I have to warn you that it contains more unorthodox English. My computer did not read it well. From username genekittenkelly:

hey. maybe you won't believe me. but i know where ur mom is.
i live somewhere really boring and maybe that's why i'm always

*trolling but anyhow, since you asked everyone 2 look 4 ur mom
i went to all the places i like, spamming things like 5chan and
fumblr and seddit and i posted her pic everyywhere for two weeks
and even hacked some sites and made that picture the homepage.
it was pretty sick, but the fbi was getting real pissy. but whatever.
i have my ways.*

anyhow. *someone on the board, username area51? ze sent me
an sms saying ze knows this lady, like she's zir's actual neighbor in Arkansas. i told zir, yeah, so give me proof. and ze sent
me this:*

My frustration knew no bounds. Screens tell me nothing!
I printed the picture and clicked at it. Heart in throat.

A face shadowed by a sun hat. But a face I knew. I knew
the hollows under its eyes and the lines around its mouth.
Could almost feel the chill.

I have those lines.

I wanted to write you. I wrote to the board instead:
We may have found her.

I thought the rapid-fire responses and emoticons would
have been audible even if my computer had been voiceless.

Not even five hours after I announced we had found my
mother on a separate continent the Blunderkinder gathered
funds to send me to Arkansas. I did not ask them to, but still
they did. I did not refuse this charity.

Some things are more important, Oliver.

I arrived at the airport four hours early. Frau Pruwitt
joined me on the sidewalk. She looked younger to me when
we picked her up. Somehow.

"I won't shake your hand, Moritz. You stopped coming to work."

"You stopped coming to our apartment," I replied.

"Your father came to mine instead. You didn't think he was working *all* the time?"

"But . . . but why?"

Did she blush. I regretted asking when she said, "You hear too much, Moritz Farber."

"Right." Prepared never to look at her again. She pulled me into a stiff embrace.

Father stood behind me, uncertain and silent. For fare-wells, we revert to quiet. He asked whether he should come in with me. I shook my head.

"It'll be noisy in there. I'll see too well." I did not want to see good-bye.

Neither of us said anything else. There are things I can never manage to tell my Father. My gratitude that he saved me. That he appreciates the loneliness and the silence. We do not say these things.

A minute passed. I stood on the sidewalk. He shook my hand. Set down my suitcases. They got in the car and pulled away.

I stepped into the terminal.

A small line of people awaited me. You may wonder how I knew it was me they waited for, in a place so bustling and bright. I knew. All of them, understand, were wearing goggles. Presumably black. Not haunting, this time. Hoping.

One by one, they introduced themselves by username.

Two of them had joined after seeing the video. One of them had been there from the beginning. Five of them were my age; three of them were a decade older, and one was in her sixties. They shook my hand. Embraced me. Wished me well. Were we all friends?

At the end of the line of Blunderkinder who wanted to hold me were four people who weren't strangers at all.

First came Klaus and Molly.

"I've already replaced you in Stagecraft. Don't come back expecting we'll take you. You and your stick-insect limbs are stuck in America until you sort this mess. Or longer."

"Don't drown," Molly told me from both sides. Her arms on my neck. She stands on steady feet again. Smelling of cherries and sawdust now.

"There are worse things," I whispered into her shoulder.

I could hear that Fieke's piercings were not made of metal today, but of plastic. Her boots remained.

"Fieke. I—"

"Let me get a fluffing word in, will you? Username nadi-aproblem. Username cortexualann. We will fluffing find your fluffing motherfluffing mother, motherfluffer."

"Should I applaud?"

"No, but take my suitcase." She tapped a wheeled bag. "I'm delicate. And don't look at me like that. I took your job at the library after you left. I just happen to want to go to the States now that I've graduated early."

"*Fieke!*"

"Yeah. This graduate wants to meet Wes Anderson. No argument."

She stepped aside. Of course I had known he was behind her from the moment I entered the terminal. Terminals are noisy places. The echoes of him are familiar. But I have come to appreciate dramatic gestures.

Owen looked taller than when I'd last seen him. Older. In his hand he held a spiral notepad. He held up his finger and wrote: *Moderator. Username bachandbeyond.*

"Owen." I focused my regret directly on him, but gently. Granted him some sense of how I felt without crushing him. "All you've done. The board. This flight. I could thank you a thousand times, and you'd deserve more."

Owen lowered his notebook. Looked at me. He did not look regretful. He did not look angry. What did he look? Did we have any branches left to us?

"Have I ever known you, Owen?"

Even if he could speak, he would not have answered that. This was all. He leaned forward—

I removed my goggles just in time, savored that final branch before the tree fell for good. When I pulled the lenses down once more, the warmth of his lips stayed trapped beneath them.

Surrounded by a circle of hope holders. It would not do to upset them. It would not do to let them feel my sadness. Owen and I parted in silence.

Fieke and I turned away from the group of friends and strangers in the security line. I did turn my head so they'd know I was looking. The begoggled group waited for us to pass out of sight.

For them I would smile in this airport. It is not the same

as hiding. It is more like entrusting others to know what you feel. As you must trust them to convey their own feelings back. Or some such moral lesson. Don't laugh, Oliver.

Fieke and I raised our hands and passed beyond the glass wall.

Not drowning. Waving.

Fieke just elbowed me: "Close the fluffing window. The glare's in my eyes."

It's given me a perfect thought. Do you know what gives many people cancer? The sun, Ollie.

Even though I've never seen the sun, I would never give up that which keeps me alive.

chapter thirty-nine
THE LEAVES

Moritz, that's so messed up.

What's more messed up: I'm writing you again. I'm still here.

Maybe all your poetic nonsense makes me want to irradiate you.

Or maybe you brought me back a little, *Geborgenheit*.

I didn't trip. I walked until I couldn't walk anymore, skirting around people on sidewalks. Beyond the Megamart were more businesses, followed by more neighborhoods, and I walked past those, too, and I started to wonder how long it would take to walk back to the woods. I wondered what the road signs for entering Michigan would say. "Welcome Back, You Murderous Freak," maybe.

By the time I reached the end of Fayton's sidewalks and started dragging my feet down the shoulder, dusk made all the approaching headlights bright as daggers. Falling on a dagger is pretty Shakespearean, Moritz. I stopped on the shoulder and took a step closer to the road. I don't know what I was thinking. I don't think I was thinking. But really, Moritz. Logically, if there's one person who'd always hurt other people, you give them the Max treatment. You make them stare into dark lenses. Or the bright lenses of head-lights.

I'd gotten used to the passing cars whipping up the air, but suddenly the air moved differently behind me—

Before I heard her footsteps, I'd been tackled to the ground.

Bridget sat on my back. I buried my face in the gritty shoulder of the road, squeezing grass with my hand.

"Bridget, get off me."

She didn't budge.

"Seriously, Bridget. You shouldn't *touch* me. I'm probably killing you. Right this minute I'm making you sick."

She shrugged; I could feel it.

"You have to get off me! *Please*, Bridget. Please. Please."

Bridget shrugged.

"Please. I killed my mom."

Bridget reached a warm hand down to my face and pulled my beanie over my ears.

"Don't touch me! You can't touch me—"

"Breathe, Oliver Paulot."

"I can't," I sobbed. "There's all this . . . *weight* on me."

We both knew I didn't mean her.

"Breathe. You can survive anything if your blood keeps flowing."

I inhaled damp asphalt, let the tension leave my neck. "The world doesn't want me."

Bridget shrugged. "Never wanted me, either. We've still got to live in it."

"How did you find me so fast?"

"I always know where the pieces of me are," Bridget said simply.

"I'm not a piece of you," I told her.

She shrugged. "Just stating my opinion."

"Since when . . . do you . . . have opinions?" I asked the pavement, grit on my lips.

Bridget got up, kneeled down next to me to find my eyes.

Moritz, her face was *alive*. Eyes welling with tears, puffy bags underneath, tracks down her cheeks from hours of feeling.

I let the grass in my hands go.

"Since I felt like it," she said, and smiled the saddest smile I've ever seen.

Turns out Bridget didn't run all the way to the edge of town. Turns out Brian answered the door when Wharton came looking for me, scattering the torn pieces of my School Daze certificate up on the doorstep, threatening to give me a living autopsy until Brian slammed the door on his fingers. Turns out Brian ran straight out the back, leaping fences like hurdles on his way to Bridget's house, and she took one look at his face and demanded her heart back. Turns out Ms. Arana got home in time to find Bridget gasping, full of feeling again. Turns out she drove Brian and Bridget to the Megamart and beyond, all over town, asking if anyone had seen Ollie—yes, *that* Ollie, the weird, new transfer student. Turns out Ms. Arana's were some of the headlights I'd stared into, the brake lights that stopped up ahead.

By the time Bridget got me off the ground, Ms. Arana was barreling my way—

"Don't touch me—"

Warm arms almost broke me in half. "Ollie! I've just heard from your doctor! He's coming to get you! Just make it to the weekend! I don't let my strays die on me."

"Don't touch me." I couldn't get loose. "I'm radioactive."

She leaned back to look at me. "Always have to stand out, don't you? Now, get in the car."

"No. You don't get it. I might be *killing* you."

"Honey, there are so many things in this world that could kill me. Cars and bullets and heart attacks and shark bites and falling trees in storms. A hug won't kill me, and won't kill you."

Brian punched me on the shoulder when she pushed me into the backseat.

"Don't touch—"

"You're not my mom."

Bridget reached back from the passenger seat to pat me on the knee. That was it.

The whole drive home, no one complained about my tearslaughtery racket. Yeah, I was laughing under the sobs. This was ridiculous, Moritz.

I can't let the sort of people who'd hug me anyway just . . . hug me anyway.

By the end of the week, I thought school might have been a dream. Or I would have, if classmates hadn't arrived on my doorstep every day with get-well gifts. I saw Chelsea and Whitney and Patrick through the curtains, watched Ms. Arana thank them and refuse them entry. So even if she was okay with me killing her, she wasn't sacrificing the high schoolers anymore.

Not only was I killing her, I was stealing her vacation days. And Brian was driving me nuts, too. He kept coming home late, but now

374

he had this shit-eaten grin, which probably meant he and Bridget were having lunch together. And he kept sitting on my couch with me.

"Don't. I'll kill you."

"I'll fight you."

"I've seen you fight."

"And you couldn't even kill elementary schoolers. Come help me feed the dogs."

The next day I got your news about Arthur and my official doom. Brian found me sitting in the backyard husky kennel with Kushla. He cleaned the straw around me, lovingly ruffled her fur, and patted me once on the head before leaving the cage.

Through the bars, he mumbled, "You remember I told you I don't like you?"

I buried my face in my knees.

"Well, sometimes I also tell people I don't like dogs. Brianism, I guess."

The Tearslaughter Shit-Com.

The following Monday, Auburn-Stache parked the Impala across the street from Brian's driveway. I watched him scratch his head and knock on the neighbor's door for almost a minute before I stepped outside.

He looked about ten years older, and he was no spring chicken to start with.

"'Lo, stranger!" I called. He froze. It took him forever to turn around. Another forever to cross the street. By the time he reached me, I'd settled onto the stoop. "How's it hanging, Ass?"

"Ollie, don't smile like that. I can hardly bear to look at you."

"Why, does looking at me cause cancer?"

I wish he'd laughed, Moritz. I tried to pretend I couldn't see how red his eyes were. "Of course Moritz told you. I might have known that." He plopped himself down next to me.

"You *did* know that. Next time save us the trouble and just tell me yourself." I took off my hat and handed it to him.

He took his hands from his face. Eyes wider than flying saucers. "Ollie . . . how?"

"Just had to calm down a bit. Sit still. You were always right about that. Not that it matters now. It's not worth the risk, huh."

He stared at my hairline where the fuzz was more of a layer of fluff now.

"It's all there. It's not falling out," I told him. I pulled the hat back on and released the air in my lungs. "But you already knew that, too. And you let me meet people."

Auburn-Stache shook his head a little. "I wasn't certain."

"I wonder if Liz is sick, too. I wonder if Mom knew and let her play with me anyhow. Now *that'd* be fucked up."

"People do fucked-up things. I left you, for instance." He peeled off his glasses and wiped his eyes. His back was hunched and trembling.

"I'm sorry about Arthur, Auburn-Stache."

"Yes. So am I. It wasn't your—"

"Don't—" My voice broke. "It is my fault, even if I didn't know it. Not knowing the truth doesn't make the truth go away."

"Ollie, it may well be that Moritz's mother will offer us a solution. And perhaps I'll find a way to, I don't know, restrain or insulate or immunize—"

"In the meantime, I don't want to be a murderer."

"It's so unjust, Oliver."

"Yup. You guys really fucked things up for a lot of people. But I'm not going to. Arthur's enough." I cleared my throat. "Auburn-Stache, you know what sounds awesome to me?"

"What, Ollie?"

"I'd kill to go home. Like, really. Can you give me a ride?"

Tears slipped down his nose, and it felt like something I shouldn't be watching, so I looked at the trees instead. Some had blossoms. Different yards, different trees. And they had leaves now. A few of them were on the grass and no one had squirreled them away yet.

And I wrote this by hand, but now Auburn-Stache will have to type it up. Now that you're on the move, my letters won't reach you. Electricity can. Shocking.

chapter forty

THE HEART (REPRISE)

Ollie,

This isn't a story. These aren't worthless words, blocks of frozen sound. These aren't lines of logic. These are words written with my heart in. These are words of joy and grit and grass and slush and winter-into-spring. Here are all the things I feel when I want to feel them, things I want to feel because there is a sun and because water looks blue but isn't and because you cared for my words even when they were ice blocks and not words at all.

They aren't words of love. Love is a strong thing to feel and right now everything is a strong thing to feel.

But gratitude. I am feeling grateful for the wind through rolled-down windows and the heat of car seats when you leave them and the smell of steaming petroleum at gas stations and the way the window-washing fluid dries out my hands.

This is sunlight through car windows. This is the smell

of things that pierce through metals as you drive past them and the strange pangs of missing someone you've only just left behind. These are words with my heart in me.

I had to wait for spring break before I could go. The Tidmores smiled and wished me the best, and when I come back I think maybe I'll smile at them, too. When I told Brian where I was going, he waited at the end of the driveway in his hoodie.

"Will you keep it in?" Brian asked me.

He has asked what you haven't. He has asked what made me put my heart back in the first place, and in the driveway I gave him the same answer I'll always give to those questions:

"None of your business."

He smiled and said, "Same old Bridget."

I am writing this with a body full of heart. I am writing words that spill from me like creek water over stones, that swirl around me like clouds torn apart by passing planes.

It has taken me so long to get to here. Hours in a car, beautiful hours. I am impatient. Maybe we're the same Ollie.

Hope blossoms from me, Ollie. I am not ready to feel that yet, but one day I might be. I know when you left us I worried about blenders.

Be stubborn. Be strong. You know me and I know you. That counts for something red and beating. Stay alive.

I hope the house in the purple hills looks the same as it ever did, the orchard stretching out in front of it.

I hope my sister can teach me how to braid happiness.
Heart beats, heart bursts, with our hearts in us.
with feeling,
Bridget

chapter forty-one
THE FICTION

Bridget,

It's funny—when we met, I downright begged you to share your story with me. When Dr. Auburn-Stache handed me this letter, I did a double take. Because that was your handwriting, I knew, but the letters curled together. But the thing is, you could have been like Arthur. You didn't have to write me. I kind of get what Auburn-Stache was saying: your story doesn't belong to me.

It's amazing that you sent it to me anyway.

And, Bridget, I'm so glad I didn't kill you.

I'm trying to listen to you. Because you listened to me, which is nuts.

I'm trying to stay alive, or find reasons to, and I won't go for the blender if you won't.

Deal?

April or not, snow held on to northern Michigan a whole lot

harder than it did Ohio. The driveway I grew up on was slushy. We got stuck halfway down it, so I got out of the Impala and helped Dr. Auburn-Stache rock the car. I don't know why, but it felt too quiet between the trees. I couldn't even hear that one crow you always hear on winter days, the one always cawing "I'm here."

After seeing electricity every single day, the woods felt colorless.

The A-frame looked the same, except that I couldn't really look at it. The first thing Auburn-Stache did after we slurped our way to the front porch was remove the rusting padlock from the door and pocket it. "We won't be locking this door anymore, Oliver."

"How am I going to keep you out, then."

"Oliver—I know you're upset, but—"

"I'm not upset." My lips were numb. "I just don't like the idea of killing my father figure."

He leaned against the wall. "Oliver, if this lot belongs to anyone, it's me. I'd die to undo what I've done to you. And I'm not leaving you alone here. I'm done wandering about."

"But . . . the Blunderkids . . ."

"I've done enough damage, thank you. Let them live." He smiled.

I stood in front of the door like a stranger. Exactly where a mud-monster named Liz—the girl I was in lovesickness with, Bridget—stood a long time ago.

"Auburn-Stache?"

"Yes, Ollie."

"Don't tell Liz I'm back."

Some doors you have to lock.

The cabin in the woods is full of ghosts. Do you believe in ghosts, Bridget?

I was scared of coming home to an empty house. I thought I'd get back and fall out of the world into this gaping well of how things used to be, but that's not what happened.

Home should have smelled musty, and it did. A few months of winter had passed with no one to warm the insides of that place. But Mom used to keep potpourri in bowls on the windowsills, potpourri she dried herself from her garden and spices. That smell snagged the air.

The floorboards moaned "hi" in exactly the same places as they used to. The terrible paneling on the walls was brown and bleak as ever. The mosaic tiles in the kitchen. Tapestries on the walls. In my bedroom, my human anatomical model remained whole and dull and nothing like a Blunderskeleton would be.

In Mom's bedroom, I smelled the first ghost. And I saw it, too—when I passed the mirror on her vanity—

I don't really look like her, Bridget. I take after my long-dead dad. Except Mom was basically bald before the end, and she was pale and confused by the end, too.

I've thought a lot about what she knew or didn't know. If she knew that I was gonna cut the world. If she knew I gave her cancer. (Auburn-Stache keeps telling me we can't say that for sure, don't hate yourself.) When I had poison ivy, she told me to share it with her, but she tried really hard not to share death with me. The fact is, I never really knew my mother. She kept a lab coat in the closet. She hid a guitar under her bed. And whenever she didn't want to think about the past, she made new things, a future out of pottery and overgrown flower beds.

You told me she's gone. I know you were trying to make me feel better, in that heartless way of yours. But she's not gone. She's haunting me.

I don't think that's the worst thing.

I'll take whatever company I can get.

Days after we got back, I sat outside and waited for a comet to pass by. I know my charts were correct, and the sky was clear over the trees, but I waited until I was blue-shivering and I never saw it. I kind of thought maybe I'd blinked right when it went by, or maybe I wasn't reaching high enough, not stretching myself like Arthur would have, just not doing *enough*, and I refused to go inside when Auburn-Stache told me to. He stayed on the porch behind me, smoking his cigarettes.

So the second ghost was the invisible comet.

The third ghost appeared in the backyard.

I sat on the stoop with my bare feet in the long grass, pulling the longest strands into a weave pattern. Mom used to weave baskets, but it was one of those hobbies I never bothered with, so who knew if I could make those tiny strands of green a solid whole. The brisk spring air made my nose run, but there was enough sun to leave me sweating in my beanie.

I felt the ghost before I heard it.

"Our mutual friend tells me, Oliver Paulot, that you have not made a single scatological joke since your return. What a travesty." The ghost's *w* wasn't totally a *v*, but almost.

I lifted my eyes.

He wasn't exactly how I imagined. He'd told me he was short, but I'm taller than most people who aren't Arthurs. Unless I was talking to a hobbit, I wouldn't notice someone's exact degree of shortness.

He stood perfectly proportionate and, I dunno, *proper*. Delicate, almost, like the origami cranes I suck at making. There was so much else to see about him: his dark hair so *neat*, apart from bangs that hung too long over his forehead down to his cheekbones, those black goggles, sleeker than I'd pictured—closer to the kind used for swimming than the kind used for flying planes. I could see more of his face than I'd thought I would, his narrow cheeks and pointed chin.

He wasn't exactly how I imagined.

But there was this silver beating of his chest—well, of the *pacemaker* keeping time inside his chest. That gleam was hard to look at. Every few seconds the silver light faded and lit up again, brighter than any comet.

I took one look at Moritz Farber and I wanted to say everything I'd ever thought all at once, and say it four times louder than usual, and maybe while coughing and laughing and gasping and shouting at the same time. I wanted to scare the chirping things from the rustling trees.

I dropped my patch of basket.

"You're . . . what about your mom . . ."

"Every quest can afford detours. The hobbits had Rivendell." He crooked his chin up at me. I saw white sky reflected in his goggles, the shadows of leaves caught there. My silhouette and the endless trees behind us, bent green and brown and strange.

You could get lost in lack-of-eyes like that.

I took three steps back, shaking my head the whole time. "I could kill you."

"What else is, ah, new?" I never guessed his smile would be crooked. "That's where we've always stood."

Suddenly, I felt this sort of flicker of warmth in the air. It had nothing to do with the white sun—it hit my head instead of my body, like someone poured milky tea through my ears—without the burning. Just the comfort. *Geborgenheit*.

"Please say something."

"Like what?"

He smirked. "Since when does 'what' matter to Oliver Paulot?"

"Moritz. *Moritz*." I choked on a laugh. "Call me *Ollie*."

Moritz can't see blushing, but that's exactly what he did. "I'm, ah, working up to it."

"Did you know something?" I blurted. "Your pacemaker glows silver!"

"Ah. What does silver sound like?"

I just kept shaking my head, trying to shake the happiness loose, happiness I didn't deserve but couldn't fight forever. Maybe life really is about meeting people under strange circumstances. If that's true, Bridget, I've lived one helluva life.

Moritz clicked his tongue against his teeth—a sound like a branch snapping. "*Ollie?* You promised to hug me first. Where are you?"

"Right here." I threw my insulated arms around Moritz's shoulders and held him like I've never held anything. We were boundless.

This is not science fiction.

ACKNOWLEDGMENTS

Many people who read *Because You'll Never Meet Me* assumed it would be a stand-alone. Readers told me that one of the book's strengths is that it doesn't *need* a sequel—a sentiment I still take as a compliment.

The trouble is, the world isn't like that. We don't have endings. We continue to grow and struggle and mourn and triumph and *live*. Ollie, Moritz, and company have always felt like characters clawing to survive, countering anything that might deny them that right. They deserve all the joyful, horrible mess the universe entails. *Nowhere Near You* was written even before its predecessor sold, because life simply doesn't stand alone.

I need to thank those who refused to let *me* stand alone during this process.

My Bloomsbury family. Specifically, kudos to Mary Kate Castellani for insightful editorial coaxing, Beth Eller for timely advice and wry humor, Linette Kim for keeping our brains in order, Emily Ritter for bringing joy to the party (even though she saw *Hamilton* without me), and Lizzy Mason for general kindness. This book is in your hands now only because I sniffled something about a sequel to Cristina Gilbert, who seemingly pulled Cindy Loh from thin air so they could say, without hesitation, "We want that."

Lana. My patient, tenacious agent. You're raising me up right.

Librarians. To be taken under their collective wing and pushed from the nest into the hands of readers is an honor. Visit libraries! They're full of *books*, people!

Likewise, because of indie bookstores, a thousand Little Books That Could *can* and *do*. Readers, please populate these places.

My friends. From the ladies of Craft Group and my cosplay and convention crew (you make San Diego worth it), to fellow artists near and far, from supporters distant but felt, to the good ol' Clarionites, I am embraced on all sides. I could lose my footing and be held up, made to levitate. Special nods to Karin Tidbeck, Courtney Alldridge, Jessica Hilt, Patrick Ropp, and Ann and Jeff Vandermeer.

My family. Mom and Dad, for giving me books and reasons to read them. Erin and Evan and Bryn, I love you despite your horrendous puns. Extended family on both sides, know that your encouragement is perpetually appreciated. Grandma, I promise one day I'll write something "normal." Or at least . . . I'll try. Maybe.

My students. My god, you are brilliant. The world has much to learn from you all. Please, always love what you love. Anything you love has value. Share that notion.

Finally, my readers. I have thousands of words, but for you I'm wondering if there's one word in some language for gratitude so deep the pit of it pierces the whole world and leaves a glorious gap through which you can see the stars on either side? That's what I have for you. (Thanks for the digital kittens, Chloe Smith.)

A few books in, I still feel like I'm constantly coming of age. I would never want that process to stop for anyone. Please keep reading. Keep growing. Be boundless. Know that you don't stand alone.

THERE ARE TRUTHS YOU CAN ONLY TELL A STRANGER

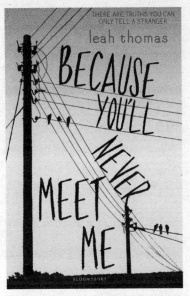

READ OLLIE AND MORITZ'S FIRST STORY OUT NOW